The bad boy is BIG trouble...but then, so is she!

"*I'm No Angel* is a delightfully witty read.
Once I started, I couldn't put it down."
Lori Foster

"Fresh! Fun! Fabulous!
Patti Berg always makes me smile."
Millie Criswell

"Patti Berg delivers an irresistible
story complete with snappy and
engaging characters."
Christine Feehan

"Patti
Vic

"Alw
Step

"Charming, sexy and fun!"
Cathy Maxwell

*With his hands pressed against
the small of her back,
they danced cheek to cheek,
very close and very personal.*

The scent of cloves drifted from his skin to her senses. It was more intoxicating than a chocolate martini, more tingly than bubbling champagne, more seductive than all the schoolgirl dreams she'd ever had of being romanced and loved by a man who'd treat her right.

Warm lips hovered over her ear, shooting a shiver of delight all the way down to her toes, then up again to quiver in that intimate place where all women love to quiver.

And then he whispered, "You know, Angel, I would have told you anything you want to know about me. You didn't have to pick my pocket."

PATTI
BERG

I'm No Angel

AVON BOOKS
An Imprint of HarperCollinsPublishers

AVON BOOKS
An Imprint of HarperCollins*Publishers*
10 East 53rd Street
New York, New York 10022-5299

Copyright © 2004 by Patti Berg
Party Crashers copyright © 2004 by Stephanie Bond Hauck; *And the Bride Wore Plaid* copyright © 2004 by Karen Hawkins; *I'm No Angel* copyright © 2004 by Patti Berg; *A Perfect Bride* copyright © 2004 by Sandra Kleinschmit
ISBN: 0-06-054476-7
www.avonromance.com

First Avon Books paperback printing: July 2004

Avon Trademark Reg. U.S. Pat. Off. and in Other Countries, Marca Registrada, Hecho en U.S.A.
HarperCollins® is a registered trademark of HarperCollins Publishers Inc.

Printed in the U.S.A.

10 9 8 7 6 5 4 3 2 1

As always . . .
for Bob

Acknowledgments

Many thanks to Kate Donovan, dear friend and confidante, who spent long hours with me on the phone brainstorming this book. Although the final story bears little resemblance to that original plot, your laughter and insight helped kick-start my creativity.

Tons of heartfelt appreciation to Robin Rue, the best agent a writer could ever have. Your guidance, your support, and your encouragement mean the world to me—so do the swift kicks to the behind you dish out when I need them!

I'm more than grateful to all the Floridians who gave this Californian advice as I wrote *I'm No Angel* (whether I used the information—or not!). Private investigator Marcia Gillings, owner of Baker Street Investigations—great website; terrific English accent. Jan Jackson for insight on swamps, alligators, snakes, and pesky insects. Kyle Smith, for the fabulous information on St. Augustine past and present, even though the story that was in my head at the time didn't get written!

And to Chery, Jan, Kim, Linda, Steph, and Susan—your friendship is something I will cherish forever. Here's to great times past and fabulous times future! You're the best!

Dangerous men are my business. And I love my job.

ANGEL DEVLIN

1

*H*e hadn't aspired to be a cat burglar.

He'd wrestled alligators in the Everglades. He'd charmed water moccasins to entertain tourists, and spent long nights in the swamps, gazing through cypress, palm, and mangrove branches at the distant stars, with not much more than mosquitoes and frogs for company.

But tonight Tom Donovan faced his most treacherous challenge—breaking into the home of the man he despised. And he was going to be up to his ass in trouble if he got caught.

He climbed cautiously from one branch to the next, each foothold steady, precise. The fernlike leaves of the tall and spreading royal Poinciana shimmered in the moonlight, camouflaging his black-clad body as he made his way toward the mansion's second-story window.

Breaking and entering wasn't his forte. Hell, he had no clue what he was doing, but Holt Hudson had allowed Tom little choice.

The reclusive billionaire had refused to see him

in spite of a dozen polite and maybe-not-so-polite requests. Didn't the bastard realize that all Tom wanted was for Holt to tell him face to face, man to man, why he'd emptied a .25 automatic into Chase Donovan—Tom's dad—twenty-six years before?

It seemed a damn simple request, yet Holt had sealed his lips on the subject the moment the Palm Beach police had closed their investigation all those years ago. No one but Tom believed there was more to the story. No one but Tom believed that Chase had been shot in cold blood.

Money could buy a hell of a lot, Tom realized. It could buy the police; it could buy isolation from the world; it could buy respectability. Money had bought an end to the tragedy for Holt Hudson, and he'd come out of the nightmare completely unscathed.

Chase Donovan had ended up dead.

Tom Donovan had come out of it scarred inside. And angry as hell.

But Tom had his own money now. A ton of it. He'd hoped his recent inheritance could buy him information. Answers to what had truly happened that night so he could put his bitterness aside and move on with his life. But damn it all, his newfound riches were buying him nothing but frustration.

His only course of action now was to go out on a limb—literally and figuratively—to find what he wanted. What he needed. Since Holt Hudson wouldn't talk to him or even allow him into his inner sanctum, Tom Donovan hoped and even prayed that somewhere within the gilded walls of

Palazzo Paradiso he'd find the truth that would make his endless nightmares go away.

He had to know that his dad, the man who had been shot inside the palatial mansion and then escaped to the Everglades, where he'd bled to death in his son's scrawny, four-year-old arms, had been framed not only for robbery, but for assaulting Holt Hudson's wife.

Ducking under a branch of feathery leaves, Tom placed one foot in front of the other, cautiously negotiating limbs that fought him every step of the way. The foliage rustled. Twigs splintered.

He wiped his brow with leather-gloved fingers, wishing the night wasn't so damn hot and humid, so calm and quiet. The only sounds around him were the gentle lap of salt water on the beach and the sweet strains of Mozart coming from somewhere inside the mansion.

A man could make all the noise he wanted wading through the towering mangroves and the endless sawgrass in the Glades. But silence was imperative now.

Take your time, he told himself. Don't get caught.

The window ledge jutted out of the mansion's limestone façade. At least two feet deep and four feet wide, it was the perfect platform for a six-foot-three-inch man to balance on while figuring out the best way to get inside. Unfortunately the glistening remnants of late afternoon rain that had puddled up on the ledge glared at him. If he took a flying leap, he could easily hit the water, slide right off the window edge, and end up on his butt in the prickly bougainvillea below.

That would surely set off an alarm or two; then the cops would come; then he'd be dead meat.

He needed to move a few more feet out on the tapering limb and then, if his luck held out, he could latch on to the ornamental arch and swing onto the windowsill.

His heart thudded as he took another step. It hadn't beat this hard since the teeth of a gator got too close to his balls.

A bead of perspiration coursed down his temple, slipped over his jaw. The tension in his body was palpable, and his eyes and ears were on such high alert for even the smallest unwanted noise around the estate that he could almost hear the drop of sweat hit the ground.

And then he made his move.

Tearing one hand from its hold on the branch above him, Trace reached across the void for the intricately carved limestone archway, but it was still too far away.

The limb beneath his feet wobbled. One foot slipped and he knew damn good and well he was going to fall if he didn't move fast. Without giving his next action a second thought, he ripped his other hand from the branch above, used the limb he stood on as a springboard, and propelled himself through the air toward the window.

His gloved hands slapped against the wall and he grabbed hold of the jutting limestone, digging his fingers into the crevices. The toes of his shoes landed on the very brink of the ledge, all the hold he needed to keep from careening down the side of the mansion. A moment later, after careful maneuvering, he managed to gain a firm foothold within the alcove.

His chest swelled as he took a deep, calming breath.

He'd made it—at least to the window.

He was safe—so far.

Tom looked around for any signs of an alarm. God knows Holt Hudson probably had something far more sophisticated than the pretty damn cheap mail-order security system he and his grandfather had installed at their gator farm in the Glades. Of course, they'd had alligators and water moccasins for extra protection, and there weren't all that many crooks anxious to tangle with reptiles that could poison, mutilate, or kill with one snapping bite.

Seeing nothing that looked remotely like wires or even laser lights protecting the window, Tom touched the glass gently. He peeked inside but saw little more than darkness and a faint light shining under a door on the far side of the room.

He ran his fingers around the sill, wondering if he should try to slide the window open or use the glass cutters tucked into his back pocket.

His dad would have known what to do, *if* the stories were true about Chase being a cat burglar. Tom didn't want to believe it but, hell, his grandfather had served time for jewelry theft. So had his great-grandfather. Larceny ran in the family.

But it sure as hell seemed that he'd missed out on some of the villainous genes that made breaking and entering more instinct than out-and-out hard work.

Dragging in another deep breath of muggy salt air, he opted for what he hoped would be the easiest way to open the window. He pressed his hands against the sash and was on the verge of pushing upward when a woman's whispery voice broke through the nearly silent night.

"I've had a wonderful evening, Mr. Hudson. The dinner was extraordinary, and once again, I have to tell you how thankful I am that you're allowing me to throw the gala here in your lovely home."

"You're quite welcome."

Tom craned his neck to peer around the limestone arch. The mansion was cast with shadows, but he was used to wandering through the mangroves at night, his eyes were attuned to the dark, and it took no time at all to find where the voices were coming from.

Staring past Grecian urns overflowing with flowers and through the tall neoclassical columns standing like sentries in front of the massive entry, he set eyes on Holt Hudson, a man he hadn't seen in twenty-six years. The man who was supposed to be his godfather, who'd promised to take care of Tom if anything happened to his parents.

The man who had killed Tom's dad.

It was all Tom could do not to jump from the window ledge, sprint up the circular entrance stairs, and, when he reached the doorway where Holt was framed by the light, slam his fist into the man's face. Then he'd drag Holt into the mansion, tie him into a chair, and force him to talk.

After that bit of lunacy, it was a damn safe bet he'd get hauled off to jail.

To a minuscule cell.

His nightmarish and baffling dread of being imprisoned in a small space was the only thing that held him back. The one thing that gave him second thoughts about breaking in.

He stayed frozen on the window ledge, watching Holt and listening to the woman's sultry voice.

"I know how much you value your privacy but I assure you, Mr. Hudson, every step will be taken to make sure the evening goes as both you and I envision it."

"You're right, Miss Devlin, I do value my privacy. But the gala is just one night," Holt said, facing Miss Devlin, who stood within earshot but completely out of sight. "You know as well as I do the heartbreak Alzheimer's can wreak. It's too late for my wife—God rest her soul—and, sadly, it's probably too late for your mother. But if there's anything I can do to help raise money for research, I'll do it."

"That means a lot to me and my family, Mr. Hudson," Miss Devlin said, a hint of sadness touching her voice. "Thank you again."

Holt extended his hand as if he were bringing the evening and their conversation to an end. In turn, the woman slipped her long, slim fingers into Holt's outstretched hand, and at last she stepped into view.

A burst of lust almost overpowered Tom's need · for answers. Damn, she was beautiful. Almost ethereal, with the cloud of light surrounding her.

Tall. Built to thrill. The platinum highlights in her honey-blond hair shimmered. It was twisted into some elegant and sophisticated style on the back of her head and showed off a slender and lovely neck.

A neck ripe for tasting.

She withdrew her hand after a short, almost perfunctory shake, and held her head high and proud as she floated down the steps and across the drive to the red Jaguar parked beside a bubbling fountain. She walked with a regal gait, her slim hips swaying only slightly beneath her tight white skirt. Tom couldn't help but notice the way it was cut up the front of her right leg, revealing a hell of a lot of nicely tanned and very bare skin.

He liked bare skin.

He liked women.

He particularly liked this woman. It wasn't just her beauty. It wasn't the way he wanted to investigate her subtle curves or to slowly unbutton her tailored white jacket to see if she wore an industrial-strength cotton bra or something lacy, something provocative, something that would let the tanned flesh of her breasts jiggle as she strolled across a room.

No, it was more than that.

She had access to Holt Hudson.

Tom smiled in the dark. If he could get close to Miss Devlin, if he could get into her good graces, mesmerize her as he did snakes and gators, she just might help him get into Holt Hudson's private world.

Getting into the lovely Miss Devlin's good graces—as well as getting up close and personal with the stunning lady—sounded a hell of a lot better, as well as easier and safer, than breaking into Palazzo Paradiso.

He could get his face slapped if she learned he was using her. But an open-handed wallop or even a fist smashed into his nose was a far sight better than a jail cell. And if good fortune were smiling down on him, she might never learn the truth.

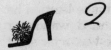

2

$\mathcal{A}$ngel Devlin wasn't used to being followed, and she sure as hell didn't like the fact that a strange vehicle was dogging her trail up and down the streets of Palm Beach, its bright lights bouncing off her rearview mirror and smacking her in the eyes.

She wasn't in the mood to play games with a stalker. She wanted to hightail it to her favorite club and have a cool drink with a friend. But the conspicuous black Jeep—ragtop down, roll bar thickly padded, and four big off-road lights mounted above the windshield—had appeared out of nowhere, not long after she'd left Holt Hudson's estate. And even though she'd done her best to shake the too-close-for-comfort four-by-four, it was still hot on her tail ten minutes later.

She zipped down South County Road to Royal Palm Way, hung a right on Brazilian Avenue, a left on Cocoanut Row, and another left on Australian, wondering if or when she would lose the guy—

and it seemed a pretty good guess that the person tailing her *was* a guy.

A guy who apparently didn't want to lose her; but he obviously didn't mind being noticed.

If he was a P.I., trailing her for some unknown reason, he was pretty darn lousy at his job.

Of course, *she* was a P.I. and she couldn't escape the man. That didn't say too much about her abilities, either.

Reaching up, she adjusted her rearview mirror and tried to get a good look at the license plate. It bore the distinctive Florida orange, but she couldn't make out the letters and/or numbers. Turning the mirror a tad higher, she did her best to check out the driver, but in spite of the streetlights, it was far too dark to make out any details.

Another five minutes of playing cat and mouse flew by. It didn't seem as though she could shake the Jeep or the mystery man behind the wheel without driving like a bat out of hell, and she wasn't going to do that on the streets of Palm Beach. Besides, curiosity was getting the better of her.

What the hell did this guy want?

Making one last turn onto Worth Avenue, Angel pulled her Jag up to the curb in front of Jazzzzz, her usual Tuesday, Wednesday, and Thursday night hangout. The classy pastel pink Mediterranean exterior and the pale lime- and white-striped awning over the entrance was a far cry from what awaited her inside. The outside of the building was understated. Inside the place was a cacophony of music, laughter, and conversations that went on and on until the wee hours of morning.

One of the two valets who'd been parking her car for the past couple of months was at the Jag's side in an instant, and opened the door. He was a cute young thing, who'd look as if he'd just stepped from the pages of *Town & Country* if it weren't for his lime green and passionate pink satin vest, festooned with a sequined black and white piano keyboard that swirled across the front, over one shoulder, and down the back.

Liberace would have loved it.

His name was printed on the piano-shaped name tag he wore, but Angel would have known him without the vest or the badge. Brent—a good name for a young man hoping to make it in Palm Beach—took her hand and helped her out of her car.

"Good evening, Miss Devlin," Brent said with a smile. "We were expecting you almost half an hour ago."

"I was tied up."

Angel winked as she handed Brent her car keys, and let him think whatever lascivious or not-so-lascivious thing he wanted. It was good for a P.I. to have an air of mystery wafting around her. No one needed to know the truth about her sex life—or lack thereof.

"I take it Miss Claire is waiting inside?" she said, tugging the strap of her white crocodile zip bag over her shoulder.

"Yes, ma'am."

She might have told him to call her Angel if she hadn't been scrutinizing the Jeep parked slyly—

yet visibly—near the corner of Worth Avenue and Cocoanut Row. Finally she was able to catch a shadowy glimpse of the driver, enough to see that his hair was dark, that it brushed against the collar of his leather jacket. He gripped the steering wheel, and his steely-eyed gaze was aimed at her face.

Instinct told her to march over to the guy and ask him straight out what the hell he was up to. But she wanted a cool drink far more than a confrontation.

Hell, maybe he was just a jerk who got his jollies by intimidating women.

Well, she wasn't intimidated.

Angel tucked a few crisp ones into Brent's hand, thanked him, then took her merry sweet time sauntering into the club, making sure the guy in the Jeep got an eyeful.

She'd learned a long time ago that the best way to get a man to open up while being interrogated—or to show him just how much power she wielded—was to blatantly flirt. To smile slyly. To absently touch her lips with her middle or ring finger. To dress with style but keep her skirts tight and no longer, no shorter than mid-thigh. Jackets had to be cinched at the waist. Necklines needed to plunge just enough to reveal a hint of cleavage.

Tantalize and tease—that's how she played the game with men.

Of course, she also knew how to protect herself if the come-on proved too strong.

Angel Devlin carried a stiletto. Better yet—she knew how to use it.

It was 10:27 when the doorman greeted her

with a smile and let her into the club. She expected to hear Jorge at the piano, playing Duke Ellington or George Gershwin. Instead, the thrum of a bass guitar wrapped around her, the distinctive mix of soul, rock, funk, and jazz that belonged to Blues Traveler pulsing through hidden speakers.

It made her want to dance, to let her hair down and maybe, just maybe let herself go, something she hadn't been able to do completely since . . . since before her miserable mistake of a marriage to the lowlife she'd divorced five years ago. But the cat-and-mouse game that had just ended, her two-hour-long meeting with Holt Hudson, and the late spring heat and humidity made her opt for nothing more than good conversation and a cold drink.

She made her way across the room, which was alight with hot pink and lime green neon letters spelling out the word JAZZZZZ. Some men, still dressed in their Brioni and Hugo Boss suits, tossed back champagne to dull the stress of their jobs, while others flirted with their wives, their mistresses, or their wannabe lovers. Women paraded around the lounge in Ferragamo and Manolo Blahnik stilettos and little black dresses accented with their great-grandmamma's pearls, gossiping about the day's events or who wore what to the charity ball they'd attended the night before.

It was a chance to show off, to see and be seen, or to compete with self-made millionaires and billionaires or trust fund babies to determine who could be the most uppity, obnoxious, or vulgar, or drink the most champagne without sliding under a table.

The Palm Beach club scene was far more interesting than anything that could be found on TV. The filthy rich were definitely a breed apart.

But she liked working for them. They kept her busy, she could charge them exorbitant rates, and knowing who's who in Palm Beach was good for her fund-raising efforts on behalf of Alzheimer's research—the most important cause in her life.

If it hadn't been for her connections in this town, she wouldn't have met Holt Hudson and she'd be paying an arm and a leg and a whole lot more to rent a ballroom for the gala coming up in a little over two weeks. Of course, if she hadn't met Holt Hudson she wouldn't be so exhausted right now. That man, in spite of being suave and debonair, sure knew how to make a person jump through hoops.

Skirting around a couple who were lip-locked and pelvis-rubbing on the dance floor, Angel spotted her best friend Emma Claire, her waist-length blue-black hair pulled up in her trademark ponytail, waving at her from their regular black-lacquered table not far from the unoccupied grand piano that was unobtrusively tucked into a dimly lit corner of the room.

"Sorry I'm late," Angel said, plopping down in the chair in a most unladylike fashion, which would have made Mrs. Alexander of Portia Alexander's Academy, the snooty school for young ladies in the English countryside where Emma and Angel had met, roll over in her grave.

"You should be." The tiny diamond purse dangling from the platinum and diamond chain on Emma's wrist glistened in the neon lights as she wagged a hot pink swizzle stick at her friend. "I was hit on by a guy who smelled like a chimney, by another guy who had to be a hundred and seven if not older, and by Chatsworth Longfellow."

"*The* Chatsworth Longfellow? As in Chatsworth I-own-my-own-island-in-the-Mediterranean-and-I-want-to-seduce-you-there Longfellow?"

"That's the one."

"Did he ask you to hop in his jet and fly off to erotica land with him?"

"Of course he did."

"And of course you said no."

With a perfectly manicured yet decidedly short pale pink fingernail, Emma pushed what looked to be a freshly ordered Lady Godiva martini across the table and straight into Angel's waiting hand. "I said I'd think about it."

Angel frowned at her friend's response. "You're not serious, are you?"

"I'm thirty years old, Angel."

"So am I, but I wouldn't go anywhere with Chatsworth Longfellow."

Emma shrugged, then took a sip of her Manhattan. "You know"—she sighed—"I do nothing but work all day, seven days a week, except when I'm catching a few hours of sleep or I'm here with you. I could use a trip to erotica land."

Angel took a drink of the cool, minty chocolate martini. "May I make a suggestion?"

"Of course you can."

With the stem of her glass clasped in her fingers, Angel leaned forward and whispered just loud enough to be heard over the music, "Get a vibrator."

"I have. Five, to be exact. All shapes, all sizes, all colors." Emma plucked one of Jazzzzz's signature pink and green flour tortilla chips from the black lacquer bowl on the table and held it close to her mouth. "Plastic. Lucite. And an unidentified fan sent me one that I swear is plated in eighteen-carat gold, and it vibrates like . . . well, suffice it to say it's quite enjoyable."

"*But?*" Angel asked, knowing there had to be more to Emma's admission.

"I'm bored. A vibrator doesn't hold you or kiss you or whisper sweet nothings in your ear."

"And men do?"

Emma took a bite of her chip and chewed on it slowly. Thoughtfully. "I know we haven't talked about this in a long time, because I know you don't like talking about it, but please don't tell me you haven't been with a man since—"

"Could we change the subject?" Angel didn't mind talking about Emma's sex life, but her own was completely off-limits.

Emma grabbed another chip. She looked over Angel's shoulder, deep in thought, then aimed her uneasy gaze directly at her friend. "I saw Dagger today."

An icy chill raced up Angel's spine. Talking about Dagger Zane was synonymous with talking about distasteful sex, but she couldn't pretend she hadn't heard Emma's all-too-serious comment.

"You didn't have the misfortune of talking to him, did you?"

Emma nodded. "He came into the shop with Stephania Allardyce."

"He isn't dating her, is he?"

Emma shrugged. "They looked more like friends out for a day of shopping, but who knows? Anyway, while Stephania was looking at those cute little clutches I've just put on the market, Dagger took me aside to catch up on old times, as if I care what that bastard is up to." Emma took a sip of her Manhattan. "For what it's worth, he said to tell you he'd heard about the gala and if he could be of any help—"

"He wasn't any help when we were married, why would I want his help now?"

"Hope you don't mind"—Emma grinned—"but I said something quite similar to him. Although I think I might have thrown in a few swear words, even that four-letter one that Mrs. Alexander said no proper young lady should ever, and I mean *ever*, utter. He in turn laughed in that vile way Dagger always had of laughing."

"What other charming things did he have to say after that?"

"That he's living on his boat, which, as you know darn well, probably means he's broke and that he's going to hit you or some of the rich ladies in town up for a so-called loan. Fortunately he didn't ask me for a penny or I would have told him he could go to hell and I'd help him get there. Instead, he just smiled that slick, greasy Dagger smile and told me his boat is moored at the marina and that he'd love to see you if you want to pay him a visit."

"I might pay him a visit if he's embalmed and stretched out in a coffin. On second thought, I doubt I'd visit him even then. As for him living on *his* boat"—Angel's muscles tensed—"I should have rigged a bomb to the thing when I handed it over to him in the divorce settlement."

"You were better off giving it to him."

"I gave him the house, too. The one I bought with *my* hard-earned money, and he ended up selling it to pay off the bills he wracked up because I was no longer supporting him."

"You got another boat. Someday you'll get another house. But all that really matters is that you got rid of him."

"I didn't get rid of him until my dad broke his nose and my brothers threatened to take their merry sweet time dismembering him bit by despicable bit."

"Seems to me you threatened him in a similar manner."

"What can I say?" Angel shrugged, as a slight but very sardonic smile touched her lips. "Quadruplets have a tendency to think alike."

Emma dug around in her glass to get the cherry out of the bottom. "Speaking of your brothers, will Ty, Hunt, and Trace be coming to the gala?"

"I'm not sure yet," Angel said, wishing she and her brothers could be together more often. "Ty said he'd show up as long as the food was good, but it's not all that difficult for him to get here from Miami. Hunt hasn't committed yet, but you know Hunt, always on the go, always mysterious about what he's doing. And Trace—"

"Would rather be plunged in boiling oil than get dressed up." Emma popped the cherry into her mouth and chewed slowly. "You know, Trace could be knock-down, drag-out gorgeous and a great catch for someone—"

"Like you?" Angel interrupted. She took a sip of her martini and watched a frown furrow Emma's brow.

"God, no. Trace and I have never agreed on anything. We're as different as night and day. And I seriously doubt he'll ever forgive me for that jock strap incident."

"You did dye his underwear and jock straps pink."

Emma laughed. "Don't forget that I hand-sewed white lace to everything, too."

"You could have warned him before he headed off to baseball camp."

"He didn't warn me before he tossed me into the mud and ruined my favorite white sundress."

"I don't think he tosses women into the mud anymore."

"Maybe not, but you know darn good and well I prefer sophisticated men to jocks. Which means Trace isn't even in my line of vision. On the other hand, I'm dying to know more about Holt Hudson." Emma's ever-present smile widened. "Is he still as dreamy as all the older women in this town remember?"

"If you like a guy with black hair that's graying at the temples, flat abs in spite of being sixty-four years old, a complete perfectionist who wants things done his way or not at all, plus an air of mystery surrounding him."

"Except for the control freak thing, he sounds divine."

Angel shrugged. "To each his own."

"Did you get him to open up about why he hasn't been out from behind the gates of Palazzo Paradiso for God knows how long? Why he's the only filthy rich person in Palm Beach who doesn't retreat to a twenty-million-dollar *cottage* up north when the season is over?"

"You don't retreat to *your* twenty-million-dollar cottage up north when the season is over."

"That's beside the point. We're talking about Holt Hudson's problems, not mine, and I'm dying to know all the nitty-gritty details about why he's walled himself up inside his estate."

"You know I couldn't ask him anything personal, but my best guess is that part of it has to do with the thief he shot. What was his name? Chase?" Angel frowned. "I know it was Chase something."

"Well, yes, there was that incident, but that's old news. I doubt anyone in Palm Beach even remembers it."

"Holt remembers it and I've heard gossip about it off and on for years."

"You're a P.I. You're supposed to know all the gruesome details about people."

"Only the people I work for. Unfortunately I don't know much more about Holt now than I knew before I met him. He doesn't talk about himself, he doesn't let down his guard, so all I can do is guess at his reasons for being a recluse."

"But you think it has to do with that killing?"

"The killing, his late wife's Alzheimer's, and the fact that he wouldn't leave her side."

"Your mother has suffered for years but your father hasn't shut himself away. Neither have you or your brothers. And you've all done a damn good job taking care of your mom."

"I'm just guessing, Em. Maybe Holt had other reasons for shutting out the world for twenty-some-odd years, but I'm not about to pry."

"I suppose you're right. Stirring up bad memories could make him change his mind about holding the gala in his ballroom."

"Don't even think those words, Em. It's like walking on pins and needles around him, making sure I don't breathe incorrectly or smile at the wrong things, just to make sure he doesn't renege on his offer."

"Is it really that awful?"

"It's not awful. He's just picky. The flower arrangements must all be tropical because he detests roses. Cristal is the only champagne we're allowed to serve. No red wine, only white. And he not only had to approve the guest list, but he insists on seeing an updated RSVP list every other day just to make sure one of the invited guests isn't going to be accompanied by someone he doesn't approve of."

"And you're going along with this? I mean, really, Angel. Isn't he being a bit unreasonable?"

"Of course he is, but I've worked too long and too hard to pull off this gala. Getting Holt to open up his estate was a miracle. Getting him to make an appearance is a godsend. And he's also donating some of his wife's jewels for the auction. I'll bend over backwards to make him happy."

Emma waved her swizzle stick again. "Holt's actually going to bring those jewels out of the safe for all the world to see?"

"Not exactly. He's going to have fakes on display, but they'll look almost as perfect as the real thing. In fact, I get to see them in a few days."

"Well, I'll be on hand ready and willing to bid on whatever strikes my fancy that night. And . . . you're going to love this"—Emma's eyes widened in delight—"I've created a new evening bag especially for the auction. It's stunning, Angel. The most fabulous purse I've ever designed."

Emma Claire purses were hotter than Kate Spade. More fun that Lulu Guinness or Isabella Fiore. And they cost a pretty penny, exactly the kind of froufrou stuff Angel wanted to auction off at the gala.

"How much do you think we can get for it?" Angel asked.

"At a minimum . . . twelve grand."

Now it was time for Angel's eyes to widen, but in absolute shock. "You don't really think we can start the bidding high enough to get up to twelve grand, do you?"

"Angel, darling, I said a *minimum* of twelve thousand. That's where I'm going to suggest the bidding start."

"But—"

"You just don't understand marketing. I've already spread word about the purse. I've got posters in the most fashionable boutiques in town and women are clamoring to learn more about it.

They'll all want to own it by the night of the gala and they'll be willing to pay just about anything."

"It's just a purse."

Emma rolled her eyes. "It's an Emma Claire original. A one-of-a-kind, not unlike that crocodile bag you're carrying and *all* the other purses you own."

"I'm not saying you don't design fabulous purses, but—"

"Trust me on this, Angel. The purse will—" Emma's gaze darted across the lounge and her words came to a dead halt.

"The purse will what?" Angel asked.

"Forget the purse. Oh, my God, Angel. You should see what just walked in the door."

Angel twisted in her chair. It took less than a heartbeat to see what Emma was gawking at—a tall guy whose broad shoulders nearly filled the doorway. His hair was long and dark and brushed the collar of his leather jacket. He was absolutely gorgeous, with mesmerizing eyes and— "Oh, my God." The words rushed out of Angel's mouth. "I'd completely forgotten about him."

"You know him?" Emma asked without turning around.

"No. He followed me around town for a good fifteen minutes before I got here. In a big black Jeep, if you can believe that."

"Well . . . he does have that rugged look to him." Emma twisted around and flashed a smile at Angel. "Any idea who he is?"

"Haven't a clue."

"Which means you don't know why he was following you."

"Exactly."

"Aren't you curious?"

"Very."

Angel turned her attention from Emma and concentrated solely on the stranger. He stepped out of the doorway and into the lounge, looking about the crowded room as if he were trying to find someone.

Sipping her martini, she studied him over the top of her glass, taking in his long, slightly wavy hair, his black T-shirt, and tan leather jacket, all that she could see of his attire through the horde of expensive designer suits and dresses. "I have to admit, he is rather gorgeous," she said offhandedly to Emma.

"Sadly he's not my type," Emma tossed back. "But he is the kind of sinful hunk I'd indulge in if I ever had the chance to take a vacation. Can't you see him stretched out on the beach in a Speedo, all bronzed and buff and dusted with specks of sand—in all the right spots, of course? *And*"—Emma fanned herself with an elegant hand—"it just so happens you've got nothing better to do than get really close to his body so you can blow the sand off all those not-so-little spots."

"Calm down, Emma." Angel was always the voice of reason. "We don't know the first thing about him, least of all why he was following me."

"Does it matter?"

"Of course it matters."

"Then why don't you go and ask him who he is and what he's up to?"

Angel crossed her legs and leaned back casually in her chair. "All in good time."

Angel wanted to study him first. Needed to check out his actions in the lounge. That was always a great place to analyze a person's character. If a man acted like a jerk in a bar, you could bet your last dollar he'd be a jerk ninety-nine percent of the time.

As he strolled through the room, he ignored the men who glared at him out of the corners of their eyes, hoping the stranger wouldn't catch on that they were gawking. How easy it was to read their little minds. They definitely weren't thinking, This guy doesn't belong here. Oh, no. They were thinking, This guy could be a threat. If anyone can get the girls, he can.

But he didn't seem all that interested in the girls. Not that he didn't look. He just didn't ogle. He seemed far more focused on the black Steinway grand tucked into the corner not far from where Emma and Angel sat. He approached it slowly, then ran tanned fingers over the tops of the keys, as if he longed to play it but didn't know how.

"Could I get you another drink?" the waiter asked, blocking Angel's view. "An appetizer?"

Angel hated to tear her concentration away from the stranger, but an idea suddenly struck.

"Could you bring another Manhattan for my friend? And I'll take two more Lady Godiva martinis."

"Two?" Emma spun around to face Angel. Her eyes narrowed. "You'll get drunk."

"Ignore her," Angel said to the waiter. "But on

second thought, make one of those martinis a bottle of beer."

"Any kind in particular?" the waiter asked.

"Oh, I don't know. Something strong and dark and masculine. And if there's any way you could get me those drinks in a hurry, I'd appreciate it."

"I'd be happy to, Miss Devlin."

The moment the waiter walked away, Emma confronted Angel. "Mind telling me what you're up to?"

"You told me I should get the goods on the guy who just walked in, and I plan to."

"What? You plan to get him drunk?"

"Maybe."

"Well, don't do anything dangerous."

Angel smiled wryly. "I wouldn't think of it."

Emma shook her head in utter disbelief. "I've heard those words before."

Sipping on her martini again, Angel concentrated once more on the man at the piano. He wasn't alone now. Jorge, the regular pianist, leaned a tuxedo-clad elbow on the Steinway and was having what appeared to be a heart-to-heart with the stranger.

The man in leather pulled a bill out of his pocket and tucked it into Jorge's hand, then sat down on the piano bench, while Jorge took a seat with his friend Lorenzo, who came every night to listen to Jorge play.

The stranger tinkled the ivories with the fingers of his right hand. The notes sounded very amateurish, but that was nothing new. A lot of regulars tried their hand at the piano when they were drunk, and most often they all played lousy renditions of "Heart and Soul" or "Chopsticks."

Angel wasn't big on making snap judgments about people and she hated to stereotype anyone, but the man who'd been following her looked as if he should be on stage with a band of bad boys, holding a mike and belting out "Light My Fire" while ogling the sweet young things tossing their panties at him.

The last thing she expected was for him to take a deep breath, close his eyes for a long moment as if in prayer, then open them again and reposition his strong tanned fingers on the black and white keys.

Suddenly he looked more like a concert pianist than Jim Morrison.

He couldn't really play, could he?

A moment later she had her answer.

The deep and dark tones he played resonated through the lounge, sounding as if the Phantom of the Opera was playing a funeral dirge, a mournful lament, or as if the stranger was taking years of heartache out on the keys.

The voices in the lounge grew silent, and Angel watched as nearly every eye turned toward the dimly lit piano. The stranger had their attention and he knew it.

A somewhat wicked smile touched his lips and the sorrowful tune eased. Without warning, the fingers of his right hand traipsed up the keyboard. Lightly. Expertly.

The melody echoed through the room. He wasn't playing Scott Joplin or blues or jazz, he was playing something classical, a refrain that was one moment light and airy, the next mind-numbingly erotic, then heart-poundingly savage.

The music transported her to another place. To the beach, where two lovers frolicked on the shore as foam and cool water lapped at their feet. Then the sky darkened. Lightning struck. Wind tore at the lovers' hair. Powerful waves crashed against them. They grasped on to each other, the fear that they would be torn apart so strong that they locked themselves in each others' embrace. They kissed, as if there would be no tomorrow for them, and then the sun came again, brighter than ever before, and right there on the beach, in the sand and foam, they made love.

Long moments passed before Angel realized she had gotten so caught up in the music, in the stranger's masterful playing, that she was barely breathing.

He intrigued her, fascinated her, more than she ever imagined a man could.

Far worse. His music and the way his fingers floated over the keys as if he were making love to each one, tenderly one instant, with great passion the next, set her on fire.

If she closed her eyes, she knew she'd feel those fingers floating over her skin.

The man could be trouble. Dangerous.

But, she thought, swallowing back the intensity of the emotions thundering through her insides, so could she.

Standing, Angel slung the strap of her handbag over her shoulder, picked up the martini and cold bottle of beer the waiter had just set on the table, and strolled toward the piano. Most everyone in the room had already lost interest in the stranger. They were chatting among themselves again, gossiping and laughing, and Angel felt as if she now had the gorgeous hunk all to herself.

Just the way she wanted.

She set both drinks beside the Steinway's music stand and studied the stranger's strong, overwhelmingly handsome face and his darkly tanned and powerful hands as he continued to play slow and easy.

A casual passerby would have thought he hadn't even noticed Angel's presence. But she couldn't miss the way his dark brown eyes trailed from the piano keys to the slit in her white skirt, up the tailored jacket nipped and tucked at her waist, over her breasts, to her fingers, which were whispering across the nape of her neck.

"It's warm in here tonight," she said. Her words were little more than a sexy whisper, but loud enough so he could hear her over his music. "Thought you might like something cool to drink."

He smiled the same wicked smile Angel had seen when he knew he'd become the focal point of the crowd. "Thank you."

"You're very welcome."

She slipped behind him and with the wall at her back and no one watching her but Emma, Angel rested her left hand gently on his shoulder. He didn't move a muscle, but something told her he wasn't completely unfazed by her I-want-to-know-you-better gesture.

Slowly, cautiously, and oh-so-suggestively, her right hand skimmed down his side. Even through his leather jacket she could feel his power, the kind of strength a man didn't develop working as a stockbroker or corporate bigwig.

What did he do for a living? she wondered. Did he pump iron in his spare time? Was he a hit man out to get her? After all, there were some men in town who hadn't taken kindly to her spying on them and then handing over the dirty little photos she'd taken to the wives or lovers who'd paid for her discreet and expert services.

Well, speculation wasn't in her current game plan.

Seduction was.

"You play Liszt beautifully," Angel said, the fingers of her left hand trailing over his chest, making small, sensuous circles to tease him, to distract him, only to find that she really, really liked the bulging muscles she felt, so much so that she knew she should pull her hand away. But his broad chest and the heavy beat of his heart worked on her like a magnet.

His allure was overpowering. Breathtaking.

A woman with less control could easily succumb to his charm.

She, however, would not. Falling under his spell was an impossibility, and even if there was the remotest chance of him mesmerizing her, seducing her, she'd fight tooth and nail not to tumble into his sensual trap.

"You know classical music?" he asked, his voice as deep, resonant, and enthralling as the notes he continued to play.

"I know a lot of things. Liszt's Hungarian Rhapsody No. 9 is just one of them."

With his left hand still on the keys, he reached out for the bottle of beer Angel had brought him, took a long, cool swallow, returned it to the piano, then went back to his music without, it seemed, missing a note.

"Do you play?" he asked casually.

"All depends on what you have in mind."

She could feel the calm beat of his heart beneath his T-shirt, but also the way his muscles seemed to tighten when she made her bold, coquettish statement.

He twisted around to give her one quick look, one wry grin. "Do you always flirt with strangers?"

She smiled mischievously. "Only ones who intrigue me."

Again he watched the piano keys as he played. "What intrigues you about me?"

Leaning closer, she allowed both hands to traverse his rock-hard chest. "That someone who looks like he belongs in Texas—"

"The Everglades," he corrected.

"All right, the Everglades. To be truthful, it doesn't matter where you're from. But you don't look like you belong here in Palm Beach."

"I've never been one to follow the norm."

She whispered against his ear, "I like that in a man."

He tilted his head again, just the slightest bit, and her lips brushed gently across a day's growth of his dark, prickly beard. Her insides tingled but she forced herself not to dwell on the lustful sensations this stranger was making her feel.

She was working right now, trying to figure out what he was up to, and she needed to remember that.

"What else do you like in a man?" he asked.

She leaned close. Real close, sliding her hand up his side. She inhaled slowly, her breasts rising, brushing against his back as she reached artfully into the pocket of his jacket.

Exhaling slowly, she could feel her own warm breath wafting against his ear. And then she whispered, "That's an answer best left for another time."

Standing straight, looking at ease and totally unflustered, Angel tucked the wallet she'd effortlessly picked out of his pocket into her handbag. What she'd just done wasn't legal by any stretch of the imagination, and if he found out she'd swiped his wallet he'd probably call the cops and she'd go to jail.

But she needed to know a few details about him, and something told her he wouldn't be forthcoming with straight answers if she blatantly asked him what the hell he was up to. Taking the wallet had been a necessity.

Angel stepped back to his side and took a cool, calming drink of her martini, watching his sparkling dark brown eyes over the top of her glass. After a slow perusal of his deeply tanned face, a chance to memorize the tiny little laugh lines at the corners of his eyes and the way the neon lights danced across his coffee-colored hair, she set her glass back on the piano.

"I need to powder my nose," she lied, then

smiled her best I'm-going-to-charm-you-if-it's-
the-last-thing-I-do smile. "You will be here when
I return, won't you?"

"I'm not going anywhere until I get an answer
to my last question."

"Just give me a few minutes," Angel said, trailing candy apple red fingernails across his shoulder, "and I'll try to come up with a proper
response."

She strolled away, winding through tables and
little cliques of men and women, wondering if he
was watching her—hoping he wasn't, yet knowing deep down inside, in a portion of her that
hadn't thought about rollicking on satin sheets in
a very long time, that he was.

She didn't dare rush, although she was dying
to take a quick peek inside his wallet to hopefully
find a few truthful details about the stranger
who'd been following her—the stranger who excited her—before hurrying back to the piano and
returning the leather billfold to its proper place.

With every word he'd said in that seductive, almost hypnotizing way, and with every note he
masterfully played on the piano, she longed to
know more about him.

The little girl's room was almost as spiffy as the
lounge, large and luxurious, with stalls nearly as
big as her bathroom at home, and as luck would
have it, every single one was empty.

She ducked inside the first stall. Without turning around, she slammed the door closed behind
her, but it slammed right back. It smacked her in
the derriere and if she hadn't thrust her hands
outward to stop her forward momentum, she

would have crashed into the wall or, even worse, dove head first into the toilet.

Her heart thudded heavily inside. A lump caught in her throat. She was afraid to turn around for fear of what she might see—that the stranger had caught on to what she'd done and that he'd followed her to this lonely little place, where no one could hear her screams above the raucous music outside.

And then she heard the voice.

"Let me in. Now!"

3

"*W*hat on earth do you think you're doing?"

Angel grabbed Emma's bare arm and tugged her into the bathroom stall, slammed the door shut and locked it. All of her nerves stood on end and she felt her eyes narrow at her friend. "I thought you were . . . were . . . Damn it, Emma! You nearly scared me to death."

"Sorry."

Angel forced herself to take a deep, calming breath. "You know, Em, I came *this* close to pulling my knife on you. Do me a favor—next time you try to accost me in a toilet, announce yourself first."

Emma shoved her fists into her hips. "If you hadn't been so preoccupied, you would have heard me call out your name."

"I'm not used to people following me into the restroom."

"Yeah, well, I want to know almost as badly as you do who the stranger is, *and,* I might add, I'm here to protect you in case he figures out that you picked his pocket."

"You saw me?"

Emma rolled her eyes. "You used to practice the fine art of pickpocketing on me and your brothers. I know your moves."

"I was that obvious?"

"The flirting was obvious. I noticed. The bartender noticed. I'm sure half the people in town will be talking about it over their morning mocha and I'm sure a lot of guys will be vying to be the next victim of your amorous attentions. *But*, you're good at picking pockets, Angel. *Really* good. And I don't think the Piano Man or anyone else but me has the remotest idea what you were doing in addition to fondling his abs."

Angel sighed with the greatest relief. "Thank God."

"That doesn't mean you should stand around here lollygagging," Emma continued. "He could catch on at any moment and then, sweetie, he might call the cops and you'll be up shit creek."

"Seems to me you're the one doing all the lollygagging."

"And I'll keep right on lollygagging if you don't open up that wallet so we can find out who he is."

Angel pulled the battered leather wallet out of her handbag and even though she felt guilty opening it up, she felt a bigger desire to get the scoop on the guy she had—to be perfectly honest—just robbed.

"Let's see," Angel said, examining the contents.

"Florida driver's license under the name Thomas Donovan."

"Just call him Tom for short."

"All right," Angel said, "Tom the hunk from your beach vacation dream lives in a post office box in Everglades City."

"I imagine it must be terribly crowded in there, especially for a guy his size. Those P.O. boxes can be awfully small and what is he? Six-two?"

"Six-three. Two-ten," Angel said, looking up from the wallet to smile at Emma. "And let me tell you, that two-ten, at least the part I fondled, is *all* muscle."

"I'm beginning to think *I* should have checked him out."

"You would have been far too blatant."

"I can be sneaky when necessary."

"I'll remember that the next time I need someone to go undercover with me."

"All right, forget it. I can't be sneaky but I can be nosy. So tell me, how old is he?"

"Thirty." Angel thumbed through the wallet's contents. "He's got four crisp hundred-dollar bills, a few twenties, a five, and a couple of ones. No business cards. No emergency information card. No photos."

"And maybe he has nothing to hide," Emma added.

"Maybe." Angel closed the wallet and tucked it back into her handbag. "But when I get home, I'll see what information I can dig up on our Mr. Donovan."

"That's *when* you get home. Right now you'd better get the wallet back into his jacket before he realizes it's gone, puts two and two together, and you end up in the can."

Angel strolled out of the bathroom, calm, composed, and trying not to look like the thief she was. Nabbing the wallet had been a cinch. Of course, when she saw Tom standing beside the piano instead of sitting at it, she realized that returning it to the pocket inside his jacket was going to be a bit more difficult.

Jorge was back at the bench and Tom was watching him do his best Scott Joplin imitation. Jorge had a unique, jazzed-up style of piano playing. He, along with the best chocolate-with-a-hint-of-mint martini in town, were the stars of the club. Angel could nurse one drink all evening, and listen to Jorge's entertaining style late into the night. Still, Jorge's talent couldn't compare with Tom's inimitable artistry.

Tom was a master pianist. His music soul-searing. Breathtaking.

He was pretty damn breathtaking, too, from the top of his long, wavy hair, to his sleek, bun-hugging black slacks and black alligator boots.

Why it popped into her head she hadn't a clue, but she couldn't help but wonder if Tom played a woman's body with the same finesse, coaxing sweet sounds out of his lady as they lay together in a sweaty tangle of legs and arms. She wondered, too, if he could coax sweet sounds out of a woman who hadn't had sex in five years because she was too afraid of being hurt.

Damn it all. She didn't want to think about sex or having sex. She needed to get Tom's wallet back in his pocket, then get the heck out of Jazzzzz, go home, soak in a tub of hot bubbles while imbibing some mind-numbing chardonnay. After that, she'd get on the Internet and see what kind of dirt she could dig up on the Piano Man.

Tom seemed to be lost in Jorge's music when she slipped up behind him and put a light hand on his arm. "Care to dance?" she asked.

He turned and leaned against the Steinway. Downing the last of his beer, he put the empty bottle back on the edge of the piano, then gave her body a shameless and ever so deliberate perusal. "Fast isn't my style," he said, an easy smile touching his perfectly kissable pair of lips. "I prefer slow and easy."

She tried not to focus on his mouth. Tried not to think about sex. Unfortunately the man oozed sensuality. It was in his walk, in his talk, in his smile. Not thinking about him in a carnal way would be physically and mentally impossible. She'd fight it, but how could she, when she'd elected to flirt with him in order to accomplish her mission?

Hang on to your libido, Angel warned herself as she moved in close and put on her most charming and enticing smile. "I thought you didn't follow the norm."

His eyes sparkled. "I don't."

She took another step closer and his gaze trailed to her fingers as they whispered down the sleeve of his leather jacket, settled on the back of his hand, and feathered over his knuckles. "Then dance slow and easy with me in spite of the music."

When he didn't refuse, she slipped her hand into his and drew him out to the dance floor. That, however, was the only leading Angel had to do. Once they were in the midst of the swarm of people, Tom wove his hands around her waist and tugged her against his warm, hard body.

Their hips melded. The friction of their thighs and legs rubbing together could have caused sparks to fly about the room. Angel's breasts brushed against Tom's chest, her suddenly hard nipples chafed against her lacy bra, and summoning up all the willpower known to woman, she held back the I'm-dying-to-taste-your-lips-right-this-very-instant sigh that begged to escape her nearly heaving lungs.

God, it had been a long time since anything had felt so good.

And they'd just begun to dance.

Tom moved slowly, his bristly yet ever so soft cheek caressing hers, his warm breath drifting like a downy feather over her ear. Inside, way down deep, her body pulsed and butterflies flitted around in her stomach. They were the loveliest yet almost foreign sensations.

Dancing with Tom had been a mistake. Yet everything about him felt right, as if they should have been together years ago but by some unfathomable force of nature they'd been torn apart before they'd had a chance to meet.

And since it felt so right and she knew that was oh so wrong, she figured she should push away. End this silly little tease before, heaven forbid, he should want to take her to bed.

But she couldn't back off. She still had to return

his wallet. It had been her mistake to play with fire, and she couldn't pull away from the flame until she'd finished her little game.

Somehow she gathered her wits together. Of course, that's when Tom chose to tug her even closer, something she would have thought impossible when it was already difficult to tell where her body ended and his began. With his hands pressed against the small of her back, they danced cheek to cheek, very close and very personal.

The scent of cloves drifted from his skin to her senses. It was more intoxicating than a chocolate martini, more tingly than bubbling champagne, more seductive than all the schoolgirl dreams she'd ever had of being romanced and loved by a man who'd treat her right.

Warm lips hovered over her ear, shooting a shiver of delight all the way down to her toes, then up again to quiver in that intimate place where all women love to quiver.

And then he whispered, "You know, Angel, I would have told you anything you want to know about me. You didn't have to pick my pocket."

Anxiety tightened her chest. The shiver of delight twisted into cold, stark panic. But she was good at hiding her emotions, and she wasn't about to show them now.

Drawing her cheek from Tom's, she tilted her head back just enough for their eyes to meet. His were tinged with devilish laughter. Hers, she knew, were filled with a mixture of surprise and annoyance. She'd hit him with a questioning glare, as if she had no idea what he was talking about, but something told her the Piano Man wouldn't buy her innocence.

Instead, she smiled. "I'd lie and tell you you've imagined things, but I doubt you'd believe me."

The grin never left his face—not when he plucked his damnable wallet, which had borne not one bit of useful information, from her handbag; not when he waved the blasted thing before her eyes; not when he tucked it back inside his jacket. And he kept right on grinning when he said quite smugly, "I don't like liars."

Angel shrugged, hoping she wouldn't appear the least bit vulnerable. "What about pickpockets?"

"I haven't yet made up my mind."

In the same graceful way he played the piano, Tom waltzed her to the far side of the dance floor, guiding her with a gentle nudge of his hand in hers, his legs pressing against her legs, his entire body twisting and turning her, holding her intimately close, until they reached a quieter, more secluded place.

"Now," he said, his brown eyes narrowing, "are you going to tell me why you felt compelled to take my wallet?"

She wove her fingers into the silky dark hair at the back of his head, not only because it felt so darn lovely, but because she wanted to claim some measure of control. "Because," she whispered close to his lips, "I wanted to know who you are."

"And now you know. I'm Tom Donovan and if I'm not mistaken, you're the ever-so-delightful Angel Devlin."

"Did you pick the wallet out of my purse to find that bit of information?"

"Fortunately Jorge was very forthcoming with everything," Tom said, swaying effortlessly with the bluesy tune Jorge had begun to play. "I asked the questions and paid him for his answers before your pretty little hands went digging into my jacket for something to steal."

"All right, so now in addition to my name, you know I'm an expert pickpocket."

"Not so expert." He grinned wickedly. "I caught you."

"But you didn't come after me."

"I hoped you'd come back."

"Why? So you could personally haul me off to jail?"

Tom shook his head. "Because I liked the feel of your hands on my chest and your lips on my cheek. If I hauled you off to jail we'd end up enemies. The fact that you came back means there's a chance for more."

"You know nothing about me but my name." And the feel of my body, Angel thought, just barely hanging on to her composure as Tom's hands glided down the curve of her spine, then flared over the sides of her waist and settled on her hips. "Why would you want more?"

"I paid Jorge for a lot more information than just your name," he said. "I know you're a private investigator and that you cater to the ultra-rich. I know that your office-slash-home is right here on Worth Avenue in a building you share with Ma Petite Bow-Wow, the local pamper-your-pooch shop. And if Jorge knows what he's talking about, you're thirty years old, five feet eight inches tall, weigh one-thirty-two—"

"Thirty-one dripping wet."

Tom grinned, his laughing gaze locking onto hers. "Should we get naked and dripping wet and weigh each other?"

"Not tonight."

"It's close to midnight. It'll soon be tomorrow."

"Are you always in such a rush to get naked and dripping wet?"

He shrugged lightly. "Depends on the woman."

"Trust me, I'm the wrong woman."

"I disagree."

The music picked up tempo and so did Tom's moves. He spun around with Angel captured in his arms, the heat of his embrace, the closeness of their cheeks, and the scent of his spicy aftershave overwhelming her, making her dizzy.

And then he slowed again. His heart beat against her breasts. Warm breath whispered against her ear. "From what Jorge told me—that you wear Donna Karan's Cashmere Mist and Manolo Blahniks if you can get them on sale—you could easily be the right woman. Of course, there's also the fact that you're soft in all the right places. And going back to your original question, *that*, Angel, is why I want more of you."

Angel laughed lightly. "Jorge was a virtual font of information."

"I figured the soft-in-all-the-right-places part out for myself," Tom said, his hands drifting slowly from her waist to her bottom.

She leaned back slightly and gave him the evil eye. "Excuse me, but we don't know each other well enough for you to touch me where you're touching me."

A grin sparkled in his eyes. The dimple at the side of his mouth deepened, as his fingers began to slide again, but not up to her waist. Oh, no, lascivious Tom Donovan's fingers slithered down to her thighs.

That was the first really big mistake he'd made since he'd chosen to follow her.

His fingers stilled. His eyes narrowed, and she knew he'd found the one thing she didn't want anyone to find.

Again his hand began to move, to explore, gliding up and down, over and around the not-so-little lump on her right thigh. His eyes narrowed even more as his gaze held hers and locked. "That wouldn't be what I think it is, would it?"

Angel grinned slowly. Wickedly. At last, she again had the upper hand. "If you think it's a slim but extremely sharp stainless steel stiletto that could carve out a man's Adam's apple in the blink of an eye, you've guessed right."

One of Tom's dark, bedeviled eyebrows rose. "I never would have expected a sweet thing like you to carry a stiletto."

"That, Mr. Donovan, just goes to show that you really don't know as much about me as you think you do."

Strong masculine fingers continued to whisper over her thigh, over her knife. "Do you have a permit to carry a concealed weapon?"

Angel nodded, drawing a perfectly manicured fingernail across his warm, taut throat. "And, my dearest darling Tom, I know how to use it."

"You wouldn't be planning to use it on me, would you?"

"All depends."

"On what?"

"How fast you can get your hands off my thighs."

In spite of her threat, there was laughter in his eyes. "You've got nice thighs. I'm not too sure I want to move my hands. But, gentleman that I am—even though you're thinking I don't have a gentlemanly bone in my body—I'll remove them."

"Thank you."

He slid his fingers and palms back to her derriere, causing deliciously lovely tingles to scatter through her insides, in spite of her attempts not to feel anything, and rested them there. "You know, Angel, you not only have nice thighs, but you've got a nice butt, too. I noticed that when you sashayed into the club tonight."

She'd had her fingers in his overly long but irresistible-to-the-touch hair but suddenly, instinctively, and ever so gracefully, one hand shot down to her skirt, through the slit at the front of her right leg, and she wrapped her fingers tightly around the hilt of her knife. "If you prize that bit of manhood between your legs, I strongly sugest you put your hands back where they belong."

He winked. "As you wish." Once again Tom caught her waist, then did another little spin with her in his arms. "For now."

The man was insufferable. On top of that, he wanted to be in charge of what was going on between them just as much as she wanted to be in charge. That probably didn't bode well for either of them.

She should walk away. She should put an end to the dance they were sharing—both mentally, physically, and emotionally. But between Tom's overabundance of testosterone and her sudden desire to have sex with a stranger—she couldn't leave.

Not yet.

She still needed some answers from the Piano Man.

"So, Mr. Donovan—"

"Tom. Mr. Donovan was my dad."

"All right, Tom. Why were you following me?"

"I like sleek red Jaguars." His lips were close to hers as he spoke. His brown-eyed gaze held her transfixed. His voice was as deep and melodic as the music he'd played and his hair felt like threads of silk winding lightly around her fingers.

Stay calm, she reminded herself. Stay in control.

"I also like women with honey-blond hair and long, slender necks," he continued, "and the second I saw you at Holt Hudson's place, I knew I wanted to get to know you."

Mention of Holt's name was like a splash of cold water on her libido. "You were at Holt's?"

"I was on my way to his place when I saw you pulling out," he answered, as if that shouldn't have been any surprise.

"Do you visit him often?"

Angel felt the muscles tense in Tom's neck. "I haven't been inside Palazzo Paradiso in twenty-six years."

"I see."

His brow rose. "Do you?"

She shrugged. "All right, maybe I don't. Holt Hudson doesn't allow just anyone into his home or even onto the grounds. So why don't you tell me how you know Mr. Hudson?"

"I'm his godson."

That was an answer she never would have expected. "I didn't know he had a godson."

"Are you privy to his personal life?"

"No, but I wasn't aware anyone else was, either."

"If you must know, I'm not privy to anything in Holt's life. Like I said, I haven't seen him in twenty-six years and I thought it was high time I paid him a visit. After all, he *is* the one who killed my dad."

Angel ceased to move. But no sooner had she stopped swaying with the music than Tom had her dancing again, as if his admission shouldn't have come as any shock.

"Your father was *that* Mr. Donovan?" Angel asked. "The cat burglar?"

Tom's eyes narrowed. "So I've been told."

How easily it would be to turn the conversation toward his dad, to the reason or reasons why Tom didn't believe his father was a cat burglar, but right now she had to concentrate on his feelings about Holt Hudson. She needed to find out what he was up to. If his motive for wanting to see Holt, who was about to come out of seclusion after twenty-six years, could foul up her plans for the gala, she had to keep him from seeing the billionaire.

She toyed with the hair drifting over the collar of his leather jacket. "I can't imagine what it must be like to lose a parent in such a horrid way," she said, knowing it was tough enough watching Alzheimer's kill her mom a little more each day.

"Not many people can."

"But . . ." She sighed lightly, her eyes filling with concern. "I'd think seeing Holt Hudson would be the last thing you'd want to do."

"Why do you think that?"

"I imagine you despise him. God knows when I despise someone, I make a point of keeping my distance."

"I've kept my distance for twenty-six years."

"So why see him now?"

"Because until a few months ago I didn't know he existed." He twirled her around, then tugged her against his chest.

Angel drew in a deep breath as her breasts pressed against his pecs, as their hearts beat hard and fast, in time with each other.

"I blocked the first four years of my life out of my mind," Tom continued, his dark brown eyes turning black and intense. "I couldn't remember my dad, my home, the kids I'd played with, or the night my dad was shot. And now all of a sudden bits and pieces of long-forgotten memories keep flashing through my mind, like my dad's blood and his pain and his tears, and they're all so clear, so real, that they could have happened yesterday."

Angel could see the muscles tighten in Tom's jaws, felt the tension in his back. "I need answers, Angel. Answers only Holt can give me, beginning with the reason why he put six bullets into my dad when they were supposedly the best of friends."

"Because your father broke into Holt's home." The words flew out of Angel's mouth without forethought. She should have kept silent, but Tom's dad had been a thief. And if what she'd read about the break-in was true, if the gossip she'd heard could be believed, Chase Donovan had been on the verge of attacking Holt's wife when he was shot. That thought alone made her believe Tom's dad had deserved everything he'd gotten.

"Read the newspaper accounts of what happened," Angel said, trying to sound like the voice of reason. "Get the police report and you'll know exactly what took place. Your dad opened a safe that was supposed to be impossible to crack and took a statue that was and still is worth a king's ransom. And—"

"And that justifies killing a man who was unarmed?"

"Your dad was attacking Holt's wife."

"I don't believe it. I *won't* believe it." Tom swirled her in his arms, holding her tight. Close. His breath was warm against her mouth as he spoke. "Something else happened that night. Something Holt Hudson has kept secret all these years, and I'm going to find out what."

"You plan to harass him?"

"I plan to talk to him. I don't care how I make that happen."

Angel wove her fingers into his hair. Her narrowed eyes were filled with an impassioned warn-

ing when she looked him straight in the eye.
"Leave him alone."

"Why?"

"Because he's a good man who doesn't deserve
to be badgered. He's decent and honorable and
he's lived with a lot of pain and heartache the last
twenty or so years."

"And my father spent three days bleeding to
death from six goddamned bullet holes."

"Did you ever stop to think that if your dad
hadn't hightailed it out of Holt's place after he
was shot, if he'd gone to the hospital or even
called the police—which an innocent person
would have done—he might not have bled to
death?"

"Of course I've thought about it. I've also wondered why the hell we ended up in the Everglades, stuck in a miserably hot car in the middle
of nowhere with nothing to eat or drink." Tom's
fingers bore into her back. "I want to know why
my dad had to die slowly and painfully, with no
one to care for him but his four-year-old son who
was scared out of his mind."

Slowly Tom eased his grip, his touch light as he
held her close, but his eyes were red with fury and
grief, and they held on to hers as if looking for
compassion and understanding.

"I'm sorry," Angel said softly.

Tom plowed a hand through his hair. For a moment she thought he was going to walk away, go
someplace where he could brood by himself. Instead, he caressed her cheek gently, then curled
his warm, callused fingers around the back of her

neck. "I may never get all the answers I want, but I'm sure Holt could clear up a few of the things I need to know. Is that too much to ask? To want?"

"*I* don't think it's too much," she answered honestly. "But Holt obviously doesn't feel that way. And no matter how much you want him to tell you all he knows, I don't think you'll ever get him to open up."

"You're wrong, Angel. I will see him. I will talk to him—if it's the last thing I do."

Angel shook her head in frustration. The man was too damn stubborn for his own good—or hers. And if he harassed Holt in any way, she had the sickening feeling the plans for her gala would meet a tragic death.

"Look, Angel," Tom said, taking her hand and tugging her from the dance floor to a place close to the entry, "this evening wasn't supposed to be about Holt or my dad or what happened twenty-six years ago. It was supposed to be about you and me."

Angel laughed lightly. Nervously. As much as she might have liked this evening to have been about her and Tom, she knew the gala—and Holt—came first.

"At this stage of the game, there is no you and me, but"—she smiled—"if you'd like to change that scenario, promise to leave Holt Hudson alone."

"That's a promise I won't make."

"Then I'll have to keep an eye on you. Make sure you don't do anything that would annoy the hell out of Mr. Hudson."

One of Tom's damnably sexy eyebrows tilted. "Does that mean you're going to follow me wherever I go?"

"Oh, I'll be following you, Mr. Donovan, but I won't be as blatant about it as you were when you followed me tonight. And if I'm not following you, rest assured someone else will be." It was all a bluff, of course. She worked alone. But Tom Donovan didn't need to know that.

"You sound as if you don't trust me," Tom said, all sweetness and innocence, a phony, playful grin plain as day on his face.

"You've given me a lot of reasons not to." Angel moved in close to Tom and tilted her head so she could glare at him eye to eye. "I have a lot of connections in this town. On top of that, I'm one hell of a knife thrower. And let me tell you something, Mr. Donovan." She poked a finger into his chest. "If you do anything, and I mean *anything*, to hurt Holt Hudson or to upset him, I'll get even."

"What? You plan to cut off my balls?"

Angel's gaze darted to the zipper on the black slacks that fit Tom snugly. Nicely. Slowly her smiling eyes drifted back to his face. "If I have to."

Tom laughed. "You'll have to get your hands on them first. And let me tell you this, sweetheart." He tugged her against his rock solid body and whispered close to her lips. "If, or should I say when that happens, using your sweet little stiletto on me will be the last thing on your mind."

4

It was half past midnight when Tom climbed down the steps leading into the living quarters on *Adagio*, the sleek yacht moored in his estate's private dock. The scent of his grandfather's always brewing coffee drew him through the cozy living room to the galley, where he found a plate of Pop's freshly made peanut butter cookies. They'd been Grandma's favorite, at least that's what Pop had told him. She'd died before Tom was born, but Pop talked about her every day, as if she were still by his side.

Tom tossed his leather jacket over a small table cluttered with fishing magazines, pinched off a piece of a chewy, sugar-dusted cookie, and popped it into his mouth before filling the sink with hot water and dish soap, to clean up Pop's mess.

He plunged his hands into the suds and a memory slammed into him. A memory that was so damn vivid, so damn real.

It was hot. The humidity thick and heavy. He

could hardly breathe as he sat inside Pop's rattle-trap pickup and struggled to see over the dash. He heard the crunch of gravel beneath the wheels as the old man he'd met just a couple of days before drove down the narrow winding road and stopped in front of the cabin that stood on stilts.

"This is your new home," the man had said. "And by the way, why don't you call me Pop? That's what your dad called me, and I kind of like the sound of that better than Grandpa."

Tom had slid out of the truck and hid behind the open door until Pop was able to coax him toward the house with the promise of a peanut butter cookie and a big glass of milk. He remembered his stomach growling. Remembered being hungry, because he'd pushed away the food the cops and the psychologists and all the other people who'd questioned him and poked and prodded him had shoved in front of his face.

He remembered hearing the strange noises coming from the swamp. The mosquitoes. And he remembered being scared, until Pop slipped his big hand around Tom's little one and led him toward the cabin. They'd walked up the stairs together, Tom tripping over the laces of his untied tennis shoes as he tried to keep up with the man who was still a stranger to him.

Finally Pop pushed open a squeaky screen door and they stepped into a big old kitchen with glass doors that led out to a porch overlooking sawgrass and water. It wasn't the ocean he'd seen through the glass doors at home, but Pop had told him he needed to forget his other house. Needed to forget everything about the past and move on.

There wouldn't be any more fancy clothes or expensive dinners in restaurants. There'd be gator tail to eat. Fish that they'd catch right outside the back door. And cookies.

Tom remembered the first whiff of Pop's peanut butter cookies. Remembered dipping one in a big glass of cold milk and nibbling on the edges as he looked out the window at the mysterious place he would now call home.

He also remembered the piles of dishes, and Pop patting him on top of his head. "You're a big boy now," he'd said, leading Tom toward the sink and showing him how the dishes were supposed to be washed. "Time you start earning your keep."

Tom laughed at the memory. Hell, he'd never done a dish in his entire four years of life, and suddenly he was faced with a week's worth. Pop still hated to clean the kitchen and Tom still made sure the dishes got done. It was the least he could do for the grandfather who'd taken him in, raised him, and loved him after the pampered life he'd always known came to a screeching halt.

Through the window over the sink Tom could see the tall palms that framed Mere Belle, the oceanfront chateau where he'd lived until Pop became his guardian; the home he'd completely forgotten, like so many other things, until a couple of months ago when he'd inherited a fortune from the grandparents he'd never known, and Pop was forced to tell him about the past.

There was still so much he didn't know, a lot he couldn't remember, but bit by bit the memories were returning.

He scrubbed brown coffee stains out of a SEE YA LATER ALLIGATOR mug, one of the few they hadn't been able to get rid of when he and Pop sold their gator farm in the Glades and moved to Palm Beach. He thought about hiring a housekeeper to help out in the three-story chateau. Someone who wouldn't mind coming out to the yacht to clean up after Pop so Tom would have more time to refurbish the Gilded Age mansion and landscape the rest of the estate.

But Tom knew his eighty-seven-year-old white-haired grandfather would pitch a fit if Tom paid someone good money to do the dishes. Hell, Pop had pitched a fit about leaving the Glades and living in a house *and* a town that was far too fancy for him.

There were times when Tom was sure the man was more trouble than he was worth. But when Pop said he'd leave the Glades if Tom got him a fishing boat to live on, Tom hustled down to Miami to find just the right boat, one with doors wide enough for a walker or a wheelchair for that day when Pop set aside his pride and accepted the fact that arthritis was crippling him and he needed more than a cane to help him get around.

He'd found a barely used eighty-foot Dalla Pietá in Miami and named her *Adagio,* then personally stripped the master bedroom of all the fancy furnishings and fitted it with the bed Pop had slept in with his wife. He'd hung his grandmother's mirror on the wall over the dressing table where she'd brushed her long silver hair, and placed the knickknack shelves Pop had lovingly built in pretty much the same places where they'd hung in the cabin. After that he'd carefully placed all of the Hummel figurines she'd collected for over forty years.

It might not be the cabin in the Glades, but Tom had transformed every room and now the so-called fishing boat wreaked of home. Still, Pop put up a stink over Tom paying an arm and a leg for the big and much too fancy yacht. Hell, if they weren't arguing over Pop's fishing boat they'd argue about something else. It seemed to be a way of life for them, but damn if he didn't love the old man.

After wiping the last cookie sheet, Tom poured himself a cup of Pop's thick as sludge coffee and let his thoughts drift back to another sparring match, one with not-so-sweet-and-innocent Angel Devlin, the lady with the extremely sharp stainless steel stiletto strapped to her thigh and a tongue that was just as sharp. She intrigued him. So did her curves, and he'd done his best to run his fingers over every silk-covered speck of her heavenly body. He would have touched the specks that weren't covered with silk, too, if her protests hadn't been so pointed.

There wasn't one doubt in his mind that Angel hoped she'd never set eyes on him again, but Tom had no intention of ending what had begun tonight. Angel Devlin didn't know it, but she was going to get him into Holt Hudson's mansion, and at some point in time, before or after that event—and the sooner the better—he was going to get her into his bed.

Taking a swallow of the bitter black coffee laced with chicory, he headed out to the sun deck, where Pop sat until one or two most every morning. Tom could smell the cherry tobacco from Pop's pipe and heard the soft creak of the wooden rocker Pop had crafted for his wife fifty-plus years ago.

The light breeze rustled through Tom's hair when he stepped outside. His footsteps could barely be heard over the lap of salt water against the hull, but Pop seemed to sense that he was there.

Rocking gently as he stared out at the starry sky, Pop took the pipe he'd been puffing on out of his mouth. "Did you talk to Holt?" he asked, setting his pipe in the green alligator-shaped ashtray Tom had made him in second grade.

Tom walked across the deck and leaned on the railing, facing the water instead of his grandfather. "I saw Holt, but we didn't talk."

"Did you get inside his mansion?"

"I got as far as a second story window."

"Couldn't do it, huh?"

"Nope," Tom said, shaking his head as he remembered standing on the window ledge and the dread that had engulfed him when he'd thought about the cramped prison cell he'd be stuck in if he was caught. He remembered the way his gut had clenched when he saw Holt and the way he'd wanted to twist his hands around the neck of his father's killer.

He drew in a deep breath and let it out slowly, glad he hadn't gone through with that damn foolish plan. Glad he now had another means of getting to Holt—the lovely Miss Devlin.

Turning, Tom watched his grandfather strike a

match and hold the flame over the bowl of the old meerschaum pipe so he could once again puff on it. "You giving up on your plan to confront Holt?" Pop asked, looking at Tom as he shook the burning match to put out the fire.

"I gave up on the plan to break into his home." Tom grinned. "Now I've got another plan in the works."

The rocker stopped its creaking. "I don't like the sound of that."

"Don't worry, Pop. I know what I'm doing."

Pop shook his head slowly, a sure sign that he was annoyed with Tom for pursuing Holt. He wanted Tom to forget the past. But Tom was on a mission, and he wasn't about to let anyone or anything get in his way.

"Did you catch any fish today?" Tom asked, changing the conversation.

"Nope. Ended up calling Jeb's place in the Glades and ordering fresh gator tail since you can't get it anywhere in *this* town. He's sending it FedEx so tomorrow night I plan to have me a feast." Pop puffed easily on his pipe, and smoke swirled in front of his face. "You want to join me?"

"I might have a date."

Pop grinned. "Met someone, huh?"

"Met someone and already had a fight with her." It was more than Pop needed to know, but he'd never kept anything from his grandfather.

Pop's grin disappeared. "That's not a good way to start a relationship."

"It's not going to be a relationship," Tom said adamantly. "She knows Holt and I figure she can get me in to see him."

"I see," Pop said, disappointment ringing in his words. "You're going to use her."

"I've got more important things than a romantic relationship to think about now."

"You know," Pop said, his pipe gripped between his teeth as he pushed his arthritic body out of the rocker, grabbed his cane, and maneuvered slowly toward Tom, "your dad used to use people. In fact, he tried using your mom when he first met her."

It wasn't often that Pop opened up about Chase or Amélie, and Tom was anxious for his grandfather to tell him more about the father he'd barely known and the mom he hadn't known at all. "Did he?"

"Sure as hell did." Pop wrapped his gnarled fingers around the railing to help support his frail, bent body, and stared across the water. "He figured if he wined her and dined her and made her think he was in love with her, he could get into her parents' safe and steal a diamond and emerald necklace, a family heirloom that was worth a quarter of a mil."

"Did he get it?" Tom asked, standing beside his grandfather, inhaling the scents of cherry tobacco and salty air.

"Didn't take long before your dad figured out he liked the lady more than the thought of putting his fingers on her parents' jewels. In the end he married your mom and she was given the necklace on their wedding day." Pop took the ever-present pipe from his mouth and gazed at his grandson. "I guess you could say he had his cake and got to eat it, too."

"What happened to the necklace?"

"It's in my safe-deposit box. Before your mom's parents—your grandparents—died, I promised them I'd give you the necklace when you marry."

Not that that was ever going to happen, Tom thought. He preferred bachelorhood, coming and going as he pleased, and not being cooped up. But now that he had Pop talking, he wanted to know more. "Is there anything else you're keeping from me?"

"Nope, that's about it. You've got the big fancy mansion your French grandparents bought your mom and dad for a wedding present. You now own their apartment in Paris, the one in Monte Carlo, and their villa in Milan."

"And every penny they amassed when they were alive," Tom said bitterly. "Would have been nice if I'd known they existed. Would have been nice if they'd offered me the pleasure of their company just once or even sent a postcard. That would have been worth a hell of a lot more than all their wealth."

"They didn't want any reminders of their daughter," Pop said, as if that were a good excuse.

"More likely they didn't want to be reminded of the man she married."

"They didn't like the fact that your mother abandoned her chances to be a concert pianist, just to be with your father. They didn't like the fact that Chase dragged your mother from one European city to the next, or that she introduced him to her wealthy friends, only to have him steal their jewels and other priceless objects."

"There's no proof he did any of those things."

"No, there's no proof. But your other grandparents knew it was true just as I knew it was true. And they hated what he was."

"You hated what he was, too."

Pop stuck his pipe back between his teeth, turned slowly and made his way back to the rocker. Lowering his feeble body carefully, he made himself comfortable in the chair.

Pop's gaze found Tom's, and through the swirl of smoke Tom saw the redness in the old man's eyes. "Your father told me he'd gone straight. He told me after your mother died that all he wanted to do was spend time with you, give you the same kind of love your mother would have given you had she lived."

Pop took the pipe out of his mouth and sighed sadly. "He said he'd never again get himself in a dangerous situation—in other words, break into someone's home for the sole purpose of stealing. But he lied to me. I can't forgive him for that. And yes"—he nodded—"I hate what he was."

"Isn't that a bit like the pot calling the kettle black?"

Pop shrugged. "I did the crime and I served my time. I went straight after that. Your father, unfortunately, couldn't bring himself to give up the life."

Tom's eyes narrowed. "Why can't you believe he was framed?"

"Because I know the thrill that comes from stealing something worth a lot of money and not getting caught. Because after I married your grandmother, I had to fight tooth and nail not to turn to robbery when times were rough. Because your father had it all. A beautiful home, a loving wife, good friends, and all the money he could possibly want, but when your mother died giving birth to you, a part of him died, too. And I know that's why he chose to steal again. He didn't need or want another woman to excite him, so he got high on being a thief."

"That's not true, and I'm going to prove it."

Pop's pale brown eyes flashed fury at Tom. "This obsession of yours has brought you nothing but heartache."

"And your refusal to believe that your son was a changed man has made you old and crotchety."

"I don't think about my son unless you bring him up. As far as I'm concerned, for the past twenty-six years you've been my son. You grew up in my house. You've worked beside me, listened to me go on and on about your grandmother, and you've seen me through three heart attacks. But for the past few months, ever since you inherited that godforsaken fortune, you've been a different man. Someone I don't always like."

Pop sighed heavily, and the tenseness that had drawn up his shoulders seemed to disappear. "It saddens me to watch you pour all your energy into the past, when you could have a promising future."

"I can't move on until I learn the truth."

"Even if Holt Hudson has a different story to tell, why would he tell you after all this time?"

"Because he owes me. And because something tells me he'd like to move on with his life, too, but he hasn't been able to do it because the real events of that night are weighing too heavy on his conscience. And his heart—if he has one."

5

The dressing room inside Morganna's on Worth Avenue was cooled to a perfect sixty-eight degrees. Crystal wall sconces and a matching chandelier cast just the right amount of light on the apricot-colored taffeta walls and sparkled in the myriad mirrors scattered here and there.

Champagne cooled in a sterling silver ice bucket. Bottles of Perrier sat on a Waterford crystal tray along with fine glassware, cheese, crackers, fruit, and Godivas. And Morganna herself, dressed as always in a knee-length black shift and rope upon rope of pearls, flitted around as Angel tried on the designer's latest fashions.

"That's not you at all," Emma said, seated on a pillow-strewn sofa, sipping Perrier as Angel paraded the floor in a lacy pink gown that looked an awful lot like lingerie. "You know you look hideous in Easter egg pastels. You need something shockingly bright. Fuchsia, maybe, or neon green."

"I thought I'd try to look a little more demure

for the gala," Angel said, checking the saggy behind and overly tight bodice of the gown in one of the full-length mirrors.

"There's nothing demure about you," Emma quipped. "And the earrings Cartier is donating for the auction—you know, those dangly diamonds you'll be wearing the night of the gala—won't go with baby bottom pink. They're far too extravagant."

In the mirror Angel could see Emma cast an all-knowing smile at the ever-patient owner of the boutique. "We'd like to see everything you have in red," Emma said. "Scarlet. Crimson. Ruby. The brighter and more glitzy the better."

"I believe I have two or three gowns in back that will be just what you're looking for," Morganna said, twirling one pearl-encrusted hand in the air as if she could make the gowns magically appear in the dressing room. "Please, have some champagne while I get them ready for Miss Devlin to try on."

Morganna literally breezed through the glossy apricot-painted door and closed it behind her, while Emma took a sip of Perrier, studied the god-awful pink lace gown, then crossed her legs and settled in for what was bound to be a lengthy dress-buying process.

"What's with you this morning?" Emma asked. "You're usually so decisive when we're clothes shopping. And good heavens, Angel, you know how much you hate pastels. But here you stand, making dreadful decisions about your attire. Where on earth is your mind?"

"Totally and completely preoccupied, I'm

afraid," Angel said, struggling to get out of the gown on her own. "There's so much left to do for the gala. Checks to collect and meetings with the caterer and the florist. And Mom was having a bad morning when I stopped by to fix breakfast for her and Dad.

"And then"—Angel swept a wayward strand of her long, wavy blond hair behind her ear—"Mitzi Christafaro called me on my cell right in the middle of eating my first piece of bacon to tell me that her not-so-discreet husband Oliver had been out all night and she found lavender lipstick on Oliver's white silk boxers. *And*—now, this is a quote direct from Mitzi's lips—'My God, can you believe that any woman with any class would wear lavender lipstick *or* for that matter put her lips *there*? I mean, *there*, right in the middle of his shorts?'"

Angel grinned in spite of her struggle to get out of the itchy pink gown. "And then, before I could even swallow the piece of bacon I'd been chewing while Mitzi went on and on, the woman insisted I drop everything and pop over to her home—not the twenty-eight-room mansion on South Ocean Boulevard but the smaller, fourteen-room cottage in town—and search Oliver's Bentley—not the black and white one but the new burgundy one—for signs of, dare I repeat Mitzi's words"—Angel whispered—"'fornication of the most perverse kind.'"

"Did you?"

"Did I go to Mitzi's or did I find signs of 'fornication of the most perverse kind'?"

"Both."

"Of course I went. Mitzi might be a kook but she's more than willing to donate whatever I suggest to *my* favorite charity, she pays her bills on time, and she has an Oliver emergency at least once a week and she insists that I'm the only one she trusts to check into her personal matters."

With the bodice of the ugly pink gown dangling around her waist, Angel adjusted her flesh-colored satin and lace push-up bra as she headed for the table laden with goodies. She poured a speck of champagne into a glass and took a sip, something she rarely did before four P.M.

"If it weren't for Mitzi and some of the other ladies in town who know I handle their domestic matters with the utmost discretion," Angel went on, "I wouldn't be able to buy a Morganna gown and Manolo Blahniks for the gala or be able to drive a Jag, and I wouldn't have as much time for the other things I need to take care of, like throwing a yearly charity gala."

"You're digressing, Angel. You were very discreetly telling me about Oliver's *perverse fornication*, which is far more interesting than your budget or your time management. So . . . did you find any signs?"

"I've already said far too much." Angel stepped out of the gown and, standing in only her matching lace bikini and bra, took another sip of champagne.

"You've said just enough to pique my curiosity," Emma said, twirling the end of her ponytail. "I love tales of perversity. So spill."

She shouldn't tell a soul, but Emma was the height of discretion and Angel just had to share some of the zany stories about the things she'd done for many of the socialites in Palm Beach.

"Well," Angel said, "I found a tube of lavender lipstick under the front seat and, don't you dare repeat this to a soul, but Mitzi gasped with utter shock when she saw the lipstick and noticed that it was, God forbid, one of those drugstore varieties."

Emma clapped a hand to her chest and giggled. "Oh, my heavens! How could anybody be so unrefined?"

"I was wondering the same thing myself. Of course, I forgot all about the lavender lipstick when I found fuzzy purple handcuffs, a satin blindfold in the same shade of purple, and, of course, a handy-dandy whip."

Emma's nose wrinkled. "You didn't touch any of that stuff with your bare hands, did you?"

"Of course not."

"So what did you tell Mitzi?"

"I didn't have to tell her a thing. She was peeking over my shoulder as I was going through the car with gloved hands, and when she saw all the bondage equipment her face turned redder than my Jag and she ever so discreetly told me that she'd been after Oliver for years to do something to spice up their behind-closed-doors life, and she'd completely forgotten that he'd taken her out in the Bentley and parked in a lonely swamp, someplace, Mitzi said, where frogs croaked and moss dripped from trees and mosquitoes the size of Cora Lee Noble's five-hundred-and-sixty-three-thousand-dollar engagement ring kept crashing into the windows. *Then* he plied her with champagne and, once she was drunker than a skunk, bound her up, stripped her naked—"

"Please. Stop." Emma threw up her hands. "I can't possibly listen to any more of this."

"Well, let me tell you, I didn't want to listen to any more of it, either, but I heard every sordid little detail, and then"—Angel grinned—"I was given quite a lovely check for my services *and* my discretion. So you can't repeat any of this to a soul."

"You know I only talk about sex with you."

"And speaking of sordid stuff," Angel said, then took a quick sip of champagne, "Frederike LeVien's butler called to tell me he thinks the Countess is having an affair with a much younger man, someone he's sure is out to screw her."

"Isn't that the purpose of an affair?"

Angel rolled her eyes. "*Screw* her as in take her for all her money."

"The Countess has oodles of money," Emma said. "That's how she managed to buy her title, and I'm sure one little affair couldn't possibly break her bank account. *And* . . . now, this is going to sound vicious . . . but I really have no sympathy for a woman who lost her husband at the very beginning of the Palm Beach season and put him on ice in some lonely mortuary so she wouldn't have to deal with the intricacies of a funeral until the season is over. Heaven forbid that she should miss one or two balls or polo games or tea parties."

"She *is* a little eccentric," Angel admitted, "but that's neither here nor there. Tonight I'll be keeping an eye on her place and if she goes out, I'll tail her."

"And what are you supposed to do if you find out she *is* having an affair? I mean, it's not like she's underage."

"I won't do anything but report my findings back to her butler. It's up to him if he wants to have a little tête-à-tête with the Countess, or let her children know she might be squandering their inheritance."

Emma leaned back in the chair and hit Angel with a questioning frown. "Don't you get bored spying on the ultra-rich?"

"Boredom is spying on people who may or may not be guilty of worker's compensation fraud, or serving subpoenas on deadbeat drunks living in squalor. And you know, Emma dear, if I got bored around the ultra-rich or, as in your case, the far more classy blue-blooded filthy rich"—Angel grinned—"I wouldn't spend most all of my free time with you."

"God, we're beginning to sound like old maids who can't get a date on Friday night." Emma took a sip of her Perrier. "Perhaps we should work on our sex appeal."

"There is absolutely nothing wrong with your sex appeal," Morganna said, breezing back into the room after she'd obviously been listening to part of Emma's and Angel's conversation through the closed door. "And that sex appeal will be completely enhanced when you slip into one of my creations."

Morganna swept an elegant hand toward the door. "Just take a look at what I've found for Miss Devlin," she said, as two of her assistants floated into the room with not three but five gowns for Angel to try on.

"Oooh," Emma cooed, after the assistants hung the flamboyant dresses for all to see, then exited the plush room. "The feathery one is *so* you, Angel."

"I was thinking exactly the same thing," Morganna said, slipping the knock-your-socks-off crimson gown off its hanger. "Come, Miss Devlin. Let me help you try it on."

"It is rather . . . unique." Angel smiled as Morganna slipped the shreds of gauzy silk over Angel's head.

"It's absolutely scandalous." Emma's eyes were wide and bright with delight. "Everyone in the ballroom at Palazzo Paradiso will be concentrating on you, thinking you're the loveliest creature they've ever seen."

Angel twirled around, the tendrils of dazzling fabric whipping about in the air she'd stirred up. "It's fabulous, but . . ."

"But what?" Emma said, her eyes narrowed as if she couldn't believe Angel could possibly have any complaints.

"I want the auction to be the center of attention, not me."

"You could always put yourself up for auction."

The all-too-familiar male voice took Angel by surprise, jerking her around to see Tom Donovan silhouetted against the bright April sunlight streaming through the windows that faced Worth Avenue.

She wasn't, however, surprised by his thorough

perusal of her body and the sexy crimson gown. But his overt scrutiny *did* annoy her, as did his suggestion that she might be for sale.

"*I* won't be on the auction block," Angel stated.

"How about that dress? I'd pay a pretty penny to—"

"Excuse me, sir," Morganna interrupted, her tone contemptuous to say the least. But a smile touched her dark red lips when Tom stepped out of the glaring light and into the dressing room. "Ah, it's you, Mr. Donovan. I didn't recognize you at first."

"That's quite all right, Morganna."

The ageless designer flitted across the room and touched Tom's darkly tanned forearm. "I'm terribly sorry, Mr. Donovan, but this is a private dressing room and even though you're one of my most favorite people on this whole entire planet, I'm afraid I must ask you to step out of the room, that is, of course, unless Miss Devlin invites you to stay."

Actually she'd love to have him leave, but she had the feeling Tom was up to something, and she wanted to know what.

"He's more than welcome to stay," Angel said, examining him just as thoroughly as he'd studied her, fastening her gaze on Tom's crocodile cowboy boots, the slim cut of his faded Levi's, the snug fit of his white T-shirt, and the muscles that threatened to burst through the fabric. Slowly she inclined her head toward Emma and Morganna. "But would you mind terribly if I asked the two of you to leave so I can share a few private words with Mr. Donovan?"

Emma's eyes narrowed. "Sure. No problem. Keep me in the dark about what the two of you have to say."

Ever the good and proper albeit nosy businesswoman, Morganna smiled and moved to the door. "I'll take Miss Claire into another dressing room. I have several items I'm sure she'd love to try on."

Emma bounced out of her chair, her raven-colored ponytail swishing to and fro. "You wouldn't by any chance have something in lime green, would you?"

"Of course I do, Miss Claire. Please follow me."

When the room was empty, Angel turned her full attention to Tom. "Mind if I ask what you're doing here?"

"Last night ended on a rather sour note. I was thinking maybe we should try again."

Angel ignored his statement and strolled across the room, more than aware of his eyes on the feathery red dress that revealed an awful lot of her chest and nearly every speck of her back, right down to her tailbone. In a gracious-host gesture that would have made Mrs. Alexander of Portia Alexander's Academy proud, she filled one of the delicate pieces of crystal stemware with champagne and offered the glass to Tom.

As he took it from her, she watched his gaze trail lazily over her barely hidden breasts.

"Very nice." Tom took a swallow of champagne, his eyes sparkling at her over the glass. "Is that what you plan to wear to your gala?"

"I haven't decided yet."

Angel took a sip from her own champagne

glass. "So, Mr. Donovan, how did you find me this morning? Did you follow me here?"

"It's Tom, remember. And no, I wasn't following you or anyone else. As a matter of fact, I was across the street talking with an antiques dealer when I saw you come in here with your friend." He wandered about the room, taking in every speck of Angel's anatomy, trying, she assumed, to make her nervous and failing miserably. "Since I never saw you come out, I thought I'd drop by and see if you were still here."

Angel turned. She smacked him with a radiant smile, eyes bright and alluring. She didn't bat her lashes. That was for amateurs. She just made damn sure he saw the twinkle in her eyes and got him to focus on her face instead of her body. "So now that you know I'm here, what do you want to discuss?"

"How I can buy the dress you're going to wear to the gala, since you won't be putting yourself on the auction block."

"You can't buy me *or* my gown. And why you'd want to is beyond me."

"My reasons are quite easily explained. If I own it, I'll have the right to take it off of you whenever I want."

Angel felt one of her perfectly plucked eyebrows raise. "Don't forget I carry a stiletto, Mr. Donovan."

"I haven't forgotten a thing about you."

Angel picked a chocolate-dipped strawberry from a plate and bit off the very end. She chewed it slowly, watching Tom as he sat in one of the easy chairs and crossed a crocodile-booted ankle over his knee.

"Since we both know you didn't come here to try and buy me or my dress, why don't you tell me your real reason for interrupting my shopping."

"I took a look at my social calendar this morning and noticed that the date of your gala wasn't marked." He took a sip of champagne. "Then I went through my stack of invitations and, what do you know? Someone must have left me off your guest list."

Angel smiled, knowing where this line of conversation was leading. "You're new in town. I imagine your name hasn't shown up on a lot of guest lists."

"But now that you know about this oversight, you *will* send me an invitation. Right?"

"I could. Unfortunately, Mr. Hudson has the final say on who's invited and"—Angel shrugged—"you've already told me that Holt refuses to see you. If I'm not mistaken, he wouldn't want you at the gala, either."

Tom's eyes narrowed. "I was under the impression that you were running the show, but obviously Holt's the one in control."

"Holt has donated his home for the night. He's contributing a lot of high-priced items to the auction and he's asked for very little in return." That last part was one whopper of a lie, but Tom didn't need to know just how much power Holt was actually wielding.

"In other words, giving me an invitation is out of the question?"

"You're very perceptive."

"I can be quite devious, too, if I have to be."

"And what's that supposed to mean?"

"Why don't you sneak me in through the back door?"

Angel shook her head. "No."

"Wouldn't you like to know how much I'd be willing to donate to your charity, if you'll just get me into your little party and then share a dance or two with me?"

"No."

Tom took another swallow of champagne, emptying his glass. "Your interest isn't the least bit piqued?"

"All right." Angel shrugged, curiosity getting the better of her. "How much?"

"Ten grand."

A lump settled in Angel's throat at the stunning amount of money he'd just suggested. Unfortunately, no amount of money would be enough, because she knew damn good and well that Holt would throw a fit if she sneaked Tom or anyone else who hadn't been invited into the mansion.

"Ten thousand is quite generous, but as I said before, I can't accommodate your wishes."

"Fifteen."

"No."

"Twenty."

Angel's eyes narrowed. Could that offer possibly be sincere? Or was he merely teasing?

"Am I to believe you have that kind of money burning a hole in your pocket?" Angel asked.

"It's in the bank. Want to check out my account, or have you done that already?"

"I planned to do that later this afternoon or to-morrow."

"I told you before," Tom said, shoving out of the chair and crossing the room to pour himself more champagne, "if you want to know something about me, just ask."

"All right," she said, wondering if she could get a donation from him and still not allow him into the gala, "do you have twenty thousand to spare?"

Tom twisted around to face her. His eyebrow rose. "I have far more than that."

"Do you have twenty-five?"

"You're getting greedy." He raised his glass as if to salute her bravery. "But tell you what. Have dinner with me tonight and let me dance at least every other dance with you at the gala, and we have a deal."

"Your offer is tempting, Mr. Donovan. But you haven't been invited to the gala and even if you were, my dance card is pretty full. On top of that . . . I'm working tonight."

"What? A stakeout?"

"Possibly."

His lips tilted into a smile. "Then I'll give your charity twenty-five thousand if you'll let me spend the night with you." He walked toward her and extended a hand. "Do we have a deal?"

Angel studied his hand, then concentrated on his devilish brown eyes. "You're still not getting an invitation to the gala."

"I didn't mention the gala in my last proposal."

"Twenty-five thousand is a lot of money," Angel said, wondering what sinister plot was being hatched behind his wicked grin.

"You're worth it, aren't you?"

"I'm worth a hell of a lot more than twenty-five grand, Mr. Donovan."

"I'll give you my opinion on that after I've gotten my twenty-five thousand worth."

Tom winked. His comment was so damn smug that Angel considered striking him with a hard right hook. Instead, Tom captured her hand and shook it as if they'd just made a corporate business deal. "I'll pick you up at eight."

Angel shook her head. No way was she going to let him be in control. "Meet me at Jazzzzz at eight. If you're one minute late, I'll leave without you and you can send a check to my office."

"I'm never late." He winked again. "Especially when I get to spend the night with a pretty girl."

Angel's eyes narrowed. "Let's get one thing cleared up right this very minute, Mr. Donovan. You paid for me to take you on a stakeout, not to spend the night with you."

"Obviously you weren't listening or you heard what you wanted to hear." Tom's insufferable grin widened. "Our deal was for you to let me spend the night with you, and let me tell you, sweetheart, that's exactly what I plan to do."

"I thought you said Tom Donovan was lascivious and irritating, not to mention arrogant and cocky." Emma plopped onto the sofa as Angel stalked back and forth across the dressing room. "And if I'm not mistaken, after he ran out on you at Jazzzzz last night, you heartily disagreed with me when I told you the man was a divine dancer, had fabulous hair, a to-die-for body, and the cutest dimple ever to dent the face of a devilishly handsome male. But now you tell me you're going to sleep with him?"

Angel stopped dead in her tracks, the feathery red dress continuing to swirl about her. "I never once mentioned anything about *sleeping* with him. What I said is that I'm spending the night with him."

"And we all know where that can lead."

"It's going to lead to him giving me twenty-five thousand, which is what he's paying for the privilege of going on a stakeout with me, nothing more. However, and this is a really big however, in making the deal I must have had little more than dollar signs operating my brain because apparently I told him that for twenty-five thousand he could spend the night with me, not just go on a stakeout. But let me tell you this, Emma, that sure as hell doesn't mean I'm hopping into his bed or taking off my clothes or even kissing the man. As far as I'm concerned, he can sit on one side of the car all night long and get cramps in his legs. But I am not, I repeat *not*, going to sleep with him."

"It seems to me that you're protesting far too much," Emma said, not even bothering to look at Angel. Instead, she was busy smoothing the folds out in her bright yellow and teal Lilly Pullitzer sundress.

"Give me a break, Em. The man's father was a thief."

"And a gorgeous thief he was," Morganna quipped, breezing into the room with pins, tailoring chalk, and a tape measure draped around her neck. "Why, the moment Chase Donovan set foot in this town he had all the women swooning. It didn't matter if he was a thief or an ax murderer, women wanted him. But I'm sure you already know all the details."

"Only bits and pieces," Angel said, dying to hear more. "Do you know the whole story?"

"Only the parts that interested me." Morganna smiled and, instead of working on the alterations to the fabulous red gown, poured herself a glass of champagne and took a sip. "Gossip is always so interesting—but only timely gossip. I could easily wager a guess that no one in town remembers all the details. What is done is done and best forgotten, because there is always something new to talk about."

"But you knew Chase Donovan?" Emma asked, kicking off her lemon yellow mules and curling her legs beneath her on the couch.

"I met him a time or two when he'd come here with his wife Amélie. Beautiful woman. French, if I remember correctly, and quite petite." Morganna plucked a Godiva from the crystal tray and took a tiny bite. "Poor woman died in childbirth. It was terribly sad to see Chase at the funeral, holding his newborn son in his arms, the tears flowing freely down his handsome face."

Morganna licked her lips, then patted her mouth with a linen napkin. "Carlotta and Holt Hudson—they were the best of friends with Chase and Amélie, but I'm sure you know that— stood at Chase's side through the entire service. So sad. So sad. And poor, poor Chase. He never did get over the loss of his wife."

Morganna took another sip of champagne

while twisting the ropes of pearls she wore around her neck. Her mind seemed to drift back in time, as a wistful smile touched her face.

"I visited Chase when I could get away from my business. In fact, I gave him the most darling little outfits that I'd handmade for his son and"—Morganna sighed deeply—"I tried to ease Chase's pain—you know, a massage here, a kiss there—but, sadly, he could not be consoled."

"You don't know anything about the theft of *The Embrace*, do you?" Angel asked, filling Morganna's champagne glass to keep the woman talking.

"One heard stories that Chase had been a famous cat burglar. It was all very romantic and ever so glamorous—like Cary Grant in *To Catch a Thief*—and I suppose it was thrilling to have Chase in our midst. But there was never any proof that he'd stolen anything—until that night when he broke into Holt's home. He didn't need to steal *The Embrace* because he already had more money than he could possibly spend in a lifetime. All I can assume is that his grief drove him out of his mind and he didn't know what he was doing."

"Is it true that Chase tried to attack Carlotta Hudson?" Angel asked, shifting the conversation just a bit, not wanting to dwell on any one thing too long, for fear Morganna might end her gossiping for the day and get back to business.

"As I said," Morganna explained, "it all happened a very long time ago. But as I recall, Chase's blood was all over Carlotta's bed. There were photos in the paper and of course the police had Holt's statement."

Morganna shook her head in dismay. "It is easy to make assumptions. Perhaps Chase was out of his mind and thought Carlotta was his long-dead wife come back to life. Perhaps. . . . Well . . . I suppose one can speculate about any number of reasons why Chase Donovan stole that statue or tried to assault Carlotta in her bed. But Carlotta was too traumatized after that night to ever speak of the incident and Holt, bless his heart, grieved for his wife as well as the man he shot. It was such a tragedy and, sad to say, with Tom Donovan in town, some of us are being forced to remember those horrible days."

"Do you know Tom Donovan very well?" Angel asked.

"No, no, not that well, although we are fast becoming reacquainted. He's been living in the swamps or some other detestable place for heaven only knows how long. I believe he said he'd only recently learned about the events of twenty-six years ago. Can you believe he forgot everything and that no one, not the grandfather who raised him or his grandparents in France, had the decency to tell him the truth about his parents until just a few months ago?"

"That's awful," Emma said. "Absolutely awful."

"So how did he find you?" Angel asked.

"Apparently he was doing research on his father and mother when he saw a picture of me taken with them at a charity function—so he looked me up." Morganna smiled and took another drink of champagne. "I told him about the clothing I made for him when he was a baby and, needless to say, he was quite touched."

"Did you actually talk about his mother and father?" Angel wanted to know.

"Yes, of course we did. Tom took me out for the loveliest lunch at Bice and we talked for hours on end. In spite of his ghastly attire, he's quite a gentleman and the loveliest man to settle in Palm Beach since his father came here all those years ago."

"He's living in town?" Emma asked, almost choking on the Godiva she'd just popped into her mouth.

"At Mere Belle. He inherited the mansion after his French grandparents died." Morganna smiled with great delight. "He also inherited a sizable fortune. In fact, I believe he might now be one of the richest men in Palm Beach and, Miss Devlin, if he weren't so interested in you, I dare say I'd make a play for him myself."

Angel sipped the last of her champagne, watching Morganna stick pins between her teeth and come after her and the red gown with tape measure in hand. And as Morganna worked on the alterations, Angel couldn't help but wonder how many other women in town were falling prey to Tom Donovan's charms. And wonder, too, how many other women he was willing to pay for the pleasure of their company.

She also wondered if it was the women—herself included—that he was interested in, or if his dastardly charm was all a ruse, part of a carefully hatched scheme to gain access to Holt.

There was only one way to find out. She had to follow through with the threat she'd hit Tom with last night. She had to spy on him.

 6

_T_om tugged his sweat-drenched T-shirt over his head, tossed it across a patio chair, then went back to work with a saw and clippers, cutting back the purple and orange bougainvillea that had invaded nearly every inch of Mere Belle's courtyard during the twenty-six years the chateau sat unoccupied.

Even now, a couple of months after he'd inherited everything that had belonged to his French grandparents, he found it difficult to believe that they sold most everything inside the chateau after Chase had been killed. Found it even harder to believe that they'd had the mansion boarded up. They'd paid the taxes. They'd hired a gardener to come in a few times a year to hack down the weeds.

But they'd neglected the place, ignored it—just as they had Tom.

They'd died a few months apart, of old age, Tom had been told. The will Tom had first heard about two and a half months ago left everything to their only grandchild. Every penny. Not one cent left to charity. Nothing given to friends or devoted servants. Maybe they'd had none.

Tom laughed to himself as he whacked away at a long dead royal Poinciana. He'd probably been damn lucky to have gone to live with Pop instead of getting saddled with his mother's parents. They'd pretty much disowned their daughter, hadn't bothered to come to her funeral or her husband's, and had never set eyes on their grandson.

Had they been completely cold? he often wondered. Totally without emotion? Someday he'd try to find out. Someday he'd visit the other houses that were now his. Someday he'd start doling out some of his millions to people who needed it far more than he did.

But for now, he had to learn the truth about his father's death.

And turn this mansion back into a home.

Of course, a hell of a lot of other people had their own ideas on what should be done with Mere Belle.

Half a dozen landscapers had called or stopped by the mansion in the last few days to tell Tom that in just a matter of weeks they could have the estate looking better than ever. They'd even brought pictures with them, showing him how it had looked in its heyday and how they envisioned it looking after they put a few hundred thousand dollars' worth of work into it.

Snooty interior designers had knocked on his door, too, each one telling him they had the ideal plan for turning his palatial home into a showplace. Most felt contemporary would be his style.

Black and white leather with chrome everywhere. Two wanted to create an African theme, with zebra stripes and leopard prints everywhere, and a massive bed in the master bedroom, draped, of course, in netting to go with the overall look.

No one seemed to understand why he turned them away, but he understood perfectly. Exhausting himself doing yard work and stripping and painting walls was a way of working through the anger that threatened to consume him. At least that's how it had started. But it hadn't taken more than a couple of days of toil and sweat for him to realize that making the mansion and surrounding grounds a home had become a labor of love.

Each time he walked through the nearly empty chateau he remembered long-ago days when he and his father had played hide and seek in the ornately decorated rooms, and when he was outside, images of his dad teaching him to swim in the pool or of them building sand castles on the beach came to mind.

And when he played the grand piano that had been left behind, the one that had belonged to his mom and that he'd had completely refurbished and tuned, he remembered his dad and the strength of his arms as they'd sat together on the piano bench listening to audiotapes of his mother playing Mozart and Beethoven, Rachmaninoff and Gershwin.

How he could possibly have blocked out those memories for nearly twenty-six years amazed him, because they were all so clear now.

Tom ripped a brittle brown vine away from the dead Poinciana and other memories returned. Vicious, haunting recollections of being tugged from his comfortable bed and carried out of the house.

His muscles tensed and a chill raced up his spine as he remembered his father's face, his pain-filled and loving smile, as they huddled together in the front seat of the car. He saw his dad's tie hanging loose, his always immaculate suit coat crumpled and torn, and the dark stains on his white shirt. And he felt the ever-weakening hugs of a man who hummed to him and told him everything would be all right.

But everything hadn't been all right. Everything had gone damn wrong.

His dad died in his arms.

He remembered being questioned by the police and child psychologists about the shooting. They wanted to know where he and his father had driven when they'd left Mere Belle, and over and over again they asked him where Chase had hidden that damned piece of artwork.

He remembered crying for hours on end. He remembered one face after another staring at him, sizing him up, dying to know everything he had locked up inside of his head.

In the end he'd told them nothing they didn't already know. And when they were finished with him, he'd been shuttled off to live in the Everglades with a man he'd never seen before, a grandfather who, over the course of time, convinced him that his former life had been nothing but a dream. Who'd told him that his parents had been killed in a plane crash, and never again spoke of the past.

Until a few months ago, when the attorneys showed up in the Everglades to tell Tom he was a very rich man.

Details were coming back to him now. Little by little. But there were still too damn many questions hanging over his head.

The musical peal of his cell phone jerked Tom out of the past and back to the present. He thought about ignoring the annoying ring because God knows no one called him except guys dying to invest his money and make him richer. Hell, he was already richer than sin. How much more could a man possibly want or need?

Hating the sound of the incessant ringing, he dropped the clippers he'd been gripping in his right hand, strode to the marble-topped patio table, and grabbed the phone. "Hello."

"You're being watched."

Tom frowned, troubled by the worry he heard in his grandfather's voice. "What are you talking about?"

"There's a boat out on the water and for the last half hour now, someone has been standing on the deck watching you."

Tom looked out across the vast expanse of lawn he'd mowed earlier that afternoon and saw little more than the sleek white and black *Adagio* resting at the dock.

"Are you inside the boat, Pop?"

"Figured that was the smartest place to be if I was going to watch the person watching you."

"Well, stay put."

"That was my plan," Pop said, as Tom looked for a better vantage point. "I'm half dead already and if someone's out to get you, I'm not about to put myself in harm's way and rush the inevitable."

That was a lie, of course. Pop would lay down his life for Tom. The feeling was mutual.

With his gaze focused on the ocean, Tom made his way to a life-size statue of a naked goddess standing tall and beautiful while she surveyed the gardens. Hiding behind the marble sculpture, he stared off into the distance, past the palms, the *Adagio*, and across the sparkling and exceedingly calm Atlantic.

"See it?" Pop asked. "The black ski boat with red flames painted on the side?"

"I see it, but I can't see anyone in it."

"Take my word for it, 'cause I've got my best spotting telescope zoomed in on a pretty blonde standing at the wheel. And she's got a pair of binoculars trained on you."

Tom folded his arms atop the goddess's marble breasts and smiled as he stared over her shoulder. "Is my not-so-secretive spy curvy?"

"As far as I can tell."

Well, well, well, was the captivating Miss Devlin watching him to make sure he didn't do anything to mess up the plans for her gala? Or was she just checking him out? Maybe he should wave at her. Maybe he should strip down to nothing and stroll around the grounds.

Of course, maybe it wasn't Angel Devlin.

"Look at her really close, Pop. Does she have a nice tan, great legs, and sapphire eyes?"

"Tell you what," Pop said, his words tinged with annoyance, "why don't I pull my fishing boat away from the dock, motor out to the young lady, and ask her over for drinks and casual conversation so you can check those not-so-important details for yourself?"

"Sarcasm doesn't become you, Pop."

Tom heard his grandfather sigh through the phone. "Look, Tom. You're being watched and I don't like it."

"I don't have anything to hide."

"Your father did. God knows how many people thought that statue he stole—"

"He didn't steal it."

"Yeah, well, a lot of people were sure that he did. They were also sure he hid it in the yard you're standing in now, or in that house you're living in. Hell, the police searched every inch of the place. They searched my place. And they spent days questioning you and me. Now we're back in this godforsaken town and all of that crap is being stirred up again. I don't like it one bit."

"If my dad stole *The Embrace* and hid it here, it would have been found by now. But no one has found it and no one has tried to fence it—"

"That you know of."

"Damn it, Pop, let's not argue."

"Fine by me. We hardly ever argued when we lived in the Glades and you were wrestling gators. If you ask me, we should go back. Open up another gator farm with you running the entire show this time around."

"You know I never liked wrestling gators and I sure as hell hated to charm snakes."

"I suppose you'd prefer wrestling and then charming pretty blond spies?"

"Yeah, I suppose I would."

Again Pop sighed heavily. "Look, son, I've got this god-awful feeling in the pit of my stomach that if we don't get away from this town you're going to end up in a heap of trouble."

"Yeah, well, I've already come to the conclusion that with enough money you can buy yourself out of any trouble you could possibly get into, especially here in Palm Beach. And I've got money to burn."

"I don't like hearing that kind of talk. Maybe I should just go back to the Glades by myself so I don't have to watch you become just another slick-as-swamp-scum rich guy who's too big for his britches."

"If you want to go back—" Tom bit back his words but the silence on the other end of the phone was so deafening that Tom knew Pop understood perfectly well what had been on the tip of his grandson's tongue.

"You want me to go back?" Pop asked, his voice a mixture of choked-back hurt and frustration.

"No, Pop." Tom shoved his fingers through sweat-soaked hair. "I don't want you going back any more than *I* want to go back. I can't explain it, Pop, but I get the feeling I was meant to be here."

"Well, hell, if you want to stay, stay."

"You, too?" Tom asked softly.

"I suppose. Besides . . ."

Tom heard Pop muttering under his breath.

"What is it, Pop? Is everything okay?"

"Let's just say that it's a good thing I'm sticking around because someone's got to keep an eye on all the people spying on you."

"It's *one* person spying on me, Pop, and if I'm not mistaken, that pretty blonde is the woman I'm getting together with tonight."

"I'm not referring to the pretty blonde. I'm talking about the other boat on the water and the other pair of binoculars trained on you all of a sudden."

"What? You mean I have more than one female admirer trying to check me out?"

"It's not a woman, Tom. It's a man . . . and if I'm not mistaken, he's got a devil tattooed on his chest."

7

*S*parks of light glinted off Emma's emerald-studded hoop earrings as she plucked one of Jazzzzz's signature pink and green tortilla chips out of the bowl sitting in the center of the table she shared with Angel. "You didn't really go out on your boat to spy on the Piano Man, did you?"

"Of course I did." Angel crossed her legs, adjusting the gentle folds of her black silk sundress so they covered her always-present stiletto. "But I'm not the only one who was spying on him."

Emma frowned. "No?"

"Dagger was out there, too, in what *used* to be my boat."

"Maybe he was spying on you. God knows the bastard told you more than once that if he couldn't have you—"

"He wasn't spying on me," Angel said, cutting off Emma's words. She didn't want to think about the threats Dagger used to wave around as often as he waved his knife. "He had his binoculars trained on Tom, and when I headed my boat over

to his to find out what the hell he was up to, he
took off."

"Don't tell me he managed to lose you."

"I didn't bother keeping up with him. Besides,
I had other things to do and I figure I'll have the
misfortune of bumping into him soon enough."
She took a sip of Perrier with a twist of lime. "I'll
find out what he's up to then."

Emma nibbled the edge off of her chip. "Did
you have any better luck figuring out what Tom
Donovan is up to?"

Angel laughed lightly. "Yard work."

Emma's frown deepened. "Run that by me
again."

"I spent nearly an hour watching him work in
his courtyard, ripping up weeds, trimming trees,
and drinking beer."

"As I've said before," Emma said, shaking her
head, "P.I. work sounds dreadfully boring."

"It wasn't that boring." Angel took another sip
of her Perrier, the image of Tom's nearly naked
body flashing before her eyes. "He took his shirt
off while I was watching him."

Emma's eyes sparkled as she folded her arms
on the edge of the table and leaned forward. "Let
me guess. He was bronzed and buff?"

A wide smile touched Angel's face. "Think
Hugh Jackman."

"As Wolverine with claws? Or Wolverine
nearly naked? Or in that movie with Meg Ryan?
Or . . . Oh, never mind." Emma patted her heart
in extreme delight. "Hugh Jackman is Hugh Jackman and most women would take him any way
they could possibly get him. So, now that you've

seen the Piano Man stripped down to almost nothing, what's next?"

"The lovely lady with the angel wings tattooed on her shoulder explains why she was spying on me."

Lightning streaked through Angel's insides when she heard *that* voice. When she felt *those* warm, callused fingers swirling around her crimson tattoo. Her eyes narrowed. She tried to spin around, but the Piano Man's closely shaved and intoxicatingly spice-scented cheek pressed against hers and the pressure of his fingers on her shoulders kept her still.

Trapped.

Speechless.

God, he smelled good.

His touch felt even better.

For sanity's sake, she had to tell him touching her was off limits. Of course how she would say that without sounding weak and out of control was anybody's guess.

As she did so often, she just jumped right in, tossing out the first words that came to mind. "Would you do me a big favor, Mr. Donovan?"

His face was too close to get a good look at his expression, but she could feel the brush of his lips against her cheek, felt them tilt into what she knew was an insufferable grin. "If you're going to ask me to pay you more money for the privilege of having you bestow your favors on me tonight, you're going to have to sweeten the pot."

"Getting more money from you is a delightful idea." Angel twisted out of Tom's embrace and hit him with her best I'm-in-control-tonight-and-don't-you-forget-it smile. "Why don't you have a seat and we'll discuss your ever-growing charitable contribution?"

Tom flipped a chair around, set it right close to Angel's, and straddled it. His arm brushed her shoulder and lightning struck her again.

Damn it.

He flashed his ever-so-charming smile at far-too-gullible Emma. "Before we talk about money, Miss Devlin, why don't you introduce me to your friend? We didn't have the pleasure of being properly introduced at Morganna's this morning."

Emma stretched her elegant hand across the table in the polite, sophisticated manner they'd been taught at Mrs. Alexander's. Her emerald bracelet glistened. So did her smile. "It's so nice to meet you, Mr. Donovan. I'm Emma Claire."

Tom took Emma's hand and held it tightly and far too long. Was he trying to seduce Emma now? Was he just being nice? Polite?

Or was he trying to make Angel jealous?

Ha! Like that could ever happen.

"You're the purse designer, right?" Tom said, his index finger toying with the emerald charms dangling from Emma's bracelet.

"I started with purses." Emma's eyes sparkled as brightly as her jewels. "I've recently added luggage and sunglasses to my product line, and I'll soon be dabbling in watches and perfume."

"I love a woman with many talents," Tom said, turning his dastardly charisma on Emma.

"Angel is loaded with talent," Emma cooed,

her allure just as dastardly as Tom's. "Did you know she's an expert knife thrower?"

"So she told me."

"Did you know she carries a stiletto with her at all times?"

"I discovered that just last night."

"In fact, Mr. Donovan"—Emma smiled brightly—"I wouldn't be at all surprised if she has her hand on her stiletto right this very minute."

Tom grinned wickedly. "Do you think she wishes to use it on me?"

"Not at the moment," Angel said, casually leaning back in her chair, "but the evening's still young."

Tom's undeniably sexy gaze shifted to Angel. "It would be a shame for you to slice my throat before we discuss how much more money you want from me and what you're willing to do to get it. And we still need to discuss the reason you *and* the guy with the devil tattooed on his chest were spying on me."

So much for being sneaky. Obviously she needed to try another method of operation with such a perceptive man. Maybe flat-out honesty would have to be the best policy when dealing with Tom Donovan.

Angel lifted her glass of Perrier and touched the cold and damp ice-filled glass to her chest, drawing it lightly toward the hint of cleavage visible over her strapless black dress. "My reasons were quite simple, I assure you." Angel smiled coquettishly, as Tom's gaze followed the movement of her glass. "First, as I told you last night, I'll be keeping an eye on you to make sure you don't do anything to bother Holt Hudson. Second . . . I wanted to see you with your shirt off and my efforts were well rewarded." She winked. "Your chest is quite impressive."

Tom plucked the glass from her hand and took a cold swallow of mineral water. "If I decide to bother Holt Hudson, you won't be able to stop me. As for your second reason for spying on me . . . anytime you want me to take off my shirt, just ask."

"It's far more fun watching someone strip when they're totally unaware of your presence."

"Perhaps. But"—Tom reached across the table with her drink and skimmed the cold and wet glass over her chest—"you had no way of knowing I'd be outside, nor did you know I'd take off my shirt."

Angel covered his hand with hers to keep the glass from moving, to keep his fingers from whispering over her skin. To keep that damned lightning from streaking through her insides.

"Speculation," Angel said, "is all part of a P.I.'s life. You learn a little bit here and a little bit there about a person, you add two and two together, and then you act accordingly. Sometimes your instincts pay off; sometimes they don't."

"Did your instincts about me pay off?"

"As I said, you look rather fine without your shirt on."

"Are you always so open and honest?"

"Not always."

"Is that the reason you're not telling me why someone else was watching me?"

"I can honestly say I don't know why the guy in the other boat was watching you." She *could* tell Tom who that other guy was, but she saw no reason to tell him anything about Dagger without first knowing what her ex—the bastard—was up to.

"I take it he doesn't work for you?"

"No."

"I watched you go after him in your boat. Obviously you want to know what he was up to just as much as I do."

"I admit I'm curious and I'm sure I'll find out soon."

"And then you'll tell me—won't you?"

"Perhaps."

Tom set Angel's glass on the table, then dragged the tips of his fingers lightly over her chest. "Now," he said, as Angel's heart began a rapid and far-too-heavy beat, "I believe we were going to discuss an addition to my charitable contribution. Do you have an amount in mind?"

She swallowed hard. Took a deep breath. His fingertips continued to float over her flesh, heating it, making it tingle, setting her entire body afire. Yet somehow she managed to keep a cool and calm countenance about her.

Angel smiled confidently and answered, "Five grand."

Tom didn't even blink at her words. He seemed totally unruffled. And his fingers continued to work their magic spell. "What do I get in return?"

Angel teased his cheek with the tips of her fingernails. "You're already getting all you're going to get, Mr. Donovan." Don't lose control, she warned herself. Don't let him get the upper hand. "It's not often that I let a man touch me."

"You're worth every penny." Tom traced the edge of her black silk bodice with his middle finger. Slowly, seductively, while his dark brown eyes held hers captive. "How much more can I have for *another* five thousand?"

"You're up to thirty already. It wouldn't be fair to take anything more from you—or to give you hope for anything more from me."

Emma cleared her throat. "Excuse me, but have you both forgotten that you're in a public place and that *I'm* here with you?"

Angel tore her gaze from Tom's bewitching eyes and realized that she *had* forgotten where she was. She *had* forgotten that Emma was sitting at the same table.

And if she wasn't careful, if she didn't get up right this very minute and head off to her stakeout, if she didn't stay focused, she was going to lose not only her senses but her ability to do her job.

Far more important than that—if she didn't get away from Tom's wildly hot touch, he might mesmerize her completely, and then she just might lose her soul.

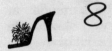 8

*H*e liked her. He hadn't wanted to. Hell, Angel Devlin was nothing more to him than an easy way to get to Holt Hudson. But he'd made the mistake of dancing with her and found himself transfixed by her smile, challenged by her bravado, and wanting to do nothing more than sit here in the suffocatingly small car and talk with her.

Well, that wasn't a hundred percent true. He wanted to do a lot more than talk. Sex sounded good. Hot, no-holds-barred sex, the kind he hadn't had in a long time. But something told him Angel Devlin wasn't the kind of woman who'd take kindly to being rushed.

Then there was the stiletto strapped to her thigh. He might want to feel every sexy and smooth inch of her skin, inside and out, but he didn't want to feel the point of her knife.

He'd wrestled an angry alligator before. Tangling with an angry woman was bound to be far more dangerous.

Leaning against the passenger door inside Angel's Jag, letting a hint of breeze blow in through the open window, and wishing the car wasn't so damn confining, Tom tossed a spear of the pineapple he'd bought from the bartender at Jazzzzz into his mouth and chewed slowly. He saw Angel cast him a quick glance out of the corner of her eye. Her jaw tightened. Eating in the car seemed to irritate her. And, hell, she sure was pretty when she was irritated.

With nothing better to do while they sat crowded together in Angel's car, which was parked across the street from the gated entry to Frederike LeVien's lavish Greek Revival mansion, Tom licked juice from his fingers and studied Angel's curves—her long and slender neck, more-than-a-mouthful breasts he hungered to taste, and luscious hips and thighs that his hands had already lingered on.

The woman was a knockout—so were her short and sleek black strapless dress and her kick-ass stilettos.

"Do you always dress to thrill when you're on stakeout," he asked, determined to break the silence that had cropped up between them a good ten or fifteen minutes ago, "or did you wear that outfit just for me?"

"I never dress for a man, Mr. Donovan." She didn't turn around. She merely stared across the street, but he could hear the disgruntled tone in her voice. "I dress strictly for me, and I rather like high heels and sexy dresses."

"Well, just so you know, I haven't got any complaints."

"Thank you, Mr. Donovan. The evening would

have been a huge disappointment for me if you hadn't told me that."

Angel was sure proving to be a challenge, and damned if he didn't relish challenges.

"Doesn't it drive you crazy sitting in a car all night with nothing more to do than stare into the dark, wondering if and when a woman who may or may not be having an affair is going to come out of her house?"

"I never get bored. And just so you know, I rarely follow women. Normally it's women who pay me to follow their cheating husbands or boyfriends or lovers. Slick, sleazy, good-for-nothing men who think with their penis instead of their brain."

"Are you lumping me into that category?"

"Should I?"

"I may not be at the top of the food chain but I don't think I've hit rock bottom yet. I can even carry on an intelligent conversation when the mood strikes."

"Does it strike very often?"

"When the company I'm keeping is willing to be civil and polite."

Tom grabbed another spear of pineapple, licked off the juice that threatened to drip from the end, then sucked it into his mouth, just to see Angel's reaction. He got exactly what he expected. Her eyes flared with annoyance when she swung her sweet, curvy body away from the driver's-side window.

"Could you be a little more careful with that pineapple?"

"I'm licking my fingers after every bite."

"I'd appreciate it if you'd stop doing that, too."

Tom couldn't help but grin. "Is there a handbook for private investigators stating that it's a sin or a crime or even the least bit unorthodox to eat inside a car while you're on stakeout?"

Angel's eyes narrowed. "It takes just one little accident for greasy food or slimy food or sugary food to go sailing onto the leather upholstery or the floor or God knows where else. And the last thing I want when I have to sit in my car for hours on end is to smell a mixture of noxious odors."

Tom licked the tip of his thumb. Slowly.

"Is the thought of an accidental spill what's really bothering you? Or—"

"Look, Tom"—Angel's sapphire eyes darkened to the color of a stormy midnight sky— "I'm trying to concentrate on my job. I need to stay focused, and having you beside me, sucking on pineapple and on your fingers and making all sorts of squishy noises, is driving me insane."

"I like licking fingers." His grin widened. "And, hell, live in the swamp as long as I have and you get used to squishy noises. But if it'll make you happy, I won't eat another bite."

"Thank you."

She glared out the window again.

"And if you find anything sticky on the seats tomorrow, just give me a holler and I'll personally take your car in to have it detailed."

Angel heaved a sigh. He'd irritated her, and God, she was pretty when she was irritated.

Slowly she turned and leaned back in her seat, gripping the steering wheel. It was damned obvious that she didn't want to look at him, but she did cast him a quick glance. "Are you always so free with money?"

"I've got a lot to be free with."

"I haven't seen a penny of the thirty thousand you owe me."

"Are you worried I'll back out of the deal?"

"No."

Tom reached into the pocket of his Levi's and pulled out a folded piece of paper. "Here you go. One check in the amount of twenty-five grand. I still owe you an extra five thousand for giving me the pleasure of touching your chest."

Angel plucked the check from his fingers, opened the purse that had been resting on the console between them, and shoved it inside.

"You know," she said, a hint of worry in her voice, "something tells me you expect far more from me in return for that twenty-five thousand."

"Thirty before we're finished."

"All right, thirty." Angel breathed deeply, her luscious breasts rising and falling and his insides fighting every instinct to reach out and caress her.

"So," she said, "what are you really hoping to get in return for your generous donation to Alzheimer's research?"

"A chance to sit here with you to see how an ace private investigator handles a stakeout. If your surveillance lasts only one hour, fine, but we're not parting company until the sun comes up. We can talk; we can be quiet. I'm not making any demands or expecting anything other than spending time with you."

"How very chivalrous."

"Not chivalrous; just patient."

"Care to explain that?"

"Want an honest answer or an out-and-out lie?"

"I'll go for honest, thank you."

"I want to make love to you, but you haven't yet decided what your feelings are on that subject. Until you do, I'll bide my time getting to know you better."

"Biding your time isn't going to get you a thing, Mr. Donovan."

"No?"

"No."

"And why not?"

"You're cocky, brash, and too damn good looking. That's a lethal combination a girl like me should stay away from."

"And what kind of girl are you?"

"I'm no angel, if that's what you're thinking."

"I never thought that for a moment. Besides, I'm not into sweet and docile."

The breeze blew lightly through the open windows, stirring the wisps of hair that had fallen out of Angel's no-longer-perfect, swept-off-her-neck hairdo. God, she was beautiful.

Reaching across her seat, he curled a lock of windblown hair behind her ear. A smart man would have withdrawn his hand. Tom wasn't feeling smart right now.

He slipped his fingers behind her neck, into soft, errant curls. She resisted his touch . . . for not much more than a second. Her eyes weren't midnight blue any longer, they were back to sapphire again. Dreamy.

She licked her lower lip.

A sigh escaped from somewhere deep in her throat.

Her tantalizing mouth parted slightly. And Tom leaned forward, drew her pretty face close . . . and kissed her. A tender, unthreatening kiss. She tasted damn good. A hint of lime, maybe lemon. He dragged in a deep breath that carried her scent. Soft. Sweet.

All of his senses fought for restraint.

But he wanted everything.

Damn moderation and self-control.

His right hand swept under her arm and around her back. Pressing a palm against the curve of her spine, he pulled her into him. Close. Real close.

Her mouth opened a little more beneath his and, sweet Jesus, she licked his lips. Slowly. Seductively.

He let her take control. Let her taste him while he listened to the purr in her throat, felt the warmth of her sigh against his lips, against his tongue.

Long slender fingers dove into his hair just as her seductive tongue dove into his mouth and tangled with his.

The hell with the stakeout. The hell with restraint.

Tom twisted in his seat, maneuvered around in the restrictive Jag so he could get up close and real personal with the devilish beauty who made him ache.

And then he heard the yap of a couple of dogs, loud and piercing, breaking through the silence, through his senses.

Shit.

Angel tore away from him. Her lips were wet. Swollen. Her lipstick smudged. Her eyes wide.

Tom's chest ached. His groin burned. Hell, he'd been on the verge of tasting her breasts for the very first time—and they'd been forced to stop because a couple of blasted dogs were barking.

Angel's long blond hair had tumbled out of its classy 'do and smacked his face as she swung away, just barely slapping some sense back into him.

"Put your seat belt on," Angel ordered, as the white wrought-iron gates leading to Frederike LeVien's mansion automatically opened and an antique yellow and green Deusenberg sailed out of the drive.

"You don't mean to tell me we're going somewhere *now*, do you?"

"In spite of what just happened, I'm working, Mr. Donovan."

"Yeah, but—"

"No buts. I've seen Frederike's chauffeur in action. He drives like a bat out of hell and if I don't want to lose her, I've got to keep up. So put your seat belt on. Now."

Tom tried to be rational as he latched his seat belt. "You know, Angel, whether you're working or not, we had a really good thing going there for a couple of minutes. So why don't we just forget Frederike and go back to my place?"

"I don't think so." The tires on Angel's Jag screeched as she whipped away from the curb and hung a death-defying U-turn right in the middle of South Ocean Boulevard. "Besides, you seem to have forgotten something vitally important."

"What?"

"Oh, come on, Mr. Donovan. Surely you know what I'm talking about."

"If you mean condoms, I've got a hell of a lot of them at home."

"Don't be silly." Angel hit him with a devilish laugh. "You've forgotten that you paid for a stakeout and as I told you before, that's all you're getting from me tonight."

Angel raced through town, driving just under fifty in a thirty-five when the Deusenberg she was tailing crossed the double yellow line and passed a doing-the-speed-limit pearly white Rolls-Royce without once touching the brakes. She was going to lose the Countess if she didn't follow suit. On the other hand, if she zipped around the Rolls, she could get stopped by the cops, have a head-on collision, or be spotted.

Since none of those options fit into her current agenda, she slowed to a snail's pace and stayed behind the Rolls, but kept her gaze glued on the classic yellow and green car.

Her plans for this evening hadn't included going on a stakeout with a brash, cocky, and far-too-good-looking-for-words male, especially one who was sucking on pineapple and licking his fingers. Nor had she planned on being kissed, but God knows she couldn't get rid of the memory of Tom's incredibly divine lips or the taste of pineapple on his tantalizing tongue, a delicious experience that made her long for an intimate night on the beach sharing a cold and intoxicating mai-tai and a whole lot more with her dream man—if such a guy existed.

Remembering that kiss made the simple act of driving nearly impossible. The lights all around her were a blur. Her muscles were tense and if she wasn't careful, a cop might pull her over and give her a sobriety test, even though she was stone-cold sober.

She really had to snap out of this ridiculous infatuation with Tom Donovan because she knew where it would lead, and she knew exactly what would happen if they ripped off their clothes.

She'd panic, he'd yell at her for being a tease, call her a frigid bitch, and she'd end up running home and using a blown-up photo of Dagger as a target, hitting him in the crotch every time she tossed her knife.

Maybe she needed a shrink.

Maybe she just needed a damn good man, and she sure as hell didn't think the sexy guy sucking on pineapple in the seat next to her was going to be the one.

"You know, Angel, you might want to keep your mind on your driving." Tom's deep, enthralling voice was one more intoxicant-slash-irritant she didn't need right now.

"That's exactly where my mind is, thank you very much," Angel snapped. Tom didn't deserve it, but it wasn't just her nerves that were prickly, it was her tongue, her fingertips, her heart, her mind, and her soul.

Tom Donovan was driving her insane.

"Be that as it may," Tom said calmly, a smug grin on his face as he relaxed against the passenger door, "you came damn close to wiping out a palm tree on that last turn."

"I did that on purpose," she lied, trying her best to sound confident and in control. "It's an old P.I. trick."

One of Tom's seductive eyebrows rose and he nodded slowly. "I see."

She wished she could smack the cocky look off of his face. He didn't see anything but her lie. He knew she was still thinking about that kiss and it made him feel all-powerful.

Damn him.

"Since you seem to know all sorts of oddball P.I. tricks, is there one that states the best way to be inconspicuous is to drive around in an eye-catching car?" Tom folded his hands behind his head, looking far too comfortable for a man who should be petrified by her driving. "I'm not a P.I., but I would have thought tailing someone in a screaming red Jag would be a no-no."

"Let me ask you this, Mr. Donovan. How many Fords or Toyotas have you seen driving around the streets of Palm Beach since you've been here?"

Tom merely shrugged.

"You'd be hard-pressed to find two or three vehicles that don't reek of wealth in this town and driving one of those two or three vehicles—and we might as well toss your Jeep into that mix—would make a person stick out like a sore thumb. My Jag blends in perfectly."

"In other words, it's pretty much the same scenario as me wearing Levi's, T-shirts, and crocodile boots when most men in Palm Beach are wearing Brooks Brothers and, God forbid, Stubbs & Wootton slippers out on the street."

"You catch on fast."

"I'm quite perceptive. I know I'll never fit into this town. Then again, I'm not out to impress anyone."

That, of course, was one of the things that made him so impressive, so irresistible. He was his own man; he wasn't trying to follow the norm.

And, damn it, he was inching his way into her every thought. This had to stop, and stop fast.

"You know, sweetheart," Tom said, stretching an arm across the back of her seat, toying with her hair that had fallen out of its once-perfect French roll, and leaning so close to her that their cheeks nearly rubbed together, "there's no one coming toward us in the opposite lane. Now might be as good a time as any to smash your foot down on the accelerator and pass the guy in the Rolls."

She'd tell him to mind his own business, but he was right.

Angel tromped on the gas, swung the Jag off to the left, and zoomed past the Rolls. She jerked back into the right lane when a pair of oncoming headlights got too close, and kept her foot firmly on the pedal until they'd once again gotten close enough to the Deusenberg to keep easier track of where the Countess was headed.

"Doesn't my driving scare you the least bit?" Angel asked, as she zipped across Flagler Memorial Bridge, and continued their cat-and-mouse chase in West Palm Beach.

"After wrestling alligators for a living, very little scares me."

"You haven't really wrestled alligators, have you?" Angel asked, skirting around a big rig, then making a screeching right hand turn from the far left lane.

"I've charmed water moccasins, too."

"How do you do that? Play Liszt or Chopin for their listening pleasure, smile disarmingly, and call them sweetheart?"

Tom wound an index finger up in a strand of her hair. "I've reserved that method strictly for you."

She glared at him out of the corner of her eye. "I'm not charmed."

"If I remember correctly, it usually takes me three or four tries to completely charm a snake. Until that happens, they do an awful lot of hissing and squirming, trying like hell to get away from me."

"And once they're thoroughly mesmerized?"

"They roll over on their backs and let me pet their soft side."

"Pretty foolish, if you ask me," Angel quipped. "I wouldn't roll over for anyone."

"You know what? Those water moccasins said the same thing." Tom winked wickedly. "But they couldn't escape my charm."

Why did she have the horrid feeling she wouldn't be able to escape his charms, either?

Hell, she couldn't think about mesmerizing men at the moment. She needed to concentrate on the Deusenberg that was rapidly making its way to the outskirts of West Palm Beach.

Almost a block ahead of her, the Deusenberg whipped along as if the chauffeur didn't have a care in the world, which made him the perfect driver for the Countess. God knows she couldn't have many cares, when she couldn't even be bothered with burying her husband until the social season ended.

Of course, who was she to judge? If Dagger had died while she'd been married to him, she would have seriously considered putting his dead body out at the curb with the rest of the trash.

Too many thoughts were ripping through her mind tonight. It was totally unlike her to have so little concentration—so little, in fact, that she blew right through a red light and didn't notice until she was halfway across the intersection.

Angel shot a nervous glance at Tom, who didn't seem the least bit fazed. Instead, he was sucking more blasted pineapple juice off his middle finger and, damn it all, an indescribably delicious twitch vibrated between her thighs.

If Tom didn't stop what he was doing, she was going to throw him out of the car at the next stoplight.

"You know, Angel"—*how many more times tonight could he possibly say 'You know, Angel' or 'You know, sweetheart'?*—"I was just wondering." Tom's eyes narrowed as he slowly, methodically, and provocatively licked another finger. *Damn him!* "Is running a red light another one of those secret P.I. tricks you like to practice?"

"At the risk of sounding foolish, I'll admit, Mr. Donovan, that that was an unfortunate accident. No one, not a P.I., not an alligator wrestler, or even a snake charmer, should practice an idiotic maneuver like that."

"Which makes me wonder why the hell you're

putting so much effort into following Frederike LeVien. She's not a murderer. She's not a terrorist."

"It's my job. I'm being paid to find out what she's up to, and I work damn hard to make my clients happy."

"At the risk of your life and possibly mine?"

"Just like you, I like to live dangerously."

"I like that in a woman."

"Is there anything you don't like in a woman?"

Out of the corner of her eye Angel saw Tom snatch the last piece of pineapple out of its plastic take-out container and pop it into his mouth. He chewed slowly, his gaze drifting up and down the entire length of her body.

"Believe it or not, sweetheart, there have been more than a few women who haven't interested me. On the other hand, there have been very few whose every action, every word, and, I must admit, every breath, have intrigued me to the point that I'd pay thirty thousand dollars just to have the pleasure of being near them. In fact, you're the only woman to hold that distinction."

Her heart slammed against her chest. God, how she wanted to believe him, but her suspicious nature got the better of her.

"If you're saying that in the hope that I'll break down and wrangle you an invitation to the gala, you're sorely mistaken."

"There you go again, thinking I have an ulterior motive."

"Don't you?"

"The only ulterior motive I have for being here now or for saying something that's the God's honest truth is having the opportunity to kiss you again."

"That last kiss came about in a moment of pure insanity, Mr. Donovan."

"I knew perfectly well what I was doing, and something tells me you never do anything you don't want to do."

"You're right, I did want to kiss you, but don't get your hopes up for anything more."

"I always have high hopes, Miss Devlin. In fact, that's why I bought a fabulous Italian Renaissance bed at the antique store across from Morganna's this morning." His fingers feathered across the nape of her neck. The dimple to the right of his lips deepened as he smiled a very wicked smile. "And just so you'll know, it was delivered shortly after you spied on me this afternoon and"—he winked, damn him!—"it's all set up and ready to go."

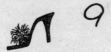

9

Of all the places in all the world Frederike could have picked for her night on the town, why did she choose the Tropical Lei, a gaudy, red, yellow, and green neon-festooned "gentlemen's" club on the outskirts of West Palm Beach? Everyone knew the place was a den of iniquity. But if Frederike went inside, Angel had no choice but to follow—and boy oh boy, wouldn't that just put the frosting on the cake for Tom Donovan's expensively purchased stakeout?

The Deusenberg turned left after pulling into the seedy strip joint's parking lot. Angel turned right, trying to keep an eye on Frederike's vehicle, while looking for a parking space. Tom, of course, relaxed in the passenger seat, sporting a lascivious smirk.

"Well, well, well," Tom said. "Who would have thought the grand dame of high society would frequent a place like this?"

"Don't jump to conclusions, Mr. Donovan." Angel slipped her Jag in between a mud-splattered monster truck and an old pink Cadillac with black-and-white-checkered upholstery and fuzzy dice hanging from the rearview mirror. "There's always the possibility that her chauffer needs to dash inside for a moment."

"What? For a quickie?"

Angel shut off the engine. "Maybe he needed to use the little boy's room."

"I don't think so, sweetheart. If a man stops at a strip joint, he's got more on his mind than taking a leak."

"Guess we'll just have to wait and see."

Angel folded her arms on top of the steering wheel and kept an eye on the Countess's car. Frederike's bat-out-of-hell, black-suit-wearing chauffeur climbed out of the Deusenberg, walked to the far side of the long and elegant vehicle, and offered a hand to Frederike as she stepped out of the car with both of her little dogs cuddled in her arms.

The short, pudgy woman who dressed like Cruella De Vil pressed an overly long kiss to the furry head of one skinny little pooch, then the other, before handing her prized and, as everyone in Palm Beach knew, much-loved dogs to her driver.

"Looks like it's Frederike who's going inside," Angel said, her eyes narrowing. "But why?"

"Maybe she's a lesbian."

Angel rolled her eyes at Tom's ludicrous statement. "She's been married eight times."

"Obviously the men in her life haven't made her happy. Switching to women could be the best thing for her."

"I'm not even going to venture a guess about what's in the Countess's mind or what's best for her."

Tom reached across the car and curled a wind-tossed lock of hair behind Angel's ear. A mischievous smile touched his lips. "Does that mean we can call it a night? Head back to your place . . . or mine?"

Angel shook her head slowly. "Sorry. This job won't be over until I figure out what Frederike is up to, which means we follow her wherever she goes."

"Guess you've gotta do what you've gotta do, and if you insist I accompany you, well, I suppose I'm up for it." Tom's grin widened. "After all, I haven't been to a good strip club in . . . months."

"How many bad ones have you been to?"

"Far too many to keep track of." Tom winked again, an annoying yet far too charming habit. "How about you? Do you frequent strip clubs?"

"I danced in one to pay my way through college." That was a big fat lie, but at least it shut Tom up long enough for Angel to reach over the back seat and grab one of the bags full of disguises that she carried around at all times.

"That wouldn't be filled with G-strings, pasties, and feather boas, would it?" Tom asked, his voice sounding hopeful.

"Close."

Plopping the satchel on the console between her and Tom, Angel unzipped it and pulled out a pair of five-inch shiny red hooker heels that she dangled in front of Tom's overexcited eyes. "What do you think?"

"I think they'll look damn good on you."

Angel slipped off her Manolos and tucked them under her seat, then slid her feet into the cheap mail-order stilettos and crisscrossed the long fake leather cords around and around her legs until she tied them off just below her knees.

"Is there anything else of interest in there?" Tom asked, digging into the bag.

Angel swatted his hand lightly. "Why don't you keep an eye on Frederike instead of me?"

"Where's the fun in that?"

"For your information, Mr. Donovan, P.I. work isn't all fun and games."

One of Tom's eyebrows slanted. "No?"

"No."

Angel touched an index finger to his strong, just-sprouting-a-hint-of-beard jaw and pushed until his eyes were facing the window. "Keep an eye on Frederike, please. She may or may not be going inside. If she does—or doesn't—we need to be ready to follow her."

Tom fastened his gaze on Frederike, but Angel couldn't miss the way he continually cast quick glances in her direction, as she rummaged through her bag of tricks.

"Mind telling me why you have to change clothes to go into this place?" Tom asked.

"So I won't be recognized if I see someone I know," Angel said, shoving her blond hair under a sleek, perfectly straight black wig that Cleopatra would have killed for.

"You don't think guys are going to stare at you in the getup you're putting on?"

"They might stare but"—she popped a piece of

gum into her mouth and gave it a quick couple of chews—"honestly, sugar, I don't think anybody's gonna realize or even care that under all this black hair is a blond lady of impeccable taste."

"You're still wearing a dress of impeccable taste, if I do say so myself."

"That's the next thing to go, honey bunch."

Angel whipped a shimmering ruby tube dress out of the bag.

"Let me guess," Tom said, his eyes growing dark and hot, as his gaze raked over the dress. "You're going to change into that right this minute?"

"That's the plan."

"Right here in the car with me sitting beside you?"

"Do you have a problem with that?" Angel said innocently.

"My libido does."

"Well, hon"—Angel dragged a red fingernail down the center of his chest—"you just keep that libido under control because I don't have time to deal with it and even if I did"—she smiled—"I wouldn't."

Angel peeled her black silk Calvin Klein over her head and frowned when she caught Tom staring first at her strapless satin bra and then her barely-there thong. "I thought I told you to keep an eye on Frederike."

"I listened but my libido didn't."

"Take one last look," she said, trying to appear stern but failing miserably, "because most of what you're gawking at is going to disappear in just a couple of seconds."

"I'd ask if I could touch, but something tells me you'd have an instant comeback, something having to do with your stiletto and my balls."

"You're a very astute man, Mr. Donovan." She winked. "Now, if you don't mind, would you and your libido *please* turn your attention back to the Countess?"

"Whatever your little heart desires."

Angel wasn't too sure what her heart desired. Unfortunately, she was beginning to realize that every other part of her anatomy, with the exception of her brain, had an uncanny desire to climb into the back seat and take Tom with her.

Thank God her brain was telling her "No way!" because climbing into the back seat would more than likely prove disastrous.

Wiping that thought from her mind, she slipped her hooker heels through the top of the spandex dress and wiggled her body into it. When the bodice was sufficiently in place, she unhooked her bra and peeled it out from under the dress, then leaned over and shook her breasts into some semblance of order inside the spandex.

"Now, that's a maneuver a guy like me doesn't see every day."

"And one you shouldn't have seen just now, since you're supposed to be on lookout." Angel's eyes narrowed. "Is Frederike still with her dogs?"

"She just went inside."

"Then we'd better hurry." Angel dug into the bag again, pulled out a black fishnet tanktop and a couple of thick gold necklaces, then hit Tom with a grin. "Take off your T-shirt."

Tom's eyebrow rose. "Excuse me?"

"If I'm going into that place looking like a hooker, you can dress appropriately, too."

"No."

"Don't argue."

"You know, sweetheart, I'd rather have you slice off my balls a quarter of an inch at a time than go into that place looking like an asshole."

"You're supposed to be doing what I want you to do, but since that's obviously an impossibility on your part and since I don't have time to go around and around with you on the subject of what you should wear inside this place so you won't be recognized, either, I'll let your inability to do as you're told slide."

Angel shoved the shirt and gold chains back into the bag. When her hand reappeared, she held an enormous floppy felt sunflower studded with beads and sequins.

"If you think I'm going to wear that," Tom growled, "you're sorely mistaken."

"*This*, Mr. Donovan, is to cover up the bulge dangling down my right thigh." She pinned it to the dress, right over her stiletto. "It's tacky, but so is the rest of the outfit."

Tom slid a finger up her leg and curled it around the floppy flower. "I like tacky."

Angel picked Tom's hand off of her thigh. "I'm sure that once we're inside, you'll find all the tacky things your little ole heart desires."

Angel threw open the door to the Jaguar and climbed out. When Tom was at her side, she pressed the lock button on her key ring, tossed it into her much-too-expensive-to-wear-with-hooker-clothes Emma Claire original handbag, and sashayed toward Tropical Lei.

A bouncer cruised the neon-lit, palm-tree-lined red carpet leading to the shiny black entry doors. The guy was a big bruiser with a flabby and flat nose that looked like it had been broken far too many times. His swollen right eye must have taken a beating at one time, too. Tropical Lei was supposed to be a classy joint, but truth be told, it didn't look like a decent place for man or beast—or a woman, especially one dressed as a hooker.

For safety's sake, Angel latched on to Tom's arm. He seemed all too willing to have her close to his side as they sauntered up the carpet, so willing, in fact, that his hand drifted from her waist—where it belonged—to her butt, where it had no business going.

"That's for effect, sweetheart," he whispered, taking a quick nibble on her ear in the process. "Any hooker worth her weight in gold would allow her john to keep his fingers on her derriere. You do want to look authentic, don't you?"

Angel paid Tom back, latching on to his earlobe with just the slightest bite of her teeth. "You can touch my butt, Mr. Donovan, but try to make this hooker-and-her-john masquerade look too authentic and I'll make a eunuch out of you."

"You do say the nicest things, Miss Devlin."

Angel smiled widely. "I try, Mr. Donovan."

They had to pay two hundred each, up front, to become members of Tropical Lei, an American Express charge that would show up on an item-

ized expense invoice that Frederike's butler
would receive at the end of the month. Of course,
paying a membership fee to a private "gentlemen's" club meant a whole lot more could be going on inside than one would find in a
run-of-the-mill Palm Beach County strip joint.
Drinking was allowed in the private clubs. Full
nudity, too.

Oh, this was going to be fun, Angel thought
facetiously.

Throwing back her shoulders, she stuck out her
boobs, and fought for composure as she and Tom
stepped through the double-door entry, with no
telling what they would find inside.

The garish club reeked of perfume, aftershave,
and sweat. Bump-and-grind music pulsated
through speakers barely concealed by plastic
palm trees, ferns, and birdcages stuffed with fake
parrots. The bigger, at-least-six-foot-tall birdcages
were stuffed with nearly naked, undulating
women.

But the pièce de résistance were the three white
wicker daybeds suspended atop bamboo-studded
revolving columns. Of course, it wasn't just the
daybeds that caught Angel's eye, it was the two
young honeys decked out in nothing more than
leopardskin thongs who cavorted on each black
fur-covered mattresses.

"Kind of seedy, isn't it?" Angel said, as she and
Tom made their way through the crowd.

"Sure the hell is." Tom grinned, his gawking
eyes sparkling with splatters of color from the
strobe lights. "Just my kind of place."

"Don't get too comfortable," Angel ordered. "As soon as we find out what's going on with Frederike, we're out of here."

Since it didn't appear Tom was in any hurry to move away from the action on the daybeds, Angel threaded her fingers through his and jerked him away, steering them around the outer edges of the massive, underlit room, keeping an eye out for Frederike, but in spite of the fabulously gaudy hats the Countess always wore, she seemed to have disappeared into the crowd.

Angel and Tom wove their way through the throng of men high on testosterone and booze, accidentally dead-ending at a circular stage rimmed by a bar, barstools, and drooling voyeurs. And smack-dab in the middle of the stage a spotlight beamed down on a busty babe whose rusty red hair had been teased at least ten inches high and ten inches wide. She wore nothing more than a gleaming red rhinestone in her belly button and stripper heels that must have been an inch higher than the pair Angel herself was wearing.

Tom stopped dead in his tracks, tugging Angel tightly against his side, as his libidinous gaze fixed on the redhead's bobbing breasts.

Angel's jaw tightened. Her eyes narrowed as Tom thoroughly scrutinized the woman's curves, that cheap red bobble in her navel, her strobe-lit thighs, and the speck of red curls that hadn't been ripped out by a bikini wax.

Angel elbowed Tom in the ribs. A slow smile touched his face and slowly, far too slowly, he tilted his head away from the stripper, focused his silly-assed and mesmerized grin on Angel, and winked. "Pretty nice, huh?"

"Her boobs are fake. She's got rouge on her nipples—"

Tom spun Angel around and into his embrace. His fingers slid to her derriere and he tugged her hard against his hips. "Don't worry, sweetheart." His words fell against her lips. "She's not my type."

His breath was warm against her mouth, his hold strong, tight. On instinct alone, Angel's eyes drifted closed and she waited for his kiss. But it didn't come.

Damn it!

Suddenly Tom took control, weaving his fingers through hers tightly—protectively—and Angel's eyes flashed open as he led her through the mass of perspiring men and found a table and a couple of chairs amid the hubbub.

"Stay here while I get us something to drink."

Angel regained her composure, and latched on to Tom's belt buckle before he skirted away. "Here's another one of those handy dandy P.I. tricks," Angel said. "Keep your hands to yourself. Keep focused on your objective—which is looking for Frederike. And don't forget that you're with me."

Tom leaned down, cradled Angel's face in his hands, and moved in really close and personal. "There's only one naked lady I'm interested in being with tonight, and that's you."

"But I'm not naked."

His lips touched hers. His blessedly sweet

tongue teased her mouth. His eyes glittered. "Not yet, sweetheart. But the night's still young."

Tom straightened, winked, then walked away like a man with a purpose, and all Angel could do was admire the view of his magnificent behind as he strolled through the crowd, looking all-powerful and far too virile.

He'd charmed her. Fighting it had become impossible. She'd tried; she'd failed miserably. Hell, before the night was over he might have her rolling over and allowing him to stroke her soft, sleek skin, just like his blasted snakes.

Get a grip, she told herself. She was becoming so fixated on Tom that she was forgetting why she'd come to the Tropical Lei. She'd been paid to concentrate on Frederike LeVien. Of course, Tom had paid her, too, and from all outward appearances, he was getting pretty damn close to what he'd probably wanted from her right from the get-go.

The red accent lights scattered about the club suddenly turned several shades of lavender. The wicker daybeds began to twirl around and around as the leopard-thonged babes stalked each other atop the mattresses. But it was the stage that took on new life. Crisscrossing pink spotlights shot down center stage, Jimi Hendrix's "Purple Haze" blared through the speakers, and a man and woman painted in swirls of glittering pink and lavender slithered from the darkness into the light, and started a nearly naked dance that was on the verge of leaving nothing to the imagination.

"Like what you see?"

Tom set a martini on the table in front of her, scraped a chair across the black concrete floor until it touched Angel's, and sat down. He took a swallow of beer, grinning at Angel over the top of the bottle.

"I really didn't expect to see anything this graphic."

"They don't go all the way, if that's got you worried."

Angel sipped at her martini. "I take it you've watched this kind of action before?"

"I'm no more of an angel than you are, sweetheart."

Angel forced herself to look away from Tom's mesmerizing eyes, and did a quick scan of the club, looking again for a little woman of great girth wearing a gigantic, raspberry-colored hat trimmed with some kid of white fur—which was probably real.

"You didn't by any chance see Frederike when you went to the bar, did you?" Angel asked.

Tom shook his head. "I thought about looking into one of the private rooms to see if she might be involved in her own personal fantasy, but figured it wouldn't be polite to interrupt."

"Afraid you might be embarrassed?"

"There's not much that embarrasses me."

"Does that mean you'd get up on that stage and do a few nearly naked bumps and grinds for the right price?"

Tom tilted his beer to his lips, took a swallow, then set the bottle back on the table. He wove the fingers of one strong hand around the back of Angel's neck and leaned in close. "I do my bumping and grinding in private—just me and the woman I'm with. And I wouldn't charge her to watch."

It was all too easy to imagine Tom bumping and grinding. Angel pictured him sweaty, with his shirt off, and all of that gorgeous bronze skin sliding over satin sheets. Better yet, she pictured all of that bronze and beautiful and oh-so-hot flesh sliding over her. It wasn't something she thought she should be thinking about right now, but it was hard not to when he kept his eyes focused on her face.

He wanted her. There was nothing more to that want than a roll in the sack. Uninhibited sex. Down-and-dirty sex. Unquestionably the best sex she'd ever had in her life. The kind of sex she and Emma had talked about late into the night at Portia Alexander's Academy.

But she'd freeze if Tom got too close. She'd get scared. And then she'd run.

Dagger had done that to her. Dagger had ruined her fantasy of what love should be.

Angel touched the cool martini glass to her throat and wondered if Tom could make even one small portion of that fantasy come true for her. She wasn't in love with him. God, no! They knew next to nothing about each other and she'd made the horrid mistake with Dagger of thinking lust was the same thing as love. Four days after meeting the jerk she'd married him.

And he'd never even cared for her; he'd simply been using her.

The warm touch of Tom's hand on her face jerked Angel back to reality. "Are you okay?" he asked, his fingers gently caressing her cheek.

"I'm fine. Why?"

"Your eyes are red, and you had a faraway look that made it seem like you'd retreated to some dark corner of the world, where no one could get to you."

"It's smoky in here, that's all," she tossed back, peeling his fingers from her cheek even though they felt damn good. She couldn't let him see her vulnerability. "And I suppose I was thinking that I've been a bit remiss in my duties the past few hours. Frederike is my main concern tonight. Not the nearly naked dancers on the stage. Not the ladies frolicking on the beds. And . . . not you, Tom."

Tom stroked her lips with the tip of his thumb, and she tried to stifle the tingling ripples of desire that zipped through her body.

"Why do you work so hard at fighting me?" Tom asked, his eyes narrowed, filled with questions. Concern.

"Because no matter how much I'd like to trust you, I don't. Because I'm sure you've got some underlying motive for being with me and because I'm sure that something has to do with Holt Hudson."

"Yet in spite of all that, you're here with me now."

"On the contrary. You're here with me." Angel grinned, refusing to give in to what she was feeling for Tom. "You paid to be here and having you close by makes it easier for me to keep an eye on you, just to make sure you don't do something that will in any way harm Holt Hudson or jeopardize the relationship I've worked hard to form with him."

"You could have asked one of your minions to keep an eye on me."

"I don't have minions working for me."

"How interesting." Tom took a swallow of beer. "Last night you led me to believe that you had an army of P.I.s working for you, and that you could have any number of them watching me at any given time of the day or night."

"I lied."

He curled his fingers around her cheek. "You don't have to lie to me, you know. And you don't have to hide anything, either." Slowly, and ever so lightly, he again caressed her sensitive lips with a rough but tender thumb. "You might be surprised how good a listener I am."

"This isn't exactly the kind of place where one pours out their heart."

Tom grinned as he looked around the room. "Okay, so maybe the time isn't right for you to pour out your heart, but maybe you have some deep, dark secrets you'd like to share."

Angel tugged Tom's hand from her cheek and took a sip of the already warm martini. "I'm afraid I don't have any deep, dark secrets."

"You're not being very cooperative," Tom said. "I'm trying to make light, civil conversation. Trying to get to know you better."

"Deep, dark secrets are things you share with someone you already know quite well. If you want to ask a question, why not make it a little less personal?"

"All right," he said, smiling softly, as if he were slowly, and easily, drawing her under his spell, making it nearly impossible to resist his charm or unburden her soul. "Why don't you tell me why you work alone?"

"Easy enough," she answered. "I had an assistant-slash-quasi-partner once, but I fired him for being interested in no one but himself. After that I divorced him and by the time our attorneys got through, I'd given my ex our home, our boat, and our measly savings, just so I could hang on to the P.I. business my dad gave me when he retired."

Angel took a cool sip of her martini to wash the foul taste of Dagger out of her mouth. "My poor excuse of a marriage lasted seven years, I've been divorced for five, and nowadays I prefer to work all by myself."

"So let me guess," Tom said, elbows on the table, his bottle of beer poised close to his mouth. "It's not just me you distrust, it's men in general."

"Not all men. I do know a few good ones—my dad and my three brothers are prime examples."

"But you're not willing to lump me into that quote-unquote *good* category?"

"I don't know you well enough."

"That could be changed, if you'd just loosen up."

"I've already let my guard down too much tonight." Angel took another sip of her drink. "And now I'm going to tell you just one more thing—another handy-dandy P.I. secret."

"Which is?"

"A good P.I. is always professional—and I've been anything but professional tonight. That's changing—beginning now."

A slow, challenging smile touched Tom's face. He raised his beer and clicked Angel's martini glass. "Here's to professionalism." He hit her with another one of his damnable winks. "For now."

Ignoring the comment, and realizing that it was far too easy for Tom to mesmerize her, Angel pushed back her chair and stood.

"Going somewhere?" Tom asked, then took a swallow of beer.

"Not until I find Frederike," Angel offered. "She's got to be here somewhere."

"We could check out the back rooms, give you a bird's-eye view of what goes on behind closed doors."

Angel hit Tom with her own wink, deciding playfulness with Tom was far safer than heart-to-heart talks. "In your dreams."

"Trust me, Angel, the things that go on in my dreams are a hell of a lot more exciting than what's going on in those back rooms. Be nice," he said, "and I might share one or two of those dreams with you."

She shook her head, but couldn't help but smile. Tom Donovan had an uncanny way of turning every single subject into something sexual, something highly sensual and erotic. And, damn it all, she was beginning to enjoy it.

Standing over six feet tall in her five-inch stilettos made looking over the heads of most of the lascivious jerks swaggering around Tropical Lei a piece of cake. Unfortunately, Frederike was nowhere around.

Angel checked her watch. She'd give this on-the-verge-of-becoming-ridiculous escapade another half hour, and then she figured it would be time to call it quits for the night. Tomorrow she could call the Countess and come up with an excuse to see her. They could talk about her precious dogs and Angel could dig for information. Frederike was always forthcoming with gossip about herself and others—whether she knew what she was talking about or not.

Angel swallowed the last of her martini, keeping her gaze focused on the partiers and off of Tom, who was too much of a distraction.

The front entrance door opened and closed over and over again, with far more men coming in than were going out. The noise level was almost unbearable. Lights flashed everywhere—and then one spotlight landed on the face of the man she despised.

Dagger Zane.

10

The room began to spin. A raw, burning pain twisted in Angel's stomach. And suddenly it was her wedding night all over again.

God, she'd been so excited, ready to give her new husband anything. They were in a seedy motel, all they could afford after their justice-of-the-peace wedding. Dagger had smoked a joint. He'd drunk a few bottles of beer, and then he'd stripped off her clothes, threw her on the bed, and straddled her hips.

He'd kissed her and she'd closed her eyes, waiting for that special moment—a special moment that never came. Opening her eyes slowly, wondering why he'd stopped kissing her, wondering why he didn't touch her, she saw Dagger staring at the knife he'd produced from out of nowhere.

When he kissed the twelve-inch blade, she'd turned cold. Numb. Scared out of her mind. The man smiling down at her, the man holding the knife, was her husband. A man she'd sworn she would love, honor, cherish, and even obey—

forever. She refused to believe she'd made a mistake. Refused to believe what he was doing would be more than a onetime game.

God, she'd been so wrong.

He'd reached out with the knife that night. She'd shuddered; he'd laughed. And then he sliced off a lock of her hair, told her he'd carry it with him forever, then clenched the knife between his teeth as he plunged into her.

She might have screamed when she felt the pain, but something told her that would give him too much pleasure. So she endured everything that night, just praying it would soon be over.

For seven long years she'd put up with his games. For seven long years they'd worked together, she'd taught him everything her dad and brothers had taught her, and she'd hoped and prayed that he'd change. But when night rolled around, he'd pull out his trusty knife. That's when she knew just how much she abhorred him, but she wouldn't give him the satisfaction of showing her fear.

And damn it all, she wasn't going to let him interfere with her life or her career. She wasn't about to let horrid memories and Dagger's presence ruin her evening, not now, when—after so many years—she'd finally come *this* close to wanting a man with every fiber of her being.

Shaking off the nightmare of her past, Angel became suddenly aware that the spotlight had circled the room and settled on her. That's when she saw Dagger's nasty lopsided grin.

She spun around. With any luck he hadn't recognized her through the disguise because she knew damn good and well that if he had, he'd come over to the table and make her life pure misery.

That's what he thrived on. He'd never beat her. Never drawn blood with his knife, but the threat was always there. Menacing. Ominous, especially when he'd told her again and again to remember that he owned her, that he could do anything he wanted to her.

And not for the first time, she wondered why on earth she hadn't filed charges the one and only time she'd found the courage to call the police on Dagger. Why she'd felt so bad after the cops hauled him off to jail that she'd told the district attorney's office that she'd lied when she'd said he hurt her, that she'd merely been angry because he'd cheated on her.

God forbid that he should now be treating another woman the way he'd treated her.

"Something wrong?" Tom asked, standing in front of her, gripping her shoulders.

She drew in a deep breath. Forced herself to relax. She offered him a tremulous smile.

"The devil just walked into the room."

"The devil?" Tom asked, his eyes narrowed.

"My ex. And the last thing on earth I want to do is bump into him or have him bump into me."

"Tell you what." Tom's fingers tightened on her arms, offering her comfort. "Why don't you sit down and I'll go have a little talk with him?"

"No. Please." Angel shook her head. "I despise him. I don't want to talk to him. And—"

"Then let's get the hell out of here. Sneak out the back door."

"We've got to stay here and keep an eye out for Frederike."

"Can't you just forget about your work for a little while? Maybe think about your safety?"

"I'm not afraid of my ex and I'm not going to run from him. I'd just rather not be seen."

An I've-got-a-devious-idea grin sparkled in Tom's eyes. "Then give me a lap dance."

"*Excuse me?*"

Tom collapsed in his chair and grasped Angel's hands. "Straddle me, wrap your arms around me, and . . . well, we can play the rest by ear."

Angel's frown deepened. "And the reason behind this would be?"

"If your ex walks by all he'll see is the gorgeous back of a working girl taking care of my needs."

"You are out of your mind."

"No, I'm fulfilling your fondest desire."

"Which is?"

"Not being seen by your ex."

Angel sighed heavily. "I'm not crazy about this idea, but I don't see any other options in sight." She straddled Tom's lap, hitting him with a no-nonsense glare. "Just don't try anything funny. Which means, one hand on my shoulder at all times so Dagger doesn't recognize my tattoo, and while you're at it, you might as well keep the other hand on my other shoulder. Understood?"

Tom's callused fingers slid over her bare arms. They curved warmly over her shoulder blade where the crimson angel wings fluttered. And then he tugged her close. "Tell you what, sweetheart. I'll protect you from the devil, I'll keep an eye out for Frederike, and all you have to do is concentrate on me."

"This wasn't part of our bargain, you know."

"This is called improvisation. I would have thought that would be one of your handy-dandy P.I. tricks."

"I don't recall lap dancing or kissing ever falling into the improvisation category."

"There's always a first for everything."

Tom kissed her. Softly—and all thoughts of fighting him off went poof inside her brain. When it happened she wasn't sure, but suddenly this wasn't just a kiss. It was need. Strong, desperate need.

Angel could barely breathe but she had to, and when she did she inhaled the spiciness of his aftershave. It wafted through her senses, making her need him even more. Her fingers dug into his neck and her lips parted. She drank in his heat, his scent. His masculinity and his charm overpowered her, took away any possible desire to even think about pulling away from him.

Her breasts brushed against his T-shirt. They seemed to swell, to ache, wanting more but knowing there'd be nothing more than this for now. More than ready to take the chance with him, ready to see if she deserved to once again feel all that a woman should feel when she was alone with a man.

Intimately.

Tangled in sheets.

In an Italian Renaissance bed that was all made up and ready to go.

Without reservation, without fear, she slipped

her tongue over his lips and into the dark, inner recesses of his mouth. He tasted of beer. Delicious. Intoxicating. She explored his teeth—smooth and hard—and felt them nip her tongue teasingly, then she went back to exploring, savoring, memorizing every contour, every ridge.

And this was just the beginning.

Music, laughter, and cheers echoed around her. Her heart beat harder than the pulsing bass and drum in the stripper songs.

Her fingers tightened around his neck. She scooted closer to Tom's hips, felt his left hand slide down her side, his fingers skimming sensitive flesh, curving over her waist and then to her thigh. He settled his hand over the stiletto that must have been sticking out for all the world to see. He was protecting her—and making her feel damn good while he was at it.

And then she felt his erection between her legs. Hard as steel. Thick and long, trapped beneath his zipper yet bursting to be let loose.

Unconsciously she moved against him, her hips circling slowly, losing all focus, all thought of what she was supposed to be doing other than being turned on by the feel of him against her satin thong.

"Keep that up, sweetheart," he whispered against her mouth, "and we're going to be in serious trouble here."

She froze. Every muscle in her body tensed.

What the hell was she doing?

A lump settled hard in her throat, but somehow she fought for speech. "That wasn't supposed to happen."

Tom smiled warmly. "I'm glad it did. Hell, I'd like it to happen again."

"Maybe we should just leave. And I don't mean go back to your place, or maybe I do mean that. I'm just not sure right now but—"

"We can't leave. First off, you're hiding from your ex. Second . . . Frederike LeVien has just popped into view and I do believe the little lady is walking toward us, with some tall, dark-haired guy with a scar across his cheek."

"Shit."

"Excuse me?" Tom's warm breath fluttered across her lips. "Is that any kind of word for a sweet young thing like you to utter?"

"It's cleaner than the one I could have used, because if I'm not mistaken, the guy with the scar is my ex."

"Then don't move, sweetheart," Tom said, "just keep your hot little mouth pressed to my neck and I'll do all the talking while you remain invisible straddling my hips."

This evening was not going well at all, Angel decided. Stakeouts were usually boring. They never involved kissing or lap dances and . . . and . . . the second she heard Dagger's familiar, reprehensible laugh, she pressed her lips against Tom's warm neck and kissed him.

With her head tilted down, Angel caught sight of Frederike's raspberry-colored pumps, studded with Swarovski crystals, striding by. Then she saw a pair of spit-polished-and-shined brown loafers. More than likely they belonged to Dagger, but she wasn't about to look up and see.

"Why, what a pleasant surprise!" The excitement in Frederike's voice rang through the room. "I can't believe I've found another Palm Beacher haunting the Tropical Lei."

Angel couldn't see a blasted thing. All she could do was feel Tom's warm, taut skin beneath her lips, feel his heart beat against her chest, and the palms of his hands on her shoulders, holding her tight and hiding her tattoo.

"We haven't had the pleasure of meeting," she heard Frederike twitter, "but I've seen you about town a time or two, Mr. Donovan. I'm Frederike LeVien."

"Nice to meet you," Tom said, and Angel could easily imagine the way Frederike's always beringed fingers clasped Tom's hand and held on tight, rather than giving him a proper shake.

"And this is my friend Dagger Zane."

Beneath her lips, Angel could feel Tom's muscles tighten.

"I do believe, Mr. Donovan," Frederike chirped, "that Dagger and I have caught you at a most inopportune moment."

"Five minutes later and it would have been completely inopportune, Countess." Tom's words vibrated against Angel's lips. Another part of his anatomy seemed to be vibrating between her thighs. "You don't mind me calling you Countess, do you?" he said in his oh-so-charming voice.

"Of course not, dahling. I paid good money for the title just so my friends could call me something other than Frederike or Mrs. LeVien."

"Well, Countess"—both of Tom's hands were once again on Angel's shoulder blades, his thumbs swirling over her flesh, making her dizzy as she kissed him—"as you must know, a man doesn't come to a place like Tropical Lei if he expects privacy."

"Privacy is quite overrated," Frederike said. "Don't you agree, Dagger?"

"Wholeheartedly."

Dagger-the-devil must be the guy who had Frederike's butler all in a tizzy, Angel surmised. Either he'd changed his ways and was no longer using a knife, or Frederike and Dagger weren't having sex. Absently drawing her tongue over Tom's neck, she hoped and prayed both were true.

"Of course, there's a limit to everything," Frederike said, her voice sounding a bit miffed as she tapped cold fingers on Angel's shoulder. "Young lady."

Obviously that was a demand for Angel to stop what she was doing and pay attention to the Countess. But Angel wasn't about to turn around and be recognized by her ex.

"Yes, Countess?" Angel said, her nose still buried in the warm spiciness of Tom's neck.

"Why don't you be a good girl and leave us alone now? Take your money and run off to some other fellow."

"That's not possible," Tom said. "I've bought and paid for this charming lady—and she's mine all night."

Angel sat up ramrod straight. How dare Tom say she'd been bought and paid for. Dagger might have considered her personal property, but no other man ever would.

Never.

Fire had rushed from her toes to her cheeks and she had a damn good idea Tom could feel it flaming out of her eyes and slapping him a time or two for that insensitive comment—whether it was a joke or not.

Of course, the blasted man who'd made that blasted, offhand remark that irritated the hell out of her had the audacity to wink. Obviously he thought it was funny.

She spun around, no longer caring who saw her. She wanted to give Tom a tongue-lashing for that comment about buying her. She wanted to lay into Frederike for treating her like a second-class citizen. And she wanted to put a knee in Dagger's groin.

Instead, she kept her wits about her and plastered a phony smile on her face. "You do know why Tom has to pay a woman for *this*, don't you?"

Frederike's eyes narrowed. "I hadn't given it any thought, my dear."

"Well, I'll tell you, Countess. It's his affliction."

Frederike's hand flew to her chest in utter dismay. "Affliction? Oh, dear. Whatever is the problem?"

"Yes, sweetheart," Tom said, laughter in his voice. "Tell the Countess about my affliction."

"I'm dying to hear this myself," Dagger said, sliding his fingers possessively around Frederike's arm, but keeping his eyes planted on Angel's face. They'd worked together and lived together for so many years and from the gleam in his sinister eyes, she knew Dagger had recognized her. He knew she was playing a game. The only question now: Would he spill the beans?

"Well, Countess," Angel continued, determined not to let Dagger bother her, even more determined to get even with Tom for his wisecrack about buying her, "Tom's affliction isn't something that one usually discusses in public, and it's not something that he would like everyone in Palm Beach to know, but I do feel you should be aware of the truth since you caught us . . . well . . . almost doing the deed."

Frederike gasped. "Please. Tell me more."

"It's quite serious, you know. And such a shame. But in spite of all the shrinks he's seen, Tom can't get a woman without paying for one." Angel smiled sweetly, while dragging her fingernails along Tom's cheek. "It's that little problem of his."

"*Problem?*" Frederike's eyes widened.

"He may have money, good looks, and charm," Angel said, "but, hmmm, how can I put this delicately?" She shrugged. "Highly paid escorts like me don't care how horribly a man performs sexually."

"I had no idea, Mr. Donovan." Frederike shook her head in shock. "If you don't mind me being a bit forward, have you tried Viagra?"

"Don't care for the stuff."

Frederike's eyes narrowed in immense concern. "You have seen a good doctor, haven't you?"

"Not recently."

"Well, I'll have my butler get in touch with yours and give you the name and phone number of the man my late husband used. He worked wonders on Evan. A little implant, you know."

"That would be so nice of you, Countess," Angel said sweetly. "After all, it is just a *little* implant that he needs."

Now that Angel had stuck the knife into Tom for his vicious comment about paying her for her services, she was on a roll, and turned her anger on Dagger. "And what about you, Mr. Zane. Do you need a little something special to help you get it up?"

Dagger's eyes narrowed as he glared at his ex-wife. His anger was palpable. "I don't believe that is a subject one should discuss in the company of a refined lady like Frederike."

The Countess tilted her head to smile up at Dagger. "You are just the sweetest man. Always so considerate."

Angel thought she'd throw up.

"The two of you know each other well, then?" Tom asked, directing his question to Frederike and Dagger, as if he knew Angel would want to be privy to that bit of information.

"We've known each other a week now. And such a lovely week it has been," Frederike said, all smiles as she held on tight to Dagger's arm and looked adoringly into his still-handsome but despicable mug. "Mr. Zane is a walker," Frederike continued. "A new walker, of course, recently introduced to me by Stephania Allardyce. But he's ever so good at the job."

"Walker?" Tom questioned.

"An escort," Dagger admitted. "An *unpaid* escort."

"I forget you're new to the island, Tommy,"

Frederike quipped. "You don't mind me calling you Tommy, do you?"

"Please do." Tom grinned. "In fact, I'll let you be the only one on the face of the earth who's allowed to call me that."

"You are such a lovely man." Frederike smiled. "If you weren't so wealthy, I'm sure you'd make an absolutely grand walker. There are so many women like me on the island who no longer have husbands to escort them around town. No sex, mind you, just lively conversation, a strong arm to hold on to, a pretty face to look at over dinner, and a good dance partner. Dagger is all of those things, and he does everything with a delightful smile."

"And Mr. Zane does this for absolutely nothing?" Tom asked.

"For the sheer pleasure of Frederike's company." Dagger patted the Countess's arm. A spark almost glinted off of his perfect white teeth as he smiled down at her.

"I believe, however," Angel added, "that the Countess foots the bill for everything."

"You make it sound quite sinful." Frederike hit Angel with frowning eyes. "In truth, I have money to burn, I'm of age, and Mr. Zane has been more than willing to escort me to places I've always dreamed of seeing, but never would have dared venturing to on my own . . . like this place."

"You're a lucky woman," Tom said, but Angel felt sorry for her—first that she didn't have a real man at her side; second, that she'd fallen into Dagger's clutches. It might be wise to warn Frederike LeVien, but Angel had no proof that Dagger had done anything or planned to do anything wrong.

"I am quite lucky." Frederike smiled widely. "Why, who would have thought a man who once worked as a P.I. here in town would become a walker? Of course, he was married at the time. Perhaps you've met his ex? Angel Devlin?"

"Lovely lady," Tom said, smiling at Angel when she looked his way. "Deeply involved in earning money—in any way she can—for charity."

"I don't have such fond memories of her," Dagger said, glaring heatedly at Angel when she twisted her head around to see his reaction.

"Messy divorce?" Tom asked.

"Messy marriage, too." Dagger's beady eyes slid up and down Angel's body. "The woman was far too involved in her work, tried to keep secrets from me, she even went so far as to wear a disguise once, thinking she could sneak around behind my back." Dagger grinned from Angel to Tom. "But I've put that experience behind me."

Frederike laughed giddily, waving a beringed hand around, drawing attention back to herself. "I do believe I've heard enough talk about sex and marriage for one night. I should get home before that nosy butler of mine comes looking for me."

Frederike straightened the fur-trimmed hat that had slid a tad sideways on her head. "You know, dahlings, I believe my children would like to have me declared incompetent so they can control my money. I also believe they've asked my butler to keep an eye on me, so"—she grinned—"I've gone out of my way to give the snoops ever so much to suspect me of and talk about. Why, I'm sure there's someone watching me now, and won't my children be shocked when they hear where I've spent the evening? Right now that nasty butler probably thinks I'm having an affair with a man who's out to screw me and take all my money." Frederike patted Dagger on the cheek, just like the mindful dog he was. "But we know that's not true."

"Of course it isn't true, Countess." Angel glared at Dagger. "Dagger doesn't look at all like the kind of man who'd screw a woman and take her for all she's worth."

Frederike hit Angel with another one of her condescending grins, then turned all of her attention to Tom. "It was a delight to meet you, Tommy." Frederike took Tom's hand and held it tightly. "I'm sure we'll bump into each other again. After all, we still have a good month left to the season."

Frederike air-kissed both of Tom's cheeks and gave Angel a withering glare. "Tootle-ooo!" she chirped, and, turning on the heel of her crystal-studded shoes, sashayed from the club with Dagger in tow.

Tom's warm, powerful fingers touched Angel's chin, and he drew her face toward his. His smile was hot. A wicked gleam twinkled in his eyes. "Now that that's over and done with, want to go back to my place and try that lap dance again?"

Angel's eyes narrowed. "You're insufferable. Not only that, but you're arrogant and cocky and—" She grabbed her purse and pulled out the folded check Tom had given her. She slapped it against his chest. "I may need this money, Mr.

Donovan. But I no longer want it, nor do I want to have anything to do with you."

Tom grinned. "I take it that means we won't be having sex tonight."

"Tonight, tomorrow, or any other time." Angel shoved out of his lap. "And if you don't mind, I'd like you, your libido, and your overabundance of testosterone to stay away from me, because you're making my life miserable."

11

*A*ngel ripped the wig off her head as she stalked across the parking lot. The night air was almost unbearably thick and hot and she longed to get in the car, roll down the windows, and drive fast, just to let the wind toss around her and hopefully blow away her rip-roaring fury.

She aimed her key ring at the Jaguar and heard the driver's door unlock, but before she could slip inside, Tom had his hands around her waist and spun her into his arms.

"I've learned from experience that a woman who's pissed at a man shouldn't be sitting behind the wheel."

"Excuse me?"

"You're angry. You're tense. And your mind is a million miles away, which means I'm going to drive."

Angel struggled against him to no avail. "I'm more than capable."

He smiled warmly. "Humor me."

"I think I humored you enough with that lap dance."

"That wasn't humorous. It was sexy as hell and I had the distinct feeling you were enjoying it just as much as me."

"That lap dance was a mistake."

"Mind telling me why?"

"Sure. I hate men."

"All men?" Tom asked, keeping her trapped, his big body pressed lightly against hers, his callused fingers whispering over her cheek, brushing away damp, wayward hair. "Or is it just the guy you used to be married to that you hate?"

Angel's eyes narrowed. "You think this anger I'm feeing right now is because of my ex?"

"Isn't it?"

"I can't waste my energy being angry with him. Yeah, I hate him. Yeah, I wish he'd fall off the face of the earth. But getting angry over anything he says or does at this stage of the game would mean he still has power over me. And he doesn't."

"Then would you please tell me why you're so damn angry?"

"Because you, Mr. Donovan"—Angel stabbed at his chest with her finger—"told Frederike you bought and paid for me."

"That was a joke. Nothing more than a half-assed comment to make up for the stupidity of what Frederike was saying."

"I didn't find it all that funny."

"I thought you had a better sense of humor."

Angel sighed heavily. "I told you this morning

that I couldn't be bought. It irritated the hell out of me that you'd even suggest such a thing."

"Yeah, but the only reason I'm here with you tonight is because I paid you damn good money for the privilege."

"You didn't pay for me or for sex, you paid to go on a stakeout with me and nothing more."

Tom's eyes narrowed, but more out of concern than anger. "What's this about, Angel?"

She tried to turn her face away from him, but he curled his fingers around her cheek, forced her to look at him. "Tell me. Like I told you before, you might be surprised how understanding I can be."

Angel plowed her fingers through her hair. "You're not the only one with bad memories." She sighed heavily. "I try not to think about them. For the most part I try to laugh things off, but seeing Dagger tonight, watching him leer at me, knowing that he knew who was behind my ridiculous disguise, made me remember the way he used to tell me that he owned me. *Owned* me, as if I were nothing more than one of the fancy toys he liked to buy with the money I worked damn hard for. And then you pop off with that completely insensitive comment."

"I'm sorry."

"Please don't say that unless you mean it."

"I don't say things I don't mean, Angel. I'm honest to a fault—you should have figured that out by now."

Angel looked long and hard into his eyes and something she saw deep inside him, something that he made her feel, something she couldn't understand, made her believe he was telling the truth.

"I hate losing control," she said softly. "I hate looking like a lily-livered lady who needs a man to take care of her, to soothe her."

"Never in my wildest dreams would I ever see you as a lily-livered lady."

"No?"

Tom shook his head. "You're the kind of lady who fights fire with fire, who gives as good as she gets, and you don't bow down to anyone. That's what I like about you."

She laughed lightly. "I thought it was my body that attracted you."

"I like the whole package."

Tom leaned forward to kiss her, but she moved away. "I think we've had enough kissing for one night."

"I thought we'd just gotten started."

"The stakeout's over, Tom. I know what Frederike's up to—which is absolutely nothing her butler needs to worry about. It's late, I'm tired, so why don't we head back to Jazzzzz and call it a night?"

Tom looked at his watch. "It's barely two A.M. We've got at least another four hours before morning."

Angel sighed heavily. "You're not going to give me a break, are you?"

"The last thing you need is to be alone." His fingers drifted up her arms and settled on her shoulders, digging gently into her overly taut muscles. "You need a drink. You need a massage."

"Let me guess. You're suggesting we go back to my place for a nightcap."

"Not your place, Angel. Mine. I've got a pool and the ocean out back. I've got beer and wine and I could even make a martini if you want one. And I've got something else, too."

"I know. An Italian Renaissance bed that's all set up and ready to go."

"Yeah, I've got that. But I've also got a grand piano. If you don't want me to take away your worries with a sweaty roll in the hay"—he winked—"let me do for you what I do for me when I've got too much on my mind."

"What's that?"

"Tickle the ivories." He cradled her cheeks in his hands and lightly kissed her forehead. "And once I have you good and relaxed, just say the word, and I'd be more than happy to tickle you, too."

Mere Belle was wild. Overgrown with royal Poinciana that hadn't yet burst into a riot of color. That would come in June, when the oppressive heat and humidity drove most of the islanders off to their summer places in Newport or Southampton.

But Tom liked the heat.

Especially the heat of the woman beside him in the car. She was tempting and beautiful and . . . and he knew he'd have to move slowly. Angel wasn't the kind of woman a man could rush.

Hell, she was the kind of woman a man should take his time with. Every second with her was worth savoring.

That, of course, didn't negate the fact that he

wanted to spend long hours with her in the sack. He just needed to bide his time, treat her right, gently, until she was damn good and ready.

The drive up to the chateau wound through palms, wild orchid, and a thicket of twisted bougainvillea in every color known to man. The stone driveway was torn up in places, but he didn't apologize for the mess that he'd already grown to love.

Apparently he didn't need to apologize for anything, because Angel looked at the mansion and the five-acre estate with wide-eyed wonder.

"It's beautiful," she whispered. "Not at all like the overly manicured mansions in town, places where you're afraid to walk on the grass or pick a flower for fear you might mess up the carefully planned aesthetic value."

"Living in a place like that would drive me crazy. I'm used to the Everglades—where everything is wild."

"Do you miss it?" she asked, as Tom pulled the Jag to a stop in front of the white stone chateau.

"I haven't had time to miss it." He reached across the car and, resting his hand on the back of the passenger seat, coiled a lock of Angel's soft, silky hair around his fingers. "I've got a lot of landscaping to do. Cleaning. Painting. Decorating."

"You could hire someone to do all of that."

"And then what? Sit around on my butt all day, drinking beer, watching ESPN, getting fat, and being lazy?"

"Join a country club or two. Play polo. Tennis. Go sailing."

"Do I look like the country club type to you?"

Angel shook her head. "That's what makes you so attractive. You're not like anyone else in town."

That was a come-on for a kiss if he'd ever heard one, and he didn't waste time making his move. He curled his fingers around Angel's neck and leaned toward her. Her lips were ripe. Warm. And he could already taste their sweetness.

Her sapphire eyes darkened. Turned dreamy.

She licked her lips, and he closed his eyes, moving in for the kill.

Before he knew what was happening, Angel's silky hair pulled free from his grasp. He heard the click of the car door opening, and the clack of high heels on the cracked stone drive.

His eyes popped open to see Angel peering at him from outside, a wide smile on her face. "Did you forget that you were going to play the piano for me?"

He'd like to forget, but he had a damn good idea that she'd remind him again and again if he tried to do anything tonight that even remotely smacked of sex.

Tom threw open the driver's door and climbed out. Skirting around the Jag, he took Angel's arm, trying to ignore her heat, the way her breasts jiggled when she walked, and her smile. He ushered her up the white stone entry and through a pair of double doors that still squeaked from lack of use.

"It's empty," Angel said, a frown narrowing her eyes as she stood in the massive entry hall. "I expected the walls to be covered with portraits and landscapes, and I was sure the place would be scattered with seventeenth-century European furniture."

Tom leaned against the wall he'd recently begun to strip of its peeling wallpaper. He folded his arms across his chest. "You sound disappointed."

"Just surprised," she said, her spiked heels clicking on the marble flooring that needed to be cleaned and buffed. She strolled to the center of the ballroom, closed her eyes, and inhaled, her luscious breasts swelling, rising, close to tumbling out of the tight red dress she was wearing.

"Someone's been using lemon oil in here."

"Me." Tom joined her, the thud of his crocodile boots on marble echoing through the room. "There's a lot of wood that needs polishing. A lot of walls that need stripping." He turned in a circle, imagining the beauty of the place once he finished his work. "I figure I've got a year or two of work to do, but I'm in no hurry. As for furnishings . . ."

He looked across the room, at the shiny black Steinway grand that stood not far from the doors leading out to the courtyard. "I've got a piano down here and another one upstairs in my bedroom, right by the big screen TV and that big old Italian Renaissance bed I just had delivered." Tom smiled. "What more could a man want? Or need?"

The smile she offered was filled with just one answer. "A family to fill up the empty spaces."

Tom laughed uncomfortably. Family wasn't something he normally talked about with a woman he eventually hoped to have knock-down-drag-out sex with.

He didn't want to even think about commitment.

He walked to the doors leading to the courtyard and looked out toward the dock and the yacht that was only dimly lit at this time of morning. "My grandfather lives on the yacht out back," Tom said, "and before you ask why he doesn't live inside with me, let's just say he prefers living on the water. But"—he shrugged—"that's about as close as family's going to get to Mere Belle for quite a few years."

"I can certainly understand that."

That hadn't been the comment he'd expected. Part of him expected Angel to talk about her own desire for a family—she was a woman, after all—but instead she walked to the piano and caressed the ebony wood. "Did you really wrestle alligators in your past?" she asked, "or are you a concert pianist who likes to tease?"

Tom turned away from the French doors. "I would have thought you'd know everything there is to know about my past by now."

"I ran out of time to do a thorough search into your past. And you did tell me if I had any questions about you, I should just ask. So"—she glanced at him out of the corner of her eye—"no more joking. You *are* a concert pianist, aren't you?"

"That was the dream my grandparents had for my mother, but she married my dad instead. As for me," Tom said, strolling toward the piano, "I must have inherited her talent, but there aren't

many concert pianists living in Everglade City."
He sat down on the shiny black bench. "There are
tourist attractions, though."

He put his fingers on the keys and as he did so
often, let the music he felt so deeply inside him
come out.

Angel sat beside him, her arm brushing against
his as he played, sending a thrill through his body
that he didn't need right now—since sex was off-
limits.

He tried to remember what he'd been talking
about, and couldn't help but wonder how she'd
managed to mess so completely with his mind,
since he usually had so much control. It must have
something to do with wanting something he
couldn't have.

Yet.

He launched into a little Chopin, and concentrated on conversation instead of his libido. "My
grandfather opened an alligator farm in the mid-
fifties. It wasn't much, just a neon sign, fresh
lemonade, a fenced pond, and a couple of gators
that people driving down the highway would pay
fifty cents to see. Over the years he bought a little
more land, added snakes, rare birds."

Tom gave the keys a little trill, interrupted
Chopin to add an improvised birdcall, and
grinned at Angel, whose sweet, lush breasts were
rising and falling lightly with each breath she took.

His libido was winning the battle.

"When my dad died I went to live with my
grandfather. Pop's kind of a curmudgeonly old
guy and he wasn't all that keen on having me live
with him in the beginning."

"Why?"

"I was four and scared to death of just about everything. I hated the gators, screamed when I saw the snakes, and refused to get close to anything that had fangs or slithered."

"But not anymore?"

Tom shook his head. "Pop used bribery. He said he'd buy me a piano if I'd touch one gator and one snake every day for a month. Took a few weeks before I got the nerve to do it and once I did, and I didn't lose a hand or my head or anything else, I decided I liked the thrill. Before long I was posing with the things while tourists took pictures."

"And you got your piano?"

"It wasn't much of a piano and it had to be tuned, but every night I'd sit down and play silly little songs while Pop rocked in his chair and smoked his pipe."

"No lessons?"

Tom shook his head. "I can't read music, either. I just listen to the songs and play what I hear."

"Did you ever think about becoming a concert pianist?"

"If I became a concert pianist, playing would become a job instead of a passion."

"Was wrestling alligators a passion or a job?"

"I liked working with the gators. I liked the tourists. But I could take it or leave it. Pop and I sold the farm a few months back and I haven't missed the place. But there's not a day that goes by when I don't want to sit down at the piano and play."

"Is yard work a passion of yours, too?"

"More a labor of love," Tom said. "Or does that sound too sentimental?"

"I wouldn't have expected words like that to come out of the mouth of an alligator wrestler, even a former alligator wrestler."

"There's more to me than just what meets the eye." He ran his fingers over the keys, wishing they were running over her body. "You said you knew Liszt. Do you know this one?"

Tom's hands glided over the keyboard, the rippling broken chords and seamless melody divided almost equally between both hands.

"It sounds familiar," Angel said, "but I couldn't give you a name."

" 'Un Sospiro'—'A Sigh,' " Tom said, adding his own sigh to the notes he played. "After I went to live with my grandfather, I forgot pretty much everything about the first four years of my life. But I did remember the music. I didn't know why, it was just there, in my head. A couple of months ago I inherited a lot of things, including Mere Belle, and when I walked in the doors the first time, I remembered my mother playing this song."

Angel frowned. "I thought she died in childbirth."

"She did, but my dad had taped dozens of songs that she played, and after she was gone, he'd play them over and over again. This was his favorite."

Angel closed her eyes while he played. She breathed deeply, her breasts rising and falling, almost keeping time with his music. He could easily get used to having her around—of course, he'd have to be able to touch her.

"We used to sit here on the bench listening to my mom play," Tom continued. "Dad talked about her and about the plans they'd had for their firstborn child. I might have been a concert pianist if she'd lived. I might have met you when I was younger. I seriously doubt I ever would have wrestled alligators."

"You might have grown up to be a jet-setting snob, and I might have ended up working for your wife or mistress, following you around, snapping pictures of you in indecent situations."

Tom grinned. "Or I might have grown up to be the exact same man sitting beside you now."

"That's the one I'd prefer."

Angel touched his cheek softly. Gently. He fought the urge to grab her hand, to pull her into his lap and kiss her until her lips were swollen. He wanted to drown out his bitterness in the softness of her. But her touch was all too brief. She turned away from him, walked across the room, and looked out on the view of the swimming pool.

"That's one of the first things I had refurbished," Tom said. "I try to swim at least twice a day. It's a luxury I didn't have before coming here."

Angel opened the French doors and a breeze blew her honey-blond hair. Everything about her mesmerized him. Her soft curves. Her long legs. Her hooker heels and that tight red dress.

How he was going to keep his hands off her he hadn't a clue. And if he didn't keep his hands off her, he doubted he could go slow.

He wanted her. Plain and simple.

He pushed away from the piano and walked to where she stood in the doorway. Slipping his hands over her shoulders, he leaned close. His bristly cheek caressed her smooth skin. "Want to go for a swim?"

Her quick nod surprised him. He'd expected her to say no, to insist he take her home. But she'd nodded yes—that was a pretty damn good start to what Tom hoped would happen later.

He took her fingers and led her to the pool. Slowly, taking his time, he peeled off his shirt and stood before her in nothing more than faded Levi's and crocodile boots.

Angel's gaze trailed up and down his body, settling on his chest, except for that one brief instant when she zoomed in on his crotch. A gaze like that was destined to get her in trouble.

"Maybe this isn't a good idea," she said, her voice barely a whisper. "After all, I don't have a swimsuit."

Tom unlatched his belt, popped the top button on his jeans, then the second button. "Swimsuits," he said, flashing a grin in her direction, "are for wimps."

"Is that so?"

He nodded. "Some people might disagree with me, but it's my expert opinion that wearing clothing of any type while swimming just gets in the way."

He tugged her against him. Slowly, ever so slowly, his palms slid down her sides. He could feel the soft curve of her breasts, the slenderness of her waist, and the flair of her hips. He wrapped his fingers around the hem of her dress, peeled it over her head, then dropped it on the cobblestone deck.

He felt her body tremble at his touch, at his gaze roving over her blessedly sweet breasts and skimpy thong. God, how he wanted to make love to her. Forget the swim. Forget playing the piano. He wanted to lose himself inside her, but something deep within him again screamed go slow.

With the tenderest of touches, he kissed her forehead, the bridge of her nose, her lips, her chin, then tasted her neck, his lips, his tongue lingering there for long seconds. Tasting. Tempting. And beneath his mouth he felt her quiver.

Again his hands swept over her cool, bare shoulders. Her pebbled nipples brushed over his chest, setting him on fire.

His fingers whispered along the curve of her spine, flared out over her bottom. Again she trembled. Again he touched. Explored.

When her breathing eased, when she seemed calm in his embrace, he slipped his thumbs under the straps at the side her thong and—

She slapped his fingers. "This is as naked as I get."

"A guy can try, can't he?"

"He can try. And I can stop him."

Tom's gaze darted to the knife and the white leather garter on her thigh. "What about the stiletto?"

"I only take that off when I feel I can trust the person I'm with."

"Trust me, Angel. The last thing on my mind right now is hurting you."

There was worry in Angel's eyes when he

touched the stiletto. A little more worry when his fingers slid beneath the leather garter and slowly, methodically dragged it down her leg. He peeled it over her high heels, then went back to the ties crisscrossing up to each knee, and just as slowly, he unwrapped each long leather strap, pressing warm, lengthy kisses to her calf, her ankle, the bridge of each foot until he tossed the shoes off to the side.

Her entire body wobbled. He thought she might turn to butter and melt right in his arms. Okay, so he was hoping she *would* turn to butter and melt in his arms. But she was still controlling her emotions. Fighting him every step of the way.

Wrapping his fingers around her waist, he rose just far enough that he could kiss her stomach. Her skin was cool; begging to be heated.

And again he felt her tremble beneath his touch.

She pulled away as if she were afraid of his fire and walked to the deep end of the pool, her stunning body radiating in the dim lights that shone down on the water, the palms, and the deep purple bougainvillea. Mounting the diving board, she walked to the very end, curled her toes over the edge, and raised her arms high over her head. Her full, round breasts rose, too. And then she dove, a magnificent, perfectly executed flight through air and into the pool.

She came out from under the wavering blue water in the shallow end. Her blond hair swept away from her face. Rivulets of water coursed over high cheekbones, over glistening tanned skin. Hard nipples beckoned to him.

Jerking off his boots, ripping off his jeans and boxers, he jumped into the water, executing a masterful, knee-hugging bomb. Water exploded around him. And to his surprise, so did Angel's laughter. And damn how he liked that sound.

He swam toward her, circled her, studying her body as the water rippled around her waist, hips and thighs.

At last he stood. Close. Real close. Half a head taller than her. Her breasts heaved, those budding pink nipples just barely above the water jutting out to meet him, but he kept his distance. Not touching her.

Yet.

He circled her again, then curled his hands on her shoulders, kneading the muscles running up her neck, along her shoulder blades. "God, you're tight."

"It comes with the job. I'm always on edge."

"Are you sure it has nothing to do with being here in the water with me? Naked? And knowing what's going to happen soon?"

"I'm not afraid of you, if that's what you want to know."

"Something's making you awfully tense," he said, massaging her shoulders. "If I'm reading you right, you're uncomfortable with the way I'm touching you."

She swam away, to the far end of the pool, and Tom joined her, taking long strokes until he reached her. Through the water he could see her legs scissoring back and forth, keeping her head and shoulders from sinking below the water's surface.

He slid his hands around her waist and pulled her against him, his own legs moving with hers. He was hard. Damn hard, and he rubbed against her pelvis. He wanted her, and her eyes widened. Was it fear he saw?

He could ask, but he didn't want to get into some long psychological discussion right now. Didn't want her to tell him it was too soon.

Dragging her hands from where they rested on his chest, he placed them around his neck and then softly, ever so softly, he touched her mouth with his.

He'd tell her he wanted her, but there was no need for words. His body said far more than he could utter.

With his hands clasped around her waist, he kicked away from the deep end, needed to put his feet on something solid. As soon as his toes touched bottom and his shoulders were above the water, he deepened the kiss, savored her sweetness.

Angel tried to pull away, that damnable fear again creeping up on her, until his fingers swept into her hair. He didn't force her against him, he just cradled her head in his hands and tasted her lips with the tip of his tongue. Gently.

He heard her deep intake of breath. A soft purr; an even softer sigh. And at last she leaned into him, opening her lips and letting him taste the inside of her mouth just as she tasted the inside of his.

And then he danced with her. A serene waltz, their bodies cutting through the water, her soft breasts and pebbled nipples pressed against his chest. He wanted to taste her. All of her. He wanted to be inside her, hot and tight and slick.

Her fingers were in his hair, tugging, but she wasn't trying to escape. She was grasping for more.

Fighting the urge to rip off her panties and take her now, right in the middle of the pool, he tore his lips from her sweet, hungry mouth and touched them lightly against the base of her throat.

A sigh tore from her lips and her head fell back as her breasts heaved against him. Her throat was warm and wet and soft, and as he kissed her she began to pant and her breasts rose higher. She seemed as desperate for more as he was.

He grasped her thighs and spread her legs to wrap around his waist, and then, when her fabulous, succulent breasts floated atop the water, he took one cold, beaded nipple into his mouth.

A deep moan escaped his throat. "Oh, God," he whispered against her dusky pink flesh. He suckled her, teased her with the tip of his tongue, circling that nipple lightly, then firmly, kissing her puckered flesh before taking the other breast into the palm of his hand, kneading her, tasting the tempting, heavenly body that thrust against him as the water lapped around them.

Again he captured her mouth, with urgency now. With need. Desire. She was every bit as hungry for him as he was for her, and that spurred him on.

He lifted her in his arms, and her hands tightened around his neck so their lips wouldn't part. He carried her up the pool steps. Water dripped from their bodies and the warm breeze hit them. It should have cooled him off, but he was burning, every inch inflamed. Throbbing with need.

He was careful not to slip on the marble floor, bounded up the circular staircase, and headed straight for the master bedroom at the end of the hall. There wasn't much in the room other than the intricately carved Italian Renaissance bed he'd bought yesterday morning.

He laid her on the high, soft, and thick mattress, and his body screamed at him to take her right then and there, to spread her legs and climb between them and thrust hard and deep, once, twice, three, four, five times, and come with an all-powerful force. He wanted her that desperately. That urgently.

He climbed onto the bed beside her, feeling the mattress give beneath his weight. He kissed her as his fingers slid down her belly, under the tiny scrap of thong she wore, through tempting curls, to the heat he longed to feast upon and make love to.

God, why was she so damn tense? He could feel it in her stomach muscles, in her shoulders, in the way her fingers grasped his hair, pulling painfully.

Opening eyes he'd kept shut so he could feel each stroke, each touch, each movement deep in his insides, just as he felt his music in his soul, he watched her eyes. They were tight. Her teeth were clenched.

"Easy, sweetheart," he whispered, kissing her lips gently. "I'm not going to hurt you."

He slipped his middle finger inside her. She

was hot and wet and tight and her legs were like a vise.

Muscles clenched inside her as he worked his finger in and out. God, he'd never known a woman to be so tight, to clamp around him. He slipped a second finger inside her, needing to release some of her tension, needing to stroke her deep and make her feel everything he wanted her to feel.

He swirled his thumb over that warm, tender little nub of flesh and nerves and her body froze. Her eyes flashed open in something close to horror.

"Stop," she nearly screamed. "Please."

It took a second or two for the words to register, and then he halted. His breathing came in ragged gasps as he withdrew his fingers. His entire body ached with the need to be inside her, but not like this. Not if she fought the pleasure he wanted to give her.

Not if she was afraid of him.

He rested on top of her, cradling her face in his hands and trying to understand what was going on inside her head. "What's wrong? Did I hurt you?"

Angel shook her head, then pushed at his chest and rolled out from under him. "I need to go."

He grasped her arm, but not so tightly that she couldn't pull away if she was desperate to leave. "Maybe you should stay so we can talk about what just happened."

"There's nothing to talk about."

Angel tugged out of his grasp, rolled out of bed, and ran from the room, disappearing from his view, from his arms.

Tom's gut tightened. He'd had women leave his bed before, but not before they had sex. It was always afterward. After they'd found pleasure in each other's bodies and they'd both been drained of energy. There was usually a quick kiss, a smile, and a wave, because the women he'd known hadn't wanted a commitment any more than he had.

But Angel was different.

Damn it. He didn't want her to be different. He wanted to have sex with her. Wanted her to enjoy it. Didn't want any commitments.

Hell, he didn't want her to be scared. Or special.

And he didn't want her to run away. He wanted her too damn much.

What the hell was she doing? Angel wondered, as she breezed through the French doors, struggling to pull the tight spandex dress over her breasts, clutching her shoes plus her stiletto and garter in one hand and searching for her purse.

She needed to get away before Tom confronted her, before he called her a tease and a frigid bitch like the last guy she'd allowed to go almost as far as Tom had gotten.

But it didn't appear she needed to worry about that. Tom was nowhere in sight. He was probably fast asleep in bed, figuring she wasn't worth yelling at or berating.

She spotted her purse on top of the piano. Grabbing it quickly, she turned to run for the front door and her car, and ended up running into Tom's powerful chest. His fingers dug into her arms, holding her almost at arm's length.

Slowly she looked up and saw the chill in his eyes. She tried to avoid them by gazing at the door, by wishing that she could will herself through it, into her car, and into her home, where she could pretend that none of this had happened.

God, she needed to get away.

"I have to go home, Tom."

"No, you don't," he said brusquely. "We need to talk."

"There's nothing to talk about." She twisted out of his hold and ran for the door, but he caught her again, spinning her around, holding her tight.

"Tell me what the hell happened upstairs."

"It's pretty damn obvious, isn't it?"

"The only thing that was obvious to me was that for some goddamned reason you were scared shitless. You were so damn tight I could hardly get my fingers inside you. But it was also pretty damn obvious that you wanted me to make love to you, and you can bet your bottom dollar I wouldn't have stopped and you would have enjoyed every second of it if you hadn't brought everything to a screeching halt."

Her jaw tightened. "I brought it to a screeching halt because it shouldn't have happened in the first place."

"You said the same thing about kissing me when we were parked in front of Frederike LeVien's place, but you know damn good and well you enjoyed that kiss and all of the others we shared tonight just as much as I did. You liked that lap dance, too. Didn't you?"

"Of course I did. But—"

"But what?" His hold tightened. His eyes blazed. "Do you have some dreaded disease you're afraid to tell me about? Are you going to turn into a frog if we make love?"

"Maybe I'm just frigid," she lied, knowing he wouldn't want to hear and probably wouldn't care about the real reason. "Maybe I hate sex."

"Bullshit. You were hot. You were wet. You were slick, and I could hear every moan, every purr, every growl deep down in your throat. I felt your muscles tighten around my fingers. I watched your breasts heave. Damn it, Angel, a woman who's frigid or hates sex doesn't react in any of those ways. A woman who's frigid or hates sex wouldn't be a turn-on to a man, and let me tell you, sweetheart, you turn me on more than any woman I've ever laid eyes on. Now," he said, his breathing hard and deep, "are you going to tell me what the hell happened up there?"

She wasn't ready to tell him. How could she tell him what she didn't understand herself?

She jerked out of his arms and walked back to the open French doors. The cool breeze fluttered around her as she stared out at the brightly lit palms.

Behind her she heard Tom's labored breathing. Heard it calm, then felt his hands sliding around her waist, his fingers clasping over her stomach. He cradled her back against his chest, his cheek brushing against hers. He didn't say a word, he just held her close for the longest time. Comforting her in a way no man had ever comforted her.

Slowly, ever so slowly, she relaxed in his arms.

"Want a glass of wine?" he asked softly.

Angel shook her head. "No, but thanks."

"Chocolate? I might have an old Hershey bar lying around somewhere."

His teasing made her smile. It surprised her that he could laugh or even want to comfort her after what had happened, and she couldn't help but ask, "Why are you still holding me?"

"I like the way you feel." His voice whispered against her cheek. "I like everything about you, Angel, and I'm not about to let you out of my arms until you tell me what's wrong. I can't help unless I know."

Could she put her trust in a man she'd known only two days? Could she bare her soul to him?

She folded her hands over his, and his warmth and strength seeped into her. She felt his compassion and an unexplainable need that seemed so much like her own.

Slowly she let her words, her thoughts flow out to Tom. "Do you have any idea what it's like to want someone desperately? To want to be held and touched and kissed? To have your insides ache with a need you can't even express?"

"I'm feeling all of those things right now," Tom answered.

Angel turned in his arms. Her breasts rubbed softly against his chest and her heart beat gently, as she looked deep into his eyes. "Before you had sex the first time, do you remember having dreams that it would be wonderful and exciting?"

He laughed, but Angel knew it wasn't her question he found funny; it had to be the memory of that first time. "It was a long time ago, but yeah, I remember those feelings."

"Is it always wonderful and exciting for you?"

"I'm a man. It always feels good. Some times are better than others." He kissed her softly, his lips lingered a moment, and then he pulled back just the slightest amount, and looked at her with gently caressing eyes. "Sometimes you know it's going to be good even before you get to the sex. There's a connection. Something that just feels so damn right."

"And then it's great when you get to the sex. Right?"

"Well . . ." He laughed again. "Yeah."

"This is crazy," Angel said, bolting across the room. "I've told you way too much."

Tom stopped her retreat, tugging her back into his arms. "You haven't told me a thing, you've just asked a lot of questions. But you know what?" His eyes narrowed. "I seem to be getting a pretty good picture of what's going on here."

"What do you mean?"

"You're a tease, Angel." She felt her body stiffen at his words. "You dress to kill wearing kick-ass high heels and tight dresses and stripping in front of a man and telling him he's not getting anything more."

"You think *I'm* a tease?" she tossed back. "You've hit me with one sexual innuendo after another from the first second we met."

"Yeah, but I'm not the one walking away right now."

"Most men do." Anger erupted inside her. "They get pissed off because I won't go all the way."

"Does that piss you off, Angel, or do you secretly enjoy making men horny, letting them get to the point of no return, then slapping cold water in their faces by saying stop?"

Her back stiffened. "You don't know a thing about me."

"But I want to."

"You want a good roll in the hay. Nothing more."

"If that's all I wanted, you'd be gone by now and I'd be at Jazzzzz or some other club looking for a woman who'd guarantee me a great time. But you're here. I'm here. And you know what, sweetheart, I'm not going to let you go until you tell me what's going on in that head of yours."

The intensity in his eyes bore into her as if he really and truly did want to know what was troubling her. And God knows she'd looked long and hard for a man she could trust. It might be a mistake to open up to Tom. Then, again, it might be an even bigger mistake not to, because if she pulled away once more, he might give up on her completely.

"She ran her hands through still-wet hair. "If I tell you everything, you'll tell me I need a shrink."

"I hate shrinks." Tom's words were blunt. His smile soft, coaxing, and she found herself leaning into the comfort of his rock solid body.

"You're sure you want to hear this?"

"Positive."

Angel took a deep breath, then let it all spill out. "Marrying Dagger was the biggest mistake I ever made. My dad told me not to. My brothers,

Emma, my mom. They didn't like him but, I don't know, I was young and rebellious and . . ."

"We've all done stupid things in our lives."

"Yeah, but I married a man who slept with a knife, who introduced me to making love by teasing me with a blade, and kept on teasing me with it for seven long years because he couldn't get excited any other way."

Tom's fingers clutched her arms. She could feel his anger. His concern.

"He said it was all fun and games," Angel continued. "He said he'd never hurt me, but every time we were together I felt as if I were being raped, felt if I didn't spread my legs for him and let him do what he wanted, he'd use the knife on me."

"Did he?"

"No, but the threat was always there."

"Why didn't you leave him?"

"A million reasons, which seem ridiculous now."

"Such as?" Tom asked.

"I didn't want my parents or my brothers to know I'd made a mistake. I didn't want to look like a failure. Most of all, I'd never believed in divorce. I always thought there was something wrong with a man or a woman who couldn't make their marriage work."

"But you finally walked away?"

"My mom got hit with Alzheimer's and I watched how gentle my dad was with her. He brushed her hair if she forgot. He'd sit for hours reading books and magazines to her even though some days she'd just stare at the wall. That's when

I realized that if I ever got hit with a fatal disease, Dagger might slice my throat so he wouldn't have to deal with an invalid. That's when I realized I didn't have a marriage. I had nothing."

"And now?" Tom asked.

"I've tried to wipe Dagger from my memory, and for the most part I've been successful. But when it comes to sex—I'm just so damn scared. Petrified. Afraid I'll be hurt."

Tom smiled gently. "Kind of like me at four, when I first had to touch an alligator. Scared shitless until I knew I was going to get something good in return. All I had to do was relax, take that first step, touch the gator, and Pop bought me a piano, which was the thrill of my life."

Angel found herself smiling. "That's an interesting analogy."

"It *was* damn good, wasn't it?" Tom laughed as he stroked a lock of damp hair away from her face. "You might be scared of me, Angel, but just touch me—and let me touch you—and I'll prove you have nothing to fear. And then I'll show you how good it can be for both of us."

"This isn't a ploy just to get me back into your bed, is it?"

"I could be a real asshole and tell you every lie in the book, but the truth is, touching you excites me, Angel. Looking at you, feeling you, watching you stroll around in kick-ass high heels makes me want you. I don't need a knife, I don't need threats, I just need you to say, 'Make love to me.'"

"I'm still scared shitless."

Warm fingers caressed her cheek, curled beneath her chin, and held her gaze captive. "Hurting you is the last thing on my mind. Making you feel good, making you moan and squirm and come over and over again . . . that's what I want."

A moment's hesitancy continued to hang over her. "You'll go slow?"

"If that's what you want."

"You'll stop if I tell you to?"

He kissed her lips lightly. Gently. "I'm not going to hurt you, Angel. Trust me. Please."

He swept her up in his arms and headed for the stairs. "I'm going to go slow, Angel. I'm going to make you feel all the things you should have felt for years. And if you get scared, if you tell me to stop, I'll stop. It may be the hardest thing I've ever had to do in this life, but I don't want to make love to a woman who's frightened. I want to make love to a woman who wants me."

Angel sighed, letting go of the tension. The fear. Her fingers tightened in Tom's long, silky hair, and then she whispered against his lips, "I want you."

12

Moonlight poured through the open French doors and danced across Tom's body as he stretched out beside Angel in the massive Italian Renaissance bed. He was gorgeous and mesmerizing, and even now, as he slipped an arm beneath her neck and caressed her cheek with a callused palm, she couldn't believe he'd run after her. That he still wanted her.

His first kiss was tender. Cautious. He breathed deeply, his eyes open, watching her with a gentle smile, just as she watched him.

"How's that?" he whispered against her lips. "Too much?"

"I've got no problem with your kisses," she said, curling into his body, slipping fingers into his hair, praying that this time she wouldn't fall apart when he got too close. "In all honesty, I could lie here all night doing nothing more than kissing."

Tom skimmed the tip of his tongue over her bottom lip. "Kissing's fine for starters, but we're going all the way, sweetheart. All the way."

And God how he wanted her now. This very instant. But he'd promised to go slow. Taking his time, he touched her neck, his fingers feathering over soft, warm skin. Slowly, ever so slowly, he caressed her side, listening to each breath she took, waiting for the hesitancy and fear to go away. Inch after precious inch he captured each curve, each little mole in his memory.

He rested his fingers on the flare of her hip and deepened his kiss. Her lips parted. Their tongues touched. Mingled. And then they danced—a waltz, sweet and smooth and rhythmic. All the while he could feel the tension easing where his fingers cradled her shoulder, could hear small sighs deep within her.

While her senses were caught in the magic of their kiss, he rolled her onto her back and swept his palm to her belly. She flinched. He could have stopped kissing her. Could have said, 'It's okay. I'm not going to hurt you,' but he told her in actions what she might not believe in words.

His hand merely rested on her stomach. A light touch, nothing more. He could feel every breath she took and they came closer together, grew shorter, heavier, as his lips strayed from her mouth. He kissed her throat, drawing lazy circles with his tongue over her collarbone, her chest, at last arriving at her breast.

A sigh escaped him when he found her sweet, hardened nipple. God, that little nub tasted like manna from heaven, a feast he sorely doubted he could ever get enough of.

But now he wanted more.

Angel could feel every hard inch of Tom's body

pressed against her, could smell his heat, the scent of his aftershave, the chlorine that still lingered on his skin. He nibbled on her nipple, suckled her, and was driving her mad with a need she'd never felt before.

Slowly, tentatively, she reached out and threaded her fingers into his hair. He moaned when she touched him, and he looked up from her wet and swollen breast and smiled.

"How are you holding up?" he asked, a twinge of laughter in his eyes.

"I think I'm going to survive."

"Then let's try this again."

With his dark brown eyes sparkling as he watched her face, he slid his hand down her belly and between her legs.

"You're nice and warm," he said. "And wet."

"That's your doing."

"Let's see what else I can do."

One finger slipped inside her, moving in and out gently, and she couldn't believe the feeling, the way electricity skittered through her veins, how her heart thumped, how her stomach quivered.

A second finger joined the first and then he swirled his thumb over the most sensitive spot of all. She jumped as a spasm of sheer delight hit her.

"Too much?" he asked.

She shook her head bravely. "Not enough."

"I was hoping you'd say that."

Without another word, Tom moved over her. The muscles in his arms flexed as he nudged her legs apart with his knees and before she had any idea what he was doing, her legs were resting on his shoulders and he was smiling at her from between her thighs.

Her body tensed. Her legs clamped around his neck.

"Relax, sweetheart," Tom whispered. "Just relax."

She felt the tip of his tongue against her sensitive flesh. Hot. Powerful. Cautious but in full command, leaving no doubt in her mind that he wanted to please her, wanted to send her over the edge and beyond without going too fast and scaring the living daylights out of her.

Did he know she'd never been touched that way before? Or did he only guess?

Tom's tongue swirled around and around and she throbbed down deep inside, wanting more. Needing more.

It had to have been instinct that made her hips thrust toward him when she was certain Tom was going to pull away.

"That's what I like," he said. "A woman who knows what she wants."

He kissed her softly and then with passion, right there between her legs, his tongue dancing over her flesh, setting her ablaze and stoking the flame when his fingers again found their way inside her.

Blood pulsed through her veins. Her heart beat fast and heavy. Her breathing was labored and with every skillful thrust of his fingers, every sweet stroke of his tongue, every kiss, a moan escaped her throat. A sigh. And then her entire body convulsed in blissful pleasure.

She felt a desperate urge to pull away, to keep

from screaming, but Tom captured her legs in his
arms and held her close, keeping her against him,
while he carried her into sweet, blissful ecstasy.

He sucked, he teased; she panted and cried out,
"Stop, please stop."

He rose above her, a powerful man. Chest heaving, eyes black with desire. He touched her face,
his palms settling on her cheeks. "Please tell me
that 'Stop, please stop,' wasn't for real. That you
really meant, 'I'm having a hell of a good time
and if you stop, I'll never speak to you again.'"

Angel reached up and cradled his beautiful face
in her hands. "You do have a condom, don't you?"

"A few dozen, and I can have the first one on
before you can say, 'Make love to me.'"

"Take your time and get it on right," she said, as
he reached toward the far side of the bed, opened
the drawer in the nightstand, and pulled out a little pouch. "This isn't a race, Tom. It's a pleasure
trip. My very first one, and I want to enjoy all the
sights and sounds and everything else."

He rolled the condom on. "And I'm ready to
depart."

"Then make love to me."

Tom smiled as he balanced the length of his
body over hers with one muscle-bulging arm. He
reached between them and she could feel him
guiding his erection against her, sliding the head
back and forth over slick skin. And then, ever so
slowly, he pushed inside her.

It had been so long. So damn long. And he was
so big that she was afraid she'd dry up from
panic, from the initial pain of being stretched, but

he felt so right taking his time getting inside her, inch by inch by inch.

"You all right?" he asked, his breathing labored, as he buried what had to have been his entire length inside her.

"Couldn't be better."

"We both could be better. I'll show you how."

He thrust hard and fast and she was sure he'd touched her heart. And then he began to move in that same way he had played the piano, calmly one moment, then with all-consuming power. His wasn't the in-and-out, wham-bam, not-even-a-thank-you-ma'am kind of lovemaking—or just plain one-sided sex—that she'd had before.

Tom made love. His style was soulful, with a bit of jazz and rhythm and blues thrown in. There was a touch of rock and then the classics, played by a master, each stroke designed to evoke intense, fiery emotions.

This was what she'd fantasized about. This was what she imagined making love would be. And now that she'd experienced it, she had the feeling she'd never get enough, and ask for more whenever and wherever the mood struck.

As long as she was with Tom.

How simple it was to enjoy and take immense delight in all that she was feeling. It seemed crazy, but she laughed, and Tom's intense eyes focused on her face.

"You find my lovemaking funny?"

"Oh, God, no. It's the best thing I've ever experienced in my whole entire life."

"It'll get even better."

"I'm sure it will."

Her hips rose to thrust against him. "Roll over and let me take charge."

A grin eased across his face, and suddenly she was above him, kneeling over his body, her mouth lowering over his.

She kissed him deeply and lingered there, her tongue memorizing the contours of his mouth, the slick feel of his teeth, the pleasure of his tongue tangling with hers.

Rotating her hips, she clenched her muscles, and as her insides tightened she felt his erection throb. She kept him trapped inside her, wanting to keep him long and hard and hot and thick, and buried in the heart of her as long as she could.

"I like the feel of you inside me," she whispered against his mouth.

"I kind of like being there."

Her lips drifted lower to caress his jaw, and lower still, licking away the salty perspiration on his neck. She traced his collarbone with her tongue and slowly, steadily kissed her way to his small beaded nipples. She flicked first one and then the other, just as he had done to hers, all the while watching the smile on his face as he folded his arms beneath his head so he could gaze at her.

"You do that quite well."

"This is a first for me." She smiled back. "I listened intently and with great interest while my girlfriends read their romance novels out loud. There were so many things I wanted to do and try when I made love."

"Feel free to use me as your testing ground."

His hips thrust upward. He added a little bump

and grind, and a zillion shock waves zapped through her insides.

"Oh, God, Tom. Do that again. Please."

And he did, bucking her, filling her completely, stroking every nerve ending.

It was amazing how good it felt to be on top of him. She wasn't in control, but she wasn't under his control, either. They were enjoying this together.

Together . . . because she wanted it to be that way, not because he had demanded it of her.

She rose above him, straddling his pelvis and holding on tight, like a woman riding a bronc gone wild.

His breathing grew hard and heavy and she moaned with each mounting thrust.

Shivers of need and want and desire and almost unbearable pleasure ripped through her, and then she was beneath him again, her ankles locking around his back, his hands clasping her bottom and holding her tight as the pounding beat of his lovemaking deepened and gained momentum.

"Stop, Tom, stop," she cried, and with her very next breath beseeched him, "No, no, please. Don't ever stop."

She threaded her fingers into his hair and drew his face close. His dark eyes were barely open, but she could see the intensity there. The passion.

And then his mouth slanted over hers. Hard. Needy. A cry for more and then . . .

Everything inside her and around her quaked. Her muscles tightened. Her fingernails nearly dug into his scalp. Tom groaned, his body stiffened and stilled, except for the tightness of his

hands holding her against him, as if he were
afraid she'd want to pull away.

Deep within her she could feel him pulse. And
when he laid down softly on top of her, when he
kissed her tenderly, she could feel the beat of his
heart.

He didn't move. He didn't get up and leave her.
He stayed there, holding her, kissing her, showing her that even her wildest fantasies about what
true lovemaking was like were not nearly as wild
and wonderful as the real thing.

Tom watched Angel sleep. Mascara and eyeliner
had darkened the hollows beneath her eyes and
the long honey-blond hair trailing across his arm
and over the black satin pillows was a mass of
tangles.

They should have taken a shower at some point
during the night. He should have washed her hair
and brushed it out for her. But he hadn't wanted
to get out of bed. Hell, he hadn't wanted to be
anyplace but inside of her most of the night. And
he had been.

How he'd managed to get it up so many times
was a mystery. He only hoped they could do the
same thing again and again.

Beneath her eyelids he could see the slight
flicker of her eyes. Was she dreaming? About him,
he hoped, and not about the bastard she'd been
married to.

In all of his life he'd only wanted to wreak
vengeance on one man—Holt Hudson. Now
there was another man he despised—Dagger
Zane. If the man got within spitting distance

again, Tom would make him regret that he'd ever been born.

Angel rolled onto her side, as if his thoughts had awakened her. Or maybe it could have been his fingers tracing the curve of her waist, the flair of her hips; or the sound of his breathing when he remembered the taste of her nipples, and the feel of her tongue when she'd teased his hard-as-granite erection.

He touched her lips with his middle finger. They were cool and plump and red, and she opened her mouth just the slightest bit and sucked his fingertip inside. She licked it, nibbled on it, then reached under the covers and touched his abs.

He sprang to life in an instant, and her hand wrapped around him, kneaded him, slid up and down, up and down, before she straddled his hips and, with eyes now open wide, lowered herself onto him.

"Sleep well?" she asked, rising to within a fraction of an inch of him slipping out of her, then lowering herself again in slow motion until their bodies melded together and became almost one.

"I don't remember you letting me sleep."

Angel smiled slyly. "Want to sleep now?"

"I'd rather just lie here and watch your breasts while you do all sorts of nasty things to me."

"You mean I don't get anything in return?"

"You get the benefit of me being hard as rock for the third time is as many hours. I don't know if I'm capable of anything else."

"In that case . . ."

The confounded woman had the nerve to climb off of him, off the bed, and then smirk.

His eyes narrowed while he did his best not to grin. "I'll get you for that."

Angel laughed. "You have to catch me first."

Tom bounded off the bed, but Angel was far faster than him. She raced out of the bedroom and down the stairs, with him hot on her trail. She threw open the French doors leading to the pool and was halfway there when he caught her and twirled her around.

He trapped her in his embrace and kissed her lips. They were hot and her laughter echoed in his mouth, then turned to moans as his tongue dipped inside.

Her hands stretched up around his neck and he lifted her. Her ankles locked around his back and he carried her to a marble bench and laid her down.

The marble was cold and hard. On the other hand, he was on fire and just as hard as the stone, and he entered her with one deep trust.

And then he came to a sudden, jerking halt. "Shit."

Angel's eyes flew open. "What? Are you hurt? Is something wrong?"

"We seem to have forgotten all about protection."

She cradled his cheeks in her hands. "I haven't got anything you need to worry about."

"Me neither."

"And the timing's okay."

"You're sure?"

"I know my body."

He tried not to worry. He tried to concentrate on just how good and tight and hot and slick she felt. And he thrust again. "I'm getting to know it pretty well, too, and I like it a lot."

"Shut up and just make love to me."

And he did.

Angel knew she should leave. It was nearly seven in the morning and she'd told her dad she'd drop by to make breakfast for him and her mom. It was a ritual she performed three or four times a week to give her father a break, to give him someone to talk with, and, for her own sake, to maybe catch a glimpse of the mother she used to know, the mom who remembered her daughter's face, even if she couldn't always remember her name.

Instead, she sat on the piano bench, tucked between Tom's legs, the warm bare skin of his chest pressed against her back, clothed in the red spandex dress she'd donned after they'd made love and taken a quick dip in the pool.

Tom's strong, darkly tanned fingers were a sharp contrast against the white and black piano keys. They were the hands of an alligator wrestler, a snake charmer, callused and rough and tanned from long days in the sun. Yet he played Beethoven and Chopin from memory, as if the music were a part of his soul.

Tom kissed her neck lightly. "What's on your agenda after you have breakfast with your parents this morning?"

"I need to talk with Frederike's butler about what we witnessed last night—which was pretty much nothing. I've got photos to deliver to another client, I have to prepare for a court case I need to testify at tomorrow, and make my every-other-day meeting with Holt Hudson about the gala."

Tom's fingers stilled on the piano. He kissed Angel's neck. "Why don't you take me with you?"

She shook her head. "I don't think so."

"Why not?"

"I told you already. I don't trust you around Holt."

"That was before you knew me."

"Just because I trust you around *me* doesn't mean I want to take you into Holt Hudson's home and let you confront him about something that's best forgotten."

Tom sighed in frustration. "Holt Hudson might think it's best forgotten, but I need to know the truth about that night."

"The truth was published in the newspapers. The truth was in the police report."

"All lies."

"I read every word of it and—"

Tom's laughter cut off her words. "You got a copy of the police report?"

"I told you yesterday that I was going to check out your background. I might not have gotten around to finding out anything about you, but I was lucky enough to get a copy of the police report off of microfiche—and I did find out what happened that night."

"I told you that you could ask me anything you wanted to ask and I'd give you the lowdown."

"You can't give me the lowdown about something you know very little about."

"I know the police report is a piece of crap."

"I read it, Tom. Your dad's fingerprints were on

the combination lock leading into the safe where Holt Hudson keeps his valuables. The same fingerprints were *inside* the safe where Holt kept *The Embrace,* and they were also on Carlotta Hudson's headboard."

"I read the same report and I know exactly what it says. But there's got to be some other explanation for those fingerprints. My dad and Holt were friends. He probably went into that safe on a lot of different occasions."

"Not according to Holt. Besides, Tom, there is no explanation for his fingerprints being on Carlotta's headboard unless—"

"He *wasn't* having an affair with her."

"Damn it, Tom. Let's not talk about this. Let's not ruin what was such a perfect night."

"You're the one who got a copy of the police report. You're the one who isn't able to understand my need to talk to Holt."

"Your father's blood was on Carlotta's bed." The muscles in Angel's neck stiffened. Her jaw felt tight. "If he hadn't been guilty, why did he run? Why didn't he go to a hospital after he was shot? Why didn't he call the police?"

Tom shoved his hands through his hair. "I told you before. If I knew the answers to those things I wouldn't have any need to see Holt. He has the answers, and I'm going to get them from him whether you help me or not."

"I'm not going to help you."

Tom shook his head, exhausted, frustrated, and hurt. "I should have known you wouldn't help me. I should have known—"

"Wait a minute." Angel's eyes were cold. Narrowed. "Is that what this whole thing between you and me has been about? Is that the reason you followed me that first night, so you could get close to me, so you could get into my pants and make me want you . . . so that I'd end up so grateful for your lovemaking that I'd do anything for you?"

"Yeah," Tom muttered. "I thought you might help me, but—"

"But nothing," Angel threw back. "You used me, and I fell for it."

"You fell for me just like I fell for you."

"You haven't fallen for me. This was all a game to you, just like I was a game for Dagger."

"Do you really think I spent the night screwing you instead of making love to you?"

Angel fought to keep the tears from sliding down her cheeks. "That's the way it appears."

"Let me tell you what screwing is, Angel. Screwing someone is claiming to be their best friend, as Holt Hudson did with my father. Screwing someone is shooting them six times for no reason at all."

Angel grabbed her purse and her shoes and headed for the door. She threw it opened and was halfway out when she looked back at Tom. "You might as well have shot me in the back, too, Tom. Because everything I was beginning to feel for you is dead."

13

"*Y*ou look like hell," Jed Devlin said to his daughter when Angel opened the screen door and stepped into the kitchen in the small four-bedroom home in West Palm Beach where she and her brothers had grown up. "Rough night?"

"Yeah," Angel said, but didn't offer any explanation as she took a mug out of the ever-present dish drainer on the countertop and poured herself some coffee. "If you don't mind, I'm going to use your shower, bum a T-shirt, and then I'll come back and fix breakfast."

"I can do breakfast."

"You burn the bacon. I don't." She smiled and gave her dad a peck on the cheek, then walked past him and into the laundry room. She'd come here straight from Tom's knowing her dad would worry if she were late. She hadn't even bothered to change clothes, but now wanted out of the clothes she'd worn since last night. Grabbing one of her dad's freshly dried Sacramento Kings T-shirts and a pair of his jogging shorts, she disappeared into the small bathroom that she and her three brothers had shared.

She twisted the knob in the shower and cold water burst out of the nozzle. It would take a good minute for it to heat up, and while it did, she stripped out of her god-awful red dress and panties and stared at herself in the mirror.

She *did* look like hell. Her eyes were red from anger and tears. Her hair was a mass of tangles, as if a mouse had nested in it. Mascara and eyeliner smudged the tender skin beneath her eyes. Her lips were swollen and, oh, God, she had a hickey on her neck.

She rested her forehead against the cold mirror. What the hell had she done? She'd spent the past five years of her life making sure she was always in control, making sure that no man ever again got the better of her, and then she'd tumbled into bed with the first man who didn't run away from her when she froze up at the onset of sex—only to find out that he'd stuck with her because he had more on his mind than making love.

He'd wanted to use her.

What a fool she'd been.

When the mirror was steamed over, she climbed under the hot, pulsating water and scrubbed away a night's worth of being screwed.

She'd never again let that happen.

Never.

Her father raised his eyes from the newspaper spread over the table when Angel walked back into the kitchen. Her hair was wrapped on top of her head in a fluffy green towel, the back of the

T-shirt was wet where water still dribbled from her hair, and even though she had her dad's running shorts cinched up, they rested low on her hips.

Jed Devlin was a big man. Six-four and a good two hundred sixty pounds. But he was as solidly built as he was solid in character. An ex-private investigator who'd worked hard at a job he'd loved so he could support the family he cherished.

And he'd never screwed anyone.

"How's Mom this morning?" Angel asked, as she took a carton of eggs from the fridge.

"I don't know." Jed took a swallow of coffee. "She didn't want any help getting dressed, got angry when I mentioned that her dress zipped up the back instead of the front, and before I came out here she was putting on makeup so she'd look pretty for Ted Cushman. That's the kid who took her to the senior prom."

Angel cracked an egg and dumped the insides into a bowl. "Want me to look in on her?"

"Let's wait and see what happens once the scent of bacon and eggs fills the house. If my guess is right, she'll know you're here and want to see you."

"She thought I was her mom two days ago."

"I'm hoping today will be a better day."

Jed got up from the table, turned the fire on under the big frying pan on the stove, and dropped some cut-up strips of bacon into the skillet. "Why don't I give the bacon a try? If I get close to burning it, holler at me."

"Okay, Dad."

They worked side by side in silence for nearly a

minute before Jed angled a questioning glance at his daughter. "Gonna tell me where you were last night that called for wearing a hooker dress?"

"The Tropical Lei."

"I hope you were there for business."

"Come on, Dad, you know I wouldn't be there for any other reason."

"Were you spying on anyone I know?"

"Frederike LeVien. Her butler's worried about the company she's been keeping."

Jed laughed. "How you can stand to work around those Palm Beach types is beyond me. You should have kept the business in West Palm Beach where normal people live."

"The pay's better over there."

"You live in an apartment and it's over a pampered pooch boutique."

"Yeah, but I drive a Jag, I wear designer clothes, and I'm socking away money for a rainy day—something you taught me to do."

"Well, at least you listened to something I had to say when you were growing up."

"She didn't listen when we told her not to marry Dagger." Angel spun around when she heard the familiar voice.

Trace Devlin, Angel's oldest brother by five minutes—Ty was eight minutes younger than her and Hunt was the baby, delivered twelve minutes later—pushed through the swinging door that led from the small living room to the kitchen.

"What are you doing in town?" Angel asked her brother.

Trace, all six-foot-four of him, kissed Angel's

forehead, grabbed a carton of orange juice out of the fridge, and took a drink, not bothering to get a glass.

"I'm heading to Miami right after breakfast," Trace said, looking at his watch. "I've got a meeting at eleven with a possible witness to a cold case I'm working on. A guy I've been looking for for over a year now and with any luck he won't flake on me."

"You weren't going to come by and see me?" Angel asked.

"I knew you'd be here to fix breakfast, otherwise I would have gone out to eat." Trace winked at their father. "You know Dad has a bad habit of burning the bacon."

"At least I can put a meal together. That's more than you ever bothered to learn," Jed tossed back, his booming laughter ringing through the house. Alzheimer's may have changed the future Jed had always envisioned for himself and his wife, but he refused to give in to the disease that was ravaging the woman he loved. Laughter and his family got him through the worst of times.

"Are you going to see Ty while you're in Miami?" Angel asked, grating cheddar cheese to throw into the omelet she was making.

"If I get a chance," Trace said. "And before you ask about Hunt, I saw him in Manhattan a couple of days ago. We shot some hoops, then went out for beer."

"He didn't say anything about coming to the gala, did he?" Angel asked, slapping Trace's hand when he dug into the bowl of cheddar she'd just grated.

"Hunt doesn't tell me anything more about what he's done or plans to do than he tells anyone else."

"He's a CIA operative," Jed said. "I'd bet my bottom dollar on it."

"I'm sticking with hit man," Trace stated. "Seems to me someone gets killed everywhere he goes."

Angel tuned out the banter between her brother and dad, and just took comfort that she had a close-knit family, even though Hunt was a bit of an enigma.

She beat the eggs with a whisk that her mother had used eons ago when cooking for her family had been one of her favorite pastimes. Her father stirred the bacon in the pan, making sure it didn't burn, and Trace set the table, something he must have learned after he left home.

When they were little, the boys were taught to be boys and Angel was taught to be a girly-girl, although that was the last thing she wanted. Trace, Ty, and Hunt were men in the making. It was their job to change tires and mow the lawn and lift heavy things. Angel had the pleasure of cooking and being sent off to Portia Alexander's Academy to become a fine young woman of impeccable breeding because God knows Jed Devlin wanted his tomboy to grow into a lady—not follow in his footsteps as she'd always threatened, and become a P.I.

Jed ended up with a rebel for a daughter, an eighteen-year-old who met a good-looking guy on the flight home from London, and brought the unemployed, tattooed knife thrower with a penchant for B.S. home to meet her family. They despised him right off the bat, but she was in love, full of starry-eyed dreams of romance.

Four days later, wearing cutoffs, a tank top, and flip-flops, she and Dagger stood in front of the Palm Beach County Clerk with no family members at their side. She carried a single red rose and Dagger had had her name tattooed on his chest, right below his devil tattoo. He gave her a ring he'd picked up at a pawnshop—something she found out on one of those horrid nights when they lay together in bed—and she married Dagger Zane, for better or for worse.

Seven years later she'd divorced him. It wasn't until then that she told her mom, dad, and brothers the truth. It wasn't until then that she'd accepted the truth herself—Dagger had never loved her; he'd merely used her.

The bastard.

Angel whacked an onion in half with one of her mom's extra-sharp kitchen knives, and went to town chopping the thing into little bits and pieces.

Her dad frowned; Trace wrapped his arm around her neck. "Got something you want to talk about?"

"Nope."

She whacked the onion again. It was amazing how much frustration a woman could get rid of while chopping food.

"I heard through the rumor mill that Dagger's in town," Trace said, putting the knives, forks, and spoons on the wrong side of the plates as he set the table.

Bitterness rose in Angel's throat as she whacked a bell pepper. "Yeah, and I had the misfortune of running into him last night."

Trace's eyes narrowed. "He didn't ask you for money or try anything with you, did he?"

"Hell, no," Angel blurted. "If that man ever touches me again, I'll gut him."

"That's my girl." Jed dumped the crisp, slightly burned bacon onto a plate lined with paper towels. "If you want, you can stick around here with your mom this morning and Trace and I will go have a talk with that asshole you married."

"I don't want either one of you tangling with him. You did it once and you all ended up in jail overnight. God only knows what would happen if you got into it with him again."

"So what's he doing here?" Trace asked.

"Working as a walker."

"What woman in her right mind would want to go anywhere with that son-of-a-bitch?" Jed asked, dumping the bacon grease into an old coffee can.

"He's tall and handsome," Angel said, striving to think of any other good qualities Dagger might have—but they were very few and far between. "I guess he can also be rather charming."

"He's got a goddamned devil tattooed on his chest." Jed's anger rang through the kitchen. "He took your house, he took your money, and he would have taken the business you built without any help from him if—"

"Can we change the subject?" Angel asked, but had the feeling her father hadn't yet finished his tirade, and she couldn't blame him. Dagger Zane had hurt Jed's daughter, and he'd never let the guy forget it.

Jed sighed heavily, then took a swig of his coffee. "Why I ever hired that worthless, good-for-nothing sack of shit is beyond me."

"You hired him because I asked you to. And I'm the one who married him in spite of all your warnings. But it's over and done with, Dad. I'm divorced. He can't get another penny from me."

"Yeah, but—"

Angel couldn't miss the grim look on her dad's face. "But what, Dad?"

"Yeah," Trace said. "That *but* had an ominous sound to it that I don't like."

Jed pulled an envelope out of his back pocket. "I was debating on whether or not to talk with you about this this morning."

"What is it?" Trace asked.

Jed pulled the piece of stationery out of the envelope. "It seems Dagger has decided to sue me over the broken nose I gave him."

"What?" Trace's eyes narrowed. "That was five years ago."

"Yeah, but his nose is crooked and the asshole says an extremely wealthy woman turned down his marriage proposal because of it."

"That's the most asinine thing I've ever heard," Trace said, snatching the piece of paper from his dad's hand.

"It's a nuisance suit, nothing more," Jed added, "but I haven't got the money for an attorney."

"If Dagger thinks he can get away with this," Angel said, "he's sorely mistaken."

"Dagger always gets away with crap," Jed said.

"He pulled all sorts of shit on you and the only punishment he ever got was a beating from me and your brothers."

"He's not going to get away with any crap this time," Angel stated. "He's living on his boat and I know where he keeps it and—"

"I don't want you messing with him on your own," Jed said.

"I don't want either one of you messing with him," Trace added. "I'll have a talk with him after I go down to Miami."

Angel sighed. "I need to take care of this now—the sooner the better."

"It can wait, Angel," Trace stated. "I'll come back—"

"I don't want either of you getting into the middle of this. Trace—you've got to leave for Miami right after breakfast and I know you can't stay away from work long. Dad—you've got Mom to take care of. And me, well, Dagger knows damn good and well that I can use a knife. He also knows damn good and well that if he tries anything funny with me, I'll cut his heart out."

"Maybe we should just pay him off," Jed said. "Get him off our backs."

"If we pay Dagger off," Trace said, "he'll find another reason to come back for more."

"No one's paying Dagger a penny, Dad." Angel shook her head. "I should have pressed charges when I was married to him. Should have made him serve jail time for what he did to me, but I didn't. That was my mistake, and I'm not going to make any more mistakes where he's concerned."

"Let who get away with what?"

Sarah Devlin walked into the kitchen wearing an old ski coat she must have dug out of the back of her closet. She was still so darn beautiful on the outside, but there was so little of the Mom everyone knew and loved left on the inside.

"It was nothing, Mom," Trace said, giving her a kiss on the cheek and pulling out a chair for her at the table.

"Good morning, Mom." Angel kissed her mother on the other cheek. "I'm making your favorite omelet for breakfast."

"I don't like eggs," Sarah said, frowning. "Do you serve Swedish pancakes here? My husband and I had them when we came here for our honeymoon."

"Of course we have Swedish pancakes," Jed said, tears pooling at the corners of his eyes. "We'll have them for you in a jiffy."

Sarah ignored the chair Trace had pulled out for her and slowly walked across the kitchen. She stared through the window into the backyard, where an old, just-starting-to-rust swing set had been overtaken by climbing roses that needed to be pruned. Gardening had been Sarah's passion once. Now she claimed to hate the scent of roses.

Angel cut the omelet she'd made in two and slid the heavy concoction onto plates for Trace and her dad. Her own appetite ceased to exist.

She grabbed flour and sugar out of one of the cabinets, hoping by the time she figured out how to make something resembling Swedish pancakes her mom would still want to eat them.

"Aren't you going to eat, Angel?" Jed asked, as he carried the two plates to the table.

"I'm not all that hungry."

"I'm sorry we got on the subject of Dagger," her dad added. "Obviously you had other things on your mind this morning."

"It's no big deal, Dad."

Angel grabbed one of her mom's cookbooks and thumbed to the index.

"Hey, Dad?" Angel said, digging another skillet out of one of the lower shelves.

"What is it?" Jed asked, giving his wife a hug that she didn't react to before he sat down at the table.

"Did you by any chance know a man named Chase Donovan?" Angel asked.

"The cat burglar?" Jed said. "The guy who was shot by Holt Hudson?"

"That's the one." Angel pulled a bowl down from a cabinet so she could mix up the Swedish pancake concoction. "You don't by any chance think the police could have falsified information on their report into his death, do you?"

"If I remember correctly, Chase Donovan was shot during a robbery." Jed scratched his ear, his eyes squinted in thought. "I don't remember there being much controversy over the whole thing. It seems to me that it was all cut and dry and the evidence proved everything that Holt said."

"Didn't that happen thirty years ago or so?" Trace asked, holding a forkful of omelet close to his mouth.

"Twenty-six," Angel said, stirring the pancake mix.

"Why all the interest in an old case?" Jed

asked. "I'm sure the file on it was closed a long time ago."

"Chase Donovan's son is in town," Angel said. "He thinks there's a lot more to the story than what Holt Hudson told the police."

"Well . . ." Jed laughed. "He could be right. You know those Palm Beach types. They're loaded with money, and money can buy just about anything."

"So you think the police report could have been falsified?" Angel asked her dad.

"You know I don't like to speculate. But if it were me, I wouldn't write off Chase Donovan's son's beliefs. Personally, I wouldn't put anything past Holt Hudson."

"He's the one having the party, isn't he?" It was Sarah who spoke, and Angel, Trace, and Jed all turned toward her as she continued to stare through the window. "I saw his picture in the paper. It was the same day as your fourth birthday party."

Angel remembered the police report. Remembered the date of the shooting—it *was* just the day before Angel and her brothers turned four. Some days Sarah couldn't remember her husband's name; yet some days she remembered all sorts of inconsequential things from the past.

"That was a great birthday party, Mom," Angel said. "Do you remember the cakes you decorated for us?"

Sarah's eyes narrowed. "Birthday cakes?" she asked, as if she'd completely forgotten what they'd been talking about.

"You decorated two different cakes—one that looked like Strawberry Shortcake for me," Angel said, hoping her mom would remember everything someday, "and a G.I. Joe for Trace, Ty, and Hunt."

"We all got bicycles that year," Trace added.

"And Angel refused to use training wheels," her dad said, cutting into his omelet. "If I'm not mistaken, she fell down and broke her two front teeth."

"They were going to fall out anyway," Angel said.

Slowly Sarah turned and tilted her head toward her daughter. "You really should try to be less like your brothers, Angel, and dress like a girl. I've bought you so many pretty dresses."

"I know you have, Mom. In fact, why don't we go shopping later and I'll buy you something extra pretty to wear to the gala?"

"A hat?" Sarah asked. "Like the ones I used to sell."

"Of course we could buy you a hat. Better yet, we could go to Emma's and get a pretty purse for you."

"I like purses. I sold those, too," Sarah said, her gaze and her mind both far away. "I had a pink one for Easter last year. And a pink dress, too."

"And you looked awfully pretty." Jed pushed up from the table and squeezed his wife's hand. God only knows how long ago she'd had a pink purse and shoes for Easter. It was an old memory, like so many other old memories that would crop up at the strangest of times.

They all held out hope that Sarah's memory

would return for good. That she'd be the same mom and wife that they loved. But in truth, they knew it was too late for Sarah. They'd just enjoy every minute they possibly could with her now—whether the times were good or bad.

Jed put his arm around his wife. "Why don't you sit down now and have some juice?" He ushered his wife to the table and pulled a chair out for her.

Angel lifted one of the Swedish pancakes onto a plate, filled it with apricot and pineapple preserves, her mom's favorite, rolled it up and sprinkled it with powdered sugar, then set it on the table.

"What's this?" Sarah asked.

"A Swedish pancake."

Sarah frowned, then pushed the plate away. "I don't like Swedish pancakes."

Angel sighed heavily. Her mom was slipping away far too fast, a torture Angel could hardly bear. And as she took her mother's plate away, tears slipped down Angel's face for all that she'd lost so far, and all that she'd lose way too soon.

14

Tom stood in the center of the nursery, remembering the days when he'd slept in this room. The paint was only slightly faded, and he decided that this was one room he'd have a specialist restore. His parents had worked together to make this room special, painting a chivalrous scene of fairy-tale castles, jousting knights, and damsels in distress. He might never use the room as a nursery, but it would be impossible to cover up the love that had gone into every paint stroke.

Even the ceiling was painted with cherubs floating around, and puffy white clouds dotting the sapphire sky. Hell, the sky was the same radiant color as Angel's eyes.

God, he'd sure made a mess of things this morning. Who would have thought a night of almost unending and fabulous no-holds-barred sex would end with a fight? And not just any fight. He'd pretty much told her he'd used her. A man couldn't get much stupider than that.

Damn. He didn't want to think about Angel

now. She wasn't about to help him get in to see Holt Hudson, so why should he bother trying to get back into her good graces?

It wasn't as if he wanted to have a relationship with her.

Or did he?

He plowed his fingers through his hair. He didn't need a woman messing with his mind. He had more important things to do. And right now—all he wanted to do was pour his energy and his frustration into the mansion he'd inherited.

He swept a broom across the floor, gathering up a cobweb thick with dust from a far corner. He wrapped the web around and around in the broom, stopping to pull out a piece of old construction paper that had been lying there for God knows how long.

Heading to the trash can that was filled almost to the brim, he started to throw away the paper when he noticed the childish printing on the front. And a memory smacked against him. A long-ago day when he'd lain on the floor in this room, fat crayons in hand, and made the Valentine for his dad.

So much had been cleared out of the chateau. Most everything Tom remembered had been sold at auction. He had few pictures of himself with his dad. Few mementos of their time together. But all of a sudden he had a Valentine, old and faded and covered with years of dust.

He brushed it off gently, and suddenly other memories came back to him. The pressure of his father's strong and loving hands against Tom's back when he'd pushed him on the swing that had once been a prominent feature on the lawn that spread down to the ocean. His dad's laughter when they lay together on the floor watching cartoons on Saturday morning. His father's cold, still body as they sat together in the Everglades, his eyes wide open even though he didn't talk, didn't smile, and didn't breathe.

He didn't want to think about those days in the Glades, trapped inside an insufferably hot car. God, he wished that had all been a dream, just as Pop had told him.

Maybe some of it was a dream, because, damn it all, there were things he remembered that couldn't possibly have happened. He'd been home in bed when his dad came for him, yet . . .

Tom slammed his fist against the wall. Why did he remember being in the dark and all alone and afraid for what seemed an eternity? Why did he remember sitting all hunched up inside a box with nothing to drink and nothing to eat?

That part was a dream. A frightened little boy's nightmare.

"Find something interesting up here?"

Tom turned at the sound of Pop's voice, and leaned on the handle of his broom. "A lot of dirt and cobwebs."

Pop hobbled about the room, using his cane for support. "Pretty room."

"It will be."

"Your dad could have been an artist, you know. He used to paint pictures for your grandma and me."

More and more things Tom didn't know kept surfacing, as if Pop wanted to dole each little bit out slowly, afraid Tom might not be able to handle all of the details about a forgotten life all at once.

"Do you still have them?" Tom asked.

"Nope."

"Why not?"

Pop sat on top of an old and dusty toy castle. "Your dad tried giving your grandma an emerald necklace once. He was twenty-two or twenty-three at the time. Your grandma was so dang proud of your dad and she couldn't stop smiling when Chase gave her that necklace. It was the prettiest thing she'd ever seen and it sure as hell wasn't something I could buy for her. The next day I heard about a cat burglar breaking into a home in Miami and the newspaper ran pictures of the things that were taken."

"The necklace?" Tom asked.

Pop nodded. "I should have turned your dad in to the cops. He might have been alive now if he'd gotten arrested and served some time in jail. But no, I lectured him instead."

"Did Grandma lecture him, too?"

"No. She just cried, 'cause her only son had broken her heart. After that I gave him back the necklace, got rid of every reminder I had of him—including the pictures he'd painted for me and your grandma—and told him I never wanted to see him again."

"But you did."

"I talked to him a time or two, but I didn't see him again until his funeral." Pop's eyes had reddened. "If it wasn't for you I wouldn't have any reminders of my son." Pop shrugged. "I was a foolish old man."

"You're still a foolish old man," Tom said, using the broom to knock down cobwebs, needing something to do to tamp down his frustration over all the bitterness of what might have been. "You still think Chase stole that statue and attacked Holt Hudson's wife."

Pop shrugged. "I've been thinking a lot about that."

"What? You've had a change of heart?"

"No, but I don't want to die believing the worst of your dad." Pop sighed heavily. "If you can find any proof, no matter how small, that he might have been innocent, I might be able to muster up the same kind of faith in him that you've got."

Those were the most encouraging words he'd heard from Pop in months.

"I'm trying to find proof, Pop, but I'm sure as hell bumping into a lot of obstacles. Seems like no one wants me to learn the truth."

"What about that girl you were gonna use?"

Tom knocked down a big cobweb. "That didn't work out."

"Told you it wouldn't."

"Yeah, well, you've told me a lot of things over the years and I haven't always listened."

"Which reminds me," Pop said. "I came up here to tell you something important."

"And you're just now remembering?"

"It takes a heap of energy just getting up all the stairs in this monstrosity you insist on living in. I can't be expected to huff and puff for half an hour and then remember why I came here in the first place."

"So, what did you want to tell me, and why didn't you just call?"

"Your cell phone was turned off and you haven't bothered to install real phones in this place yet."

"All right, I'm at fault for making you expend so much energy. Now tell me what was so important it couldn't wait."

"You're being watched again."

Tom grinned. "The pretty blonde?"

"Nope, the guy with the devil tattoo on his chest."

Tom went to the window and pushed back the dusty curtains. "I see the same cabin cruiser that was out there yesterday, but I don't see anyone on board. Do you have your spotting scope with you?"

"I can't use a cane and carry a scope at the same time. Take my word for it, that's the same guy who was out there yesterday. And I don't like it one bit."

Tom squinted, trying to get a better look, but all he saw was another boat speeding toward the one that he was watching. A black boat with red flames. Angel's boat.

What the hell was she up to, and why on earth was she pulling up close to the boat belonging to the other guy who'd been spying on him? Tom didn't have a clue what was going on, but he was damn sure going to find out.

* * *

Dagger Zane should have known better than to mess with Angel's family. She was livid, and as soon as she confronted Dagger, he was going to get an earful. And after she'd given him a piece of her mind, she might also give him a mouthful of broken teeth.

She tied her speedboat next to the cabin cruiser she'd given Dagger as part of their divorce settlement. That, the house and their savings should have been enough to keep him happy. But Dagger always wanted more.

Trying to tune out the annoying noise of the speedboats and Jet Skis racing by, she climbed the ladder leading to the sun deck and stepped over the railing. Dagger stood in the sunlight, grinning at her.

"Well, well, well. I hadn't expected the pleasure of seeing you again so soon." Dagger grinned that despicable, sleazy grin she remembered from years ago. "I should tell you, Angel, that I liked the getup you were wearing last night a lot more than this preppy sundress you're wearing. You looked kind of trampy last night, and I always liked that in my women."

"I don't give a damn what kind of women you like. This isn't a social call."

"Then you've come to thank me for not blowing your cover at Tropical Lei?"

"I'm sure you had an ulterior motive for not giving me away."

Dagger slapped a hand over his chest. "You wound me, Angel. Always thinking I have an ulterior motive, when the truth is, it was damn fun seeing the anger in your eyes—that touch of fear when you saw me—and I didn't want the fun and games to come to an end."

"Cut the crap, Dagger, I'm not here to bullshit with you. I want to know why the hell you're suing my dad, what the hell you're doing out here spying on Tom Donovan, and last but certainly not least, what the hell you're doing back in Palm Beach."

Dagger grinned. He peeled off his shirt and stood in the sun in nothing more than a Speedo and all of his tattoos, including the blasted one that said ANGEL right below the devil on his chest. "That's an awful lot of questions."

"If you have trouble remembering any of them, I'm sure I can tick them off for you one at a time."

"I don't see any need to be so nasty. We had a good thing once upon a time."

"That's not a subject I want to discuss, Dagger, not now, not ever."

"From the hot and heavy look of things last night between you and Tom Donovan, you're having quite a good time now. Is he as good as me?"

Angel fought for breath. She also fought to keep her fingers from wrapping around the stiletto she wore under her sundress. Fought to keep from shoving him overboard and hoping that he'd get bumped off by a noisy Jet Ski or a speedboat. He could scream as loud as he wanted, and no one would hear him over the noise. And then, with any luck, he'd become shark bait.

Somehow she regained her composure. "Why are you back in Palm Beach? I thought you were working in Miami."

"I was. Had a pretty decent job working for a

P.I. down there until your brother Ty got wind of it and fed my boss some shit about me not being the most upstanding guy on the face of the planet. I was pretty damn pissed, Angel. I mean, your family's done a good job screwing me over ever since you and I called it quits."

"There's only one person who deserves any blame for your problems, Dagger, and that's you."

The asshole laughed. "You're being awfully cruel, Angel."

"Quit playing games and tell me why you're in town."

Dagger shrugged. "Frederike told you. I'm a walker."

"Why any woman in her right mind would want you as an escort is beyond me. You've got the manners of a bloodsucking hyena—"

"Frederike LeVien doesn't think so. Neither does Stephania Allardyce. In fact, I've been in town several weeks now making friends with a number of women. I treat them nice. They treat me to dinner and wine and parties. And if I'm really good, they buy me trinkets. Some quite expensive."

"And let me guess—you've hocked them all."

"Most of them." Dagger grinned repulsively, then picked up a bottle of suntan lotion, poured it on his chest, and began to rub the oil into his still-hard but reprehensible body.

"So you really came here just to be a walker?"

"I've got a nice boat to live on, thanks to our divorce settlement, and the ladies I accompany are quite good to me. Breakfast, lunch, and dinner at all the best places. Leisurely afternoons lying around their pools. All I need is a designer wardrobe and my charm. If I'd known how enjoyable it is being a walker, I would have taken up the profession a long time ago."

"That still doesn't explain why you've been out here spying on Tom Donovan."

"That's easy, Angel." Dagger leaned against the cabin and cockily folded his arms over his devil tattoo. "One day while I was lounging by Stephania's pool reading the local gossip rag, I saw something quite interesting. A new, filthy rich almost-a-billionaire had moved into Mere Belle. There was a slight mention about a cat burglar who had lived there twenty-six years before, a few brief lines about *The Embrace*, a robbery, and the fact that the statue had never been found."

"So you put two and two together and decided that Tom Donovan knows everything there is to know about *The Embrace*, that he's moved to Mere Belle because he just might have some idea where it's hidden, and you're going to watch him and take it away from him if and when he does find it—then sell it, illegally, of course, to the highest bidder."

Dagger frowned. "You and your family have accused me of a lot of things, Angel, but I'm not a thief. If you must know, if and when it turns up, I fully intend to give it back to Holt Hudson. I'm sure he'll be quite pleased and offer me a handsome reward for my trouble."

"I would imagine Holt Hudson is no longer interested in the piece. It disappeared twenty-six years ago and I'm sure the insurance company paid him quite handsomely for his loss."

"You're wrong, Angel." Dagger grinned smugly. "I did quite extensive homework, and what do you know, I found out that the insurance company didn't pay Holt Hudson a penny because a claim wasn't filed after the theft."

Angel frowned. "How could you possibly know that?"

"I have connections, Angel. You forget, you did a damn good job training me how to be a P.I. I know how to pick pockets, bypass alarm systems, and find out just about anything I want to know about anyone. It's easy when you know all the tricks. And trust me, I've done my homework on that statue, on Chase Donovan, and on your new lover."

"If you'd done your homework you'd know that Tom doesn't have a clue where the statue is."

"What makes you think that?"

"Because he's trying to prove his dad's innocence. He wouldn't be working so hard at that if he knew for a fact that the statue was somewhere on his property."

Still, Angel did find it interesting that Holt had never filed a claim. That didn't make sense at all.

"I suppose," Angel said, "the idea of finding a buyer for *The Embrace* never crossed your mind, even though it's worth close to twenty mil?"

Dagger laughed. "Twenty mil would be nice, but I'll be just as happy with the money I get out of the lawsuit I've filed against your dad. Hurt him and I hurt you."

"You'll never get a dime from my dad or anything else from me, so why don't you call off your ridiculous suit."

"Because your father broke my nose." Dagger slid his middle finger down the bridge of his nose, over the insignificant bump her father had caused, when what her father had really wanted to do was smash the bastard so hard his brain would turn to sludge. "I deserve restitution for what he did to me."

"And what suit do you plan on filing after you lose this one—if it ever gets to court?"

"Your brother Ty slandered my good name. I think that should be worth a pretty penny. What do you think?"

"I think I'd like to wrap a heavy weight around your ankles and throw you overboard."

"That's not very creative, Angel. Surely you'd like to do something with your stiletto. Threaten to cut me. Pretend you're going to make me bleed?"

"That's the game you liked to play, Dagger."

"It's a game I'd like to play right now, too." His grin made Angel want to run to the side of the boat and wretch, but she was not about to let him see anything but a woman in complete control.

"Do you still get your rocks off that way, Dagger?"

"Damn right." Dagger moved toward her and cupped her cheek. "Wanna go downstairs and let me remind you how good it can be?"

"She's not going anywhere with you."

Angel spun around just in time to see Tom swing over the side of the cruiser. He stalked across the deck and stood just inches from Dagger. "Apologize to the lady."

"Fuck off."

Tom's brow slanted. "That's not a polite thing to say in front of Angel."

"Don't antagonize him, Tom," Angel said, touching Tom's shoulder. "He's got a knife and he knows how to use it."

Dagger practically slithered toward a deck chair, slick and slimy as ever. He lifted the shirt lying there and picked up his scabbard with a twelve-inch blade stuck inside. "Angel's right, you know. I do know how to use this."

Tom walked away from Angel, circling Dagger, a smirk on his face as he moved. "You don't really think that little knife frightens me, do you?"

"It's frightened a hell of a lot of people."

"And I've frightened alligators with my bare hands and my smile." Tom grinned again. "Let me tell you this, Mr. Zane, an alligator is a hell of a lot stronger than you and smarter than you, but I've whipped them without breaking a sweat. Taking care of you will be a piece of cake."

"It took two of Angel's brothers plus her dad to get the better of me," Dagger said, bravado ringing in his voice. "And you're nothing more than a sissified piano player."

Tom clasped his hands behind his back and stood at ease, feet, legs, and chest bare, wearing only a pair of baggy surfer shorts. Sunlight glinted in his eyes. He was far too calm and Angel was getting worried as the men played a game of standoff.

Angel slipped her fingers around the hilt of her stiletto at the same moment she watched Dagger grab the hilt of his.

Everything after that seemed to move in slow motion. Tom slammed an angry fist into Dagger's gut.

Dagger grabbed his belly. Shock widened his eyes. He groaned, staggered back a few feet until he hit the cabin wall. "If you think you're going to get away with this—"

Tom slapped an open palm on Dagger's chest and got right in his face. "No, Dagger, if *you* think you can intimidate me, you're sorely mistaken." Tom ripped the twelve-inch knife out of Dagger's scabbard.

Dagger flinched, his eyes filling with terror.

Tom laughed as he studied the glistening blade, then tossed the vicious knife over the side and into the Atlantic.

"Let me make something very clear to you," Tom growled. "If you ever touch Angel again, if you don't withdraw the lawsuit you've got against her dad right now, and if you file any kind of future lawsuit against her or her family or try to extort money from them or do anything, and I mean anything, to hurt her, I'll haul your miserable ass down to the Everglades and feed you to some of the alligators I'm acquainted with."

Dagger's eyes narrowed as Tom backed away. "You don't scare me," Dagger snarled. "And if I want to touch Angel—"

Tom grabbed a hunk of Dagger's hair, latched onto the back of the asshole's Speedo, and with ease and grace, tossed him overboard.

Over the squawk of gulls and the roar and whine of a couple of speedboats and Jet Skis zipping by, Angel heard a flurry of swearing as Dagger floundered in the water. The bastard deserved a hell of a lot more. Maybe she'd be lucky and a shark would swim by. For now . . . she'd settle for seeing Dagger looking like a half-drowned rat.

Tom tossed the scabbard into the water, right next to the Jet Ski tied up to her boat.

As he turned slowly, facing her, Tom's gaze was filled with anger. He stalked toward her, standing just inches from her face. "What on earth possessed you to come out here and see that bastard?"

"He filed a frivolous lawsuit against my dad."

"Yeah, I know. I heard every stinking word the creep had to say. But that's no excuse for you confronting him on your own, especially when the whole thing could have been handled in court."

Angel stiffened. "My dad can't afford an attorney."

Tom's eyes narrowed. "You could have asked me for the money."

"Seems to me you and I were fighting this morning." Angel poked Tom in the center of his very bare, very muscular, and very bronzed chest. "Seems to me I pretty much told you I didn't want anything to do with you and that also means I wouldn't take anything from you, nor would anyone else in the Devlin family."

"Seems to me I just saved your pretty little ass."

"I could have taken care of myself."

"You could have gotten yourself killed."

"Well," Angel tossed back, "I didn't."

Tom shoved his fingers through his hair. "I came out here ready to give you hell for spying on me again, for joining forces with the other guy who'd been spying on me—"

"What?" she said aghast. "I'd never join forces with that asshole ex of mine."

"Yeah, well, I didn't know it was your asshole ex you were motoring out here to see, and when I did realize it was him, when I heard all the shit he was dishing out, when I saw him touch you—"

Angel saw Tom's muscles tense. Saw him swallow hard, then watched his chest rise and fall heavily.

"Damn it, Angel, I don't remember a time when I wanted to kill someone as much as I did just a few minutes ago."

A gentle smile touched Angel's face. A dizzy happiness rippled through her insides. And she walked up to Tom, wove her fingers around his neck, and kissed him softly. "I owe you one."

Tom gazed into her eyes. His were the darkest of brown, touched by anger and fear. Then, slowly, ever so slowly, he smiled. "I think you owe me at least two or three, and it just so happens I don't have anything planned for the afternoon, so why don't we—"

"Go fool around in that big old Italian Renaissance bed?" Angel asked, brimming over with happiness and excitement.

Tom pulled her into his arms and kissed her lightly. "That'll do for starters."

15

Tom sucked Angel's big toe between his lips, and over her cute little pinkies, he watched a smile brighten her sapphire eyes. She relaxed against the marble tub filled nearly to overflowing with bubbles, and teased his stomach with the toes of her other slender and slippery foot.

"I thought we were going to relax for a while," Tom said, drawing the bottom of her foot against his lips and licking her sweet pink flesh. "God knows I don't think I'm up for another hour-long romp quite so soon."

"Oh, I don't know about that." She slid the ball of her foot down to his groin and teased him with a soft brush of her toes. "If I'm not mistaken, you might soon be up for just about anything."

Tom grabbed the foot that was doing all the probing and teasing and drew it toward his chest. He held on to both her ankles and sucked one toe and then the next, grinning as she squirmed, as her breasts bobbed on top of the water right along with the bubbles.

"Would you really toss Dagger to the gators if he got in my face again?" Angel asked, her words a bit breathless.

"Sure as hell would, and I wouldn't blink an eye while Bessie devoured him."

"Bessie?"

"She's only nine feet long and lost a foot to a poacher a few years back, but she's got the prettiest brown eyes you ever did see."

"Seems a shame to dump a tough piece of crap like Dagger on a sweet thing like Bessie."

"Nah, she'll eat anything. And what she spits out, her son Ralph will swallow whole."

"Is that so?"

"Yeah. He's a mere thirteen feet long and weighs in at eight-ninety-one, give or take a few pounds."

"You wrestle with him?"

"When we're both in the mood."

"What are you in the mood for right now?"

Tom nibbled on one of her heels, then swirled his tongue over her ankle. "Right now I'm pretty content with what I'm doing."

"I'm pretty content, too, but how about later?"

Tom wiggled his brows. "You have something in mind?"

"How about chicken-fried steak, mashed potatoes, and gravy?"

"If I'm going to lick something off that sweet little body of yours," Tom said, then slid his tongue along her arch, "couldn't we make it chocolate? Or maybe boysenberry?"

"I'm talking about dinner. Tonight," Angel said adamantly. "I'm cooking for my mom and dad."

"You're inviting me over to meet them?"

"My opinion of men isn't always the best. I figure I should let them check you out and tell me what they think."

"You wouldn't by any chance be thinking of turning this thing between us into a long-term relationship, would you?"

"It's already a relationship. Whether it's long-term or not remains to be seen."

"I've never been in a long-term relationship. Hell, I've never had a relationship that could withstand more than one or two dates."

"We haven't even had a first date yet," Angel said.

Tom slid his hands over her sudsy legs. "What do you call this?"

"Two close friends exchanging a bit of witty repartee . . . with some knock-down-drag-out sex thrown in for good measure."

"Sounds a hell of a lot better than eating popcorn in a stuffy theater or—"

"Not so fast," Angel said, tugging her feet out of his hands and kneeling in the tub, one knee on each side of his legs. "I like stuffy theaters and popcorn."

"All right," he said, drawing his palms up her silky thighs and settling them on her hips. "If you want to go out on a real date—"

"I like candlelight, too," she said, lowering her heavenly body back into the water, her breasts speckled with suds. "I like caviar and fine wine. Linen tablecloths and napkins and seven-course meals."

"I suppose you like flowers, too?"

Angel moved a little lower, her hips swaying

gently. His own body throbbed and his penis went into active duty, ready to take on anything she wanted to dish out.

"I like red roses," she said, her fingers sliding around the base of his erection and slowly, tightly, moving to the very tip. "I like white orchids and orange lilies."

"Anything else I should know about?"

"I like dark chocolate." She licked her lips, then purred as she rubbed the very tip of his penis between her hot and slippery folds of soft, begging-to-be-fondled skin.

"How about whipped cream?" Tom asked.

"With fresh, plump, juicy strawberries."

"Ice cream?"

"Rocky road and black walnut."

"What about me?"

She sighed deeply. "Oh, yeah, I like you, too."

Tom thrust into her to ease his agony, and Angel smiled, her eyes closed as she allowed herself to sink fully onto his erection and let Tom please her.

He caught her hips and held her against him, loving the feel of her soft, pliant body, the tightness of her insides, and the way she moaned when he deepened his plunge.

She leaned forward, bracing her hands on the edge of the tub, and her succulent breasts brushed lightly over his mouth.

Capturing one nipple, he feasted upon it, suckled, almost tasted her heartbeat.

His breath turned ragged as he poured his energy, his soul into their lovemaking. He thrust upward, driving into her again and again, listening to her purr and moan.

Her tangle of wet hair fluttered across his face as she rose, stealing her breasts away from his tongue, his lips. Tearing the tight, hot, and slick haven of her insides away from his erection.

He grabbed her arms as sheer dread ripped through his insides. "You're not planning on running away from me right this instant, are you?"

Angel grinned wickedly. Her tongue slid around her lips and then slowly, devilishly, she slipped a finger into her mouth and sucked it in and out. "No, sweetheart"—she winked—"I don't plan on running away. I have far too much to do right here in the tub with you."

She slid down, down, down, her skin squeaking on the bottom of the marble, the curling ends of her long blond hair puddling on top of the bubbly water.

And then she slipped her hands beneath his butt, dragging his body up until his erection poked out of the bubbles, and she licked the very tip.

"Now, that I like a whole hell of a lot better than the thought of you running away," Tom said.

She sucked the swollen head and he moaned, trying his damnedest to keep control of his body, to enjoy the pleasure of her mouth and her tongue and the nip of her teeth as she teased and almost consumed him whole.

He threw his arms over the sides of the oversize tub and held himself just high enough in the water so she'd have all the access she wanted, needed.

And he let her taste him. Taunt him. Drive him mad, bringing him nearly to the brink, then pulling away just long enough to lick one of his nipples, to fondle his balls, rolling them around in the palms of her hands, before going down on him again.

"You know, sweetheart"—the words came out of Tom's mouth in a rush, along with a groan when her tongue flicked back and forth, back and forth over the very tip of him—"I don't think I can last much longer."

Her smile was wild. Her eyes blazed. And she swept over his body, her legs straddling his hips, and lowered herself onto him. Down, down. Deep.

He had to be touching her heart by now, as every speck of him squeezed inside her. She was tight and wet and hot, and her blessed hips began to swirl and grind and bump, sending him almost over the edge.

But he'd be damned if he'd go without her.

He latched on to her hips and they rode the waves together, the water sloshing between them and over the rim of the tub as their abandoned ride grew wilder by the moment.

By the heartbeat.

With every moan and purr and groan.

Angel's breasts heaved with her raspy sighs. Her eyes closed, flickered. Her lips tilted up into a soft I-love-the-feel-of-this smile.

And then he felt her shudder inside. Tremble. Her whole body quaking, shivering, as spasm after spasm ripped through her and her smile became tinged with unrestrained passion.

He wove his fingers about her neck and

dragged her mouth down to his, tasted her, teased her, their tongues dancing together wildly.

Her cries of sheer, unadulterated pleasure rippled through his mouth and he knew, without a doubt, that somehow, in some strange way, something he'd never expected happened.

He fell in love with her.

Never wanted to leave her.

Ever.

And when every muscle in his body tightened, when he chose not to hold back any longer and let his life and his heart and his soul flow into her, he realized that even if he never found the answers that he wanted about his past, he could be whole.

And happy.

As long as Angel was at his side.

It was late afternoon when Tom watched Angel sweep her crimson sundress off the top of the big-screen TV in his bedroom and tug it over her head. Her body was made for loving, he thought as he zipped up his jeans and went to his dresser for a clean white T-shirt.

"You know, Angel, I've been thinking about tonight."

Angel studied his still-naked chest and moved toward him, swirling her fingers over his pecs and tracing one perfectly polished red nail down to his abs and toying with his navel. "Chickening out?"

"I don't chicken out of anything. But . . ." Tom frowned. "Isn't there some unwritten rule that says a guy shouldn't meet a girl's parents until they're engaged?"

"Why?" Angel teased. "Are you thinking you should propose to me before I leave this morning?"

"At this stage of the game, I'm heavily into sex. I hadn't given any thought at all to a proposal, and I sure as hell haven't given marriage any thought."

"You think I have?"

"Don't all women think about getting married?"

"I've been married. I'm in no big rush to do it again."

"So the fact that I'm worth somewhere close to a billion dollars hasn't made you picture a ten-carat diamond on your wedding finger?"

Angel contemplated that for a moment, rubbing her chin with her thumb and index finger. "A billion dollars, huh?"

"Pretty damn close."

"A ten-carat diamond?"

"That was something I threw out off the top of my head. If you wanted a twenty-carat diamond you could have that. But, and this is a big but, I haven't proposed and I have no plans to propose."

Angel laughed. "Relax, Tom. It's just dinner. Chicken-fried steak. Mashed potatoes and gravy. And if there's a basketball game on tonight you'll have to watch it with my dad and root for his favorite team."

"I don't root for the Lakers."

"He doesn't, either."

"He sounds like my kind of guy."

"Yeah, but he might grill you."

"Suddenly this isn't sounding so good."

"It's just dinner, Tom. No strings attached."

His hand slid around her waist. "You know, you never did tell me why Dagger's been watching me."

"He seems to think you're looking for *The Embrace*."

"Doesn't he realize that the police gave this place a thorough search after that blasted statue was stolen?"

"Understanding Dagger is like understanding the inner workings of a cesspool. I told him you don't have the statue. I told him you're not interested in the thing. Whether that keeps him from spying on you or not remains to be seen. But"—Angel smiled—"you might like this bit of information. According to Dagger, Holt never filed an insurance claim for *The Embrace*."

Tom frowned. "That doesn't make sense. He must have had it insured for a small fortune."

"I don't know any of the details, but you're right, it doesn't make sense. If it was stolen, he had every reason to claim the money."

"And if it wasn't stolen and he knew it hadn't been stolen"—Tom grinned—"and he put in a claim, he'd be guilty of insurance fraud."

"So," Angel sighed, "if he didn't put in a claim, more than likely that means the blasted thing was never stolen. And if it was never stolen, why did he say your dad took it?"

"Now do you see why I want to talk to Holt?"

"Of course I see, but there's still the fact that Holt doesn't want to see you."

Tom pulled her into his arms. "Talk with him,

Angel. Make him see that I'm not out for revenge. Make him see that I just want to talk—and ask him to see me."

"I'll have to think about it."

Tom kissed her softly. "Well, that puts us a few steps ahead of where we were this morning."

"I'm warming up to the idea."

"How about me warming you up a little more after dinner tonight? I'll rent a movie. I'll buy dark chocolates and strawberries and whipped cream."

"Will you light a few candles?"

"Something tells me, sweetheart, that I just might do anything your little heart desires."

Tom pulled her into his arms and kissed her, not yet ready to walk her out to her boat and let her go. He wanted to make love again, but those thoughts came to a halt when the doorbell rang.

"Don't leave yet," Tom said, leaving Angel at the base of the stairs when he went to the entry and opened the front door.

"Tommy, dahling!"

Frederike LeVien stood on the doorstep, her face nearly invisible beneath a bright sunflower-shaped hat, complete with a couple of crystal bees hovering above it on thin gold wire. Her gigantic handbag matched the hat. So did her shoes, and her short round body was bedecked in flaming yellow.

"Good afternoon, Countess."

Without invitation, she breezed into the mansion, carrying her two yappy dogs. It wasn't that he had anything against dogs, he just didn't like little ones, or ones that barked or snapped. Frederike's dogs were everything Tom despised. Especially since they'd interrupted his kiss with Angel.

"Oh, my." Frederike's ultra-high heels clicked on the marble floors as she sauntered toward Angel. "Isn't it fortunate that I should find you here, too? Of course, why wouldn't I find you here? It's all over town that the two of you are an item."

"Is it?" Tom asked, when Angel appeared to have lost her voice.

"I believe it was Morganna who told CoCo Roxborough, and naturally CoCo called me, and I dare say there are so many others we'll have to notify so Miss Devlin can be added to all of our guest lists."

"You know I'm not the partying type," Angel said.

"Nonsense. Now that you're moving up in the world, it's imperative that you be seen in all the right places."

Frederike flitted toward Tom and whispered, "I promise not to breathe a word to Miss Devlin about the woman you were with last night." She winked. "That will remain our little secret."

"Thank you, Countess."

"Now . . . I can only stay a moment, dahlings, and then I must dash off. So many people to see today, so many things to do."

Frederike wandered toward the piano, looking about the empty room. "You know, Tommy, I have the best decorator in all of Palm Beach at my service whenever I need him. Since it's obvious you're in desperate need of a mansion makeover, I'd be happy to give him a call and put the two of you in touch with each other."

"Thanks for the offer, but—"

"It's no bother, Tommy. In fact, I'll give him a call as soon as I get home and have him get in touch with you."

Just what he needed.

"Was that the reason you dropped by?" Tom asked.

"Of course it isn't. I'd assumed you'd already had Mere Belle decorated and landscaped, but I should have realized that some people move faster than others." She gave both dogs kisses on their little black snouts. "Actually, the reason I stopped by is to invite you to Cosette and Celine's birthday party tomorrow afternoon at four. You will come, of course?"

"Cosette and Celine?" Tom questioned. "Your daughters?"

"No, you silly man." Frederike looked down at the dogs in her arms. "My *papillons*, or, as I prefer to call them, my little butterflies."

"I'm not sure I'll be able—"

"Nonsense, Tommy. It'll just be a couple of hours." Frederike turned her attention on Angel. "You must come, too, Miss Devlin. It's at four o'clock, at Mirasol, of course."

"I have to be in court tomorrow afternoon," Angel explained.

"I quite understand, dear. If you must be late, Cosette and Celine will understand. And I'm sure Tommy won't mind if you meet him there."

Tom was on the verge of bursting into laughter. A birthday party for two spoiled dogs, thrown by a woman whose dead husband was on ice until the social season was over, had to be worth attending.

"I'll be there," Tom said. "I can't speak for Miss Devlin, however."

"I'll be there, too," Angel answered. "With bells on."

"Oh, no, please don't wear bells," Frederike said. "Their ringing is so terribly hard on my butterflies' ears."

She nuzzled first one dog and then the other, then looked at her diamond-crusted watch. "Goodness, it's getting terribly late and I've so much to do. The florists will be coming at two tomorrow but I still have to pick out the cake and gifts for my little ones."

"Cake?" Angel asked.

"A lovely little confection of chopped liver and all the other tasty treats that Celine, Cosette, and all of their friends, love."

"There'll be other dogs there?" Tom asked.

"Oh, yes. Seven have RSVP'd already, and they'll be dressed in their prettiest frocks. And just so you know," Frederike whispered, "Cosette and Celine absolutely love the Swarovski crystal collars they sell at Ma Petite Bow-Wow. Cosette favors seashell pink; Celine absolutely adores any shade of purple."

"What about you, Frederike?" Tom said. "What do you adore?"

She patted Tom's cheek. "Handsome young men."

16

"So..." Jed Devlin said, sitting in an overstuffed easy chair in the cluttered living room, his beady and questioning eyes staring at Tom across the big square coffee table. "What do you do for a living?"

"This isn't the inquisition, Dad." Angel set a bottle of Budweiser on the coffee table in front of her father and shoved another cool bottle into Tom's hand. "Tom's a friend. Nothing more."

Jed's eyes narrowed. "Since when is it illegal for a man to ask another man what he does for a living?"

"It's not illegal as long as you remember that this is just a friendship thing. Tom and I *aren't* engaged."

"I should hope the hell not," Jed barked. "You just met."

This wasn't going all that well, Tom realized, as he took a swallow of his beer. God, how he wanted to get out of the place, take Angel home, and make love to her.

Looking over the top of the bottle, he saw Jed glaring at him. Maybe it wasn't such a good idea to think about Angel and sex right this minute.

Angel's dad grabbed a handful of chips and popped a few into his mouth, then washed them down with beer. "So, Tom . . ." Jed said again, "what do you do for a living?"

Tom smiled his best I-really-don't-want-to-be-meeting-the-parents smile. "I used to wrestle alligators."

Jed scooted to the edge of the chair and leaned his elbows on his wide-spread knees. "Like that guy on TV?"

"Kind of, only he's Australian and I never had a TV show."

"You want to be a TV star?"

"The thought's never crossed my mind."

"Let me get this straight," Jed said. "You said you *used* to wrestle alligators,"

"He charmed snakes, too, Dad," Angel added, as if she felt that could help Tom's cause. "He and his grandfather had a gator farm in the Everglades."

Jed frowned. "You know, everything I keep hearing is in the past tense. Mind telling me what you do now?"

"A little landscaping. A little interior decorating."

Jed scratched his head. "You don't make the jobs sound all that stable."

"What does it matter, Dad?" Angel tried coming to Tom's rescue again. "He's just a friend."

"Like I said, Angel," Jed continued, "this is just a man-to-man chat. And Tom can ignore any questions he's uncomfortable with."

"If you'd like me to be brutally honest, Jed," Tom said, wanting to get the interrogation over as quickly as possible, "I can sum up my life story in less than a minute or two."

"I'm not all that concerned with your life story. In fact, I've just got a couple of questions."

"Such as?"

"Have you ever been in jail?"

"No," Tom answered. "Have you?"

"A couple of times. Once for beating the crap out of Angel's last husband."

"Did Angel tell you I punched Dagger out this morning and threw him into the water?"

"No, as a matter of fact, she didn't." Jed took a swallow of beer and grinned. "I might decide to like you after all."

"Dad." Angel's jaw had tightened. "Would you lighten up a bit?"

"I've only got a couple more questions," Jed told his daughter, then faced Tom again. "I've always believed in setting money aside for a rainy day. Do you sock money away for the future?"

Tom took a swallow of beer. "My savings account isn't hurting."

"Well, it can't be all that big if all you've ever done is wrestle alligators and worked construction."

"It's big enough."

"You get paid weekly, monthly, or what?"

"I don't get a paycheck at all."

Jed threw his hands up in the air. "Then how the hell do you expect to take care of my daughter?"

"I take care of myself, Dad," Angel growled. "I

have for a long time and you know darn good and well I don't like the idea of a man taking care of me."

Jed looked deep into Tom's eyes and shook his head. "I sent her to some fancy school in England where she was supposed to learn how to be a genteel young woman and she comes back to me tattooed, wearing a stiletto, and—"

"That was a long time ago, Dad."

Tom liked this guy. He was a lot like Pop. A lot like the kind of dad he would have loved. Most of all, he liked him because he cared so damn much for his daughter.

"You know what, Jed, let's stop beating around the bush. If you want to know my financial status, all you've got to do is ask."

"All right, do you own a home?"

"Four of them. One in Palm Beach, one in Monte Carlo, one in Paris, and one in Milan."

Jed frowned. "You aren't one of those jet-setting Palm Beach types, are you?"

"I'm just a guy who grew up in the Everglades, wrestled alligators and charmed snakes for a living, and then had the good fortune of inheriting a few dollars."

"How many is a few?"

"At last count, around seven hundred and seventy-two . . . million. That doesn't include the four homes, my Jeep, or the eighty-foot yacht I bought for my grandfather."

Jed coughed. Then he took a swallow of beer. "In other words, you're worth somewhere in the neighborhood of a billion dollars?"

"Yeah, that's about right."

Jed's eyes narrowed again. "I hope you don't think you're good enough for my daughter just because you have all that money."

"Dad!"

Jed ignored his daughter's aggravated appeal. Tom just grinned.

"You don't play polo, do you?" Jed asked.

"Nope."

"Do you attend tea parties?"

"I hate tea," Tom said.

"You like basketball?" Jed asked.

"As long as the Lakers are losing."

At last Jed grinned. He reached across the scuffed coffee table and shook Tom's hand. "Welcome to the family."

"Angel, darling."

Angel's mom, Sarah, had sat quietly through the entire exchange, doing nothing more than staring at Tom. The moment she spoke, all eyes turned toward her.

"What is it, Mom?" Angel asked softly.

Sarah turned toward Tom. "Are you the one who plays the piano?" she asked in a voice so much like Angel's.

"Yes, ma'am."

"Would you play something for me?" Sarah asked, a faraway look in her eyes.

Tom stood and walked to the old black upright standing in a far corner of the room, the top littered with a myriad of picture frames and family photos.

"It's not exactly a Steinway," Angel said, "and it hasn't been played in a long time."

"I keep it tuned," Jed said, "just in case we ever have grandchildren who want to play. Sarah gave birth to quadruplets, but not a one of them was interested in tickling the ivories."

Tom sat on the bench, pulling Angel down beside him. He opened the lid and put his fingers on the keys. "Do you have a favorite?" he asked, looking back at Sarah.

She frowned, as if trying to recall a tune, a title, and then she smiled. " 'Yesterday.' " A tear slid down her cheek. "I didn't have any troubles then."

Jed moved to his wife's side on the sofa. He held her close and kissed away her tear.

Tom kissed a tear from Angel's cheek too, and felt a lump settle in his throat when she smiled softly at him. This was the closest he'd ever come to being part of a real family, one with a mom and dad. Not that he didn't love Pop, but it felt special here. Like he belonged.

And he wanted to do something special for Sarah.

Tom closed his eyes, hearing Paul McCartney sing the words he'd written long ago. Heard a string orchestra filling an outdoor auditorium with the sweet strains of the song. He'd played it before, but it seemed to have more meaning tonight, and when his fingers floated over the keys, he gave it his all.

Angel's fingers curled around his thigh as he played, and then from the corner of his eye he saw Jed hold out his hand to his wife. She took it cautiously, then Jed pulled Sarah into his arms and danced with her, barely moving from where they stood, but holding her, kissing her cheek.

When the song ended, when Tom folded down the cover, Sarah walked toward him slowly and touched his shoulder. "Do you dance as well as you play?"

Tom smiled. "I don't trip over my feet."

"Yes, Mom," Angel said, tucking her arm through Tom's, "he dances just as well as he plays."

Sarah pressed a soft, cold palm to his cheek. "Will you dance with me at the ball?"

Tom took Sarah's hand and squeezed it. "Except for dancing with Angel, I can't think of anything I'd rather do."

"Are you sure you don't want to go back to my place?" Tom said, leaning against his Jeep parked at the curb in front of the Devlin home. "I picked up strawberries and whipped cream and—"

"I've got a lot to do tomorrow and I really do need a good night's sleep." Angel leaned forward and kissed him. "Unfortunately, I don't sleep all that well when I'm with you."

Tom's eyebrow rose. "Unfortunately?"

"That was a poor choice of words."

"Damn right."

Angel swept her fingers through Tom's hair when he pulled her against him. "Tonight must have been really awful for you. My dad's not exactly Mr. Warmth and Charm and I really didn't expect him to give you the fifth degree."

"It could have been worse."

"How?"

"He could have told me he liked the Lakers and I would have walked out the door."

Angel laughed. "You've got more couth than that."

"Just wait until you get to know me better."

"You did a rather nice job charming my mom, too. Of course, part of me has to wonder if you did that on purpose."

"Charming people comes easily."

"You haven't been able to charm Holt Hudson."

"That's going to be your job. Now that I need to dance with your mom at the gala, you're going to have to get me into Palazzo Paradiso that night."

Angel sighed heavily. "This could be disastrous, Tom. You know darn good and well he's not going to want to see you."

"Maybe not," Tom said, kissing her softly, "but I'm sure you can wear down his defenses."

"One little screwup and all my plans for the gala and the charity auction could go up in smoke. I've put so much effort into this, not for me, but to raise money for research. People are expecting it, so I can't let everything fall apart."

"Then wait until after the gala to talk to him."

Angel laughed. "If you'd said that yesterday or the day before I would have said sure, why not. But everything's changed since my mom asked you to dance with her. You've got to be there."

"Do you really think she'll remember?"

"I don't know. But even if she doesn't, I'd love

to see the two of you dance together. And to be perfectly honest, I don't think the evening would be nearly as special to me if you didn't sweep me around the ballroom at least once or twice."

17

"**M**r. Hudson will be with you in a few minutes, Miss Devlin. Would you like some coffee or tea while you wait?" the butler asked.

"Tea would be lovely. Thank you."

Angel had been in Holt Hudson's library at least half a dozen times since she'd first been given permission to step through the lavish gates of Palazzo Paradiso. The mahogany bookshelves were strewn with leather-bound first editions of Charles Dickens and Mark Twain and a host of classics by other authors.

With the drapes open, she could look through the massive windows at the swaying palms and the gentle waves lapping up on the beach. She'd thought this could easily be a girl's dream home. A palace of magnificent proportions, with gilt walls and frescoes painted on the ceilings.

But she saw it in another light now. It was cold and impersonal, nothing more than collection upon collection of priceless artwork and furniture. It was more a museum than a home.

Mere Belle was just the opposite. The rooms might be mostly empty, but when she and Tom had strolled from one room to the next and when they'd made love in his tub and in his bed, and he had told her about his father's love for him, she could see a family in the place. A big family filling the vacant rooms with laughter and music.

She'd known Tom such a short time, but already she felt as if she might be falling in love with him. But love and all that it entailed frightened her. She was so darn afraid of making another mistake.

Of thinking lust and love were the same thing.

Of falling in love and then marrying someone, only to find that he was so much different from what she'd imagined.

She laughed at her worry. Tom hadn't proposed. He hadn't even professed love.

He'd simply made love to her. A lot.

Maybe he didn't want anything more.

God, she hated to speculate, but there was nothing else to do while she waited for Holt to make his appearance.

"Good morning, Miss Devlin."

Angel spun around at the sound of Holt Hudson's deep baritone. "Good morning, Mr. Hudson."

Angel shook Holt's hand, then slyly tucked it into the pocket of her jacket and turned on the small tape recorder.

"My secretary tells me that arrangements for the gala are going quite well," Holt said. "And thank you for faxing over the newest RSVP list. I had an opportunity to look at it last night."

"The turnout is far better than I expected. Much bigger than last year's gala," Angel said. "I have you to thank for that."

"Don't doubt your capabilities, Miss Devlin. You have worked hard on this event for the last three years and, like all functions of this sort held in Palm Beach, they get bigger and better—and far costlier—every year."

"Fortunately this one isn't costing an arm and a leg."

Holt smiled, something he rarely did. "You have quite the knack for twisting the arms of caterers and florists. Should you ever decide to give up your private investigative business, I believe I could offer you a lucrative job working for Hudson, Inc."

"Getting rich has never been one of my goals. I like what I do for a living. I might not have the biggest and best P.I. business in town. In fact, it's probably the smallest and least diverse, but it serves my purpose, which is to give me time for my family and—I'm sure you and everyone else are tired of hearing this from me—it gives me the time I need to raise money for Alzheimer's research."

"What about your personal life?" Holt asked, clasping his hands behind his back. "You shouldn't neglect that."

"Funny you should mention that, Mr. Hudson."

"Oh? Have you met someone?"

"As a matter of fact, I have." Time to go in for the kill. "Your godson. Tom Donovan."

Holt's face seemed to melt. The sparkle that

had been in his eyes disappeared. They were dull now. The color nearly drained from him. He looked sallow. Old. Like a man stretched out in a coffin.

"I know it's been a long time since you've seen Tom."

"Twenty-six years," Holt said, as if he'd kept count of the years, and maybe even the months and the days, on a calendar.

Holt walked to the bar and poured himself a whiskey. "Would you like something to drink?"

"No, thank you."

Holt sipped on the whiskey and walked to the window. "Are you aware that Tom has contacted me numerous times in the last few months, asking if we could meet?"

"He told me. He also told me that you refuse to see him."

"I don't like to dredge up old memories, especially memories about that night."

"He just wants to know the truth."

Holt turned. His eyes had grown cold. Narrow. "The truth was in the newspapers. It was in the police report."

"But he wants to hear it from you. Don't you think you owe him something?"

"This isn't something I want to talk about."

Oh, man, she was going to be in big trouble if she kept this up, but it was getting pretty damned obvious that Holt was hiding something.

"You and Chase Donovan were best friends, weren't you?"

"Yes, we were, and that was the worst night of my life," Holt offered, when she was sure he'd just clam up. "It plays over and over in my mind like a nightmare, every single night."

"Tom has nightmares, too. Nightmares he doesn't understand. Maybe if the two of you talked, the nightmares would end—for both of you."

Holt laughed, shaking his head. "I don't see the need to justify my reasons for not seeing Tom, but I will tell you this once and once only. I have seen photos of Tom and he is the spitting image of his father. He has the same eyes, the same dimple at the side of his mouth, and the same color of hair. If Tom walked into this room right now, it would be like having a ghost stare at me. An angry spirit."

Holt's jaw clenched. "I cannot forget the look in Chase's eyes when I shot him. The hurt, the pain. And I can't bear to relive those times. So please, do not ask me about this again."

Holt's anguish was far greater than she ever would have imagined. It was as if he felt tremendous guilt over what had happened, instead of feeling justified. And maybe a little piece of her understood why he didn't want to see Tom.

"Since it's impossible for you to talk with Tom, would you tell me what happened that night?" Angel asked politely, softly, hoping he'd say yes.

"As I said, it's not something I talk about."

She put all of her P.I. skills to use and kept right on asking questions. "Did you and Chase get into an argument earlier that day?"

Holt poured himself another whiskey and slugged it down as he stared out the window. "Do you plan to badger me all morning?"

"I'm not badgering you, Mr. Hudson. I'm just curious about what happened, and I don't want to go by gossip, or even the police report. I'd really like to hear it from you."

He sighed heavily. "All right. Chase and I played golf that morning, just as we had most every day for I don't know how long."

"And you had a fight?"

Holt turned. "Why don't you just read the police report? All the details are there."

"I have read the report. Tom's read the report, too."

"Then neither one of you should have any questions."

"I'm an investigator, Mr. Hudson. I always have questions."

"All right, I'll give you the complete rundown of the events as I remember them. You can relate this information to Tom and then I don't want to hear anything more about it."

Angel sat in one of Holt's chairs and crossed her legs. "I'm listening."

"Chase and I did have a fight . . . over money, of all things. He always spent too much. He didn't invest. He didn't save. He'd bought so damn much for Amélie when she was alive and even more for his son and it was killing him because he didn't have any money coming in. I told him how to invest. I told him how to save, but instead, he asked to borrow money. A hell of a lot of money, and I said no."

"Was that the first time he asked you to help him out?"

"No. He'd asked Amélie's parents to begin

with, but they'd already given them Mere Belle. They'd washed their hands of Tom after that. Even when Amélie died, they refused to come to the funeral. They wanted nothing to do with their grandson—while they were alive, at least, although I hear they provided for him quite well when they died."

Holt looked out the window again. "Chase came to me time and time again asking for money. He was my best friend and God knows I would have done anything for him, but there came a time when I had to tell him no."

"And that happened the same day you . . ." Angel paused, almost afraid to go on.

"You can say it, Miss Devlin. Yes, it happened the same day I shot him. It was in the morning. Chase was angry. Furious, in fact." Holt's entire body was reflected in the window, and Angel could see him wipe his eyes, as if tears had built up inside. "Chase told me a friend always helps a friend, no matter what, and when I told him again that I wouldn't give him another penny, he said our friendship was over. He said he'd get money one way or another, and then he'd get even with me. Never in my wildest dreams did I think that meant he'd break into my home, steal one of my most prized possessions, and then"—Holt took a deep breath—"attempt to rape my wife. If I hadn't heard her screams, Chase might have gone through with it. But I was here in this room and I grabbed the gun out of my desk. I ran up the stairs and saw him there in bed with Carlotta."

Holt turned slowly. His eyes were clouded as he poured whiskey into the glass he hadn't even touched. "I begged Chase to stop what he was doing, but he just looked at me and laughed. Carlotta was screaming and . . ." Holt sighed heavily. "And I shot him."

"Six times?"

"Yes. Six times. One bullet just inches from his heart, the other five in his back because he wouldn't stop what he was doing, and I couldn't let him hurt my wife."

Holt walked across the room and slumped down in an easy chair. "Chase should have died right then and there, but he didn't."

"He escaped through a window?"

"No. He left the same way he came in—through the front door, although the papers wanted to sensationalize the whole account by printing that he went through a window. If you read the police report carefully, you'll see the truth. As I've said, Miss Devlin, everything that happened is in the police report."

"Do you know why he went home to get Tom? Do you have any idea why he drove to the Everglades?"

"Maybe he knew he was going to die and needed to be with Tom when it happened. That's my best guess. As for the Everglades . . ." Holt shrugged. "Perhaps he was trying to get to his dad's place. But we'll never know for sure."

"And he had *The Embrace* with him when he left?"

"He was choking my wife with it. If you'd seen the entire police file you would have seen the photos of the bruises on her neck, pictures of Chase's blood in our bed. I wasn't paying all that much attention to what he was holding in his hands when he ran out of the house, all I could think about was taking care of my wife."

"So you're only assuming he stole the statue?"

Holt's eyes flashed with anger. "The statue disappeared that night and I haven't seen it since."

"Then why didn't you file an insurance claim?"

Holt's eyes narrowed. "You've talked with my insurance company?"

"I haven't, but I did hear that bit of information from a fairly reliable source." That was a lie, but . . .

"I'll answer this last question, Miss Devlin, and then I suggest you leave. I didn't file an insurance claim because I had too many other things on my mind. My wife was traumatized that night, and afterward she sank into a horrid depression. Long before Alzheimer's hit her, she was little more than a shell of the woman I loved."

Holt heaved a heavily burdened sigh. "That statue had always been my most prized possession. My friendship with Chase was something else that I cherished. But none of that mattered to me after that night. I needed to care for my wife. To protect her in a way that I'd never protected her before. Getting a couple of million dollars in insurance money meant nothing to me, Miss Devlin—that's why I never filed a claim. It just didn't matter."

"I'm sorry I've made you rehash bad memories."

"As I said, those memories are rarely gone from my mind." He stood. "Now, if there's nothing else, I'd like you to leave."

"I have just one more question, Mr. Hudson."

He clasped his hands behind his back again. "What is it?"

"I'd like to invite Tom Donovan to the gala—as my guest."

"No. That's where I draw the line, Miss Devlin. If he walks through the door that night, I will order everyone to leave."

18

Tom wanted to get the hell out of Frederike's freakish maze of a home. The woman collected "everything, dahling, simply everything!" or so she'd told him when he arrived at Mirasol with two extravagantly wrapped six-hundred-dollar-apiece dog collars he'd picked up at Ma Petite Bow-Wow.

Everything dominated every nook and cranny of the thirty-one-room mansion, the main attraction being a brightly lit full-size 1913 musical carousel that twirled around and around in the massive entrance hall from nine in the morning until midnight, every day of the year.

Frederike liked carousels almost as much as she liked outlandish hats. Dogs, of course, were the loves of her life. If her late husband Evan LeVien had been a dog, he might have been buried by now instead of cooling on ice until Frederike could take the time to throw a proper—and opulent—funeral.

Tom slugged back a glass of champagne and

grabbed another, figuring if he got drunk he might make it through the birthday party. One minute in the chaos of Frederike's home and he'd found himself longing for the Glades, for his grandfather's fishing boat, Jed and Sarah Devlin's small but comfortable and inviting home in West Palm Beach, and most of all his own empty mansion.

As long as Angel was there with him.

"Are you really the son of *that* Chase Donovan?" Stephania Allardyce, the diamond-bedecked woman who'd been conversing with him for the past five minutes about her *lovely* little dog, Flagler, interrupted his faraway thoughts, her surgically young face—with skin stretched to the limit—beaming up at him.

He'd been asked the same question by two other people since he'd arrived at the party. Rather than saying anything, Tom nodded.

"Oh, my!" Stephania giggled. "Here come the dogs."

Tom slugged down the rest of his champagne as Cosette and Celine tramped between his legs for the second time in the last fifteen minutes. A moment later a pooch the size of a swamp rat snapped at the toes of his best crocodile boots, and Stephania's overly male Schipperke humped his right leg.

Stephania batted her false eyelashes at Tom, put a diamond-encrusted hand on Tom's chest, apparently for balance, and bent over to have a little chat with her puppy. "Now, now, Flagler, darling, you know you're not supposed to do that."

Flagler let out a loud, piercing bark, humped

Tom's leg one more time, snapped at Stephania's scolding finger, then scampered across the room to annoy someone else.

Tom snatched another glass of champagne as one of the waiters passed by and thought about Bessie and her appetite for new and different things. If Flagler didn't watch himself, Tom just might snatch the nasty little dog in the middle of the night and hightail it to the Glades to feed the thing to his favorite gators. Bessie and Ralph would love him forever.

"They're such darling little creatures, aren't they, Mr. Donovan?"

Again he nodded, forcing a smile.

"As I was saying," Stephania went on as if they hadn't been interrupted, "your father was such a lovely man. And your mother . . . What was her name?"

"Amélie."

"Yes, yes, that's right. She had such a divine accent. Hungarian, I believe."

"French."

"Oh, yes, French. She was always the life of every party—until she died, that is." Stephania took a dainty sip of her champagne. "All of the men loved her but she wanted nothing to do with anyone but your father."

"Is that so?"

"Yes, I do believe I have my facts straight on that, although it is difficult at times to stretch one's mind back twenty-six years."

For half an hour Tom had wanted to get the hell out of this place, but Stephania had finally caught his full attention. He wanted to know everything possible about his parents—the good, the bad, and even the ugly. It was the only way he had of knowing them.

"Tell me everything you know, Mrs. Allardyce," Tom said, taking Stephania's empty champagne glass from her fingers, putting it on the tray of a passing server, and grabbing her a crystal-clear flute full of the best bubbly money can buy.

"Thank you so much," she said politely, taking the glass. "If I remember correctly," she continued, "Holt Hudson was quite enamored with your mother, too."

Tom's eyes narrowed. "Holt Hudson and my mother?"

"They weren't an item, of course. Carlotta never would have allowed that, not after she fought tooth and nail to win the attentions of Holt Hudson in the first place. She was desperately in love with him, you know."

"Was she jealous of my mother?"

"No, no, of course not. They were the best of friends and went everywhere together. All four of them were friends. I remember Carlotta crying uncontrollably at your mother's funeral. You were a newborn, of course. And your poor, poor father looked like a zombie that day."

"What about Holt Hudson?"

"He was, I daresay, as lovely a man as your father." Stephania frowned, as if thinking back to that day so long ago. "I remember Holt comforting his wife, then sending her off with their chauffeur so he could stay at the grave with your father as everyone else departed. It was quite the funeral, you know."

"No, I didn't know."

Stephania pressed a hand to Tom's arm. "I suppose you wouldn't." She smiled warmly. "Holt planned the entire affair because your father was too distraught. There were flowers everywhere. Unimaginably beautiful bouquets.

"I remember Holt holding you in his arms while your father wept on your mother's casket. I remember him crying, too, as if his heart were broken."

A waiter passed by for the umpteenth time and Stephania picked a canapé from his silver tray and nibbled on the edge. "It's terrible what happened that night—when your father was shot. I only saw Holt and Carlotta once after that, when I went to Palazzo Paradiso the next morning to offer my support. Frederike went with me. She took a lovely little cake and I took chocolates." Stephania smiled sadly. "We always exchanged gifts when we saw each other. Poor Carlotta. She was beside herself, running around the room looking for something to give us in return. The doctor had given her something for her nerves and"—Stephania sighed deeply—"it was all so terribly sad. Carlotta was never the same after that. Neither was Holt. Their lives were shattered, I believe. Such a shame."

Stephania put a cool, age-worn hand on Tom's cheek. "Just between you and me, I never believed your father did any of the things he was accused of. He may have been a cat burglar in his youth, but the man I knew would never have broken into Holt's home and stolen a statue. And never, ever would he have attacked Carlotta."

"Yoo-hoo! Tommy!"

Damn it. The last voice Tom wanted to hear right now was Frederike's. He wanted to spend more time with Stephania, but she blew him an air kiss and rushed off, trying to get to Flagler, who was humping the leg of Frederike's stuffed giraffe—a gift, she'd told Tom, from an African king.

Tom thought about rushing after Stephania, but when Frederike called his name again he turned, and thanked the gods for smiling down on him. Angel strolled alongside the Countess, looking beautiful in a bright green suit that showed off all of her curves, and, of course, was slit up the side so she could easily access her stiletto.

And not for the first time that day or the day before, he was pretty darn sure that he had fallen in love.

"Look who finally arrived." Frederike's heavily made-up eyes beamed beneath a pink and purple hat shaped like a three-tiered birthday cake. At any moment Tom expected someone to stick candles in the top and set the thing on fire.

"Sorry I couldn't get here sooner," Angel said, "but the court case was a fiasco and I ended up on the stand far longer than normal."

"You've come," Frederike said, "and that's all that matters, except, of course, for the lovely presents you brought for Cosette and Celine. We'll have such a lovely time unwrapping them later.

But come, come, now that you're both here—and together, of course—let me show you around."

"Do you have more collections for us to see?" Tom asked, slipping his arm through Frederike's and winking at Angel over the top of the Countess's hat.

"Oh, yes, of course I do. There's my hat collection, which is a must-see on any tour of my home, plus all of the artwork I've been given as gifts, and next time you come, I'll take you to the private room where Evan kept his ancient Greek phallus collection. It's quite a sight."

"Sounds intriguing," Angel quipped, and Tom couldn't help but notice her rolling her eyes.

"I like mentioning that collection to first-time visitors to my home," Frederike told them. "It's such an attraction and because I never show it off to first-time visitors, it always guarantees they'll come back a second time. After that, I tempt them with something else, not that they wouldn't come back just to see me, of course."

"Frederike! Darling!"

The muscles in Tom's arms, neck, and shoulders went on alert when he heard the voice he recognized as Dagger's. Angel's entire stance was filled with uneasiness; her eyes with out-and-out hate.

"What a lovely surprise to have you show up for Cosette and Celine's party," Frederike said, abandoning her hold on Tom and Angel and slipping her arm through Dagger's. "I trust you're feeling better?"

"Yes, darling," Dagger said. "I'm terribly sorry

I had to cancel our plans last evening, but I must have eaten something that disagreed with me."

"You had an upset stomach?" Tom said, trying not to laugh.

"Yes," Dagger admitted. "But like anything that upsets me, I bounce back quickly and make sure I'm prepared should I get caught unaware in the future."

"Goodness," Frederike said, "please don't even think about having another upset stomach in the near future. It's quite depressing. Personally, I'd rather think about hats. Wouldn't you?" she said, smiling at each of her companions.

"I'd love to see your hats," Angel said. "Are they all as unique as the one you're wearing this afternoon?"

"Just wait until you see them. They now take up three rooms here at Mirabel and I've had to hire a man who does nothing but keep them dust-free and in tip-top shape."

"Have you decided which one you'll be wearing to the Alzheimer's gala?" Angel asked, as Frederike led them up a stairway lined with portraits of all eight of her husbands—all dearly departed, she'd told Tom earlier—and each one of her past and present "little butterflies," all of them with French names and painted with their jeweled collars.

"I have an absolutely fabulous new hat that's being created for me now. It will be the hit of your gala, Angel, my dear. And what about you? What will you be wearing?"

"I haven't quite decided yet," Angel said.

"I thank God that I don't have to struggle with

such a decision," Dagger said, trying his damnedest to sound like a stuffy, upper-crust bastard. "I've just picked up a new Armani which will see me through the rest of the season, and"—he kissed Frederike's cheek—"I'll be taking it with me to Newport, too."

"Isn't it divine?" Frederike said, beaming at Dagger. "I have a spectacular oceanview condominium in Newport that was left to me by"—she frowned—"I believe it was Marcus Pennington, my third husband. It's rarely used, so I've offered it to Dagger for the summer and he's graciously accepted."

"Then you'll be leaving town soon?" Tom said, hitting Dagger with the full force of his disgust.

"When the season ends. In the meantime"—Dagger grinned—"there will be many parties to enjoy."

"Speaking of your gala," Frederike said, opening the double doors that led into a room filled to the brim with a mishmash of anything and everything gaudy, "I understand Holt will be auctioning off much of his late wife's jewelry and donating all of the money to charity. Is that true?"

"Yes. I can't begin to tell you how excited I am at the prospect."

"I'm quite excited, too. Carlotta had a hat-shaped pin that I always admired, just a small piece, about the size of . . ." She looked at Dagger's hand resting on her arm, then at Tom's hand clutching Angel's. "Oh, I'd say it was about the size of Tommy's palm. I would love to bid on that piece."

"When I see Holt next, I'll ask him if that's one of the pieces he'll have on display that night."

Frederike laughed. "Oh, don't be silly, Angel. We all know he won't have the real pieces on display. He'll have fakes made up. God forbid that anyone should walk off with the real thing. That hat-shaped pin, all by itself, has got to be worth at least two, maybe three hundred thousand, and heaven only knows how many other pieces of jewelry he has locked away."

Angel looked uncomfortable. It was pretty darn obvious to Tom that she didn't want to discuss Holt Hudson's security in front of Dagger. Maybe she didn't even want to discuss it in front of *him*.

"Mr. Hudson hasn't mentioned anything to me about having fake jewelry on display," Angel said, "and I do know he'll have all kinds of security that night."

"Well, I'm glad to hear that. I've heard rumors that Holt hates security personnel or cameras monitoring his grounds or the important parts of his house. It's all rumor, of course, but if it's true, anyone, and I mean anyone, could pretty much just walk into that place and take whatever they wanted."

"I'm sure Holt has security," Dagger said. "He'd be foolish not to, and I seriously doubt he's a foolish man."

Frederike frowned. "You're a private investigator, Angel, and you've been to Palazzo Paradiso. Have you seen any signs of security?"

"The security of Holt's home isn't something I feel comfortable discussing, Countess, but I will promise to talk with Holt when I see him about that piece of jewelry you're interested in."

"You know, dahling, if he doesn't have it on display, perhaps Holt will take us up to his safe and let us take a peek. What do you think, Tommy? Wouldn't that be—" Frederike's frown deepened as she looked at Tom. "I'm sorry. I suppose you wouldn't want to see Holt's safe, and I suppose Holt wouldn't want you anywhere near it since your dad—"

"Unfortunately," Angel said, interrupting Frederike's spiel, "Tom will be out of town the night of the gala. I had so hoped he'd be able to attend, but he had a prior engagement."

Obviously that was the pronouncement she'd gotten from Holt, Tom thought. He wasn't to be admitted to Palazzo Paradiso come hell or high water. Taking advantage of Holt's obvious lack of security may be his best way to get in, he decided. He might even have to try going through the window again.

"You have a lot of beautiful things in here," Angel said, obviously trying to change the subject. She slipped her arm through Tom's, offering him a smile that said, "I'm sorry."

"Nearly everything you see in here—except for the hats, of course—came from friends. Little gifts, you know, for a kindness here and a kindness there." Frederike walked across the room and picked up a broad-brimmed zebra-skin hat. "This came from a lovely little boutique that used to be on Worth Avenue."

"The one where my mother worked?" Angel asked.

"That's right, dahling. I believe I was with Carlotta Hudson the day I bought it, and that was twenty-six, twenty-seven years ago."

"Do you remember all the little details about every hat you own?" Angel asked.

"Of course I do. They're like husbands, you know. You remember every second of your first meeting, who was there, what you ate and drank. Even the music that was playing." She smiled fondly at the zebra-skin hat. "It was a Friday morning when I first saw this lovely piece. Carlotta was looking at purses, something dainty, not the least bit my style, and your mother, Angel, was an absolute dream, placing the hats on my head in that special way she always had, tilting it just so, then standing back as I admired the look in the full-length mirror."

Tom had no idea where Frederike's tale was going, but he listened intently, determined to relive the last years of his father's life through the eyes of other people who'd been in Palm Beach at the time.

"Was there music playing?" Tom asked.

Frederike smiled slyly. "If you think I don't remember, you're wrong, young man. It was a Beatles tune." The Countess looked at Angel. "Your mother used to play their music all the time, much to the annoyance of her customers. But she was such a delight that we never said a word about her odd taste."

"She still likes the Beatles," Angel said.

"Your mother liked this hat, too. She went on and on about how stunning it was. It was a one-of-a-kind, the only way I will ever buy a hat, and I believe I only wore it once." Frederike handed the hat to Angel. "Please, give it to your mother. A little gift from an old acquaintance."

"I couldn't possibly take this, Frederike."

"Nonsense. You've given me the pleasure of your company this afternoon and I'm giving you a gift in return. It's a tradition among my friends."

Frederike scurried across the room and pointed at a hat strewn with fake fruit. "This was a gift from Bunny Endicott, a little something to thank me for the chocolates I'd had sent to her from Belgium after she had her breasts enhanced."

"It's a lovely hat," Angel said.

"Oh, no, not the hat." Frederike lifted it off the marble statuette of a naked Greek or Roman god. "Bunny gave me the statue. It's not my taste, of course, but it is the most perfect hat stand." Frederike put a finger to her lips. "Please don't tell anyone in town what I've done with Bunny's gift. If word gets out that I use works of art like this as hat stands, my friends might stop giving me gifts, and I'd absolutely hate that."

"Speaking of statuettes," Dagger said, his eyes narrowed at Tom, "isn't that what your father stole from Holt Hudson?"

"Allegedly stole."

"Oh, but he did steal it, Tommy," Frederike said. "I remember your father talking about it at a party once. It was after your mother died, of course, and he'd been drinking too much and rumor had it that he was borrowing money from everyone in town and—"

"Please, Frederike," Angel interrupted. "I don't really think Tom needs or wants to hear—"

"But I do, Angel," Tom said, putting his hand on her arm. "I want to hear every word of what Frederike has to say."

"I don't mean to hurt your feelings by saying all of this, Tommy, but there was no doubt in my mind at all that your father took that statue. At the time I believe it was worth three or four million, which was quite a lot of money twenty-six years ago. Heavens, if it was sold today, a person could probably get ten times that much for it. And the night of the party your father said if that statue belonged to him, he wouldn't keep it hidden away. He'd either charge admission for people to see it or he'd sell the thing and buy something worthwhile."

"Sounds pretty incriminating to me," Dagger said.

"Maybe it does," Tom said angrily, "but that doesn't explain why the statue was never found."

"You mean it's not hidden somewhere at Mere Belle?" Dagger asked, a sneer on his ugly face.

"For all I know, the damned statue could still be in Holt Hudson's safe. For all I know, my dad might have had some incriminating evidence against Holt Hudson and Holt shot my dad to keep him from talking. For all I know, everything Holt told the police was a lie."

"You know," Angel said, gripping Tom's arm, "maybe we should go back down to the party."

"That sounds like a lovely idea," Frederike said. "I believe it's long past time to open presents."

And, Tom thought, it was long past time for him to make another attempt to break into Palazzo Paradiso and find out what the hell had really happened that night.

19

"I'm sorry, Tom," Angel said, sitting on top of a blanket she and Tom had taken down to the beach, her knees drawn up to her chest and her arms wrapped around her legs as the stars started appearing in the sky. "I spent a good hour this morning badgering and nagging Holt, but obviously my powers of persuasion aren't quite as good as you seem to think they are."

Tom stood at the edge of the surf, the lapping waves and foam rolling again and again over his feet. "You have nothing to be sorry about. You did all you could do to get me in to see Holt."

"It's not just that," Angel said, holding her cassette player in her hand. "It's everything Holt said on the tape about what happened that night. It's everything Frederike said that confirms Holt's story. I wanted so much for your father to be innocent—"

"He was. I listened to that tape and I swear, Angel, that story Holt told is word for word what he said in the past. It's well rehearsed. Scripted so he doesn't leave out any little detail." Tom turned. He smiled. "Stephania Allardyce believed my dad was innocent. I know he's innocent, too, and you, sweetheart, are going to help me prove it."

"I'm what?"

Tom walked toward her, his bare feet sinking slightly in the soft white sand. He had a grin on his face that made Angel a tad uncomfortable. "I said you're going to help me prove my dad's innocence."

"And how do you expect me to do that when everything, and I mean *everything*, proves his guilt?"

"You're going to help me break into Holt's place."

Angel shook her head adamantly. "No, I'm not."

"I have it all planned. We'll wait until after the gala because I don't want anything to screw up your evening."

"That's awfully kind of you, but as I said, Tom, I'm *not* helping you break into the place."

"Your dad told me that you know all the ins and outs of any security system," Tom went on, apparently oblivious to the fact that she'd flat out told him she would not break into Holt's place. "Your poor dad. It makes him mad that you don't use your knowledge of security systems and choose instead to work for the obnoxious rich snobs of Palm Beach."

"I know a lot of stuff, Tom. I can even crack combination locks if I put my mind to it, but I'm not about to use that knowledge for criminal reasons."

Tom strolled toward her, his body looking fabulous in a pair of baggy swim trunks that slung low on his hips. The muscles heaved in his chest as he got close, and then he dropped down in the sand in front of her.

"Tell me, sweetheart," Tom said, clutching the bottom of the T-shirt he'd loaned her to wear, "do you think Holt might still have *The Embrace* in his safe?"

"I seriously doubt it."

"But if he did, and if you and I found it there, wouldn't that be proof that my dad didn't steal it?"

"I suppose so."

"Then let's break into Holt's place, break into his safe, and take a peek."

"You're out of your mind."

Tom drew the shirt over the top of her head. "I've never been more sane or more sure of what I wanted to do in my entire life."

"If we got caught we'd go to jail. My life would be screwed. Your life would be screwed."

"But what if we didn't get caught? What if we got into the safe, found *The Embrace*, and then confronted Holt with what we suspect?"

"What is it that you suspect him of doing?"

Tom put his hands on her shoulders and laid her back in the sand. He kissed one nipple. Then the other.

"The only thing I suspect him of doing is lying. I don't have any proof. I just have a feeling deep down in my gut."

"Breaking and entering isn't going to get you anything, Tom. And if you do it, you'll lose me."

He kissed her belly. Licked her belly button. "Would I?"

"I'd refuse to see you again. Ever."

Slowly, ever so slowly, his warm, callused palms whispered over her bare skin, along her sides, over her thighs. He parted her legs. Smiled wickedly. Slipped a finger inside her.

"Would you really give all of this up?" Tom asked, sliding a second finger inside her.

"You want to know the God's honest truth?" Angel said, slapping her hands against his chest and trying to push him away. "I'd hate you."

Tom heaved a heavy sigh. He slid over her, resting his body easily on top of hers. "I don't want to lose you, Angel."

She threaded her fingers into his dark silky hair. "And I don't want to give you up. But I will." She felt tears threaten, but she held them back. "I spent seven years living with a man I couldn't trust. I won't do that again."

Tom drew a thumb lightly over her lips, then cradled her face in his hands. "Finding out the truth is important to me, Angel."

"More important than me?"

"Yeah, it's important. I can't begin to tell you how much I need to know the truth. But I'm falling in love with you, Angel. I'm not going to risk losing you when I've lost so many other people in my life."

"You aren't just saying that to make me change my mind, are you?"

He kissed her tenderly. "When are you ever going to put all of your trust in me?"

"I want to trust you, Tom. I want to know that

the feelings I have for you go beyond lust and are really love. But I'm still unsure of things."

"I'm not going to rush you, Angel."

"And you promise you won't break into Holt's place?"

Tom held her face close to his, his eyes full of a tenderness she'd never known before and doubted she'd ever find in another man. "I may not give up searching for the truth, but for you"— he shook his head, laughing lightly—"I promise I won't break into Holt's place. Ever."

"And now that I've exacted that promise out of you," Angel said, "I probably should do something very special for you."

"Can I have anything I want?"

"Within reason."

Tom traced her lips with the tip of his tongue. He delved a little farther, touching her teeth, and Angel parted her lips with a sigh. Tom's mouth closed over hers. His sweet, blessed tongue slipped into her mouth and made pretty music with hers.

And then she felt his erection. Throbbing. Hard. Thick and long.

She locked her legs around his waist and wrapped her fingers around his hot, solid-as-a-rock penis, and guided him inside her.

Tom moaned when she thrust her hips up and drove him deep within her core. "That's my gift to you, Tom."

"Whenever I want?"

"All you have to do is say the magic words."

"And what would those be?" he asked, taking charge, loving her, carrying her to the brink and pushing her over the edge in not more than a few heartbeats.

She sighed against his mouth. Purred. "Just tell me you love me, Tom."

"I love you," he whispered against her lips, and then he showed her just how much.

Angel curled up against Tom's chest, as she had nearly every night for the last couple of weeks. His left arm was tucked under her breasts, his right arm stuffed under her pillow. Her feet rested against his feet; their legs melded together almost as one.

She felt safe with him. Loved. And as she lay wide awake, her head spinning from a little too much wine and just the right amount of loving, she was pretty sure that tomorrow she'd be able to tell Tom that she loved him, too.

"Having troubles sleeping?" Tom's words were little more than a whisper against her ear.

"You dragged me to bed at seven o'clock and right now"—she looked at the clock beside her bed—"it's not even ten. I never go to bed so early."

"You've been going to bed early every night for over a week now. It's the sleeping part that has come much later. We just got an earlier start tonight."

"I really should get up and check my list of things to do for the gala, just to make sure I haven't forgotten anything."

"You can check it in the morning."

Tom pressed soft warm kisses down the curve

of her spine. His fingers swept over her breasts, teasing her nipples. How was it possible to go from being frightened of sex two weeks ago, to this? To wanting to be with Tom every minute of every day. Wanting to be held. Needing to be kissed.

The phone rang and Tom's arms tightened around her when she automatically reached for the phone.

"Let it ring," Tom whispered against her back.

"I can't. It could be my dad. Something could be wrong with my mom."

Tom chuckled. "Your mom's got a lot of years left. They might not be perfect years, but—"

"But nothing, Tom. I hate to listen to a phone ring." She grabbed the phone, only to be greeted by Holt Hudson's assistant on the other end.

"Mr. Hudson would appreciate it if you could come by to see the reproductions he had made of the jewelry he'll be donating to the auction."

"Would tomorrow morning be all right," Angel said, "or perhaps later in the afternoon?"

"Mr. Hudson will be unavailable tomorrow. We realize it is late, but Mr. Hudson would prefer it if you come now."

"*Now?*"

Tom frowned, shaking his head. Angel glared at him in return.

"Yes," said Holt's assistant. "Please."

"All right. I can be there in half an hour."

"Thank you. You know the code for getting through the gate, and I will meet you at the door when you arrive."

Angel rolled out of bed and ran to the bathroom. "I've got to take a shower," she hollered back at Tom. "I'll be out in a minute."

"I'll join you," he said, wrapping an arm around her waist and reaching past her to turn on the shower.

"I don't have time to fool around right now. I've got to get to Holt's."

"I'm not going to do anything to keep us from getting there on time."

"There is no us where this is concerned, Tom," she said, as they stepped into the shower.

"It's late. I've plied you with liquor all evening to make you relax, and I'm not about to let you drive yourself to Holt's when you're not a hundred percent sober."

"I'll call a cab," Angel said, sticking her head under the powerful spray.

"You'll do no such thing. You'll trust me to get you there safely, and you'll trust me to sit in the blasted car while you're inside talking to my godfather, the man I'd kill to see."

"But you're *not* going to see him."

"No, I'm not," Tom said, smoothing a bar of soap over Angel's breasts. "I promised you I wouldn't break into his mansion. I promised I wouldn't do anything to jeopardize the gala. And as far as I can tell, I haven't done anything to blow your trust."

Angel grabbed the soap from Tom and lathered his chest. "All right. You can go with me. But you'll sit in the car and you won't, I repeat *won't*, go into Holt's even if the place catches on fire."

A silly-assed grin touched Tom's face. "I might have to draw the line there."

Angel frowned. "Promise me, Tom."

He kissed her lips, the hollow beneath her ear, and took his merry sweet time kissing her breasts.

"I'm still waiting for your promise," Angel murmured between her purrs and sighs.

"I promise to do anything I can to keep you happy."

And before they left the shower, he made her very happy, indeed.

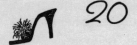 ## 20

Tom sat in the Jag's driver's seat, watching the sway of Angel's hips as she strolled across the drive, wearing the same sexy white suit she'd worn the first and last time he'd been here at Palazzo Paradiso. God, she was gorgeous, but she had a hell of a lot more going for her than beauty.

She had brains and guts. She refused to let anyone walk over her. And she refused to bend her principles.

When he'd fallen in love he wasn't quite sure, but there was no denying that that's what he felt. And every time he said those words to her, they came from his heart.

If only she could say the same words to him.

The front door opened and an elegant butler let Angel inside. He wished he were with her. He'd give anything to talk with Holt, anything to find out if there was more to the story about that night when his dad was killed.

Of course, he *was* on the grounds. He could get through that front door without any effort at all, follow the sound of Angel's voice, and confront Holt tonight. He could even bypass all thoughts of confronting Holt and just search the mansion for *The Embrace*.

And if it was in the mansion, in the safe, he'd know Holt had been lying.

Of course, he had no idea how to open a safe.

He'd also promised Angel he wouldn't break in.

He'd be damned if he broke that promise. Because if he did, he'd never hear her whisper, "I love you."

His gaze shot to the royal Poinciana he'd climbed before. He'd been crazy to try and break in. Insane.

But as he sat in the car staring at that tree, he realized just how easy it would be to do it again. Right now. He could scale the tree, push open the window, and sneak into Palazzo Paradiso. He could wander through the rooms to see if *The Embrace* was anywhere in sight. He could attempt to find the safe room where Holt apparently kept his most precious valuables.

But he could be caught. He could get hauled off to jail and get thrown in a tiny cell more stifling than the inside of Angel's Jag.

Then Holt would cancel the gala.

And Angel would walk away from him and never look back.

He couldn't do anything to hurt her. He couldn't bear to be hurt himself.

Still, he kept his eyes on the tree, wondering what would have happened if he'd managed to get inside that night. Wondering what he would have found.

He might have found the answers he sought, but he sure as hell wouldn't have found Angel.

As much as he wanted to prove his father's innocence, as much as he wanted Pop to believe in Chase again, he couldn't bear to lose the woman he'd fallen completely in love with.

Leaning back in the driver's seat, he closed his eyes and thought about silken thighs and sweet lips and the tightness of Angel's body when he sank into her. His groin ached just thinking about her. His heart beat fiercely. Blood rushed, hot and pulsing, through every vein, every artery, and centered in the one place he didn't need it to be centering right now.

His eyes flashed open in a hopeless attempt to get thoughts of no-holds-barred sex with Angel out of his head.

It was stuffy in the car even with the windows rolled down. Opening the door, he climbed out into the nighttime air, letting a hint of ocean breeze roll over him.

His body cooled. Calmed. He leaned a hip against the hood of the car and looked out across the grounds. Too perfect for his tastes. Everything sculpted and orderly, while Mere Belle was wild, like the Everglades that he'd first hated with a passion, had been afraid of, and at last had grown to love.

Strains of Mozart whispered through the mansion's open doors and windows, just as they had the night he'd met Angel, the night he'd attempted to break into Holt's home. But unlike the last time, he realized it wasn't an orchestra playing, it was simply a piano.

His mother's piano.

Tom frowned as he listened intently to the light, airy melody, to the unique play of chords, and to the short, not more than a two-second-long trill that his mother had always added to each song she played.

Did Holt have the tapes Chase had made of Amélie's masterful playing? Had he made his own? Had Amélie and Holt shared a relationship that was more than friendship?

Tom's fists tightened. He'd spent the past week trying not to think about Holt or the past. He'd sunk himself into his work around Mere Belle. He'd sunk himself into Angel, making love to her when the nightmares overwhelmed him, when he wanted to forget the past, when he just wanted to have a good time, wanted to please her and take her away from her own past.

But as much as he wanted to forget all that had happened years ago, he couldn't. That night would live on in his mind until he knew the truth.

Mozart became Gershwin. "Rhapsody in Blue" rippled through the night. So did the unmistakable sound of a splintering limb.

Tom's gaze shot to the royal Poinciana. Squinting, he saw the long, lean shape of a man leaping from a tree branch to a window ledge—the same window ledge he'd stood upon two weeks before.

The man was dressed in black just as Tom had been, but this man didn't hesitate to open the window. Unlike Tom, he placed his hands on the glass and pushed up.

An instant later, Dagger Zane disappeared through the window.

Tom sprinted across the drive, trying not to give too much thought to his actions or else he might stop, think things through carefully, and maybe do nothing.

But he had to do something. There was no telling what Dagger was up to and there was no doubt in Tom's mind Dagger's ultimate goal spelled trouble.

Tom could care less if Dagger stole all of Holt's prized possessions and got away with them. He could care less if Dagger vandalized the place.

But he did care about the ultimate results. If Holt suspected any kind of trouble at all, he'd tell Angel to forget about holding the gala at Palazzo Paradiso. He'd withdraw the jewels he was donating to the auction.

And Angel's world would come crumbling down.

Tom was running full speed by the time he neared the tree. He took a flying leap for the lowest branch, grasped on to it, and swung himself up. He tried his damnedest not to make noise. He didn't want to send up any alarms. He only wanted to stop Dagger from screwing things up for Angel. He needed to get Dagger out of the place before anyone got wise to the break-in.

He moved cautiously but quickly, every foot placed squarely on branches without twigs that could snap beneath his boots and send up an alarm. Breathing easily, trying to stay as relaxed as possible under the circumstances, he scaled the tree faster than he had weeks before, in spite of wearing crocodile boots that lacked any kind of tread.

When he reached the limb that stretched toward the open window, he slowed, moving across it inch by inch. Water again puddled on the ledge, very little of it wiped away by Dagger's entry into the mansion.

Tom's heart beat heavily now, as he looked into a near-dark room, the only light entering it seeping under the door from the hallway or room on the other side. Tom stood silently, listening for the sound of footsteps, the cast of a shadow. But all was still.

Dagger was nowhere around.

One more step. Another. He took a deep breath and leapt. His boots hit the water and limestone and he slid, his feet gliding over the edge, his hands losing their hold on the molding.

His legs, his chest plummeted. The mansion's rough stone walls scraped his fingers as he fought for something—anything—to hold on to. Just when he thought he was going to end up in the prickly bougainvillea below, he caught hold of the molding, which stopped his immediate fall, and he wedged the toe of his boot between the stone blocks.

Slowly he worked his way back up to the window. He looked around the grounds to be sure no one had seen him, then slipped into the darkened room.

Tom crept toward the light slipping under a far door. He turned the knob slowly, inched open the door, then peered out into a wide landing that looked down on the mansion's massive ballroom, where Angel's gala would be held—*if* something didn't get screwed up tonight.

He stepped out onto the landing, keeping his back close to the wall. All he had to do now was make a choice—go right or left.

Downstairs in the ballroom he could hear Angel and Holt. He heard laughter and cautiously moved to the marble railing.

"This was one of my wife's favorite pieces," Holt said. "Or, I should say, the real necklace was one of her favorites, but these faux jewels are almost exact replicas."

"It's beautiful, Mr. Hudson."

"I believe the bidding should start at somewhere close to thirty thousand for the necklace and earrings, but I would hope that you'll be able to get forty or more."

"I've been getting calls almost constantly from people coming to the gala, asking if we will be providing a catalog in advance so they can see what's going to be auctioned off."

"Better that they come and see everything in person," Holt said. "And speaking of people who will or will not be coming, I understand you are still seeing Tom Donovan."

"Yes. Have you had second thoughts about—"

"No, Miss Devlin. As I have told you, I do not want him on my estate. The only reason I mentioned his name is to once again reiterate my feelings and to remind you that if he does show up here, I will close the estate immediately."

Tom's muscles tightened. Not even the sound of Chopin—his mother's piano again—floating through the house could ease the fury he was feeling now. Anger over Holt's refusal to allow his godson into his home. Anger over the condescending way he'd just talked with Angel. Anger over his threat to renege on his promise to let her use the mansion for her gala.

Holt Hudson did not sound like a man who could have cried at Chase's funeral. Didn't sound like a man who could be tortured at all by the past.

He sounded like nothing more than a rich bastard who cared nothing about anyone but himself.

Damn it all. Tom wanted to find Holt's safe himself, take out every piece of Carlotta Hudson's precious jewelry and dump it in the middle of the ocean. He wanted to take something away from Holt to make him suffer.

But all he could do now was keep quiet, find Dagger, and get him—and himself—out of Palazzo Paradiso before trouble rained down on Angel's head.

From where he stood, Tom could see all the doors leading to rooms off the landing. Only two were open, and Tom held out hope that he'd find Dagger in one of them.

Walking softly, moving again along the edge of the wall, Tom slipped through the first open doorway. It was a bedroom of massive proportions. The walls were papered with gold brocade. The fireplace was floor-to-ceiling marble, and antique chairs and tables littered the room.

Two other doors led off of this one. Tom mentally flipped a coin and moved to the door on the right. He peered inside. A bed canopied with dark red velvet stood on the far side of the room. An elaborate cherry wood and gilt desk was on another side. And gathered in front of the open windows looking out onto the ocean was a grouping of comfortable chairs.

Just like the first room he'd looked in, the walls were papered with gold brocade, but there was something different about the wall to the right of the bed. A door had been cut into it. A seemingly secret door—and it was slightly ajar.

It was, no doubt, the room that Frederike had mentioned; the room where Holt had sat for hours on end staring at his jewels, and that blasted statue called *The Embrace*. And Dagger was probably behind that door. He probably had another knife with him. And he was probably on full alert.

Tom took a long, deep breath, then moved silently toward the opening in the wall.

Careful. Wary.

His throat tightened.

Every nerve ending was on edge.

And the door creaked open.

Tom stopped. He couldn't hide. Couldn't run. All he could do was stand in place and hope, pray, that he'd be able to surprise the person on the other side.

Long fingers wrapped around the edge of the door. A head of dark hair peered around the edge.

Dagger.

Tom ripped the door open, lunged for the man he abhorred, slapped a hand around his mouth to keep him from crying out and disturbing the peace inside the mansion.

But it was too late for peace. Dagger kicked out of Tom's grasp, stumbled across the inner sanctum filled with jewels and art a museum would have paid top dollar for. He hit a marble bust with full force and it toppled, landing with an almost deafening thud on the floor.

Tom knew he was screwed.

"What was that?"

Angel saw the fear shoot into Holt's eyes as they stood before a mirror in the library. His fingers stilled at the back of her neck, all thoughts about securing the faux emerald necklace coming to a screeching halt.

"Someone's upstairs." Holt dragged the necklace from Angel's chest. "In my bedroom."

"Your butler?" Angel asked, hoping she was right. Praying that Tom hadn't broken in. "A housekeeper?"

"An intruder." Holt spun Angel around. "It's Mr. Donovan, isn't it?"

Angel shook her head. "It couldn't be. He said he'd wait in the car."

"Someone is in my bedroom without my permission." Holt stalked across the room, ripped open a drawer in one of the many desks scattered around the house, and pulled out a gun.

"You don't need that, Mr. Hudson. Please."

Anger raged in his eyes as he raced from the room.

Damn you, Tom. Damn you.

Angel followed Holt out of the library, racing through the massive entry hall and up the stairs, keeping up with his long, angered strides. But when she heard the glass break and something hard and heavy slam into a wall, she cut around Holt.

She had to get there first.

She didn't want Holt getting anywhere close to Tom with a gun.

She ran down the landing, tore through an opened door, and continued to follow the noise until she saw Tom crash into a wall on the far side of the room.

And then she saw Dagger barrel into him, his head butting Tom in the shoulder.

Angel slammed the door behind her. Locked it. She'd be damned if she'd let Holt come into this room. Not with a lethal weapon.

Angel's eyes narrowed in something close to panic mixed with anger as ornately framed artwork careened off the walls and marble busts toppled off their stands.

"Damn you both!" she hollered, then joined the fray, grabbing Dagger by the hair as he lunged after Tom. But he spun around and as he'd done in the past—took control.

Dagger latched on to her hair. His eyes feral. His teeth bared. And with one swift jerk, he threw her across the room. She smashed into the bedpost, bounced off of it, tumbled over a chair, and before she could get her footing, upended a porcelain vase full of flowers and water.

"Let me in, Miss Devlin," she heard Holt holler. "Damn it, let me in."

"Call the police," she yelled back at Holt. "Tell them to get here quick."

She'd rather have Tom behind bars, locked away for God knows how long, than have him dead.

"Stop," she pleaded, out of breath, her body

bruised, her scalp aching, but when neither man listened to her, she raced back into their midst.

"Get the hell out of here," Tom yelled at her. "I don't want you hurt."

"I'm already hurt," she shouted back, then closed her eyes and ducked when a chair flew across the room and sailed over her head.

She opened her eyes just in time to see Tom sling a right hook and bash Dagger under the nose. Angel heard the crack, heard Dagger scream, and watched Tom grab on to the black shirt Dagger was wearing and throw the bastard against the wall.

Dagger staggered. He slumped. He held his nose, looking like he was going to pass out.

Blood dripped through his fingers. Onto the carpet.

Angel could hear her asshole of an ex-husband whimpering like a baby.

And then she watched Tom bend forward, hands on his knees. He dragged in a deep breath. Blood trickled from his nose, his lip. He tilted his head and looked at Angel, overwhelming guilt in his eyes. "I saw him climbing through an upstairs window," Tom said. "I had to follow him."

"Why?" Angel asked, anger in her eyes, her voice shaky. Furious. "Because you thought he'd lead you to the safe so you could look for that goddamned statue?"

Tom stood up straight. His breathing was erratic, heavy. "I wanted to get him out of here so he wouldn't cause you any trouble."

"You sure did a hell of a job."

"You don't believe me, do you?"

"You could have knocked on Holt's front door. You could have told the butler that you saw an intruder breaking into the house."

Tom's eyes narrowed. And then he laughed. "I thought you trusted me."

"I wanted to. Now I know I shouldn't—"

Angel's words were cut short by the blur streaking across the room. The flash of steel.

"Tom!" Angel screamed, but Dagger's blade speared into the man who'd thrown him off his boat, the man who'd just broken his nose, the man Angel loved.

Everything else seemed to happen in a split second.

Dagger ran for the window, as Tom slumped to the floor. "Stop, Dagger. Stop. Now!" Angel screamed, but her ex leapt for the window.

She wasn't about to let the bastard get away, not when he might have killed Tom. She grabbed her stiletto and as she'd done thousands of times before, she threw it with precision. The knife buried itself into the window jamb.

"You're not going to get away, Dagger."

Dagger spun around, one leg outside the window, the other ready to pull through at any moment. A sickening sneer touched his face. He pulled Angel's stiletto from the wood. "I thought I taught you better than this, Angel. Missing a target can get you in all sorts of trouble."

"I could have killed you, Dagger."

"No, you couldn't. You never had the stomach for anything like that. But I don't have the same reservations. Never have. Never will."

He raised the knife, and Angel dragged in what

could easily be her last swallow of air. Dagger's aim was always dead on, even with a moving target. If he wanted to hit her—even kill her—he would.

But she refused to go down looking like a chicken. Refused to let him think she was scared in any way. So she glared at him, defying him to throw, as she moved toward Tom, showing Dagger that the man on the floor was her only concern right now.

Just as she got to Tom, he staggered to his feet, and a prayer of thanks shot through her. She wanted to grab him. Hold him, but he had something else in mind.

Tom ripped the bloody knife out of his left arm and in what looked like a near blinding rage, threw it at Dagger.

The blade whizzed past Dagger's shoulder, and the bastard grinned.

"I knew he wasn't as good as me." Dagger laughed, but he also seemed to think twice about throwing the knife in his hand as Tom tore across the room after him.

Sirens rang out. Loud. Piercing. And Dagger hit Angel with one last hate-filled stare before disappearing outside.

Angel ran to Tom, but he couldn't be stopped. He lunged through the window, and in spite of his wound, in spite of the blood, he jumped from the window ledge to the tree outside.

Her heart thundered in her chest as one horrid thought after another tore through her insides—the worst one . . . that a man would die before all of this was over.

She raced for the window, determined to stop Tom, but she was far too late. A hot and humid breeze slapped her face. And then she heard the snap of the branch wobbling beneath Tom's feet. She saw the look of horror on his beautiful face, the blood on his white T-shirt, and in the next instant, the thick limb broke beneath the weight of two men.

Angel screamed.

And the man she loved and the man she hated crashed to the ground.

21

He was dead, a six-inch blade embedded in the word ANGEL that Dagger had had tattooed beneath the devil on his chest.

Angel rubbed her arms, trying to find some warmth amid the cluster of police and firemen. Tom—bruised, his lip and nose bloodied—sat in the back of the ambulance, an EMT treating the wound in his arm. They'd wanted to take him to the hospital but he'd refused. Stubborn to a fault.

But as he sat on the gurney, his gaze stayed fixed on Angel. There was no mistaking the sadness and hurt in his eyes. She knew he was as torn apart inside as she was. He'd promised her he'd stay in the car and he'd lied. She wanted to believe that he'd gone inside the mansion only to follow Dagger, to protect her, to keep trouble from happening, but he'd also wanted to find that statue. She knew it in every fiber of her being.

And she knew inside that he'd keep on trying to find out the truth about his father's death, even if it meant breaking promises or getting hurt.

There was no way she could fault him for that. She'd do the same thing if something bad had happened to someone she loved. She'd do anything to get to the truth.

But God forbid, she knew all that had happened tonight was going to put an end to all she had planned for. Her dreams of making a lot of money for charity.

It seemed so selfish to think about that now, when Dagger was dead, when Tom was wounded, when her own body was a mass of aching muscles and bones.

When Holt stood at her side. Cold. Emotionless.

"Excuse me, Miss Devlin." Detective Brodie stood at her side, a small leather-bound notebook and pen in hand. "Could I have a moment of your time? In private."

Holt's eyes narrowed. He squeezed her arm and nodded once.

It was time to lie.

Before the police had arrived, Holt had begged Angel and Tom not to bring up the past. He wanted this investigation to be put to bed fast. He didn't want Tom mentioning that he'd climbed through a window to get inside. Didn't want Tom mentioning that he'd been trying to see Holt for months.

"Tell the police you were my guests," Holt had insisted. "The past is history, over and done with, and I want to keep it that way."

They'd argued. Tom standing there, pale, breathing hard, pressing Angel's white jacket against the wound in his arm, saying he had nothing to hide. Holt, controlled, his eyes narrowed, telling Tom if he ever—*ever*—wanted to sit down face to face and discuss the events that happened twenty-six years ago, he wouldn't mention the past. He'd tell the police that he'd been inside the house with Angel and Holt looking at jewelry, not waiting outside.

When the gates opened and the police and the emergency vehicles drove onto the estate, Tom reluctantly agreed to do as Holt had asked. Angel agreed, too. She didn't know what Tom's true motives had been, but she knew he wasn't a thief, hadn't been out to steal anything. Because of that, she'd protect Tom; she'd protect Holt, too, even though deep down inside she knew before this night was over he'd tell her he was backing out on his sponsorship of the gala.

Angel followed the detective she'd known for years to his car. "Would you like some coffee?" he asked.

"No, thank you. I'm fine."

She leaned against the dark blue sedan and folded her arms over her chest.

"Mr. Zane is . . . *was* your ex-husband. Right?"

Angel stared at the body lying on the grass. "You know the answer to that."

"Are you okay?"

"I will be," she answered honestly.

"Want to tell me what happened?"

"Do you really need my version?" she asked. Tired. Wanting to just go home. "You've already talked with Mr. Hudson and Mr. Donovan."

"You know how this works, Angel."

She inhaled deeply, and let the air out slowly.

Fighting for composure. "Mr. Donovan—Tom—and I came here to see the jewelry Mr. Hudson is donating to the charity gala that we're holding next week. Actually, the pieces we looked at were reproductions because Mr. Hudson didn't want to take the real jewels out of his safe until he had the proper security for it."

"You knew in advance that Mr. Hudson wouldn't be showing you the real jewelry?"

"I knew. Mr. Donovan knew. Dagger Zane knew." Angel laughed lightly. "I imagine most of Palm Beach knew, since the jewelry and the subject of security came up in a conversation that took place at Frederike LeVien's home a couple of weeks ago."

Detective Brodie's eyes narrowed. "*You* brought up the subject of security?"

"I believe Mrs. LeVien brought it up. I tried to change the subject."

"Not easy to do with the Countess." The detective grinned knowingly. "Did you have any reason to think Mr. Zane would want to steal the jewelry?"

"My ex-husband was an asshole. You know that, Detective. But as far as I know he'd never stolen a thing before. Finding him upstairs was a shock."

"How did you know he was upstairs?"

"I didn't know *he* was upstairs, not at first." Angel swept her hair behind her ear. "We were looking at the jewelry. In fact, Mr. Hudson was slipping an emerald-and-diamond pendant around my neck when we heard something hit the floor upstairs."

"Then what happened?"

Holt grabbed a gun, but Angel left that part out, as she'd been instructed. "We ran up the stairs and saw Dagger running out of the room where Mr. Hudson keeps his valuables. Tom ran after him as he dashed for the window. They fought." Angel dragged in a deep breath. "Dagger stabbed Tom and I threw the stiletto I always carry at him."

"Did you hit him?"

"I missed. On purpose. As much as I hated him, as many times as I wished he were dead"—Angel shook her head slowly—"I didn't want to kill him."

"But it *was* your knife that killed him?"

"Yes, it *was* my knife. He'd pulled it out of the wall." Angel's eyes narrowed. She felt a tear slide down her cheek. "I might not have wanted to kill him, but he was going to throw the thing right back at me, and I know he wouldn't have missed."

"Did he throw it?"

"Tom stopped him. I don't know if he meant to miss or not, but he threw Dagger's knife at him and then he charged Dagger. That's when they went out the window, out onto the tree, and"— she dragged in a deep breath—"that's when the branch broke."

Angel looked toward the ambulance. At Tom's arm in a sling. His gaze hot, intense, as he watched Angel talk. "Mr. Hudson and I rushed out of the house."

"Were there any servants around?"

"If there were, none of them came out."

"What did you find when you got outside?"

"Tom was tangled in the branches but managed to stand up with my help and Mr. Hudson's. Then we went to Dagger . . . but he wasn't moving. Wasn't breathing. That's when Mr. Hudson went inside and called 911."

Angel's eyes trailed back to Detective Brodie. "There's nothing else I can tell you."

"Did Mr. Zane have any family we can contact?"

"Last I heard his dad owned a wrecking yard in Wichita. They weren't all that close." Angel looked into Detective Brodie's comforting eyes. "I don't have to deal with contacting him or anything like that, do I? I mean, we were married, but—"

"We'll take care of everything, Angel."

Detective Brodie tucked his notebook and pen inside his suitcoat. "Can I give you a lift home?"

"I can drive, thank you. I'll roll down all the windows and let in the fresh air. I think I need it."

They walked together to the ambulance.

"Sure you don't want to go to the hospital?" the EMT said as Tom climbed down from the gurney.

"I've been bit by an alligator before." Tom laughed lightly, but Angel could sense his pain, not just from the wound but from what had happened. "All I need is a few aspirins and a good night's sleep."

The EMT dished out more directions, but Tom didn't seem to hear them as he walked up to Angel and slid his uninjured arm around her shoulders. "Are you all right?"

"I'll be fine. Thank you."

She pulled away from Tom's hold and walked up to Holt.

"I'm sorry about tonight," she said. "Sorry about all of this."

"I do not want the police to hear your apologies," Holt said. "Let me walk you to your car, or shall I have my chauffeur take you home?"

"I'll drive," Angel said. "Tom lives just up the road at Mere Belle—as you know. After I drop him off, I'll be going to my parents' for a few days."

"Please give your mother my regards," Holt said solemnly.

Angel's muscles tensed. "She'll be at the gala. She's even got a pretty gown to wear." Angel smiled warmly. "Perhaps you could dance with her that night."

"I will be closing Palazzo Paradiso as soon as the police have finished their investigation. I knew it was a mistake to open my home to you. Knew it was a mistake to let my defenses down." Holt linked his hands behind his back. "You will have to find another venue for your gala, Miss Devlin."

Tom grabbed Holt's arm. "You can't do that. She's spent months planning that night. The invitations are sent. Everything is arranged."

Holt dragged Tom's hand from his arm. "You should have thought of that before you entered my home."

"There won't be any other problems," Angel stated. "I assure you."

"You gave me your assurances a couple of weeks ago that everything would go smoothly, without any trouble at all. I believe you told me the same thing when you came here a year ago asking me to open my home. You were wrong, Miss Devlin. Things haven't gone smoothly and tonight's trouble is something I don't ever want to see repeated." Holt's eyes narrowed. "Now please go."

Holt turned on his heel and strolled back to his cold, lonely mansion, without saying another word.

Angel stared at Holt Hudson's back, and felt as if she'd just been stabbed with her own knife.

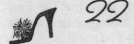 22

They sat almost side by side on the drive to Mere Belle, but there might as well have been a million miles between Angel and Tom. She was silent; he was, too, his right elbow propped on the open window, his fingers plowed into dark hair that blew in the cool night air.

Angel stared through the windshield at her headlights flashing on palm trees as she sped through the night. There were no other cars on South Ocean Boulevard. It was quiet out, except for the sound of the tires on the road and the breeze whipping through her hair, through the car.

Pulling to a stop at the gates in front of Mere Belle, she pressed the code Tom had given her into the security box recessed into a tall marble column. When the intricate white wrought-iron gates swung open, she drove up the circular drive and stopped in front of the chateau, leaving the car's engine running.

Tom turned slowly. "You're going to come inside, aren't you?"

"No. I thought we should say goodbye here."

Tom reached across the car with his right arm and switched off the engine. "I told you before, I didn't go into Holt's home to look for *The Embrace*. Yeah, I know I broke my promise about staying out of that place, but—"

"It doesn't matter anymore."

"If it doesn't matter, then why won't you talk to me? Why won't you let me touch you?"

Angel gripped the steering wheel and looked out the driver's-side window. "My ex-husband was just killed."

"I'm sorry about that, Angel." She heard Tom's heavy sigh. "If I hadn't followed him into the house, he'd still be alive."

"And you wouldn't have come close to getting killed—first by Dagger throwing a knife into you and second by falling out of a tree."

"Wait a minute." Tom pivoted in the seat and cradled her cheek in his right palm. "Are you giving me the silent treatment because I almost got killed?"

"Because you almost got killed. Because Holt backed out of his agreement. Because all of my plans for the gala have just been shot to hell."

"I'm sorry about the gala."

Angel dragged in a deep breath. "I spent an entire year trying to make that a success. A whole year doing everything right. Bending over backwards to make Holt happy. It was all going so perfectly—"

"Until I screwed it up."

Angel shook her head. "You didn't screw it up. I did."

"I'm the one that went into Holt's place when I wasn't supposed to."

"I would have done the same thing if I'd seen Dagger. Well, maybe I would have gone in through the front door. But I know you did it for all the right reasons. I know you did it to try and protect me."

"So why the hell are you telling me goodbye?"

"Because I've spent the past five years learning how to keep my emotions under control. Five years learning that I can be in charge of any situation and that I don't have to kowtow to anyone else. But you walk into my life and completely mesmerize me—"

"It's called love, Angel."

"It's called giving up everything I am for the sake of someone else. I don't want to do that, Tom."

He laughed, but she heard the hurt mixed with his cynicism. "You'd rather spend the rest of your life alone? Without me?"

"I don't know what I want right now. I just know that the gala fell completely apart because I lost control. How many other things in my life will fall apart if I let my guard down?"

"You've got to take chances, Angel."

"I know my limits, Tom. I know what I'm good at, and right now I want to crawl back into the safety of that cocoon I've lived in for the last five years."

"You know what, Angel?" Tom said, his eyes cold, filled with frustration. "You're feeling god-damned sorry for yourself. Pure and simple. When you decide you want to crawl out of that cocoon, when you decide you're willing to take chances, and be willing to get hurt, you can come looking for me. I may be around. Then again," Tom said, climbing out of the car, "I might not."

He slammed the door. He didn't look back, he merely walked away, up the stairs of Mere Belle, and disappeared inside.

She'd lost him. She knew it. And for the first time in her life, she realized what utter and complete pain felt like.

23

Tom tore off his sling and sat down at the piano, the only thing he could face at the moment. The pain in his arm was almost unbearable, but it was minor compared to the ache in his heart.

He slammed his fingers down on the keys and the deep, vibrating thrum echoed through the nearly empty room. For long minutes he played, bits and pieces of one mind-numbing masterpiece blending into another, every sound dark and haunting.

"Do you plan on pounding that piano through the floor?"

Tom's fingers stilled on the keys, and through the remnants of the music still reverberating through the room, he heard Pop's cane and the shuffling of his feet as he walked toward the piano.

"I heard something on the news tonight that sent shivers down my spine."

"What?" Tom asked, although he had the distinct feeling Pop already knew some details about Dagger's death.

Pop sat on the bench beside Tom. He touched the bandages on his arm. "The reporters said Dagger Zane was dead. They didn't mention anyone else being injured."

"There's no reason for the press to know about it. And knowing Holt Hudson the way I do, I imagine very few details will ever be released to the public."

"Are you all right?"

"No."

Tom sucked in a deep breath and played the piano again, lightly this time.

"I expected Angel to be here with you."

"She won't be back again."

Pop scratched his head. "That's too bad. I liked her."

"Me, too."

"You gonna tell me what happened?"

"No."

"You ready to head back to the Glades now and forget all about this town?"

"No."

"You gonna forget about Angel?"

"No."

"You gonna forget about learning the truth about your dad?"

"No, Pop, I'm not."

"Then what the hell are you gonna do? Sit here until you wear out those piano keys, or fight whatever it is that's got you so pissed off right now?"

Tom's eyes narrowed. And then he slung his arm over Pop's shoulder. "Shit."

"Did I say something wrong?"

"No, Pop, I got stabbed tonight and it hurts like

hell. But what hurts even more than that is that I walked away from Angel when I should have kept on fighting and I walked away from Holt Hudson when I should have made that bastard talk to me."

"So what are you going to do about it?"

Tom laughed. "I'm going to go have a talk with Holt Hudson."

"What about Angel?"

"With any luck, she'll come to her senses and realize just how much she loves me."

Tom knew the code to Holt's security gate. He'd memorized it after watching Angel punch it in earlier tonight. There'd be no more climbing trees and sneaking through windows. It might be four o'clock in the morning, but Tom was going to walk through the front door, walk straight up to Holt Hudson, and give him a piece of his mind.

And this time Holt had damn well better listen.

He slammed the car door, not caring who heard him, and raced up the circular stairs leading to Palazzo Paradiso's grand entry. He knocked hard.

He waited.

He took a few deep breaths and continued to wait.

He knocked again. Harder this time.

The massive door opened and the butler, dressed in slippers and a blue silk robe, stood between Tom and the rest of the house.

"May I help you?" the tousled old gentleman asked.

"I need to see Mr. Hudson."

"I'm afraid that isn't possible, sir. Mr. Hudson is asleep and has asked not to be disturbed."

"Unfortunately, disturbing Mr. Hudson is something I need to do."

"Please leave, Mr. Donovan. If you don't, I will be forced to call the police."

Tom grinned. "Mr. Hudson could have turned me in to the police earlier tonight, but he didn't. The way I see it, Mr. Hudson doesn't want the world—or the police—knowing that he bears any animosity against me. So . . . I seriously doubt you'll be calling anyone."

The butler tried to shove the door in Tom's face, but Tom slammed a hand against the wood and pushed. He stepped inside, skirting around the butler. "You can go back to bed now."

"I most certainly will not."

"All right." Tom winked and headed for the stairs. "I know where Mr. Hudson's bedroom is. You're more than welcome to follow me if you want."

Tom's boots echoed on the marble floor as he beat a path through the elaborate and enormous gallery where Angel's gala *would* be held. Holt may have thought he could put a stop to it, but Holt had another think coming.

He bounded up the stairs, taking them two and three at a time. The pain in his arm was gut-wrenching, but he pushed the agony aside.

Twisting the knob that led into Holt's quarters, Tom slung open the door and went inside. There was no need to be quiet. Something told him Holt already knew Tom was in the house and that he couldn't be stopped.

Holt wasn't in the bedroom. He was sitting in an easy chair staring through an open window that looked out toward the Atlantic. Smoke curled over his head, and when Tom stood in front of the man he'd learned to despise, he saw a fat cigar resting between Holt's lips.

"We need to talk." Tom shoved a chair close to Holt and sat down, facing him.

"You're wasting your time. I can't be threatened. I can't be intimidated. And I will not discuss what happened the night your father was shot."

Tom crossed a booted ankle over his knee and leaned back casually, trying to look calm and in control, when he was seething inside. "I know what the police report says. I know my dad's fingerprints were on your safe, on your wife's headboard, and that he was shot in your wife's bed. But I will never believe that he did anything wrong that night. And if it's the last thing I do, I will find out the truth, not just for me, but for my grandfather, because his heart broke the day my dad died, and I won't rest easy until he believes his son was innocent."

"As I said, that is not a subject I wish to discuss."

"Contrary to what you may think, that's not why I'm here tonight. I want to talk about the gala."

"That's as much history as that incident twenty-six years ago."

"I'll tell you what, Mr. Hudson. You get on the phone first thing tomorrow morning and call Angel Devlin. Tell her you've had second thoughts, that she can hold the gala here after all, and that you're still going to donate your wife's jewelry. It's to be your idea and your idea only. Do this, and I will never again try to talk with you about my father or that night. If you don't throw the gala, I will make your life a living hell until the day you die."

"I don't like people giving me ultimatums."

Tom shoved out of the chair and headed for the door. "And I don't like liars."

Angel's hand shook as she poured orange juice into a glass. It was five A.M. and she'd done nothing but pace the floor of her parents' kitchen since three in the morning.

She'd made such a mess of things. Tom. The gala.

Tom.

The kitchen door swung open and her dad walked into the room in boxers and a wrinkled T-shirt, his hair mussed, sleep in the corners of his eyes, and a day's growth of beard on his face.

"You know, Angel," he said, "this kitchen floor is getting old. It squeaks. And if you don't stop that pacing you're going to wake your mom the same way you woke me."

"Sorry."

He patted her cheek, then plucked the glass of orange juice from her shaky hand and slugged it down. "You going to tell me why you spent the night here instead of going home—or to Tom's place?"

"Tom's history."

"I see."

"You really don't see, Dad, but I'm not going to get into a long discussion about that now."

"Pretty bad night, huh?"

Angel sighed. "Dagger's dead."

Jed's face went blank. "What happened?"

"He fell on my knife."

"Fitting end for an asshole."

Jed put the glass on the counter and pulled his daughter into his arms. His chest was warm and solid and comforting, and she rested her cheek against him.

"You okay?" Jed asked softly.

"I don't know why I feel bad, but I do."

"Because he was young. Because in spite of all he did to hurt you, you spent seven years hoping that he'd make something of his life, praying that he'd love you, that . . ." Jed hugged her tightly. "Some people don't want to change, honey. Some people feel they're perfect and that everyone else has problems. That was Dagger in a nutshell."

Angel allowed herself to cry for all the years of pain and suffering Dagger had put her through. There was no telling how long she stood there with her dad. He just held her tight, and let her get rid of the anguish she had thought would never go away.

At long last, she took a deep breath and wiped the remnants of tears from her eyes. "You've got mascara all over you," she said, tugging on her dad's T-shirt.

"It'll wash out." He kissed her forehead. "Now, is there somebody else you want to cry over? Tom, maybe?"

Cry? Hell, no. Because it wasn't over between them. Not by a long shot.

"Actually, Dad, I think I need to go see Holt Hudson."

Jed glanced at the old kitchen clock on the wall. "It's five-thirty. Something tells me those Palm Beach types don't get up this early."

"Something tells me he hasn't gone to sleep yet," Angel said. "And even if he is in bed, I plan to give him a piece of my mind."

Angel strolled into Palazzo Paradiso, head high, in spite of the bruised and swollen eye she hadn't been able to camouflage with makeup. After her crying jag in her dad's arms, she'd headed for home, hopped into a cold shower, and painfully washed away blood and tears and anguish.

She didn't have time to grieve or feel sorry for herself. Once again, she had to retake control of her life.

Now, dressed in a crimson silk suit, an Emma Claire original slung over her shoulder, four-inch red crocodile slingbacks, and her hair twisted into a chic French roll that reeked of professionalism, she allowed Holt's butler to usher her into the mansion.

"Mr. Hudson is waiting in the library."

She'd ask the butler how he and Holt Hudson had known she was coming, since she hadn't called, but she preferred showing off an air of self-confidence, after doing such a damn good job of losing all control a few hours ago.

The mansion was silent except for the click of her heels on stone cold floors. The ever-present piano melodies were missing, as light from the crack of dawn filtered through the windows and skittered across the remnants of nighttime shadows.

They walked briskly through a maze of corridors, and at last the butler opened the massive door leading into a mahogany-paneled library.

The butler stepped inside the room. "Miss Devlin is here to see you, sir."

"Thank you, George."

Holt, dressed in a charcoal suit, not one strand of his silver hair out of place, stood in front of the floor-to-ceiling windows that looked out on his formal gardens. He puffed on a cigar, and the smoke wafted around him.

"Come in, Miss Devlin. George has put coffee out if you'd like to help yourself."

"Thank you."

It was all too polite in the room, considering that a fight had recently taken place upstairs and a man had died on the lawn not far from the main entry. It would be easy to apologize to Holt right now, but apologies weren't in her game plan.

Crossing the room, exuding poise and confidence, she poured coffee into a delicate porcelain cup, spooned in a few heaping spoons of sugar for energy, and, holding the saucer in one hand, turned toward Holt, taking a sip of the sweet, steaming brew.

Holt turned. He watched her drinking her coffee. Looked at the pot and the empty second cup, as if he couldn't understand why she hadn't played the role of subservient or even refined young woman and poured him a cup, too.

But she hadn't come here to be refined or sub-

servient. She marched across the room, sat gracefully on a white brocade sofa, and crossed her
legs. "I'm here to discuss Tom Donovan."

"That's a closed subject. Let's talk about the
gala instead."

Angel took a sip of coffee, realizing that getting
and keeping the upper hand with Holt Hudson
would not be easy. But if he wanted to discuss the
gala first, fine, she'd go there. And then she'd get
back to the more important matter.

"I assume you've had a change of heart." She issued the words as a statement, with no hint of a
question in her tone.

Holt walked powerfully across the room but
leaned casually against his desk. She'd never seen
anything casual in his stance, and couldn't help
but wonder what he was up to now.

"I made a promise to you many months ago,
Miss Devlin. I told you I would open my estate to
you as a contribution to your gala. I offered to donate many extremely valuable pieces of jewelry.
You in turn assured me that there would be no
trouble, no mishaps. You did not live up to your
part of the bargain."

If he thought she was going to get all wimpy
and whiny when he'd spoken the truth, he was
wrong. She could take criticism. She wondered if
he could take it, too, because when he was finished with his diatribe, she was going to launch
into him with one of her own.

Taking a slow, calculated sip of her coffee, she
kept her gaze on Holt and waited for him to con-
tinue.

"Contrary to what you might believe, I rarely

go back on my word. I realize that invitations have been issued and all of the arrangements have been made. Therefore, I have decided you may go ahead and hold your gala here."

Angel smiled inside. Hell, she was bubbling over with sheer, unadulterated joy. But she refused to let Holt see her excitement.

"And your late wife's jewelry?" she asked calmly.

"All of the pieces were recovered last night and"—he sighed heavily—"the security here will be upgraded. I don't want a repeat of what happened tonight."

"Did you upgrade the security twenty-six years ago?" Angel asked. She put her coffee cup on the table and stood. "Or did you decide it was easier to hide?"

"We were talking about what happened last night, Miss Devlin. I don't want to discuss the other incident with you."

"Or with your godson." Angel walked to the window and stood silhouetted in the just-rising sunlight. "Have you ever wondered what Chase would say about the way you've treated his son? Or"—she shrugged—"maybe you and Chase weren't as close as you've tried to convince me you were. Maybe the people in town who've related stories to Tom and I about your friendship with Chase were misled all those years ago. Maybe you weren't best friends. Maybe you didn't care about Chase at all."

"That's enough, Miss Devlin."

"Have I hit a sore spot?" Angel said. "If not, I'd like to. God knows, if Chase were here now—*if*, of course, you hadn't shot and killed him—I imagine he'd be pretty damn angry to learn that you'd abandoned his little boy, the little boy you promised to take care of if anything happened to his dad."

Holt turned away from Angel and stared out the window. He didn't want to hear any more and she knew it. But she was going to keep right on hitting him with truths he didn't want to hear.

"Tell me, Mr. Hudson, do you think Chase would have abandoned your child if you'd had one? Do you think he would have refused to talk to your child, to answer that child's questions, to help that child learn something about his past? Or do you think he would have thought about himself first? Wallowed in self-pity and guilt, and not once given any thought to a four-year-old boy who wasn't guilty of a thing, but ended up having to watch his father die, and had to face a grief far greater than any of us could ever imagine?"

"Tom's not a child any longer. And he's had a good life."

"How do you know anything about his life?"

"I've kept tabs."

"Then you do have something resembling a heart beneath the expensive suits you wear?"

Holt spun around, anger in his eyes. "What is it you want from me? I've told you that you can have your gala. I'm giving you the jewelry—"

"That means a lot to me, Mr. Hudson, and I appreciate it more than you'll ever know. A year ago it seemed like a miracle to me that you were going to come out of hiding after more than two decades. People in this town are so damn excited about seeing you again, which tells me that at some point in time you must have been a man with a generous heart."

"I don't need to be sweet-talked, Miss Devlin."

"All right, no sugar coating. You may have come out of seclusion, but my gut instinct tells me you're still hiding from something. Something that's haunted you for twenty-six years. And my gut instinct also tells me that you're going to be haunted by it until the day you die, unless you tell the truth to your godson."

"Are you quite finished?"

"No."

"Well, Miss Devlin, I am." Holt stalked across the room but Angel caught up with him. She blocked his exit through the door.

She moved in close. Stood eye to eye, not about to back down. "I'll be inviting Tom to the gala."

Holt's eyes narrowed. Burned. "Do whatever you have to do."

That answer came as a shock.

"Just one more thing," Angel said. "Why don't we check your calendar right now and find a time when you and Tom can meet . . . and talk?"

Holt shook his head and laughed. "I can only be pushed so far, Miss Devlin. And I feel I've been poked and prodded enough for one night."

Angel zipped up South Ocean Drive, exhausted from her meeting with Holt, but anxious to see Tom, to invite him to the gala, to tell him he might, just might, get a chance to talk with Holt.

And more than anything, she wanted to fall into his arms and beg his forgiveness. For being afraid that he could be even a little bit like Dagger. For being afraid that he'd try to control her when, in truth, he'd shown her how much power she really had.

She wanted to kiss him, to feel the warmth of his breath against her lips, the beat of his heart against hers, and the power of his arms as she gave herself up to his embrace.

And then she'd tell him she loved him.

She had no doubts at all about that any longer.

She'd never doubt it ever again.

Not more than five minutes later Angel stopped in front of Mere Belle. Her heart beat rapidly, full of excitement, anxiety, and anticipation. Stepping out of the car, she raced up the steps and knocked on the door.

And waited.

Anxiety peaked. A lump formed in her throat when no one answered the door. After knocking again and waiting even longer, she wove her way through the wild overgrowth of the estate to a winding path that led to the courtyard, hoping that Tom was working out back as he did so often.

The courtyard was empty. There wasn't a shovel, a pair of clippers, or even a wheelbarrow in sight, as there'd always been before.

She ran to the pool.

Nothing.

Walking to the French doors, she shaded her eyes and peeked through the glass. She saw Tom's piano with the lid closed—even though he always kept it open.

She dragged in a long, deep breath of cool morning air, then walked to the edge of the patio, past the shrubs and the statuary, to the long expanse of grass. If Tom wasn't inside, she'd go see Pop. Tell him that she needed to talk to Tom, or hopefully find Tom on the fishing boat sharing coffee or breakfast with his grandfather.

But when she reached the lawn and looked out to Tom's private dock, the *Adagio* was gone. And even though she didn't want to believe it, she knew the yacht, Pop, and Tom wouldn't be returning anytime soon.

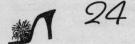 24

*N*ot one cloud marred the sky the night of the gala. Lights twinkled in nearly every tree, nearly every shrub. Bentleys, Rolls-Royces, a handful of Maseratis and Ferraris, and a yellow and green Deusenberg rounded the circular drive at Palazzo Paradiso, while young men in white dinner jackets graciously opened doors for the ladies and gentlemen, and, for those without chauffeurs, parked their cars.

The inside reeked of the tropics, with magnificent arrangements of white and lavender orchids, hibiscus, ginger, and bird of paradise placed on nearly every tabletop in Holt's fabulous ballroom.

Angel couldn't have asked for a more perfect night. Well, that wasn't true. It would have been absolutely perfect if Tom had been present, but the *Adagio* hadn't returned to Mere Belle, she hadn't heard from Tom, and all of the messages she left on his recorder in the past two weeks went unanswered.

She refused to be sad. Disappointed—definitely.

But she wasn't about to let anything spoil this evening. It was far too special, her mother looked fabulous and seemed to be comfortable in spite of all the people, and she knew without a doubt—well, maybe one or two—that she'd see Tom again.

If she had to go to the Everglades and search him out, fighting off alligators and mosquitoes and water moccasins along the way, she would.

Tom Donovan had not seen the last of Angel Devlin.

"You look marvelous tonight," Emma said, gliding toward Angel, wearing a simple white gown and the fabulous diamonds Cartier had donated to the auction.

Angel touched the glittering rubies and diamonds dripping down her own neck, a fabulous piece of jewelry Holt had asked her to wear with her feathery crimson gown. "What do you think of this?"

"Well . . ." Emma frowned. "They're not me, so I won't be bidding on them. But they're definitely you, Angel."

"I was thinking the same thing myself. Of course, there's no way in hell I can afford them."

"Maybe some sugar daddy will come along and buy them for you."

"In my dreams."

Emma smiled warmly. "Come on, Angel, we both know it's not a sugar daddy you want. It's Tom Donovan, and you'd take him even if you had to spend the rest of your life living with him in a mosquito-infested swamp."

"Unfortunately Mr. Donovan isn't around. Unfortunately Mr. Donovan hasn't been invited to this gala. So—"

"Oh, my God!"

"What?" Angel frowned as Emma's eyes opened wide.

"You should see the hunk who just walked in." Emma patted her chest. "He's gorgeous, Angel. Absolutely gorgeous."

Angel spun around and her heart leapt into her throat.

Tom strolled through the crowd. Tall. Broadshouldered. He wore the finest tux she'd ever seen on a man and it fit as if it had been tailored just for him. And, to echo Emma, he *was* absolutely gorgeous.

A Straus waltz was playing, something rousing and wonderful. Angel hoped Tom would look around the room and find her. Instead, his eyes never veered from the beautiful woman holding on to another man's arm.

A tear slid down Angel's cheek as Tom walked up to her mother, took her hand, and led her out to the dance floor—just as he'd promised. Not once did he stop smiling that warm, generous, and wonderful smile that Angel remembered and loved.

Sarah's steps were halting, uncertain, but Tom held her against him, guiding her, talking to her—mesmerizing her as only Tom could do.

"May I have this dance?"

Angel turned to the voice at her side. A much older version of Tom stood there, cane in hand, bent and a bit fragile, but looking incredibly handsome in his tux.

"Hi, Pop," she said, fighting the lump of happiness lodged in her throat.

"Bet you didn't expect to see me tonight."

"I hoped I'd see you days ago. But I'm glad you're here now. Angel slid a hand around Pop's neck, taking his free hand in hers.

"I'm not as steady on my feet as I used to be and I'm sure as hell not as tall as I was when I was forty—hell, even when I was sixty—but it's been a long time since I danced with a pretty woman and I want to make the best of this."

"We'll go as slow or as fast as you want," Angel said, as they took a couple of halting steps, then pretty much stood together on the edge of the dance floor.

"I've missed you . . . and Tom," she said, as they barely moved from the place where they'd begun their dance.

"We went to the Glades. Ate a lot of gator tail. Drank a lot of beer. Got drunk a few times and went fishing every day."

"I'm surprised you came back."

"I got to missing the ocean view. Amazing how pretty the morning is with the sun rising over the Atlantic."

"You were homesick, huh?"

"I suppose. Sure as hell didn't think I'd get to feeling that way when I made Tom take me back to Everglade City. Thought that would be the best place for both of us after that night."

"It was your idea?"

"Sure as hell was. After spending a couple of hours listening to Tom pound on the piano keys, making all sorts of god-awful racket, I figured it was best if we got the hell away from Palm Beach."

"So why'd you come back?"

"Like I said, I got homesick."

"And Tom?"

Warm fingers wrapped around her arm. Callused fingers. Familiar fingers. "Because just like Pop," Tom said, "I received an invitation to your gala from Holt, of all people. And because I got homesick, too."

Tom stood at her side, touching her gently not just with his hands but with his eyes, his smile, making her heart swell.

"Mind if I cut in, Pop?" Tom said.

"Nope. My body was about to give out anyway."

Tom spun Angel into his arms and heat radiated through her veins. Her heart beat wonderfully fast, as his smooth, heavenly-smelling cheek pressed against hers. "I've missed you," Tom whispered.

"Me, too."

He swayed with her in his arms, circled around and around, even did a little dip for everyone in the room to see, then nearly swept her off her feet as he danced her out onto the balcony in the cool night air.

"I shouldn't have left you. Shouldn't have gotten angry."

Angel put a finger to his luscious lips to stop his apologies. "I was afraid of losing control. Of doing something for others simply because they wanted it, not because I wanted it. I was scared of falling for someone and letting him take control of me. But you'd never do that, Tom. It just took me a while to realize it." She drew a deep breath. "I love you, Tom. I could never stop loving you, no matter what."

Tom kissed her. Soft. Gentle. Keeping her in his embrace. Keeping her warm and loved, and then he began to dance again, circling the terrace until they were hidden behind a cluster of palms.

His fingers swept down her sides, over her hips. "I've missed making love to you."

"We could easily make up for lost time."

"Now?" Tom asked, a gleam in his eye.

"I think we need to wait until the gala is over."

"What if I try something funny before then? Will you threaten to cut off my balls?"

Angel grinned. She placed her hand on top of his and slid it down her thigh.

Tom frowned. "Are you missing something?"

"No. I gave something up."

"You're no longer wearing the stiletto?"

Angel shook her head and wove her hands into his hair and pulled his mouth close to hers. "I don't need it any longer, Tom. I don't need to build any more of those walls you told me I was throwing up—unless I built one around the two of us to keep us together."

"Excuse me."

Tom jerked back, their long-awaited and much missed kiss interrupted before their lips had even touched.

"Pardon my interruption," Holt's butler said, "but Mr. Hudson would like to see you in his library."

Tom and Angel reluctantly followed the butler through the crowd. Everyone was having a wonderful time, drinking, eating hors d'oeuvres, and talking about the extraordinary jewels, the divine Emma Claire original purse, and all of the other items that would soon be up for auction.

Of course, that auction couldn't begin until Angel returned to offer her thanks to everyone for making the evening so special, and to encourage them to contribute with open hearts and very big checks.

They entered the mahogany library. Pop was there, leaning on his cane and the back of a chair, glaring at Holt, who stood on the far side of the room, his hands clasped behind his back.

"I apologize for dragging you away from the party," Holt said. "It appears to be going quite well."

"It is," Angel said. "Thank you."

Holt's gaze turned to Tom. "It's been a long time since you were in this house—because you'd been invited here."

"I don't remember ever being here with an invitation."

"You came here quite often with your father. I even had a swing set installed outside—just for you."

Suddenly Tom remembered feeling the weight of a man's hand pressed against his back as he was pushed in a swing, and he wondered if it had been Holt's hands he'd felt, his dad's, or both.

But why had Holt picked tonight to talk of old times?

"Have you called us here to unburden your soul?" Tom asked.

"There is a lot I want to share with you," Holt said.

"You could have picked a hell of a better time," Tom said. "This is Angel's night. She's worked hard to put this gala together and she should be in the ballroom celebrating with everyone."

Angel clutched Tom's arm. "It's all right, Tom. You've waited a long time for this. It's more important than anything going on outside. Besides, Emma is in her element. She'll make sure everything goes smoothly."

"So what do you plan to tell us?" Tom asked.

"You aren't the only three who will know the truth when tonight is over." Holt lifted a few sheets of paper from his desk. "I have a press release to fax to the newspaper. And after tonight's auction, I have a speech to give, so everyone will know what happened the night your father was shot."

"You plan to tell my grandson the truth with everyone else looking on?" Pop moved toward Holt, his cane thumping on the floor. "That's the most despicable thing I've ever heard."

"No," Holt said. "You three will see the truth first."

Tom's eyes narrowed. "*See* the truth."

Holt opened one of his desk drawers and pulled out a videotape. "Twenty-six years ago I had video monitors installed in the house. Not for security purposes, not to monitor anyone's actions as they happened, but to look at should someone break in."

"The same type of system they use in convenience stores?" Angel said.

"Pretty much," Holt said.

"So let me get this straight." Tom swept his fingers through his hair. "You expect me to sit here tonight and watch a videotape of you shooting my dad?"

"I want you to watch a videotape to see what happened that night. Please sit down, Tom," Holt said in his imperialistic way. "You, too, Miss Devlin. Mr. Donovan."

While Holt walked to the TV on the far wall and put the tape in the VCR, Tom helped his grandfather sit in one of the easy chairs, then sat beside Angel. She clutched his hand tightly, knowing this was undoubtedly going to cause him pain.

Holt dimmed the lights. Static and snow filled the screen, and then Chase stepped into the picture.

"My God," Pop said. "That's your father."

Tom stared at the screen, seeing the young and handsome man that he remembered. He was thirty then. He'd always be thirty—the same age Tom was now.

"The audio is filled with quite a lot of static," Holt said, as the film flickered on the TV screen. "But watch closely. The room you're seeing is my master suite. There's a walk-in safe in the wall. You've been in there, Tom," Holt said. "It's quite large and hidden, but any good thief would be able to find it."

"Your father had been a cat burglar," Holt went on. "He'd stopped stealing right about the time we met, and when I wanted a safe built into my home, I asked him to design it and oversee construction."

"Why would you do that?" Pop asked. "You were opening yourself up to being robbed."

"Because I trusted Chase. Amélie trusted Chase." A faraway smile touched Holt's face. "He'd worked quite hard to gain your trust, Mr. Donovan. Sadly, he died without getting it, but I hope before we leave this room that you will see what a good man Chase had become."

Again Tom turned his full attention to the monitor, and watched Chase press a spot on the wall near the four-poster bed. A panel swung away from the wall, revealing a heavy steel door and a combination lock.

Everything Tom saw was exactly what he'd read in the police report.

Holt fast-forwarded as Chase twisted and turned the lock, finally opening the safe to reveal a tall bronze statue of two lovers.

"That's the infamous statue, *The Embrace*," Holt said, as Tom watched Chase grasp it in his hand.

"He's shaking," Pop said. "Chase never shook. He was damn good at cracking safes. Knew exactly what he was doing. He shouldn't have been shaking."

"Keep watching," Holt said. "You'll soon know the reason."

Chase turned, statue in his hand, and walked out of the safe room. He didn't bother closing the door behind him, he just stared, as if someone were standing in front of him.

"I can't do this," Chase said, his voice full of anguish. "Not to Holt."

Tom frowned at his dad's words. Who the hell was he talking to?

"Do you think I care if Holt is hurt by this?"

It was a woman's voice Tom heard. Frantic. Loud.

"He loves that damned statue more than me," she said, but she never came into view. "He loves you more than me and, God forbid, he loved your wife more than me, too."

Tom saw his dad shake his head. "You're wrong, I tell you. He loves you. Only you."

"Shut up," the woman screamed. "Shut up."

"That was my wife yelling at Chase," Holt said, his voice breaking with sadness as he stared at the television. "And she was right, Tom. I did love your father. I'd never had a friend as close or as dear, and I haven't had a friend like him since. I loved your mother, too, but as nothing more than a friend. It was my wife I loved, more than life itself, but . . ." Holt shook his head. "Just watch."

Chase stood still, the damned statue clutched in his hands.

Why didn't he drop it? Tom wondered. Why was he just staring at Holt's wife?

"Where is my son?" Chase asked, his voice begging to know. Imploring the woman to answer him, and Tom felt a shudder deep inside him.

Fear.

"He's someplace where he'll never be found—unless you do exactly as I say."

Tom moved toward the TV screen to get a better view.

"She was mad," Holt said. "Completely mad, but I didn't know it at the time."

Tom kept his focus on the monitor, on his dad.

"I'll do exactly as you tell me," Chase said, his words frantic, his voice tinged with anger and pain. His hands trembled as he held the statue in a death grip. "Please," Chase begged, "just tell me what you've done with my son."

"Later, Chase." Carlotta Hudson's taped laughter rang through the library, sending chills racing up Tom's spine. "Later."

Holt fast-forwarded again, and Tom watched his father and the woman who had to be Carlotta Hudson speeding down the hallway, into a bedroom. The tape slowed. Flickered. And Holt dragged in a ragged breath as a canopied bed popped into view with Carlotta lying in the center of it—a gun gripped in her hands.

"It was a .25 automatic," Holt said, as the tape played on, almost in slow motion. "It was my gun. One I kept just in case someone broke in."

Tom found the tape hard to watch. Almost like a poorly made porn flick with the characters still clothed, but ready to take everything off. Carlotta beckoned to Chase with the wiggle of an index finger. "Make love to me," she purred. "Please, Chase, make love to me."

"I won't." Chase stood at the far end of the bed, his voice controlled but angry. "I won't do that to Holt."

"Think about your son." Carlotta laughed. "If you want him back, you'll do as I say."

Tom plowed his hands through his hair. A sickening knot had balled up in his gut.

"This is crazy," Chase said. "What is this going to get you?"

"Pregnant, perhaps. With your child." Carlotta grinned, her distorted face glaring at the camera. "And once I'm with child, I can tell Holt you're the father. Then Holt will hate you and I'll have him to myself again. All to myself."

Chase shook his head. "You're mad."

"Perhaps. But I also have your son—sweet, precious little Tom—which means you will do as I say."

Tom plowed his fingers through his hair. "I remember now. Oh, God." His chest heaved with pain. "I remember."

Holt paused the tape again. "What do you remember, Tom? Please. Tell us."

"It wasn't my dad who took me from my bed that night. It was Carlotta. She said we were going on a picnic, that we'd play hide and seek." Tom frowned as the memories came tumbling back. "We drove for the longest time, at least it seemed long to me. We sang songs in the car and it was dark out and then she stopped. We got out of the car and it was hot and there were mosquitoes flying around and—"

Tom took a deep breath, not wanting to remember, but realizing that this one memory had been right at the very tip of breaking through for a long time. "There was a wooden box." He frowned, remembering the rough texture of the wood, the way it smelled, and the heat. "It wasn't all that big," Tom said. "But Carlotta told me to climb inside because it would be the perfect place to hide.

She said no one would find me there and I'd win the game."

"You always loved playing hide and seek," Holt said. "We played it here and at Mere Belle."

"I don't remember anything else," Tom said, pressing fingers into his throbbing temples. "Just the dark and the mosquitoes. And I remember being afraid that I'd be locked away forever. Like I was in jail for being a bad boy—until my dad found me and picked me up and carried me to his car."

Tom swallowed hard, trying to get rid of the damn lump in his throat. He breathed deeply, and Angel stepped behind him, put her hands on his shoulders, and gave him some measure of comfort.

"We sat in the car together, just my dad and I, and he was humming to me and telling me everything would be all right." Tom frowned, his whole body wracked with anguish. "And then my dad just stopped speaking. He stopped humming. His eyes were open and he stared straight ahead—at nothing."

Tom looked up at Holt, standing just on the other side of the TV, and saw tears in his eyes. "You knew all of this, didn't you?"

"Not all of it." Holt shook his head. "I know exactly what happened while your father was here in the house. As for what happened between here and the Everglades, I didn't know, not until I read in the papers that you and your father had been found by park rangers."

Anger and frustration ripped through Tom.

"What I've just seen on the tape isn't what's on the police report?"

"For the most part, what you read on the police report is what I believed had happened," Holt admitted.

"But you had the tape," Angel said, her eyes narrowed. Questioning.

"I had a distraught wife who told me she'd almost been raped," Holt said. "She was frantic. Almost incoherent. On top of that my best friend had been shot. He'd disappeared and so had his son."

Holt dragged in a deep breath. "I didn't even think about the tape until days later, after the doctors had been here and the police. You've got to understand, I was nearly as grief-stricken as my wife and I wasn't thinking straight." Holt pressed his fingers into his neck, as if trying to soothe away pain. "After I saw the tape, I saw no need to let the world know that my wife had gone insane that night."

"I still don't know why you shot my dad that night," Tom said. "Were you jealous? Did you catch him with your wife?"

Holt shook his head. "It's all on the tape if you want to see it."

"I already have memories of my father dying. I don't need new memories of seeing him shot. I just want to know the truth. Why you shot him."

"It's all on the tape," Holt said. "Perhaps—"

"No, damn it," Tom said. "Just tell us what happened. It's time you bring it all out in the open the way you should have done twenty-six years ago."

Holt walked to the window again and looked

outside. "Your father did as Carlotta asked—up to a point. She begged him to make love to her. Pleaded for him to treat her in a way that she felt I'd never treated her." Holt shook his head, as if he wished he could shake off the memories. "The tape's all fuzzy. You saw how bad it is, but . . . but Chase got on the bed with Carlotta. He caressed her face. He kissed her. He told her he'd never loved anyone but her."

"And that's when you came in?" Tom asked, his breathing labored. Bitter. "Is that when you shot my dad?"

Holt turned slowly and shook his head. "Carlotta was mad. Chase must have realized it that night, just as I realized it a few days later. He played along with her. Made her believe he loved her, and then he asked her to tell him what she'd done with you."

Holt crossed the room and slumped in a chair. "Your father could charm anyone and he charmed Carlotta that night. She told him exactly where she'd left you—a place where we'd gone once or twice before, when Amélie was still alive. And as soon as Chase knew the truth, he tried to leave, but she grabbed his hair, tore at his shirt. She was wild and he put his hands around her neck to stop her and . . . ." Holt stared at Tom, sadness reddening his eyes. "Carlotta shot him. Not me. Carlotta. She shot him once, twice, but her hands were shaking so badly that she only grazed his sides. That's when he let go of her throat. He was bleeding, holding his sides, but he managed to get away from her, to get off of the bed. And he was cursing at her, telling her that if his son had been hurt, he'd come back and kill her."

Holt paused, looking into Tom's eyes.

Tom had never seen such sorrow. So many tears streaking down a man's face. And then he looked at Pop, his face pale, expressionless, his gnarled fingers gripping his cane.

"What happened then?" Tom asked.

"Chase turned to run, but Carlotta kept on shooting."

The room became deathly silent, except for the strains of Beethoven coming from the ballroom, which seemed a billion miles away.

"I'm sorry," Holt said. "Deeply sorry."

"Where were you when this happened?" Angel asked.

"Sailing. I'd been gone, just like it said in the police report. But I didn't get home to see Chase attacking my wife. I got home not more than ten, fifteen minutes later to see her sitting in a bloody bed with an empty gun in her hand."

"Why not tell the truth?" Tom asked. "Why all the lies?"

"As I told you. Carlotta told me Chase had tried to rape her. She told me he'd stolen the statue. She told me she'd shot him but he'd escaped. I didn't want to believe the worst of Chase, but I loved my wife. I had to believe her, and what she told me was exactly what I told the police, except for the part about who shot Chase."

"But why tell the police that you'd shot my dad?" Tom asked.

"Because Carlotta was fragile. Because I was afraid if she wasn't completely mad, she would be if the police questioned her over and over again. Because I wanted to protect her; and when it was over, and up until the time she died, I wanted to protect her from gossip. From prying eyes.

"If the truth had come out," he continued, his anguish unmistakable, "she would have gone to prison, but she was already in a prison in her mind. And I imprisoned her in our home, afraid of what she might do if she left. That's why very few people ever saw us after that night. My reasons were selfish, too. Carlotta had said on that tape that I didn't love her, but I did. And I never left her after that night. I did everything in my power to show her that she was loved, even when she got to the point where she couldn't recognize me."

"Carlotta's been dead for six years," Angel said, standing as close to Tom as he could hold her. "Why not tell the truth after she was gone? Why not clear Chase's name? And why wouldn't you talk with Tom?"

"Self-preservation, I suppose. Selfishness. Old friends remembered Carlotta for her generosity and I didn't want them to remember her madness. I didn't want anyone knowing what I'd done, how I'd let my best friend take the blame." Holt looked at Tom, tears in the corners of his eyes. "She used to hold you when you were a baby. She'd rock you and, just like your father and I, she'd play old tapes of your mother playing the piano. We were the best of friends once, and then everything fell apart."

Holt sighed heavily. "As for why I didn't want to see you, well, I just couldn't bear to face you, Tom. In a sense, you're the only family I have, and

I knew you'd hate me when I told you the truth."
He laughed nervously. "Who could blame you, after what I've done? I abandoned you. I allowed
your father to be called a would-be rapist. I made
a lot of mistakes, and I don't expect you to forgive
me. But now that this is out in the open, maybe I
can move on."

"You're right, Holt. I can't forgive you," Tom
said, his body aching with anger.

"I can," Pop said. "I would have protected my
wife until the ends of the earth, too. That's an
emotion I can understand. As for my son . . . I
loved him dearly, but he wasn't a saint. No, he
didn't deserve to be shot, and God knows I wish
he were here now, wish he'd been able to watch
Tom grow up. But at least now I know that Chase
hadn't turned bad . . . again. I know he had good
reasons for everything he did."

Using his cane, Pop walked toward Holt and
put a hand on his shoulder. "I've made mistakes,
too. It's gonna take me a long time to forgive you
for the mistakes you made, but something tells
me you're redeemable, just as my son was redeemable."

"What about the stories about Chase being
broke?" Tom asked Holt. "What about him asking
you for money and the two of you getting into an
argument? Was all of that a lie, too?"

"That, I'm afraid, is the truth. That's why I went
fishing that night. I hated the fact that Chase and I
had had such a horrible argument that morning. I
was trying to decide if I should loan him money
again. In the end I decided against it, not that it
mattered after that. When Carlotta told me that

Chase had broken into the safe and taken the statue, it made perfect sense. He needed money and the statue was worth a fortune." Holt shrugged. "What better way to get back at me than to take the statue and my wife—one way or another? It made perfect sense to me and it made perfect sense to the police."

"But you had the tape," Tom said. "You had proof that my dad was innocent. That Carlotta had taken me, that she'd threatened my dad."

"As I said, I didn't see the tape until later. Not until the case was closed. By then the damage was done. And as I told you, I needed to protect my wife and, yes, I wanted to protect my good name, too."

"So what happens now?" Tom asked.

"I send the press release off," Holt said. "I tell every person here the truth. And then your father's name will be cleared."

"He'll still be branded a thief," Tom said. "Unless you know the whereabouts of *The Embrace*."

"I honestly don't know if Chase had it with him when he left or if Carlotta had hidden it."

"My father didn't take it," Tom said adamantly, prepared to defend his father until the bitter end.

"No, I don't believe he did," Holt said. "I never put in an insurance claim for it because it ceased to be important to me after that night. It could be worth a billion dollars and I wouldn't care." Holt walked to the window and stood by Tom. "I lost my dearest friend that night. I lost my wife, first to madness and then to Alzheimer's. I lost the godson who I had loved." Holt put a hand on Tom's shoulder. "I owe you so much. Tonight was the first step. And right now all I can say is, can you find it in your heart to forgive me?"

Tom shrugged away from Holt's touch. He walked to the VCR and pulled out the tape. "May I have this?"

"It's yours," Holt said. "You may do with it what you want."

"Personally," Pop said, "I'd like to see it dropped in the center of the ocean and completely forgotten."

"Are you out of your mind, Pop?" Tom said. "It proves my dad was innocent."

"It happened twenty-six years ago," Pop said. "The whole thing has become a distorted mish-mash of truths and lies and gossip, and God knows, no one but us gives a damn whether your dad was innocent or guilty. I know the truth. You know the truth. That's all that matters to me."

"I want the police to have this," Tom said. "I want Carlotta held responsible for a kidnapping. For murder."

Angel stepped in front of Tom and cradled his face in her hands. "Don't do anything rash, Tom. Think about it for a while."

"I've thought about it constantly for far too long."

He tugged away from Angel, walked to the library door, and threw it open.

And then he heard the music. A recording of his mother playing the piano so beautifully. He dragged in a deep breath, then turned around and shut the library door behind him.

"Why do you play my mother's music?" Tom asked Holt.

Holt smiled, a long-ago warmth touching his face. "To remind myself of the good times in my life, when Amélie and Chase and Carlotta and I were the best of friends. To remind myself of you and Chase sitting at the grand piano in my ballroom. You couldn't even play 'Chopsticks' at the time, but your father had always hoped that you'd play like your mother someday." A tear slipped from Holt's eye and he wiped it away. "Those really were the best of times, Tom. The absolute best."

Tom looked across the room at Pop, standing as tall as he possibly could with the pain ravaging his joints. He looked at Angel—his angel—smiling at him, needing him. Both of them would stand by his side no matter what he decided to do.

And then he looked at Holt. Really, really looked at him—tired, aging, and hurting deep down inside. A man who'd made a mistake twenty-six years ago and had lived with the consequences ever since.

Tom could make a mistake tonight, too. He could ruin a man and the memory of his wife; or clear a man people barely remembered, a man who was loved only by three of the people standing in this room.

Tom stared at the videotape in his hands, then walked across the room. He tossed it into the fireplace.

"You don't have to do that, Tom," Holt said. "I gave it to you so you could clear your father."

"Let me ask you this, Holt. Did you ever once hate my dad?"

Holt frowned deeply. "He was my best friend. I

would have gone to the ends of the earth for him and he would have done the same for me. I didn't like the way he handled his money and he didn't like the fact that I worked twenty hours a day, but in all of my life, I've never known a man so generous or so loving.

"In fact," Holt went on, "you reminded me of him when you came back here the other morning and told me you'd never again ask to know the truth about your father's death if I'd call Angel and tell her she could have the gala in my home."

Angel's eyes narrowed as she looked at Tom. "You did that?"

Tom shrugged. "It was no big deal."

"And you, Angel," Holt continued, "reminded me very much of Amélie when you came here even later that morning and pretty much called me a self-centered bastard and then told me you were going to give Tom an invitation whether I wanted you to or not. Amélie would have done exactly the same thing."

"What he's trying to tell you," Pop said, "in case you can't figure it out, is that people will do all sorts of strange things in the name of love. Kind of crazy, but that's just the way it is."

Every emotion known to man rumbled through Tom's insides. He had all of his answers, he just wasn't sure where to go from here.

And then Angel slipped her fingers into his hand—and he knew. It was time to start a new chapter in his life, one that could look back at the good things from his past, and forget all the bad.

He wrapped her up in his arms, not caring who was watching, and kissed her softly. Gently. Dragging in a warmth he'd known only with her—the woman he loved.

Letting go of her uneasily, he walked to Holt's desk, picked up the speech and the press release, and tossed them into the fireplace. "Do you have a match?" Tom asked Holt, not bothering to turn around, knowing that all eyes in the room were on what he was doing.

Behind him he heard a drawer open. Heard Holt's dress shoes cross the floor, and felt their arms brush lightly as he and Holt stood side by side.

Holt handed a lighter to Tom, and without giving it another thought, Tom set the carefully typed pages on fire, watched the flare of the flames, and the tape inside the cartridge curl and crinkle as it melted—and all of the past disappeared, became ashes.

Tom drew in a breath of air and let it out slowly. There was just one more thing he had to do.

He turned to Holt and held out his hand.

There were questions in Holt's eyes. Worry. But he grasped Tom's hand and held it tightly.

"Someday," Tom said, "when I've got the energy to forgive you, I might let you tell me stories about my mom and dad."

"I'd like that," Holt said. "I really would like that."

Tom caught a glimpse of Pop moving slowly toward Holt, his cane helping him every step of the way. His grandfather slapped Holt's shoulder. "There's a party going on outside. Why don't we go see if we can get into some mischief?"

Holt grinned, a sight Tom figured hadn't been

seen in twenty-six years. "I remember Chase telling me that you like to fish," Holt said. "Was that just a passing fancy, or something you still do?"

"Oh, I still fish, all right," Pop said. "Used to have me a real good fishing partner, too, but ever since he hooked up with the pretty lady in red, I've been left to my own devices."

"I was thinking about going out tomorrow and buying a new pole or two, then heading over to the Gulf for a week or so to see what I can catch," Holt said, walking slowly at Pop's side as they headed for the door. "Care to join me?"

"Sounds pretty damn good," Pop said. "By the way, do you like gator? I've got a recipe for fried gator tail . . ."

The library door clicked shut at last, and the massive mahogany-paneled room was quiet, except for the beat of Tom's heart, and the click of kick-ass heels walking toward him.

Feathery red fabric floated around Angel, the gown he'd first seen her in a couple of weeks ago just barely covering luscious, tantalizing breasts that jiggled as she walked. Her blond hair was wrapped on top of her head in some elegant kind of 'do that begged to be let down. And her smile—oh, God, her smile—was wicked. Devilish.

She slipped into his embrace, weaving her fingers around his neck and capturing his mouth. Sweet. Tempting.

All his.

A soft purr echoed in her throat as his hands floated down to her heavenly derriere and tugged her against him. A needy moan ripped through his body.

And then she whispered, warm breath fluttering against his lips. "Are you feeling adventurous?"

Tom's heart beat wildly. "What do you have in mind?"

"A quickie." Angel's tongue slid deliciously across his lips. "Your place or mine?"

"What about the gala?"

An impish smile touched her mouth, sparkled in her eyes. "It's going to last until the wee hours of the morning. And really, Tom, if someone notices I'm missing, well"—she shrugged her sexy bare shoulders—"everybody knows that I'm no angel."

"And don't ever change, sweetheart," Tom whispered, drawing her toward the French doors and leading her out into the cool night breeze. "Don't ever change."

Epilogue

"*Y*oo-hoo! Tommy! Yoo-hoo! Angel!*"

Frederike LeVien scurried down the wooden dock with her chauffer shuffling along behind. She looked like a lemon in yellow pumps, yellow suit, and a bright yellow sultanlike hat with a bright green feather sticking out the top. Her arms waved back and forth in the air, obviously trying to catch Tom's attention before he and his brand-new wife cruised off on their honeymoon.

Behind her ran Cosette and Celine, their Swarovski crystal collars glistening in the sunlight, their leashes bobbing up and down, and the Countess's poor chauffeur holding both dogs at bay while he tried to keep hold of a gigantic gift box with a bow the size of Florida on top.

Tom climbed down from Pop's fishing boat to greet the woman who'd become a friend in the past year. She was kooky, but she had a heart of gold. She'd even buried poor, dearly departed Evan when last year's season was over, and cried during the funeral.

A week later, ensconced in her Newport, Rhode Island, twenty-eight-million-dollar cottage, she'd married husband number nine. He didn't have a title, but she loved him all the same.

Frederike latched on to Tom's arm, huffing and puffing until she caught her breath.

"Are you all right?" Tom asked.

"I couldn't be better, Tommy, dahling. That new husband of mine bought me the loveliest new hat. One he picked out all by himself, and as I was looking for an appropriate place to keep it, I stumbled on the loveliest piece of artwork. Something I thought would be absolutely perfect for you and Angel."

Frederike frowned. "Where is she, by the way?"

Downstairs, lying naked on black satin sheets, anxiously waiting for the present Tom planned to give her as soon as he could get rid of Frederike. But that's not what he told the Countess.

"She's cooking up a mess of fried gator." Tom grinned. "Care to join us for lunch before we take off?"

"Oh, my word, no! But thank you all the same."

Cosette and Celine pranced around Frederike's lemon yellow pumps and Frederike giggled. "All right, my precious little butterflies, we'll just be another moment, then Mommy will take you to Ma Petite Bow-Wow to buy you some treats."

Frederike's chauffeur inched forward, looking as if he'd like to kick Cosette and Celine over the dock and drown them, but he kept a somewhat straight face as he handed the box to Tom.

"I hope you'll love it." Frederike beamed. "I'd almost forgotten the thing existed until this morning, and then I remembered Carlotta Hudson giving it to me the day after that horrible shooting. I took her the loveliest chocolates that day. Or maybe it was a cake. Oh, it doesn't matter. She was just so touched that I cared, and she gave me a gift in return. It's a tradition amongst my friends, you know."

"I believe you've mentioned that a time or two," Tom said, smiling. "Maybe Angel and I will find a pretty hat for you while we're traveling."

"That would be lovely. Absolutely lovely. And while you're gone, please keep an eye out for carousels. You know me, the more unique the better. But now," she said, blowing Tom an air kiss, "I must be off. My little butterflies have been terribly impatient today."

"Tootle-ooo!"

The Countess scurried off, her butterflies and her chauffeur bustling along after her.

Tom climbed back onto the *Adagio*, contemplating the big, heavy gift box Frederike had given him for all of a second or two. Something told him *The Embrace* was inside, a statue that had been part of the grief of his past. And grief was the last thing he wanted to think about now.

With any luck there was a naked woman waiting for him downstairs, and he had a much better present to give her.

He set the box Frederike had given him on top of the outside bar, pulled the slim, black velvet box out of his back pocket, and raced down the stairs to the master bedroom to be with his wife.

She stood at the window, looking out at the ocean where they'd be heading soon. Her silky blond hair trailed down her lovely back, her crimson angel wing tattoo kissed her shoulder, and her sleek, sexy, blessedly naked body called out to him.

Turning slowly, a sly and wicked smile on her lips, she winked. "Is that for me?"

"Are you looking at the box or—"

"I'm looking at you, Tom. You're the best present a girl could ever get."

"Better than a ruby and diamond necklace?" Tom asked, strolling toward her slowly, methodically, taking in every speck of her luscious bare flesh, as he opened the box to show her the fabulous jewels. "It's a family heirloom. I thought you might wear it for me."

Angel touched the sparkling gems. "It's beautiful, Tom. Absolutely gorgeous. But I didn't pack anything special enough to wear it with."

"You're pretty damn special, sweetheart—dressed or undressed.

Tom stepped behind his wife and slipped the diamonds and rubies around her neck. He spun her around, gazed into her dazzling sapphire eyes, and took his merry sweet time contemplating the gift he'd given her and—with even greater pleasure—the woman who'd given herself to him completely.

"I have a gift for you, too, Mr. Donovan."

"And what would that be?"

His devilish Angel pressed her heavenly breasts against his chest. "Dark chocolate, whipped cream, strawberries, and champagne. I thought we could treat ourselves to some wickedly delicious sundaes. And while we're at it"—she traced his lips with her tantalizing tongue—"we can treat ourselves to each other."

Tom smiled warmly as he kissed his wife—the woman he loved and would always love—and then whispered against her lips. "That's the best gift of all, sweetheart. The very best gift of all."

What Every
Woman Knows . . .

Let's face it. No one wants to *admit* that they use their feminine wiles to catch a man . . . but the truth is we do! From the first moment he sees you in a sexy pair of high-heeled shoes to the moment he first glimpses you in your wedding gown, a man often doesn't know how much effort we've taken to dress to impress! And while blatantly trying to catch a guy is definitely a "don't," there are little touches that any woman can wear that will make a man take notice.

As for our Avon Romance heroines, they *all* know that a little bit can go a long, long way. And, sometimes, when the going gets tough, it's worth it to pull out all the stops.

Now let's take a peek as four intrepid heroines captivate the interest of the men of their dreams. . . .

Coming May 2004

Party Crashers
by Stephanie Bond

Jolie Goodman's life's a mess. Her boyfriend vanished months ago—with her car! She's broke and working in the Neiman Marcus shoe department, selling tantalizing but financially (for her!) out-of-reach footwear to the women whose credit cards aren't maxed out. And now, the police have come looking for her . . . thinking that she has something to do with her boyfriend's disappearance! But sometimes selling sexy shoes is just as enticing to men as wearing them.

Jolie glanced at the doorway leading back to the show-room, then to the fire exit door leading to a loading dock, weighing her options. She had the most outrageous urge to walk out . . . and keep walking.

Is that what Gary had done? Reached some kind of personal crisis that he couldn't share with her, and simply walked away from everything—his job, his friends, and her? As bad as it sounded, she almost preferred to believe that he had suffered some kind of breakdown rather than consider other possible explanations: he'd met with foul play or she had indeed been scammed by the man who'd professed to care about her.

The exit sign beckoned, but she glanced at the shoe box in her hands and decided that since the man had been kind enough to intercept Sammy, he deserved to be waited on, even if he didn't spend a cent.

Even if people with vulgar money made her nervous.

She fingercombed her hair and tucked it behind her ears, then straightened her clothing as best she could. There was no helping the lack of makeup, so she pasted on her best smile—the one that she thought showed too much gum, but that Gary had assured her made her face light up—and returned to the showroom.

Her smile almost faltered, though, when Mr. Beck Underwood's bemused expression landed on her.

She walked toward him, trying to forget that the man could buy and sell her a thousand times over. "I'm sorry again about running into you. Did you really want to try on this shoe or were you just being nice?"

"Both," he said mildly. "My sister is going to be a while, and I need shoes, so this works for me."

At the twinkle in his eyes, her tongue lodged at the roof of her mouth. Like a mime, she gestured to a nearby chair and made her feet follow him. As he sat she scanned the area for signs of Sammy.

"She's behind the insoles rack," he whispered.

Jolie flushed and made herself not look. The man probably thought she was clumsy *and* paranoid. She busied herself unpacking the expensive shoes. "Will you be needing a dress sock, sir?"

He slipped off his tennis shoe and wiggled bare brown toes. "I suppose so. I'm afraid I've gotten into the habit of not wearing socks." He smiled. "And my dad is 'sir.' I'm just Beck."

She suddenly felt small. And poor. "I . . . know who you are."

"Ah. Well, promise you won't hold it against me."

She smiled and retrieved a pair of tan-colored socks to match the loafers. When she started to slip one of the socks over his foot, he took it from her. "I can do it."

"I don't mind," she said quickly. Customers expected it—to be dressed and undressed and redressed if necessary. It was an unwritten rule: *No one leaves the store without being touched.*

"I don't have to be catered to," he said, his tone brittle.

Jolie blinked. "I'm sorry."

He looked contrite and shook his head. "Don't be—it's me." Then he grinned unexpectedly. "Besides, under more private circumstances, I might take you up on your offer."

Heat climbed her neck and cheeks—he was teasing her . . . his good deed for the day. Upon closer scrutiny, his face was even more interesting—his eyes a deep brown, bracketed by untanned lines created from squinting in the sun. Late thirties, she guessed. His skin was ruddy, his strong nose peeling from a recent burn. Despite the pale streaks in his hair, he was about as far from a beach boy as a man could be. When he leaned over to slip on the shoes, she caught a glimpse of his powerful torso beneath the sport coat.

She averted her gaze and concentrated on the stitched design on the vamp of the shoe he was trying on, handing him a shoehorn to protect the heel counter. (This morning Michael had given her an "anatomy of a shoe" lesson, complete with metal pointer and pop quiz.)

The man stood and hefted his weight from foot to foot, then took a couple of steps in one direction and came back. "I'll take them."

A salesperson's favorite words. She smiled. "That was fast."

He laughed. "Men don't have a complicated relationship with shoes."

Coming June 2004

And the Bride Wore Plaid
by Karen Hawkins

*What is to be done with Kat Macdonald? This Scottish miss is
deplorably independent, and unweddably wild. But while it's
impossible to miss her undeniable beauty, it's also impossible to get Kat to act like a civilized lady. Still, even she cannot
resist Devon St. John. A man born to wealth and privilege, he
has no intention of ever settling down with one woman . . .
until he meets Kat and realizes that his future wife will, indeed, proudly wear plaid.*

Devon lifted a finger and traced the curve of her cheek,
the touch bemusingly gentle. "You are a lush, tempting
woman, my dear. And well you know it."

Kat's defenses trembled just the slightest bit. Bloody hell,
how was she to fight her own treacherous body while the
bounder—Devon something or another—tossed compli-
ments at her with just enough sincerity to leave her breathless
to hear more?

Of course, it was all practiced nonsense, she told herself
firmly. She was anything but tempting. She looked well
enough when she put some effort into it, but she was large and
ungainly, and it was way too early in the morning for her to

look anything other than pale. Her eyes were still heavy with sleep and she'd washed her hair last night and it had dried in a most unruly, puffy way that she absolutely detested. One side was definitely fuller than the other and it disturbed her no end. Even worse, she was wearing one of her work gowns of plain gray wool, one that was far too tight about the shoulders and too loose about the waist. Thus, she was able to meet his gaze and say firmly, "I am not tempting."

"I'd call you tempting and more," Devon said with refreshing promptness. "Your eyes shimmer rich and green. Your hair is the color of the morning sky just as the sun touches it, red and gold at the same time. And the rest of you—" His gaze traveled over her until her cheeks burned. "The rest of you is—"

"That's enough of that," she said hastily. "You're full of moonlight and shadows, you are."

"I don't know anything about moonlight and shadows. I only know you are a gorgeous, lush armful."

"In this?" She looked down at her faded gown with incredulity. "You'd call this gorgeous or lush?"

His gaze touched on her gown, lingering on her breasts. "Oh yes. If you want to go unnoticed, you'll have to bind those breasts of yours."

She choked.

He grinned. "And add some padding of some sort in some other areas."

"I don't know what you're talking about, but please let me up—"

"I was talking about padding. Perhaps if you bundled yourself about the hips until you looked plumper, then you wouldn't have to deal with louts such as myself attempting to kiss you at every turn."

She caught the humor sparkling in his eyes and it disarmed her, even as the thought of adding padding to her hips made her chest tickle as a laugh began to form.

"Furthermore," he continued as if he'd never paused, "you will need to hide those eyes of yours and perhaps wear a turban, if you want men like me to stop noticing you."

"Humph. I'll remember that the next time I run into you or any other of Strathmore's lecherous cronies. Now, if you'll let me go, I have things to do."

His eyes twinkled even more. "And if I refuse?"

"Then I will have to deal with you, myself."

"Oh-oh! A woman of spirit. I like that."

"Oh-oh," she returned sharply, "a man who does not prize his appendages."

That comment was meant to wither him on the vine. Instead he chuckled, the sound rich and deep. "Sweet, I prize my appendage, although it should be *your* job to admire it."

"I have no wish for such a job, thank you very much."

"Oh, but if you did, it would then be my job to wield that appendage in such a way as to rouse that admiration to a vocal level." Devon leaned forward and murmured in her ear, "You have a delicious moan, my sweet. I heard it when we kissed."

Her cheeks burned. "The only vocal rousing you're going to get from me is a scream for help."

A bit of the humor left his gaze and he said with apparent seriousness, "I would give my life trying to earn that moan yet again. Would you deny me that?"

Coming July 2004

I'm No Angel
by Patti Berg

Palm Beach's sexiest investigator, Angel Devlin, knows that a tight skirt, a hint of cleavage, and some sky high heels will usually help her get every kind of information out of any type of man. But millionaire bad boy Tom Donovan has something up his custom-made shirt sleeve, and even though Angel is using every trick she knows, it's proving far more difficult than usual to get what she wants.

Tom grinned wickedly. "I caught you."

"But you didn't come after me."

"I hoped you'd come back."

"Why? So you could personally haul me off to jail?"

Tom shook his head. "Because I liked the feel of your hands on my chest and your lips on my cheek. If I hauled you off to jail we'd end up enemies. The fact that you came back means there's a chance for more."

"You know nothing about me but my name." *And the feel of my body,* Angel thought, just barely hanging on to her composure as Tom's hands glided down the curve of her spine, then flared over the sides of her waist and settled on her hips. "Why would you want more?"

"I paid Jorge for a lot more information than just your name," he said. "I know you're a private investigator and that you cater to the ultra-rich. I know that your office-slash-home is right here on Worth Avenue in a building you share with Ma Petite Bow-Wow, the local pamper-your-pooch shop. And if Jorge knows what he's talking about, you're thirty years old, five feet eight inches tall, weigh one thirty-two—"

"Thirty-one dripping wet."

Tom grinned, his laughing gaze locking onto hers. "Should we get naked and dripping wet and weigh each other?"

"Not tonight."

"It's close to midnight. It'll soon be tomorrow."

"Are you always in such a rush to get naked and dripping wet?"

He shrugged lightly. "Depends on the woman."

"Trust me, I'm the wrong woman."

"I disagree."

The music picked up tempo and so did Tom's moves. He spun around with Angel captured in his arms, the heat of his embrace, the closeness of their cheeks, and the scent of his spicy aftershave overwhelming her, making her dizzy.

And then he slowed again. His heart beat against her breasts. Warm breath whispered against her ear. "From what Jorge told me—that you wear Donna Karan's Cashmere Mist and Manolo Blahniks if you can get them on sale—you could easily be the right woman. Of course, there's also the fact that you're soft in all the right places. And going back to your original question, *that*, Angel, is why I want more of you."

Angel laughed lightly. "Jorge was a virtual font of information."

"I figured the soft-in-all-the-right-places part out for myself," Tom said, his hands drifting slowly from her waist to her bottom.

She leaned back slightly and gave him the evil eye. "Excuse me, but we don't know each other well enough for you to touch me where you're touching me."

A grin escaped his perfect lips. It sparkled in his eyes and made the dimple at the side of his mouth deepen as his fingers began to slide again, but not up to her waist. Oh, no, lascivious Tom Donovan's fingers slithered down to her thighs.

That was the first really big mistake he'd made since he'd chosen to follow her.

His fingers stilled, his eyes narrowed, and she knew he'd found the one thing she didn't want anyone to find.

Again his hand began to move, to explore, gliding up and down, over and around the not-so-little-lump on her right thigh. His eyes focused even more as his gaze held hers and locked. "That wouldn't be what I think it is, would it?"

Angel smiled slowly. Wickedly. At last, she again had the upper hand. "If you think it's a slim but extremely sharp stainless steel stiletto that could carve out a man's Adam's apple in the blink of an eye, you've guessed right."

One of Tom's dark, bedeviled eyebrows rose. "I never would have expected a sweet thing like you to carry a stiletto."

"That, Mr. Donovan, just goes to show that you really don't know as much about me as you think you do."

Coming August 2004

A Perfect Bride
by Samantha James

Sometimes expensive clothes and shoes aren't what does the trick . . . occasionally, men simply can't resist the power of a damsel in distress . . . an ugly duckling who unexpectedly turns into a gorgeous swan. When Sebastian Sterling rescues Devon, a wounded tavern maid, he thinks she's a thief—or worse. But underneath her tattered clothes is a woman of astonishing beauty and pride, who he quickly discovers could become his perfect bride.

Jimmy pointed a finger. "My lord, there be a body in the street!"

No doubt whoever it was had had too much to drink. Sebastian very nearly advised his man to simply move it and drive on.

But something stopped him. His gaze narrowed. Perhaps it was the way the "body," as Jimmy called it, lay sprawled against the uneven brick, beneath the folds of the cloak that all but enshrouded what looked to be a surprisingly small form. His booted heels rapped sharply on the brick as he leaped down and strode forward with purposeful steps. Jimmy remained where he was in the seat, looking around with wary eyes, as if he feared they would be set upon by thieves and minions at any moment.

Hardly an unlikely possibility, Sebastian conceded silently.

Sebastian crouched down beside her, his mind working. She was filthy and bedraggled. A whore who'd imbibed too heavily? Or perhaps it was a trick, a ruse to bring him in close, so she could snatch his pocketbook.

Guardedly he shook her, drawing his hand back, quickly. Damn. He'd left his gloves on the seat in the carriage. Ah, well, too late now.

"Mistress!" he said loudly. "Mistress, wake up!"

She remained motionless.

An odd sensation washed over him. His wariness vanished. His gaze slid sharply to his hand. The tips of his fingers were wet, but it was not the wetness of rain, he realized. This was dark and sticky and thick.

He inhaled sharply. "Christ!" he swore. He moved without conscious volition, swiftly easing her to her side so he could see her. "Mistress," he said urgently, "can you hear me?"

She moved a little, groaning as she raised her head. Sebastian's heart leaped. She was groggy but alive!

Between the darkness and the ridiculously oversized covering he supposed must pass for a bonnet, he couldn't see much of her face. Yet he knew the precise moment awareness set in. When her eyes opened and she spied him bending over her, she cringed and gave a great start. "Don't move," he said quickly. "Don't be frightened."

Her lips parted. Her eyes moved over his features in what seemed a never-ending moment. Then she gave a tiny shake of her head. "You're lost," she whispered, sounding almost mournful, "aren't you?"

Sebastian blinked. He didn't know quite what he'd expected her to say—certainly not *that*.

"Of course I'm not lost."

"Then I must be dreaming." To his utter shock, a small hand came out to touch the center of his lip. "Because no man in the world could possibly be as handsome as you."

An unlikely smile curled his mouth. "You haven't seen my brother," he started to say. He didn't finish, however. All at once the girl's eyes fluttered shut. Sebastian caught her head before it hit the uneven brick. In the next instant he surged to his feet and whirled, the girl in his arms.

"Jimmy!" he bellowed.

But Jimmy had already ascertained his needs. "Here, my lord." The steps were down, the carriage door wide open.

Sebastian clambered inside, laying the girl on the seat. Jimmy peered within. "Where to, my lord?"

Sebastian glanced down at the girl's still figure. Christ, she needed a physician. He thought of Dr. Winslow, the family physician, only to recall that Winslow had retired to the country late last year. And there was hardly time to scour the city in search of another . . .

"Home," he ordered grimly. "And hurry, Jimmy."

A Perfect Offer!

USA TODAY BESTSELLING AUTHOR OF *The Truest Heart*

SAMANTHA JAMES

"A remarkable writer." —Lisa Kleypas

A Perfect Bride

Devon St. James can't believe her eyes as she awakens wrapped in fine linens and staring into the eyes of Mr. Perfect himself, Sebastian Sterling. Surely she must be dreaming. Sebastian, marquess of Thurston, is mesmerized by the exquisite young beauty he rescued from the streets of London. Already tormented with a family scandal, he must face his burning desire for the fiery and sensual "diamond in the rough," who may just be a perfect bride.

Buy and enjoy A PERFECT BRIDE (Available July 27, 2004), then send the coupon below along with your proof of purchase for A PERFECT BRIDE to Avon Books, and we'll send you a check for $2.00.

- -